CROSSOVER

CHRONICLES
OF FEYREE: SCROLL 1

Claudia Newcorn

Theogony Books
Virginia Beach, VA

Chris Kennedy/Theogony Books
2052 Bierce Dr.
Virginia Beach, VA 23454
http://chriskennedypublishing.com/

Publisher's Note: This is a work of fiction. Names, characters, places, and incidents are a product of the author's imagination. Locales and public names are sometimes used for atmospheric purposes. Any resemblance to actual people, living or dead, or to businesses, companies, events, institutions, or locales is completely coincidental.

Ordering Information:
Quantity sales. Special discounts are available on quantity purchases by corporations, associations, and others. For details, contact the "Special Sales Department" at the address above.

Crossover/Claudia Newcorn. – 2nd ed.
ISBN 978-1942936640

Map of Lampion

Author's Note

Part of the enjoyment of a journey to any new realm is discovering the different languages and customs, as well as the people. At the back of this book you will find a convenient guide to Lampion and Nonetre with the explanation of words, as well as a who's who.

Chapter One

The cool musty shade of the toadstool was a welcome escape.

Leaning back against the thick stem, Danai watched as Feyree danced and pirouetted in flight, their colorful wings flickering in the sunlight as if a rainbow were scattering itself through the air. Some swooped down to the laden trestle tables for a goblet of goldenvine dew, a nibble of nuts. Others gathered near the musicians, laughing as they clapped along to the lively tune of skirling pipes, windhorns and throbbing tambours, laced with the vibrant thrum of harps.

Clumps of wingless sprytes stood apart, deep in conversation. Danai guessed they too were worrying about the impending Rites. She shoved away her nightmare by gazing about the meadow of the Great Dell where the trees and new grass were blushing the pale green of early spring.

What if she failed Krisalys? Then what? She had heard whispers of sprytes who did not return. One never heard why. She knew only that the Rites had to be passed by every spryte if they were to acquire the skills and knowledge necessary to live in their realm of Lampion and earn their wings to become fully-fledged Feyree. She scratched her shoulders on the toadstool, trying to relieve the itch of her wing bumps. The dream of the strangling krisalys washed back up into her memory.

Already the sun was beginning to wester, crowning the *Shehn* on whose massive branches the first oak leaves were unfurling. Clumps of Lunasaberries clung to the smaller branches, the white globes peering out from among dark green leaves. When *Lunasa* rose, his full face turned to bestow his blessing, the Rites would commence.

A merry laugh, intertwined with a giggle, passed nearby. Danai glimpsed Aaron and Tatia weaving their way through the stubby grass blades. Aaron's golden skin and hair contrasted sharply against Tatia's pearl and black. Each carried a goblet of dew. They vanished into a hawthorn bush, where new pink buds wove a concealing screen.

Despite her worries, Danai smiled wryly. The aphrodisiac qualities of goldenvine dew were well known. It was a standing joke in Goldyn Vale that Tatia had indulged so often it had caused her promiscuous personality. Since coupling was forbidden during the Rites, they both appeared to be getting in a last romp before the Mentors' summons. As if I know anything about coupling anyway, Danai sighed.

She glanced about the Dell, noting that almost all the sprytes from the outlying dells, glens, and vales had arrived, most on bird back. A few stragglers were just touching down. She spied a raven back-flapping to land beside the Trykle, the small creek that meandered from the wood across the Dell. She recognized her close friend Pook and another spryte climbing off its back.

"Danai?" Bright azure eyes peeked under the toadstool's rim, then Triasa squatted down to face her niece. "May I join you?" At Danai's nod, she folded her cobalt wings, ducked beneath, and settled down on the soft moss. "Let me guess. Krisalys?"

Danai did not answer, and Triasa found herself once again musing over her niece's unusual coloring—silver hair and skin, and emerald eyes. The old chant came to mind:

Silver, silver, green.
In youth remains unseen.
Winged, changes brings
future that has been.

She set it aside. Not even the Teaching Skalds knew what it meant, but tradition required all younglings learn the rhyme. She waited, fingering the intricate gold Charmer amulet nestled at her throat, symbol of her chosen Calling among the Feyree. Her work with the wood folk required the utmost patience for they distrusted magic and kept a cautious distance. Sometimes silence asked the best questions of all.

"I don't think I'm ready," Danai whispered, hugging her knees. "I keep having that terrible nightmare. I'm wrapped, blind, deaf, dumb. Unable to break free. Smothering while everybody stands about and laughs and laughs. I'm dying for my wings and nobody will help me. I feel myself die and exist motionless in a gray-blue silence of nothing. I never become a Feyree." She turned despairing eyes on her aunt. "I know I must sound ridiculous to you—yet...is there nothing you can tell me?"

Triasa tucked an escaped strand of silver back into her carefully plaited red hair, then shook her head. "You know I may not speak of the Rites," she gently rebuked. "Each of you must discover your Self and your Calling during the trials you will undergo." She paused, absently drumming her fingers on the ground. How could she reassure Danai that fear was to be expected when poised on an abyss of change into which there was no choice but to fall? But the Mentors and the Dolmen closely scrutinized the sprytes' actions throughout the Rites, and could discern if one knew too much. Such a violation would force both spryte and Feyree to forever forfeit their wings for breaching the cloak of secrecy that surrounded these sacred rituals.

"Listen well." She gazed out at the Dell, a relaxed smile creasing the corners of her mouth and eyes, her voice barely a whisper. "Panic is a poor leader. Only a clear mind has good judgment and can solve a problem. There is nothing to fear but your self." She paused, and her voice brightened. "The Skalds have trained you well, you are capable, smart, and if I do say so myself, quite talented."

She punctuated the last words with her rich laugh. Danai leaned over and hugged her hard, hiding for a moment in the safe return embrace. She had been fostered out to Triasa as a youngling, and loved and respected her gentle yet firm manner.

"Come. Anticipation is a *dirq* with two keen edges: delight and fear." Triasa eased from under the toadstool and held out her hand to Danai. "Only the Mother and Lunasa know the future. Even though the Rites commence this gloaming, we also celebrate Spring, the blossom time, the season of rebirth. Let us go listen to Skalds Rianya and Amryn sing the tale of the birth of our beautiful realm of Lampion. Listen! The Orpheii are gathering with them near the sacred Shehn. Come."

* * * * *

anai shivered as she stood waiting on the stream bank. Lunasa's silvery light seemed only to darken the forest shadows. Water droplets pearled her waist-length hair, and the air was permeated by the sharp scent of crushed rosemary that her Mentor had scrubbed her with during the ritual bath. After, her Mentor had slipped a plum-colored tunic over her head, then disappeared into the shadows. The first Rite, the Cleansing, so far had only been breathtaking because of the snow-chilled waters.

In the soft waiting silence, she thought of how Mentor Melitsa had strode forth with the other Mentors from among the ancient Shehn's gnarled roots. Their steps matched the beat of the pounding tambours, until each stood before a spryte. They looked as Danai imagined wraiths might appear—draped in ground-sweeping hooded robes that flowed about them like thick brown water, wings covered, faces absorbed in the darkness of cavernous cowls, hands swallowed by wide-mouthed sleeves. Cold, impersonal, silent forms that would rule their lives until the final Rite of Krisalys.

Close by a startled bird gave a half-chirp. Danai staggered, choking back a cry of pain as someone grabbed her hair and nearly yanked her off her feet. She twisted her head and glimpsed a cowled figure.

"Stand."

She stood still. Obedience was paramount when an Order was given by any Mentor. She winced as she heard the thin hiss of metal being drawn from its sheath.

The shadowy figure hacked away, showing no mercy or concern for Danai's burning scalp. In moments, a coarse silver thatch was all that remained, and the figure melted into the darkness. Danai blinked away tears, gazing down at the long silver locks curling about her feet.

"Spryte, come." Melitsa appeared and tapped her on the left shoulder, evincing no reaction to her Charge's ransacked appearance.

They slipped through the forest. Her hearing made acute from pain and nerves, Danai thought she could detect the faintest rustles as other pairs converged upon the Dell, now devoid of all traces of the earlier celebration. Glancing about she realized all the sprytes had been shorn. Why, we look like thistles, she thought, surprised to discover some shred of humor.

There were twenty-seven members in her pod, as a group of sprytes were known. Twenty-seven, one *lumna*. Lunasa's sacred number, the time it took for him to look away from, then return his gaze to Lampion, as he did tonight in full *Solas*. They were herded into a group, then encircled by a matching number of Mentors who waited like watching pillars. Lunasa hung directly overhead, austere in his realm of stars, drowning the Dell in silver light without shadows. Far off, a fox gave a shrill bark, and an owl screamed.

A Mentor detached itself from the circle, and eased back its cowl. The sprytes gasped. It was the Dolmen.

The almost unbearably white skin emitted a dull gleam, unlike the faint shimmering bodyglow of most Feyree. No wrinkles cragged its gaunt face, and the hairless skull seemed to absorb rather than reflect light. Ebony bird-like eyes glared out from silver-rimmed sockets, peering into each spryte's face, leaving them feeling as if their private self had been cored, inspected, and found wanting. Shoulders slumped or stiffened in response. In those eternity of moments, each succumbed to the Dolmen's scouring scrutiny.

Danai caught her breath. The most Revered One! The Most High of Loremasters! One that was neither male nor female, higher than even the Lord and Lady of Revelstoke. The eyes delved hers, and suddenly the urgent necessities of her life seemed trivial, self-absorbed. She bit her lip.

At last, the Dolmen raised both hands, palms out in formal greeting. "Sprytes of all Vales, all Dells, all Glens. Thrice welcome be ye. The Mother greets ye. Lunasa greets ye. We greet ye. Ye are about to embark on the Rites of Krisalys. Ye risk death, perhaps worse. Ye may choose. Leave now. Or proceed. But know that after this moment, there is only one path. Choose!" Its voice cracked like a lightning-split stone.

Daring them. Denying them. Doubting them.

Not a spryte even breathed. The surrounding woods waited in silence.

The Dolmen's arms sank. There was a barely perceptible nod. "So be it. Eight are the Rites ye shall endure. The first is passed. Survive ye all, and only then shall ye confront the ninth, the most sacred, the Rite of Krisalys!" Its pale hands retrieved the hood, extinguishing the face, and it stepped back into the circle.

Danai blinked and glanced about at her podmates. She wondered if her face looked as dull and drained. As if they had all been heaving great weights. A sudden thought pecked at her. I had a chance to leave, and I didn't take it. Why?

Unbidden, a second thought popped out. Now I'm in for it.

* * * * *

Danai collapsed by the creek, sucking for air. Her myriad scratches burned with sweat. It seemed she had been fleeing the whip-wielding Mentor for *ever*.

The Dolmen's retreat had signaled the Mentors to lunge at the sprytes, uncoiling hidden whips that nipped at shoulders, buttocks, legs. With startled yelps, the sprytes had scattered in all directions, fleeing into the woods.

Danai had stumbled and tripped over solid shadows, shoved through clinging twigs, dodging the whip's stinging lash. Dawnshine brought no respite. Every time she had tried to stop, the Mentor reappeared within moments, forcing her to lurch up and onwards.

The tangy smell of sun-warmed pine needles pierced her fog of desperation. Panic. Triasa had warned her not to panic. But how could you not when being hunted without mercy? Then figure out some way to stop the hunt, murmured a small voice from within, like a clear draught of water bubbling through mud. Danai scanned her surroundings. A heap of pine cones to the left, a blister of pine saplings further down, the stream burbling to the right. Forcing herself back to her feet, she dashed towards the stream, deliberately scuffing through pine needles, then darted behind the cones, careful to avoid their spiny points as she crouched low to earth to peer between their thick scales.

The forest duff crunched behind a nearby birch, and the Mentor appeared, whip tightly furled. It studied the ground, then followed the scuff marks. Anger coiled behind Danai's eyes. She held her breath. Five feylengths. Four. The Mentor, panting slightly, stepped past her hiding place. Now!

Bellowing with fury, she slammed into the Mentor's back, knocking the figure sprawling. She yanked the whip away, then stepped aside, and cracked the long thong, savoring the hissing snap. Slowly she raised it. Your turn, she thought, intent on paying back her tormentor for the pain, the fear, the self-doubt.

The cowl crumpled back as the figure rolled over. Melitsa studied her Charge, still a little winded. She observed Danai's posture, and took a deep breath. Revenge could be a clumsy mistress. Now came the other half of the Hunted Rite.

Melitsa's passive posture infuriated Danai. Red sparks flecked her vision. How dare she lie there so uncaring, she thought. She struck. The whip dragged harmlessly through the thick unyielding cloth. Danai lifted her arm again, determined to strike even harder, oblivious to the Mentor's disappointed expression.

In one fluid motion, Melitsa surged up, flung off the cloak, and unfolded her amber wings to fly easily out of reach of the snaking whip. She plummeted behind Danai and pinned her whip arm against her back with a quick wrench that extracted a sharp cry. Flailing her body from side to side, Danai kicked at Melitsa's legs, trying to throw her off balance. "Danai, stop! This is an Order. Stop! STOP!" The last command was a full-throated shout.

It penetrated. Danai slumped, flooded by gut-wrenching humiliation. You've already failed, she thought. Don't cry.

Melitsa released her and stepped back, content to let her suffer. It was necessary, the only way Danai could complete the Rite, despite this common failure. The silence seethed.

Trying to ignore the darts of pain in her shoulder, Danai turned to face her Mentor. "Melitsa, I...I..." There seemed no words that could excuse the enormity of her actions, she thought. No, her crime! She had assaulted a Mentor. During the Rites! Such an act could merit only one penalty, she was sure. But it was more than that. She had always taken such pride in her self-control, had felt a lofty sense of disdain when others erupted into a display of strong emotions. The savage rape of her self-image robbed her of speech. "You wanted to kill me is what you can't say." Melitsa spoke softly, plucking through the emotions that careened across Danai's face. "You wanted to hurt me as I hurt you. Didn't you?"

Danai nodded, wishing she could crawl away and hide in a squirrel hole.

"Sit." It was an Order. Melitsa settled into a comfortable position beside the trembling spryte, and gazed at the sun-splashed stream dancing over the rocks for a few moments. "Danai, how long have the Feyree survived?"

Danai responded from habit, the chants of the Teaching Skalds coming to mind. "Since the birth of Lampion."

"And why have they survived?"

The Laws of Lunasa came to Danai's lips. "Because they have avoided danger. Because they are wary. Because although they may know magic, they are not immortal. Because they learn and know their limitations. As a folk and as an individual."

"Explain."

Danai struggled to grasp this Order. Nobody explained the Laws. They just were!

Melitsa insisted. "Explain."

"I think...I think it means that we must not abuse magic?" Danai was guessing, and she knew Melitsa knew it. Her thoughts were muddled. She hurt more inside than out. The Dolmen had known she would fail. Would any others suffer such shame?

"No." Melitsa hesitated. She empathized with Danai's feelings, wanted to soften the pain. Yet this humiliation was instrumental to the Rite. She could not reveal that virtually all sprytes failed the physical part. But the true hurdle was their interpretation of the experience. If they could not..."Danai, when did you decide to become hunter, not hunted?"

Abraded by such a precise description, Danai blurted out, "Because you never let up. You just kept chasing me, hunting me, hurting. What else could I do? Run until I dropped? Let panic rule?"

"Actually, you did just that." She smiled at Danai's shocked look. "I know you think you took control of the situation, but consider your behavior."

Concentrating, Danai forced herself to re-experience the moment. She recalled her exhilaration upon capturing the whip, the power of striking back. She had been in control—or had she? The feelings—the anger she amended to herself—had been so violent, so consuming, yet...She shook her head. "I was sure I was in control. It was wonderful, such a release after all the fear I had felt! And yet I wasn't truly in control because I was reacting to your actions. Just like panic." She hesitated, then plunged onwards. "Yes, I wanted to hurt you, maybe even kill you. Anything to stop your hurting me. Oh, by the Mother..." She paused, staring at the wriggling heat shimmers rising from a flat stone nearby. "That's why sprytes aren't taught magic until the Rites, isn't it? Because we can't conceive our limitations. We really don't even know ourselves yet. If you armed us with magic, we'd probably kill each other instead of getting into fisticuffs in a rage we haven't learned how to control. And depending on our moral consciences, we might even feel proud of the accomplishment—at least at that moment. True?"

"Yes, and therein are the roots of this Hunted Rite." Melitsa's voice deepened, her dark blue eyes seeming to see far into a forgotten distance. "Many are the old tales that originate time out of mind, when Feyree were like all wild things, living the days as they came, as the Mother first intended. But there is a younger tale that you are not permitted to be told until now.

"Some thousand winters past it was, a Feyree discovered certain magics—we have no records or tales to tell us how—and grew mighty with power. Solon was his name. He gathered those about him that concurred with his ideas. He wielded magic like a whip, and tormented the folk that resisted, ceaselessly forcing them to do his bidding. Finally, many of the folk rebelled, believing how could it get any worse?

"It was a bloody war, with Feyree slaughtering Feyree. Whole dells were annihilated, and it is said that the Mother wept crystal tears of blood for her warring folk. Solon was killed during a final terrible battle, but after seasons seemingly beyond count of battles and bloodshed, the Feyree had lost their sense of purpose, of direction, of reason for being. And so more seasons passed. It was known as the Days of Dimness, a dark time for our folk.

"It is told how the Twins arose, the younglings of the Blessed One, and began to preach for thought, not emotions, as the guiding principles. These were the precursors to the Laws of Lunasa.

"Now by then, many Feyree knew fragments of magic, but it was a jumbled muddle, without reason or rhyme. The Twins collected the spells and knowledge, and working with the Chief Tains of the scattered groups, they scribed the Scrolls of Atonement. And these scrolls were copied and carried back to each group, and the new Laws were taught, and slowly the folk began to rise again."

Melitsa's eyes refocused on the enthralled spryte. "Danai, we are volatile, passionate folk. You have rightly determined that it is only by learning our own limitations that we can gain control. Only then are we fit to use magic. And even then..." she hesitated, momentarily unsure of imparting this last piece of information, yet driven by some premonition to do so. "Sometimes, despite the Laws and the Scrolls and all the Teachings, there are Feyree who have passed through the Rites and still lose control." She rose and extended her hand.

Danai gratefully took it. Getting to her feet, she realized how little she really knew of her folk and her self.

They hiked back through the woods, Melitsa pointing out the early shoots of certain flowers and plants that would provide food on journeys. "You will soon receive instruction on this and many other survival skills as well as spellcasting, weapons-making, and basic weather lore. There is much you have to learn after sheltering these one and twenty winters in your bower in Goldyn Vale." She laughed, remembering. "I did not realize how much I took for granted until these Rites, how much went on that I did not even know was happening. I think that you shall discover more than you could ever expect about your self and our folk these next six lumnas."

Danai ventured a question. "Were you afraid of Krisalys?"

"Yes and no. The unknown always brings fear. How you choose to deal with that fear is what determines your mettle. Ah! There is the Dell."

At the call of the reed pipe, the pod gathered once again, encircled by the Mentors, many of which had torn cloaks. Danai wondered how many others had also flubbed the first part of the Hunted Rite.

The Dolmen uncowled and studied the pod for several moments, waiting until they stood perfectly still. Then it asked each Mentor, "Did your Charge pass?" One by one, they stepped forward, pulled back their hoods, and answered yes. They then re-cowled and stepped back into the circle.

When Melitsa advanced, Danai felt time slow to the crawl of ice over stone. Her heart throbbed in her mouth.

"Did your Charge pass?"

Melitsa paused, her eyes holding Danai's gaze for the briefest moment. "Yes."

Neither noticed another Mentor relax at the affirmation.

* * * * *

Chapter Two

Nearly two lumnas had already passed. The forest was now in full leaf, the wood folk busy with food and frolic as the sun warmed the soil and brought forth plants and flowers in colorful profusion. The Dell, grass grazed short each night by the deer, was gemmed with wild violets, golden hearts-ease and primroses, and the startling blue of gentians. Delicate pale anemone and wood sorrel gazed from under the pink and white blossoms of tartberry and sweetberry bushes.

The sprytes had little time to enjoy it.

Under the Mentors' stern tutelage, they were acquiring the foundations of magic and essential survival lore. Some training involved the entire pod; other instruction was done in small groups. No spell came without a history. No food without a caution. No effort without sore muscles. Danai had never imagined how the beautiful hills and woodlands of Lampion could hold so much danger and power. There were moments she missed that innocence.

Clusters of friends bloomed. Danai spent her free time with five others whom she had met at previous revels. Joson hailed from Glyffshado Glen towards the eastern foot of the Anlyn Hills, while Pook came from Firebaugh Vale along the eastern shore. Rhytha was from Darlding Glen nestled in the southern Wynndowns, while Damon and Elanoria came from westerly Mireer Vale, known for its weavers.

"Who would ever have thought of using a holly leaf as a shield?" Damon commented as they trudged along the creek towards the clearing to continue defense training. "Although those edges are sharper than I thought. I scratched my hand when I shifted to edge-flinging it at Mentor Dilyn." He whirled, mimicking the toss, his bronze skin and coppery hair glinting in the sunbeams. "He told me at mid-meal that properly dried and flattened, the shield can take an enemy's head off." He shuddered. "Why would any Feyree need to know that?"

"Don't be a dim," Pook snorted. "You get out of your dell and who knows what may think you're a tasty tidbit." He grinned, then ducked as Damon took a half-swing at him.

Rhytha rolled her eyes at Danai and Elanoria. "Lads! Always at fisticuffs."

Mentors Toron, Arlymyria, Asagion, and Dilyn were waiting in the clearing. Each was a member of the Guardian Guild, trained in the craft of weaponry, attack, and defense. Toron hailed from Danai's vale, and often in the gloaming she had seen him circling the perimeter, riding his luminous nightwing. He was popular among the ladies and maids, darkly handsome with his jade skin, ebony hair, and eyes the deep blue of the sky just before dawnshine. Danai found him reserved, slow to laugh or anger, and precise in his expectations of Orders being followed.

There were weapons everywhere, if one knew where to look. Already they had learned how to locate hardwoods and other readily-available items and quickly convert them into protection.

Arlymyria not only showed them how to craft spears from oak and ash, but how they could double as staffs, useful in close combat. She had laughed at their startled looks when she selected Joson, the largest spryte, as her partner. She was slender, with creamy skin and hair the color of dandelion fuzz, and several of the lads had joked a feather's touch would be her undoing. But with a few sure strokes, she deftly knocked Joson's legs out from under him. The clearing had resounded with the clack of wood striking wood, and the grunts of the fallen as the sprytes practiced.

Asagion had instructed them on which seed pods could explode and blind the attacker or leave them helpless with sneezing. Properly dried, the spiny husk of a chestnut became lethal when dropped from a high branch, or wielded at the end of a thong. Even freshly plucked, its heavy weight guaranteed damage on impact.

They had chuckled at the sight of a Guardian pulling out a simple slingshot...until Toron split a beechnut at fifty feylengths. Washing the webs free of their sticky goo, and braiding them into flexible bands to be tied on forked twigs took patience. Elanoria was still trying to remove the last of a web that had gotten tangled in her copper curls the previous day.

Today they were making their first dirqs. "Select your wood from such hardy trees as oak, ash, and blackthorn," Mentor Dilyn explained. "All are about this clearing. Look for twigs wide at the top or long pointed thorns. Then, if you cannot break them off, call, and we will cut them."

"Do you really think a wooden dirq will be able to cut anything?" Joson muttered to Danai as they hurried off towards a blackthorn bush dense with white blossoms.

"I hope so. I guess we'll find out. We won't get our own first metal dirqs until after Krisalys. Triasa told me that later we will receive guild dirqs, bestowed when we are trained in our Calling, along with our amulets. They are both specially-crafted by the mastersmythes at the Metalworks Guild hall and are to be cherished. Her guild dirq has a beautiful design on the blade, with wood folk among trees, symbols of her Calling."

A full head taller than Danai, Joson was able to reach two wicked-looking thorns that snapped off when he hung on them. "See?" He patted his full belly. "Being a bit on the well-fed side has its advantages." Danai laughed and reached up to ruffle his curly black hair.

"Oh, I simply delight in blisters, don't you?" Elanoria grumped as they squatted, each in front of a flat stone, slowly honing a cutting edge onto their dirqs. She popped a bronze thumb into her mouth with a grimace. "I bet they made us choose a hard wood, so it would be harder to do this."

"More likely so it wouldn't break when you poked it into something Ela." Damon remarked, wiping away sweat from his eyes. He grinned as she stuck her tongue out. They were born of the same father, by different mothers, but never failed to act like brother and sister.

* * * * *

So much to digest, so much to understand. It was nothing like the Teachings, where the Elder or Skald would drone on about the Laws and the Tales as restless younglings twitched through the passing morn. You had to prove you could interpret and apply these lessons, not just dutifully repeat them. Some nights Danai collapsed onto the soft turf of the Dell and was asleep before her second breath, too drained for dreams—or nightmares. When she occasionally awoke, she observed that there were always some Mentors about, standing and watching.

There were moments she wanted to quit, yet pride—or was it fear of failure? she wondered—kept her in place.

Foraging in the forest when the season was yet young proved surprisingly hard. Seeds and fruits had yet to form, and the sprytes learned with much unpleasant trial to select edible plant parts. Young hawthorn leaves became a common meal, although later in the season, they would become tough and hard to chew. Danai gained new appreciation for the vale's Gatherers, realizing how she had always taken for granted the full *bionas* that stored the dried foodstuffs shared by all during the long cold days of winter.

During the second lumna, they commenced the First Tier Magics. This morning they had started on Fire magic, nine sprytes to a pair of Mentors. The contortions and gestures needed to control the elemental power resulted in aching arms and fingers. Mentor Melarna made it seem so simple—until one had to emulate her.

Danai waved at Joson and Pook returning from Mentor Quenton's and Mentor Shanaron's groups, and they met and hastened to the trestles for evenmeal. Carrying their heavily-laden trenchers—Joson's threatened to topple—they joined their friends under a tussock of sweet-scented white lily bells.

"I actually got a fire going!" exulted Damon, who had shown a talent for spellcasting. "Although I did singe my fingers a bit."

"Um," mumbled Rhytha through mashed dandelion leaves, "and how do you explain your Mentor's rather crisped-looking cloak?"

Damon flushed. "No idea what you're talking about." He busied himself with his food, stuffing his mouth to avoid further speech.

"I did pretty well, actually." Pook sprawled back, pushing his empty trencher aside. "It's a lot of fun. So much power bound up in words and gestures. I want to learn more about this fire magic—lots more."

Joson waved a piece of mallow root towards the Mentors, talking around a bit tucked into his cheek. "You know, it's hard to believe that all of them—and all those before—have gone through this. I mean we're all so different—even after the Rites. You would think that such intense training would grind the differences right out of us."

"Uh-uh." Rhytha shook her head. Her coloring was uncommon among the Folk—fiery red hair, topaz eyes, rosy skin with a generous handful of freckles sprinkled across nose and cheeks. One tended to look when she spoke. "Consider that even as we're learning, our individual strengths—and weaknesses—are going to appear. Remember that part of this is to help us discover our Callings."

"What do you hope to be?" Danai asked.

"I had really wanted to be a Charmer, but the wood folk just don't seem to like me. Charmer Eberle fostered me in Second Season, and I was such a disappointment to her! She released me to the easier craft of weaving. Even youngling wood folk won't let me approach. And I do so like them." She sounded wistful.

"So what?" Danai countered. "Don't tell me that just because it didn't work under one Charmer, you're going to give up your dream?"

"It's not so much that." Rhytha looked down, seeking the right words. "It's that it just doesn't feel right anymore. You know what I mean? It's as if I'm being pulled in another direction—I'm not even sure what that is—and I have to follow these feelings to find out what is right for me. Dream Council should open that passageway."

Her friends were silent, digesting her words and their meals. Eventide cast an indigo veil across the sky. Already a hem of stars twinkled on the eastern horizon, while bands of marigold, ruby, and plum dimmed in the west. About them bubbled the soft chatter of other sprytes. The final evening calls of birds slowly dissipated, save for the clear piping notes of the nightingale, Danai's favorite bird. She loved how it sang in the voices of all birds, at any time of night or day as it pleased. Such freedom!

Pook contemplated the darkening skies. He was difficult to see in the gloaming, his skin just the right shade of amethyst, his tousled locks raven black. Only his glowing aqua eyes were visible, reflecting the burnished silver of Lunasa's rising oval. "The fire magic puzzles me," he murmured. "Didn't you get the feeling that the Mentors were saying a lot less than they actually knew?"

"We're beginners. What do you expect?" Joson sucked on a bit of sweetgrass.

"It's not that. It's more of a, a reticence to say things, as if there's something else behind the basic spell."

"I repeat. We're only First Tier, you dim! There's a lot of stuff we're not being told, and they won't tell us until it's time. Quenton spent time with our group on how to do the basic spellcast, and with Balanoran having trouble, it took a bit longer. You're always the impatient one, Pook. Wanting to explore before you know what's out there. You can get into trouble that way."

"Well, why not? There's a lot of things we Feyree don't know, all nestled snug as we are in our bowers. I was talking with an Ael once—"

"You never!" exclaimed Elanoria, jerking upright. "You're just making that up!"

Pook's full-lipped mouth tightened into a thin line. "Not hardly, Ela. There are other folk out there, even if you've stayed hidden in your safe little glen all these years. I want to meet them. There's so much more I want to know about Lampion—and beyond." His eyes and skin shimmered brighter with enthusiasm.

"Isn't that unwise Pook?" Rhytha murmured with a slow shake of her head. "We don't know enough about our own folk yet, much the less interacting with others."

"But it's not like that, not like that at all!" Pook sat up and leaned forward with eagerness. "This Ael was as startled as I was when we met near the Froth—that's the big pool the Tumbledown Falls spills into near our vale. It was eventide, and I guess he didn't see me in the gloaming, perched upon the branch. He was hard to see, too— his skin was silver, like a pool of reflecting water." He paused to savor his rapt audience. "I called out a greeting, and it was actually pretty funny." Pook grinned at the recollection. "He was looking everywhere, and I had to call out a couple of times before he located my voice. When he leaned over me, his pale green eyes were so wide that you could see white all around them. He wore his gold-streaked green hair in a braid that ran half down his back; it showed off his pointed ears pretty well."

Elanoria gulped. "Pointed ears? Leaned over you? How big was he?"

"I'd guess about ten feylengths."

"As tall as that!"

"And?" prompted Danai, well-acquainted with Pook's tendency to swagger.

"He told me it had been long since he had seen a spryte. Actually asked to clasp hands with me to make sure he wasn't dreaming. Of course I let him."

"You let a being ten times your size touch you?" Rhytha's eyes shone like amber glowflies with amazement.

"Well, think on it. If he tried anything, I could have easily just let myself tumble off the branch, and disappear into the bramble bush underneath. Hard to reach for me in there! He couldn't find me until I directed him, after all. And he was really very polite. Introduced himself as Rynok, and explained he was on a journey to somewhere he called High North, where the Ael-lords hold summer court. He's like one of our Orpheii, carrying songs and news among the *hyells*—I guess that's what they call their bowers. He had the most beautiful lyre, all of beaten silver and strung with the glowing tail hairs of the alicorn, he told me. Would you believe he even strummed a melody for me? It wasn't like any of our music. Want to hear what I can remember?" He proceeded, not waiting for an answer.

> *"Come memories gone in ancient past*
> *Learn us of your grief and joy.*
> *The peace of days is passing fast.*
> *The hooded ones unwitting teach the change,*
> *sowing seeds that breed the last.*
> *Rising innocent the One*
> *whom happiness with hate shall blast."*

"What a queer song." Danai felt a shiver crawling up her back from the discordant tune. "What does it mean?"

"Actually he hasn't any clue." Pook shrugged. "That's why he's headed up north. Several of his folk dreamed a similar verse, and they believe it's a sending from the Mother—they believe in her too—and hope that their high Dream Loremaster can interpret it."

A sharp clap from a Mentor prevented Joson from asking his question. It was time for rest, and silence was mandatory. Danai found sleep long in coming.

* * * * *

Mentors Majikian and Tarlokyn called a respite in the spellcasting of Feyree dust, and Danai's little group gathered under the broad shade of a burdock leaf. The cool dampness was a welcome change from the warming sun—summer heat was starting early.

"I wonder if we'll have the same problems birds do when they learn to fly," said Pook. "You know, flapping about, falling off branches at the wrong time."

Elanoria giggled behind her hand. Danai had realized her friend was sweet on him. "Oh, I can just see you now Pook. Trying to look like a serious Feyree poised on some branch, and an Ael startles you, so instead of falling into the shrubs, you flap right up into his face."

"Face? No it would probably be his pointy ear," chortled Rhytha.

"No, up his tunic, or whatever Aels wear," teased Aaron, who had ambled over to join them. He had a well-earned reputation for mischief-making, and already several sprytes had awoken to ankles roped with braided grass, chilly drops of dew descending without warning as they sat down to eat, a catkin bed suspended in a webber's sticky net. One kept a wary eye on the golden lad when he was around. His humorous disposition refused to be quenched under the most weighty of circumstances, and more than once a Mentor had banned him from meals, or ordered him to stand alone during rest times. He winked at Elanoria.

"Ha, ha," retorted Pook, miffed at being the butt-end of the joke. "You're so graceful Rhytha,"—he knew her reputation for clumsiness—"you'll try landing and wind up on your head." He grinned at her discomfiture.

"Do you think you can damage wings?" Danai turned the conversation to a safer path.

"Doubt it," yawned Damon, his silver eyes half-lidded to dim out the sun's glare.

"No, actually you can," Joson paused his chewing on a bit of tang-grass. "Nehrani—she's Glyffshado Glen's Healer, and my *lirupai*—she's had to fix torn wings a few times. Like for Cnonklan, who isn't all there since being thrown from the back of his dragonfly. He misjudges distances all the time. Seems to forget his wingspread and just flies through areas that aren't wide enough."

"It must be nice to have a lirupai who's a Healer." Elanoria's voice bore a trace of sadness. "At least their craft is to care about folk. My Second Season foster mother was a Messenger, and much preferred to be dragonflyback than biding with her sprytes. We were a lonely little bunch, those seven winters we had to live with her." She brightened. "But my Third Season lirupai was a Skald, and Manali was grand. It made up for those empty years."

"I had a Scryer Third Season," Danai said, stretching to relieve the stiffness in her neck. "Harmona was, I guess, strange, though I always had the feeling she did care about us in her way. But her bower was so busy with Feyree coming in and out, seeking advice and guidance, that we were usually running to get herbs for smoke trances, or fallwater for the scrying bowl, or whatever else she needed. We were more like thralls than fosterlings, but she fed us, listened to our problems, and tried to be there. Her craft just always seemed to get in the way."

"Did you ever wonder why we don't stay with our own birth mothers?" Pook asked after a contemplative silence. "I can understand fostering by choice, or if you have a mother who just doesn't have time for you—or worse yet, doesn't want you. But having to rotate among foster mothers every seven winters seems a bit hard."

"It's not like you can't visit with them," Elanoria said.

"Not the same thing. I mean you have her for the first seven years of your life—maybe—then get yanked away whether you want it or no. And then have to start all over again a second time."

"We don't do lirupai that way any more in Ardmoor Vale," remarked Ayulun, who had also wandered over. He blended perfectly with the greenish shade, and in tests of search, was hard to find in the woods. "I was with my birth mother until twelve winters passed." He had their full attention. "After that, I was sent to serve in various guildhalls, under the guidance of Third Tier masters, each for a period of three winters. We call it *mancebo* instead. I still lived at my birth mother's bower, although after the first mancebo, I moved out. For various reasons." He blushed. Aaron snorted.

"But I thought all Feyree did things the same way." Danai was surprised.

"Well, you thought wrong," Pook replied. "How long has your vale been doing this mancebo thing?"

"A ways before my birthing," Ayulun explained. "My birth mother said it grew from just what you were saying earlier. A lot of them didn't want to give up their younglings. So they approached the Chief Tains and petitioned them to consider a change. Lahiri and Beriel are very open-minded, and spoke with every Feyree in the vale. Lahiri is also a Charmer, so she consulted many of the wood folk to learn their thoughts on mothering. They decided it was unfair to separate mother and youngling, and with the vale's approval, put into place mancebo. About seven pods ago, I think."

Danai wondered if the Chief Tains had consulted the Dolmen. She doubted it. It didn't seem one that would approve of such changes.

"It sure shows that change is a good thing." Pook waxed enthusiastic. "Instead of staying in the same dry creek bed hoping for water, they were willing to try a new approach for the better."

"They didn't just go and change things Pook," Danai objected. "They did a lot of thinking and consulted other folk before making a decision."

"It might not have worked," added Joson. "Then what?"

"Lahiri agreed it was a trial of one podspan of sprytes," Ayulun explained. "If at the end, it did not seem to be working—and sooner if need be—the trial would end."

Joson spat out the grass. "What convinced them to continue?"

"Two things actually. Birth mothers were a lot happier, and so were their sprytes. And the *fa-mancebo*—the ones who mentor us—could instead focus on teaching us the basics of their crafts. Ardmoor Vale has become known for the clay warework our crafters produce. It has another benefit too, I think."

"What?" Rhytha smiled at him.

"Helps us start to get an idea of what craft we may want to follow after Krisalys. I mean it's all well and good to do the Dream

Council, but I want to do something I like. What better way to find out enough about a craft than trying it out?"

"Sprytes to me!" Mentor Majikian shouted.

The group emerged somewhat unwillingly into the bright sun. Danai squinted, wondering how the Mentors could tolerate their cloaks in the humid air.

"You have all learned to create Feyree dust," Mentor Tarlokyn began. "A simple First Tier spell that can be used for pleasure—or protection. Now you must learn to direct it, to move it as an extension of your will, however it is needed. Yes, Pook?"

"Why not just simply point to direct it?"

Tarlokyn released a thin smile that slit his gaunt copper face. "That is a part of the spellcast. But what if your hands are occupied elsewhere? Or bound? Or injured? It is not enough to learn a magic and then rough handle it to your bidding. Like any craft, it must be practiced, perfected. The loremasters each have their own special talents, and it is said you can tell which loremaster cast the magic from the way the spell transpires."

"So you can become a loremaster as a craft?" Pook looked intrigued.

Majikian interceded. "Yes and no. You can be selected to become a loremaster by the Chief Tain, Guild Master, or even the Dolmen. But loremaster is not a craft that you choose at the outset. Most loremasters are found among those who show an unusual ability during the teaching of the Second or Third Tier spells."

"When do we start learning those?"

"You don't," replied Tarlokyn with an impatient gesture. "Those are reserved for the members of each guildhall and are a part of their training. After Dream Council and Krisalys, you will take on the Calling of your Dream's choosing, and then be involved in the rituals and ways of your fellow crafters. Only after you have learned the Second Tier spells of that craft will you be considered for Third Tier."

"You mean it's not a given?"

"Of course not. Not every Feyree can lead a Guild or become a loremaster. Too many loremasters would be too many leaders. Some are needed to do the basics, while others' skills allow them to advance only to a certain Tier."

"Do all crafts have the same number of Tiers?"

"Pook, Pook, you should know that answer," chided Tarlokyn, glancing at the sun. "Recall the rhyme you were taught during fire magic. You were to memorize it."

"Seven are the Tiers of Spells
born of Twin-Gathered lore
taught by Crafters in their Dells
to bend beauty to their work.
One for sprytes unwinged.
Two for Crafters new-fledged.
Three for those of special skills.
Four Guild Masters claim their own.
The final Tiers that lie beyond
The Loremasters only know
learned in the master spells
born of Twins' lore long ago."

"Does any Feyree know all the spells that there are?" Pook remained unruffled by the Mentors' palpable impatience.

"Not even the Dolmen."

Pook's casual demeanor evaporated. "How is that possible? He is the Most High, the greatest of loremasters!"

"He knows more than any other Feyree, yes." Majikian replied in the tone used with a small youngling. "But that does not mean he knows all. Did you not listen to what Tarlokyn said? Potential loremasters advance to a different apprenticeship after Third Tier. Fourth Tier spells are known only to the Guild Master and their chosen few. The Twins never again wanted all spells under the command of one Feyree." He held up his hand to forestall further questions. "Enough! The day is waning, and we will not return until this final spellcast is learned. Since you are so eager and full of questions Pook, come forth and we shall begin with you."

Pook bounced up. A pleasurable tingle shirred down his spine. How he loved spellcasting! At Tarlokyn's command, he cupped his palms and concentrated on spelling Feyree dust, envisioning the sparkling lavender flakes; the dust was always the color of its maker. He murmured, *"Pousyehr eteencel amoy,"* felt a quiver scurry down his arms, then the prickly weight coalesced.

"Very good," nodded Tarlokyn. He pointed at a rounded gray stone that stood waist high beside him. "Now you will cast it over this rock. Point your arms towards it. As with making the dust, it is a blend of mind and murmur. Envision the dust striking the stone. Now, repeat after me *'Zjet achosa lasbas.'* Good. Go ahead. Try."

The dust exploded from Pook's hand with a tinkling hiss, cloaking the stone. The Mentor blinked and stared as the last particles cascaded down. "Excellent," he said after a long pause. "I commend you, young spryte. In my many years as Mentor, I have not ever seen a spryte strike that stone on their first try."

Pook gave a self-satisfied smile.

"So, as you already have this lesson," Majikian continued, his eyes narrowed, "let me give you the next, so you can practice both as we teach the others." He strode towards Pook, pulling a supple strand of woodbine from his sleeve pouch. "I will bind your hands behind your back. So." He ignored Pook's slight grunt at the awkward position. "Now you must combine the two spells, for no longer can you gather the dust in your hands. You must form and hold it in the air before you, then cast it forth. Your target shall be that fern yonder. Is something the matter?"

Pook shifted his shoulders, trying to get more comfortable. "I don't see how you can do that. You have to have something to put something in."

"Ah, but you do not. Watch." The Mentor held his hands behind his back and seemed to gather within himself. The fascinated sprytes heard a rapid mutter, saw the gathering of shimmery dark blue dust before the tall figure, then watched open-mouthed as it looped twice, soared upwards, and dove down to burst just above Pook's head in a flickering cascade. "I could as easily have knocked you flat with the impact," Majikian said coolly. "Like all magic, it is a weapon that can increase in strength based on the skill of the user. Sohain, come. It is now your turn."

As the sprytes learned to fling Feyree dust, the air became hazy with multihued sparkles, the ground more glitter than grass. Both Mentors' cloaks were splotched with misdirected dust. Danai kept trying to suppress the tickling sneeze that interrupted her spellcasting. Occasionally she would glance over at Pook, still struggling with the second spell. He was encircled by lavender dust piles.

Sandai gave a shriek of excitement, causing the ball of bronze dust gathering before her to slump. She refocused and it rose, hovered a moment, then advanced with short jerks towards a birch tree to splatter at its roots. There were scattered cries of approval from sprytes not in the middle of a spellcast.

Danai noticed Aaron, his face crumpled with concentration, form not just a golden ball but an almost petalled shape that drifted to dapple a nearby oak sapling. "Good, very good!" called Majikian. "You are seeing that you can control the shape as well."

"Mentor, what am I doing wrong?" Pook's tone was more respectful as he realized he was one of the few who still could not master the basic hands-free spell.

"Stop trying so hard." Mentor Majikian approached with a smile. "Pook, you cannot be perfect at everything the first time. Because you did so well on the first spell, you tasked yourself with the same achievement on the second. And when you failed—as most do the first round—you let your emotions rule your mind. Emotions and magic are a poor mix. Either the spell fizzles or, worse, it can pervert itself. Now relax. Close your eyes. Inhale. See the dust before you, see it gather, and now push it towards the fern, yes push, push, push. Ah, you've done it!"

Pook's eyes flew open. The fern glittered lavender. "I did it!" He jumped with delight, lost his balance, and tumbled backwards into his piles of dust that burst upwards and scattered over his cheering podmates. The sun settled on the treetops.

"Time for us to return for evenmeal," chuckled Majikian as he released Pook's bindings. "Everyone will know what we have been doing, for you are one large pod of sparkles."

"Mentor Majikian, what happens to the dust?" Danai asked as they walked back towards the Dell.

"The wind will push it about. Some will land in flowing waters and sink to gild the streambed. It is what the Gem-Dwarves call fool's gold. Other will be caught up in the evening dew, and the next morn a field or flower or glade shall gleam more brightly than usual, even if the sun hides itself among the clouds. If it is a strong wind, some may even soar into the skies to gild the low-flying clouds. Wherever it goes, it is harmless. There are those who say it brings good luck."

The sprytes bathed in the Trykle before evenmeal. Most rinsed quickly and headed back along the stream bank to the Dell, but Danai and Aaron lingered in the cooling air. "Feyree dust it may be, but I'm sure not interested in eating it," spluttered Aaron as he splashed about the small pool formed by a backwash in the slow-moving stream. The powdery dust lifted off him in a cloud of gold, caught a ridge of current, and slipped away.

Danai sat on the mossy overhanging bank, fluffing her hair dry. It had grown a fingertip's worth since being sheared, and now formed a spiky silver halo about her head. "How did you manage to create that flower?"

"Just saw it in my mind. Actually, I should have directed it to fall on you, but I guess I don't have enough skill to get that far." He grinned slyly up at her, shaking water from his golden hair as he emerged, then scrambled up to sit beside her. "I'll get you yet with one." His dark golden eyes were inviting.

Danai blushed and got to her feet. Aaron was far too handsome for his own good, a lad of the sun, she thought. Anyway, what could he possibly see in her? "I doubt we'll have any time for that. Shall we get back? I hear the Mentor's reed pipe summoning us to evenmeal."

* * * * *

Chapter Three

A thick gray mist filled the Dell, coiling about the trees and grass, sagging the flowers with moisture. Occasionally a muffled bird call could be heard through the steady drip off the branches.

Mornmeal was a quick affair. The sprytes huddled together in their clammy tunics, some wishing they could use fire magic to warm themselves, others thinking of cozy bowers and thick coverlets. Anything to hide from the skin-chilling damp. Danai nudged Elanoria, and nodded at the cluster of Mentors off to the side in deep discussion. After a short while, they broke apart. A reed pipe summoned the sprytes into the Mentors' Circle.

"Sprytes, sit." Mentor Armerion ignored the mutters of protest as they sat on the wet moss, waiting for silence. Danai glanced around, expecting the Dolmen to appear, but the Mentor continued. "This morn begins the Sojourn of Truth. Ye will be placed in different groups, each given a journey rucksack. Ye are to seek the Truthing Well, from which you may petition but one question. Ask naught that be frivolous, lest ye waste your quest. The Well is wise in the ways of foolish young sprytes, and can as easily disregard thy presence as acknowledge it. Questions?"

Kerion stood. "Mentor, since we are all headed for the same spot, why break us up? Wouldn't it be safer and easier?"

A shadow of a smile softened Armerion's fissured olive face. "Yes. But ye are not all starting from the same place."

The sprytes glanced at each other. Kerion rolled his golden eyes as he sat down. Another elusive answer. He should have known better than to ask, he thought, but sometimes they were given useful replies. This was not to be one of those times.

"Listen well. Seek ye out Pyre Tor, a twisted stone peak crouched at the southern feet of the Rymple Mountains, northwest of the Wynndowns. It is crowned by the setting sun's fire last of all the western peaks. At the Tor's footstone shall ye find the Truthing Well. For proof of thy Journey, each group shall bring back a trefoil, the likes of which is only found there. A safe Search to ye all."

Moments later, Danai rose stiffly as Armerion called her name. Search for a Truthing Well. It sounded like an interesting Rite. Certainly nothing to be afraid of. She wondered as to Pyre Tor's actual whereabouts. Her bird journeys had never passed any such peak that she could recall.

Three others were bundled in her group—Tatia, Aaron, and Joson. She was relieved that at least one was a friend. Aaron carried his usual lopsided grin, and cocked an eyebrow at her. Danai noticed Tatia's lush smile as she approached. Oh, by the Mother! This could be a long journey with those two.

"Fetch thy dirqs and a rucksack from those on the trestles," Armerion called to the groups.

Danai hurried over to her rest spot, nearly bumping into Rhytha. "Weapons! Danai, do you have the feeling this is not going to be a lark in the meadows?"

Thong belts had been given to each spryte at the end of the dirq-crafting, and Danai girded on the birch bark sheath she had made for her dirq. The papery bark released a fine white powder onto her hands as she slid the sheath loop along the belt, and then secured her weapon.

The dark green rucksacks were surprisingly light. Quick inspection revealed a *kuis*—a hollowed acorn shell filled with water and plugged with beeswax—and six *miyacan* balls—a standard journey food of dried honeycomb, nuts, seeds, and fruits pounded into a dense paste. Nothing else.

"Doesn't look like they expect us to be gone too long," remarked Aaron, shouldering the ruck. "I hope not," grumped Joson. "That's not going to last me more than a day or two."

Danai chuckled, adjusting the carry strap. "Well, it's one way to get you to lose weight."

"Me? Need to lose weight? I'm already a wraith!"

Armerion signaled their group, his sodden cloak clinging to him like brown moss. "Follow me in silence."

As they headed out, Danai observed the other groups being escorted by their Mentors towards all points of the Dell. In moments, every figure had been swathed in gray, and her world shrank to five silent forms and the plop of dripping fog. She shivered and fell last in line behind Tatia.

Any sense of direction soon dissipated. A bone-white birch trunk veined in black emerged from the gray, then retreated. Dripping underbrush continuously soaked their tunics. The only sound was the faint squelching of their feet in the forest floor's duff. They trudged behind the Mentor, heads down, watching the feet in front of them, wrapped in their thoughts.

At some point, Danai noticed her leg muscles tightening, and realized they had started uphill. But which? The Great Dell was centered in a large bowl shaped valley, and in this fog, they could have headed off in any direction. She realized she had never paid much attention to the surrounding landmarks. Now would probably be a good time to start. Except for this dratted fog! Coarse gray stone, blotched with lichen, began to interrupt the soil. The climb steepened. She began to pant, hearing an echo among her fellows.

She glanced up. It seemed lighter ahead. Then, with a cry, Joson lost his balance and pitched forward, tumbling down into the thick mist. Giving a shout of alarm, Aaron dropped his rucksack, and lunged after him. Tatia shrieked.

"Keep screaming," bellowed Aaron, his voice echoey and distorted. "I've got him. He's not much hurt." Danai joined her voice with Tatia's, their shouts pummeling the fog, and in a few moments, the two lads reappeared. Pine needles spiked Joson's hair; a gash bloodied his left forearm. Even in the dim shifting light, his ivory skin seemed paler than usual.

"For the Mother's sake, sit down," Danai ordered, yanking off her rucksack and digging for the kuis. She pulled out the beeswax, sloshed water over the wound to clear the blood, then inspected it. Bits of dirt and gravel lodged around the torn edges of flesh. Ripping a piece from her tunic hem into two strips, she used one to carefully swab the gash clean. Joson winced, biting his lip as she pinched the wound's lips together, and snugly bound it with the other strip. "Nice fancy bandage for you," she teased, reaching up to pluck some of the debris from his hair. "Good thing my Aunt Triasa taught me some basic Healer skills when I fostered with her Second Season. We were always getting into scrapes of some sort. You'd think they'd have taught us Healer Lore over the past two lumnas."

Aaron glanced around. "Where's Armerion?" They stared at each other.

Danai jumped up. "He didn't fall too, did he?"

"No, I don't think so." Aaron was still peering into the mist. "At least I only saw Joson fall, and then everything happened so fast."

"Now what do we do?" Joson's question hung between them.

"I would say stay put until this mess lifts and we can see where we are, and if the Mentor is anywhere around," Aaron suggested.

"But what if he's hurt?" Tatia hugged herself, her tinkly voice a subdued whimper. "Shouldn't we search for him?"

"We'd only get ourselves lost into the bargain," Danai argued, "Aaron's right. This fog is bound to lift, hopefully soon, and if Mentor Armerion has fallen, he'll be somewhere down slope from us. And I would think he'd be calling out if he were hurt."

Tatia moaned. "Unless he's knocked silly."

An unseen branch gave a sharp snap. Joson looked towards the sound, frowning. "I think we had better move into a safer position," he muttered. "After all, there are creatures out here, and I'll bet we're well past the edge of the Dell."

Aaron shrugged. "So what?"

"So didn't you get that part in survival training where the Charmers have established terms with the local wood folk like they do in our glens, so that we ground-bound sprytes can poke around into the woods without having to look over our shoulders? I doubt the truce zone extends this far—which means we're just a bunch of tasty morsels for some fox...or worse."

Tatia began to sob. "They've sent us out here to die. Oh Aaron, what do we do?"

Danai wanted to shake the silly flit, even as her own stomach knotted. What a ninny! It was no time to flirt. And since when was Aaron the group's leader? "Joson, can you walk?"

"I was just waiting for somebody to ask." He heaved himself up, swaying unsteadily for a moment as red and white sparks cluttered his vision. The air was pierced by the startled trill of a robin.

"Move folks," hissed Aaron. "Joson's right. We've got company."

Fear makes for poor woodcraft, Danai realized as they hustled away through the confusing mist. Any creature would hear their stumblings and their rustles as they pushed through the bracken, and dodged around pine cones and piles of fallen leaves. Oh, for their wings!

"We have a definite problem." Aaron had been leading them single file, and they bumped into each other at his abrupt halt. Before them was a sheer black rock face, shiny with damp.

"Go left." Tatia clutched his arm, her whisper shrill.

"Can't. There's a fallen tree there. Saw it through a swirl in this blasted fog."

"Oh, Mother!" Joson cursed softly. "Listen!" Somewhere behind them, they could hear an eager sniffing.

"Aaron, quick. Was the tree rotting or new fallen?" Danai barely whispered.

He stared at her, puzzled. "Rotting. Pine I think. Why?"

"Come on! Maybe we can crawl inside and hide!"

They bolted for the tree, sliding to a halt before the furrowed black bark gashed by pale dirt-clogged cracks. "I can't go in there," panted Tatia, with a backwards step. "I can't. Lunasa knows what might be inside."

"You'll be inside of something else if you don't," snapped Joson, as he pushed forward into a moist, uninviting crevasse. "Come on."

He glanced over his shoulder. A monstrous shape emerged behind them, crouched down. "In!" He lunged forward.

The wood crumbled around them as one after the other they plunged into the trunk's hollow. An eerie shriek, like the wail for the dead, shriveled the air. Through the gap, a gleaming amber eye glared, replaced by a moist black nose giving quick short snuffs. Then a tentative scratching sound, and the crisping tear of wood.

"Determined little fellow, isn't it?" Aaron smiled grimly. "Sounds like a clawcat. I think we had better get a move on, don't you? Unless you'd rather see if he can break through."

"What's to prevent it from smelling us, and waiting at wherever we come out?" Tatia was shaking so hard, she could barely keep her balance. It was a good question.

"Well, it's obviously hunting." Joson rubbed his chin absently, favoring his injured arm. "What if we leave one of our rucks behind? Maybe the smell of the miyacan will make it think we're still here. But we should take out the food."

Aaron seized Tatia's ruck, tossing the food balls and kuis to the others, then flung it close to the long curved claw that was pulling at the crack. "Let's move."

Down the slender tunnel that cored the tree, something glowed. Motioning them to be silent, Joson lead the way, holding his good hand above his head to avoid colliding with the tunnel roof. They proceeded more by touch than sight, only faint slivers of light incising the darkness from other cracks in the trunk. The dank air reeked of pine-scented decay, and rivulets of sweat trickled down their faces. A few moments of eternity later, they reached the greenish light, bulging into a narrow kink of the tunnel.

"Root rot!" Danai leaned forward. The others looked at her in confusion. "Root rot. Foxfire. Don't you recognize it? It's the stuff the Skalds and Orpheii set up on the Tale Tells and Dancing Eves to light the revels. Glows in the dark. Joson, what's beyond it?"

"Can't see a blasted thing," he grunted, sidling around the glowing fungus.

"Well, take a piece of the foxfire!"

"I'm not touching that slimy stuff."

"Oh, please. Look, here, I'll grab some and give you a piece." Danai drove her hands into the luminescent glow. The cool mass yielded easily, squishing like an overripe fruit. With the sound of thick leaves tearing, a blob broke off in her hands, and a pungent smell engulfed them.

"Ugh, it stinks."

"Take it, you dim! Aaron, Tatia, here you take some too. At least we'll have something to light our way." Up tunnel, the scratching had halted, but quick sniffs could still be heard.

The tunnel angled down then widened, allowing Joson and Aaron to hurry forward side by side. In the foxfire's dim glow, their heads seemed to float along like the mournful night wisps of the swamp. Danai held onto Tatia's elbow, afraid the maid would collapse from tremors.

"I think we've reached the roots," Joson pointed. "See how gnarly the walls are getting? There's got to be an out here somewhere."

"Wait a second."

"No, let's go forward, go forward," urged Tatia, jerking her arm from Danai's grasp.

"No really, stop." Danai halted. "What time was it when the Mentor abandoned us?"

"No idea," Aaron answered after a moment's thought.

"Mid-day? Later?"

"I swear we hiked forever," said Joson. "But with the fog and all, I don't really know. I just sort of followed Armerion. My stomach says it's well after mid-day."

"Well let's assume it's later. So it's going to be dark soon. My guess is the clawcat isn't going to follow us down the tunnel."

"And how do you know?" Aaron leaned against the tunnel-side, studying her.

"The eye was too big for a small creature. We barely fit through that crack. Besides, it's no Orpheii-song that most of the hunters come out at gloaming. So wouldn't it just be smarter to settle in here for the night? We've got light, food, and water. At some point I'd think it will get bored and leave."

"And how will we know when it's dawnshine, oh wise Elder?" Tatia wasped as her fear subsided.

"Well, I don't know about you," Danai retorted, "but I usually wake up at dawnshine. I don't see why I shouldn't do the same morrowmorn."

Aaron nodded. "She's right you know."

Joson scuffed around, then sat down after bending over to inspect the area for possible splinters. "I like the idea of something to eat. And truthfully, my arm hurts like all daemiani, and staying put would do me fine."

"Some sojourn," Tatia groused, daintily seating herself on a smooth knob of wood, then plucking at the drawstrings of Aaron's rucksack. "And after all this, we're supposed to go search for a Well? Hah!"

"Methinks this is just the start of the fun," Aaron answered, reaching for his rucksack.

The honeyed sweetness of the miyacan was a welcome relief, and the cool water washed away the sour taste of decay permeating the air. "Don't gobble too much," Danai suggested. "Somehow I think this journey is going to take a lot longer than we expect."

"Our luck, you'll be right, again." Tatia curled up, pillowing her head on Aaron's rucksack.

He stared at her a moment, shrugged, then lay down near Joson. "Isn't it strange that none of us thought of using Feyree dust to blind that thing?" he asked nobody in particular. His question went unanswered as the others' feathery breathing filled the air.

* * * * *

Danai opened her eyes to darkness. She heard nothing but the slow thump-thump of her heart. The foxfire had dimmed to little more than bits of glow. Only the sprytes' faint bodyglow revealed their whereabouts. We'll need to get some more of the foxfire before we can move, she mused. I'd forgotten it does that. She stretched, feeling a mild protest from her thigh muscles. Some shape I'm in!

A rustle and yawn came from Joson's indistinct figure, and she sensed more than saw him roll to his knees, stand up—and collide with the low tunnel roof. "Ow!" Tatia and Aaron jerked upright.

Danai saw the startled glow of their eyes, and wondered once again why Feyree eyes flickered when frightened. "Morrowmorn's greeting to you."

"What's greetable about it?" Tatia rubbed her eyes and yawned. "Hey, what happened to the foxfire?"

"I forgot it fades when broken away from the main plant. I'll go get some more." Danai almost added a remark about Tatia never being around at the end of a revel when the foxfire had dimmed because she was probably otherwise occupied, but decided against it. She scrambled to her feet.

"I'll come help." Aaron rose and shook himself, running a hand through his hair, not noticing Danai's surprised look. Seizing two of the foxfire bits, they moved back up the tunnel.

"Fresh air would definitely be a welcome change." Aaron yawned. "Remind me to not build my next bower in a rotting pine trunk. Phew! Say, you were pretty calm yesterday. All the maids I know would have acted like Tatia. Shrieks and mushy knees."

Danai was thankful that the darkness hid her blush. "Well, maybe it's the maids you know," she replied primly, then hurried to change the subject. "Look, there's the foxfire." She tossed her piece down; it broke apart. The newly exposed portion glowed brightly. "Toads! I didn't know it did that. Would've saved us a trip. Should we grab a larger piece so it'll last longer?"

"Depends on what we're going to do next, don't you think?"

"Umm, good point. Let's grab a big chunk anyway—we can always toss it."

Aaron helped yank off two large chunks. "Yuck! It still stinks." They returned more quickly than they had come, the fresh foxfire casting weird shifting shadows.

* * * * *

"This is a worse labyrinth than bramble bracken!" Joson smeared the sweat from his eyes. It seemed like forever they had been following the intersecting tunnels to get out, with no luck.

"I don't get it." Aaron chewed his lip. "We should have found some way out of the roots a ways ago, where it toppled."

Tatia had been unusually subdued all morn, but now spoke. "Uh, what if the roots never pulled free of the dirt? We wouldn't find an out because they're still in the earth."

"By the Twins, I think you're on to something!" Joson nodded. "It has been smelling pretty earthy in here, now that you mention it. I've been so busy watching where to put my feet, I didn't bother to look around us." He held up the foxfire close to the roof. "Lots of dirt—more dirt than root. These tunnels must have been caused by the roots shifting when the tree fell. We'd better turn around."

"Oh great, so we just hiked all this distance for nothing. Frog feathers! Couldn't you have said something sooner Tatia?" Aaron shook his head with disgust.

"Well," Tatia put on what she knew was a fetching pout, "you all seemed to know where you were going, and nobody listened to me yesterday."

"You were all noise and shakes."

"Was not!"

"Were!"

"Not!"

Danai didn't know whether to laugh or scream. "Yes, I'm sure the Mentors would be impressed by us right now, aren't you Joson? Look, I just want out of here. Could you two save your little love quarrel for later?" She pivoted and started back.

"Danai wait!" Joson grabbed her shoulder. "What *is* the way out?"

"Hah?"

"I didn't make any trail marks, did you? No, I didn't think so. We've been so sure about this being the right path. Think of all the turns and crosspaths we've followed. Face it all; we're lost. Trackers we're not."

There was a long pause. The stuffy tunnel felt like a burial chamber. They strained their ears, hoping for a sound, any sound to suggest a way out. Forward or backward?

"How about something to eat?" Joson pushed the panic-laden silence away with his cheerful, practical suggestion. "You know I always think better on a full stomach." He squatted down, and began to rummage in his rucksack. "Seriously, sit down you three. We might as well figure out what we're going to do over food and water. Just tearing off in one or the other direction isn't a good idea—we've kinda done that already." Reluctantly, the other three sat down.

The few sips of water rinsed her parched throat, and Danai felt the tight sensation in her chest subsiding. Something Joson had said earlier tugged at her thoughts. "Dirt."

"Plenty of it around here," griped Aaron through a mouthful. "Want some more?"

"There wasn't any in the trunk."

"How's that again?" Joson lowered the bit of miyacan he was about to nibble, and stared at her intently.

"When we were in the tree, it was just that. Tree. Wood."

"Oh, ho. I see where you're headed," said Aaron. "The clues are all around us, if we just had paid attention. If we go backwards, we should watch for the tree—more wood means we're closer. We should be able to find our way back into the trunk."

"Exactly. And we usually were coming down, not climbing up. So we should do the opposite."

"How do we know it's going to work?" Tatia put in.

Danai sighed. "We don't. It's open discussion here Tatia. What do you suggest?"

"I don't know. But we've sure made a mess of things so far."

"Nothing escapes you, does it Tatia?" Aaron stood up, ignoring her glare. "So let's un-mess them. I, for one, have a real hankering to smell something other than stinking foxfire, damp dirt, and moldy wood. Of course, that just my opinion. Perhaps you enjoy it?"

"And our food is getting low too," Joson added, forestalling further argument. "Danai, why don't you lead?"

Oh, I hope we're right, Danai prayed silently to the Mother, as she tried to walk and simultaneously study the walls. All this time wasted going down the wrong path—and now we have to backtrack and try again. Why can't this be easy?

"Smell!" cried Joson sometime later.

"Yes it does." Aaron rolled his eyes. "Tell us something we don't already know."

"No, you snail brain. The air. It smells different." Joson's nose was twitching like a squirrel's.

"Look, more wood up ahead!" Tatia hastened past Danai and Aaron. "Oh Aaron, maybe we're getting there. I think I remember that bend!" The tunnel walls were shifting back to twined roots and further up, just at the edge of their foxfire's glow, the tunnel thickened into trunk. Tatia ran ahead and disappeared around the bend. They heard her shouting.

"Tatia, come back!" Joson bellowed. They all burst into a run, hurrying around the bend. Up ahead they saw flickers of light. Real, natural light. It was so wonderfully bright after the tunnels. Tatia was dancing with delight by the foxfire blob.

Moments later, they tumbled out of the much shredded-crack into glorious sunshine. Birdsong bathed their ears, sun-warmed air filled their nostrils. They gulped down deep draughts of it, savoring the freshness. "Oh, it's as good as goldenvine dew," Tatia exhaled rapturously.

Danai looked about, then giggled.

"And what pray tell is so funny?" Aaron arched an eyebrow as he reached into his rucksack for the kuis.

"Us! I'm sure I look as much a fright as you do! Aaron, you have all this dirt and root in your hair, and a big smear of something, only the Mother knows what, across your nose." She laughed harder. "Joson, there's miyacan on your tunic—what I can see of it under mud and wood bits."

"Well, you're no lady of springtime yourself," said Joson, as their laughter, tinged with hysteria, poured forth. "Actually, that shade of dirt is very becoming on you. And what a lovely crown of foxfire you have. What did you do? Sleep on it?"

"Some Rite," chuckled Aaron, smearing away laugh tears. "Four dirty sprytes by a rotten tree. This is how we earn our wings?"

"I think they should rename this the Rite of Dirt," groused Tatia, vainly attempting to wipe off her blotched tunic with a piece of freshly-torn leaf. Her comment sent the others off into more peals of laughter, and after a pause, Tatia finally joined in.

Their laughter subsiding, Joson shaded his eyes and stared skyward. "My guess from the sun is that it's probably mid-day. That gives us a chance to get back on track with this Rite—wherever it is we're going. Which we still have to figure out. Let's head back up the hill to where this whole thing fell apart." The others nodded and followed him.

The climb was short, and the forest peeled back to reveal the knobby stone spine that marked the ridge along which they guessed Armerion had been leading them. Before them lay a broad swath of Lampion. The ridge framed the northerly part of the Dell, which was hemmed by pines and trees robed in every shade of green. Rolling away to the west was a rumpled swell of hills that vanished into a purple haze. Northwards surged the jagged Rymple Mountains, footed by the Anlyn Hills, their muscled flanks mantled in swags of dark pine patterned with lighter green pockets of birch and aspen. In the distance, the highest peaks were diademed with snow. Somewhere to the west lay Pyre Tor.

"So which one is it?" Aaron muttered, scratching absently at the dirt on his neck.

"Those are the Wynndowns." Joson pointed at the hazy hills. "We flew to Rymple Dell a few summers ago, and our bird flapped right over them in less than a day. It would have taken us several days to walk across. Beyond that is Whittlesea. We probably flew right past Pyre Tor, but fish feathers if I even noticed it."

Danai repeated Mentor Armerion's words. "Seek ye out Pyre Tor, the twisted stone peak which is crowned last by the setting sun's fire."

"Thanks, we remember what he said, and I for one have absolutely no intention of sitting another day waiting for sundown," Tatia spat. "Let's go down. It stands to reason if we head west, we'll figure it out as we go along."

"But will we get as good a chance to see it through all the forest?" Aaron argued.

"What about following this ridge top for a while?" Danai gestured to the right. "It looks like it wraps around west towards the hills, with plenty of bald spots. We'd be headed in the right direction, and at sundown, Lunasa willing, we'll see Pyre Tor."

"But there's no water," Tatia objected, her voice growing shrill. "I'm tired. I'm filthy."

"Yes, you are definitely that. May I offer a dab from my kuis?" Aaron loosened the drawstrings on his rucksack.

Tatia shot him a glare that would have quartered a chestnut in its shell. "And I'm hungry and just want to sleep. I'm sick of this stupid Rite."

"And, of course, you're the only one that feels that way," Aaron snapped. He took a few paces along the ridge. "Look, we can't risk not seeing which one is Pyre. As it is, we'll need to forage. So let's get going. We can always hike down slope later."

Tatia looked mutinous. "And if I choose not to accompany you?"

Aaron shrugged. "I hope you can run quickly. Because you'll be alone and outside the Charmer's truce zone."

* * * * *

The sun was level with their eyes when Aaron suggested a halt on a craggy outcropping of dark red stone that commanded an excellent view of the Rymple Mountains and Wynndowns. A gentle breeze had sprung up, and the peaks were flushing pink.

They had managed to replenish their kuis from cupped leaves that still cradled the morning dew, and gathered young shoots and leaves to munch. They agreed to save the miyacan for as long as possible.

Danai dangled her legs over the outcropping's edge, the others perched comfortably behind her. The sinking sun cast long strands of honey-hued light, framing the Wynndowns and Anlyn Hills as they sank into amethyst shadows, separated by gathering mist. Thin filaments of glittering clouds striated the sky. The light deepened from gold to bronze, from bronze to copper, then blazed red, washing the mountain peaks in scarlet. Slowly it withdrew the crimson mantle until it edged the horizon, a glowing crescent.

"That must be it," breathed Joson, pointing. One twisted peak clasped the last of the sun's rays, a tortured spiral of frozen fire. A shimmering red ribbon cascaded down its distant face, bleeding into the darkness below. The sun vanished. Pyre Tor dimmed to the color of old blood, but remained visible a short while longer as gloaming swathed the surrounding hills and mountains. A magpie shrieked its raucous cry, startling them to motion.

"Well, I guess we've figured out where to go," murmured Danai, somewhat bemused by Pyre Tor's frozen flame.

"Yes, on the morrow." Aaron shook himself free of the image, and stood up, followed by Tatia. "Now we need to figure out where to bower for the night." As he spoke, Lunasa emerged above the trees behind them, a glowing egg in the darkening sky. The ridge stone reflected back his silvery light, blackening the shadows of the surrounding brush and trees that shivered in the rising breeze.

Joson stared uncomfortably into the restless shadows. "Talk about fuzz heads. We should have chosen a bower site before sundown watching. I have absolutely no urge to go rooting about in those shadows for a sleeping place, do you? Makes you wonder how any sprytes survive these Rites."

Danai stared along the bald-topped ridge. During their hike it had made for clear views and a feeling of safety. Except for a possible bird attack, little could sneak up. "What if we keep going?" She was rewarded by three pairs of startled glowing eyes. She gestured towards the silvery path. "We can see perfectly well in Lunasa's light, and the trail goes a fair distance. It would bring us closer to Pyre, and at least we wouldn't have to worry about falling asleep and becoming a hunter's dinner. I know we're all tired, but maybe this is part of the Rite. Nothing has been exactly what I'd call simple."

"True, true." Joson nodded thoughtfully, heaving himself up. "We might as well walk as sit and be eaten."

"Will you stop with something eating us already!" Tatia stamped her foot. "Eat, eat, eat! Is that all you can ever think of? Either putting something in your fat stomach or being put into something's stomach. By all that exists, I am sick, sick, sick of it! Do you hear? Sick!"

The woods had hushed their soft night sounds to listen to her shrill tirade. It was strangely quiet. Too quiet. Danai shivered, wondering what Tatia's outburst might have attracted.

A creaky groan vibrated beneath their feet. Stone gritted on stone. There was the faint 'ting' of metal scraping rock.

"Good going, Tatia," hissed Aaron, crouching down, and motioning the others to follow. "Why don't you just shriek some more, and see what other adventures you can summon to liven up this dull journey?"

Danai peered over the outcropping's edge.

Two glowing emerald eyes peered back.

"By the Mother," she gasped, leaping to her feet.

"Indeed, by the Mother," a gravelly voice replied, followed by a figure crawling over the cliff's edge. It straightened, looming over them, a club-shaped staff poised on its left shoulder.

* * * * *

Chapter Four

"It be a good thing that thee petitioned the great Mother with thy words. In the dark hours, I be more likely to swing first, speak after. State thy business here, standing like as ye be on my doorstep at Windsrest Carrig." It pointed the club at Danai.

Lunasa's light revealed a seamed and whiskered face, a shock of silvery hair bushing out from under a rounded cap to match the long silver beard. It was hard to discern where eyebrows ended and hair began. A dark loose-fitting tunic fell to mid-thigh, waist-cinched with a wide belt clasped by a glimmering buckle of intricately wrought gold. Baggy leggings disappeared into heavy-soled boots laced just below the knee.

Swallowing hard, she stepped forward and bowed. Tipping her head back to see his face, she realized she barely stood to his knees. "Good sir," she hesitated, scrambling for the correct formal words. "We apologize if we intrude on thy home. We are sprytes on a quest for truth, and halted here to spy out the peak named Pyre Tor towards which we journey. No discourtesy was meant, we assure thee." She wondered if she should have spoken about their search.

"Sprytes, hey, thee says? Hmmm. Had forgotten what short things ye are. Long has it been since any have crossed the ridgestone of Tlarg's hearth." He pondered, studying them. Then flashed a brief smile. "Would ye like a bit of a sup? Night is not the best time to be out for small wingless ones. Even short folk such as mine self are well advised to be inside."

With the question directed at her, Danai had no choice but to speak for her podmates. "Thy kindness would be most welcome good sir. And how shall we call thee?"

"Tlarg," he grunted. "Of the *Troich*. And thee?"

"I am Danai of Goldyn Vale." The others then stepped forward and introduced themselves.

When Tatia spoke, Tlarg chuckled. "Ho, ho! And was it thee who shrilled like an angry cricket to disturb the night, so loud that I heard it down my vent hole?" He turned away, not waiting for an answer. "Come. There are easy steps along here, for all thy smallness. I will wait for ye below." He slipped over the edge, and only a crunch of boot on stone proved he was not a dream shadow.

"Are you crazed?" whispered Tatia. "He may just want to eat us."

"Now who's talking about eating?" Joson said. "Do we really have a choice? Danai has accepted his hospitality. So down we go." He took a deep breath and started over the edge.

"But what is he?"

"Well, I guess we'll just have to find out. Hey, remember it's four against one." Aaron grinned, stepping forward. For a moment his golden head shimmered above the stone. "And for Lunasa's sake, please Tatia—no more shrieking." Tatia muttered something under her breath, then followed.

Danai stood alone on the ledge like a stranded shard of silver. Far off, Pyre Tor flamed blue-white under Lunasa's glow. It seemed immeasurably distant. With a sigh, she clambered over the ledge. Below she could see Tlarg waiting.

"Wondered if we'd already lost thee to some hungry one," he joked. "Come, it is but a quick step to my *tunevich*." He gestured them through the stone door. As they hastened inside, it swung shut, blocking any possible chance of escape.

Tlarg stumped along, following a well-trod path faintly lit by luminescent stones. They hurried behind, thankful he was only perhaps five times their height and not walking too quickly. In a few moments, a trembling reddish light could be glimpsed down-tunnel. Tlarg's stride lengthened, forcing them into a quick trot.

"Welcome, thrice welcome, friends." He had halted at a rough-hewn entryway and turned to motion them inside. "Come. Seat ye by the fire—my table would be too high—and I'll bring ye some food-stuffs." As he spoke, he put his knobstick in a nook by the entry, its metal shod foot tinging as it brushed against stone. A darkly grained wood, it sheened in the firelight with the polish of untold seasons. Then he turned and released a heavy hide to curtain the entry.

The well-lit cave was filled with cozy warmth. As they moved towards the hearth, they gazed about in wide-eyed wonderment. Near the left side of the hearth, a pile of coarse-shaped many-hued stones glowed dully, placed within easy reach of a bench laden with some sorts of tools, a tray, and an unfamiliar treadle wheel-driven object. Beside the tray lay brilliantly polished gems that scattered back firelight in rainbow fragments.

In the opposing corner, a rumpled bed sleeve snuggled atop a pallet of dry grasses. Several stools and benches lined the walls. A faint trickling came from behind the tool bench, where a pool of water collected in a deep basin carved from living rock, and was then carried off in a channel over to another basin beside which Tlarg stood preparing food, humming softly, his beard tucked neatly into his belt. Nearby stood a shelf, intricately carved from some dark knotty wood that held an assortment of clayware and other items.

"Ye looks like it has so far been a trying journey," he remarked, glancing at them. "If ye wishes, I can prepare a bowl of warmed water in which to refresh thyselves."

Tatia was the first to jump up and accept his offer. "Good sir, thank thee for thy courtesy to unknown wayfarers such as we be." She scurried over to where he set the bowl, considerately placed behind a wide bench leg for privacy.

By the time Tlarg had readied the meal, they were washed and refreshed. It felt good to rinse off the stickiness and sweat of the past—could it be only three days, Danai thought. They gathered on the woven hearth rug, comfortable against buttocks more recently accustomed to stone and damp wood. Tlarg brought forth a laden wood trencher and set it beside them, then returned with fey-sized mugs of water. Clearly not all Tlarg's guests were his size, Danai decided. He made a final trip, gathering up a short stool and a large mug that gave forth delicate odors of summer flowers and sweet honey. "Eat, eat, my friends," he urged, waving the mug over their heads as he settled near them. "I will talk meanwhile, as I would guess from thy many stares ye has not seen the likes of me before."

A large smile appled his full cheeks as the four sprytes eagerly served themselves from the seeds and thinly-sliced fruits. "Well enough. I be of the Troich, in the common tongue Gem-Dwarves. Ah, I see ye has heard of us, if only from thy taletellers, eh? We be harvesters of gems, the beautiful tears cried by the Mother in her joy at giving birth to the world. See ye those stones piled hither and yon? I delve them from the rocks and dirt, sometimes alone, other times with my brethren. And then these old hands shape and cut to reveal the beauty therein. Many are those that come for the well-wrought gems of Tlarg—even among thy Feyree folk. Ah—surprised be ye? And where didst ye think the stones came for thy Lord and Lady's crowns worn at the High Seat of Revelstoke on feast days?" He paused, took a long swig, then settled the mug back on his knee. "Lucky were ye that yon maiden shrieked at eventide. I choose not to go out much in the day—it bothers mine old eyes, although the youngsters will brave the light—and often go not out into the wide world for a season or two. Those seeking Tlarg come to me. Happen that I wanted to see the face of *Lugh* this night, or ye still would be there on my doorstep." He gave a deep throaty laugh. "Now that ye have taken the edge off thy hunger, tell me more of thy tale."

The sprytes glanced at each other. Joson and Aaron's mouths were full, and Danai knew Tatia would not have the nerve. Wiping her mouth, she adjusted her position to properly face Tlarg. He nodded and occasionally quirked a bushy eyebrow as she recounted their short journey. What was not told—Danai preferred to delicately sidestep some of the more emotional moments—was still unwittingly revealed to some degree on their faces. Tlarg was a long-lived dwarf; much could he see of that unspoken.

"So on the morrow, good Tlarg, we will continue our journey to Pyre Tor and the Well of Truth."

"Um," he grunted, mulling her tale as he took another swig of mead. "Be a long journey on short legs. What say ye to a shift in plans that will bring ye to the Tor, yet perhaps be a change in thine adventures? A change for the good I hazard."

Aaron's head snapped up. The fire's warmth and good food had nudged him towards drowsiness, but Tlarg's suggestion sparked him awake. "Sir?"

"My folk, like thine, are long of this realm. Yonder bright stones require much delving in the Mother's heart. Many be the chambers and tunnels that weave through the hills between here and Meall Clarsair, as we call thy Pyre Tor. It will at least be an interesting journey, mayhap the likes of which ye have never seen, and I shall perchance see some friends along the way."

There was a muffled snort. Tlarg's eyes opened wide at Danai's shaking figure as she tried unsuccessfully to control her mirth. Tears streamed from her eyes as she gave in to laughter.

"Danai, are you all right?" Embarrassed, Joson reached over to shake her shoulder.

"Ye-e-e-s, oh, oh," she gasped, the storm subsiding into chuckles as she palmed the tears away. "Oh Tlarg, forgive me. I was not laughing at your, uh, thy offer. But truly, this whole journey has been the likes of which we have never seen!"

A wry smile fissured the dwarf's face. "Youngling has a sense of wit." He chortled, then shook his head. "I forget that my winters are not thine, and much that is old to me is new to ye. Even so, we will go on march morrowmorn, and continue thy journey." Heaving up from the stool, he trundled over to the shelf, and returned with soft coverlets which he spread over the hearth rug. As the sprytes snuggled under the rumpled folds, he banked the fire then moved towards his sleeping pallet. "Sleep deep under Lugh," he bade them.

"May the Mother guard thy dreams," they chorused. Soon, gentle sighs ruffled the air, punctuated by an occasional crackle from the glowing hearth, and a throttled snore from the corner.

* * * * *

Tlarg was already bustling about preparing for the journey when they awoke. "At most four days march," he answered Aaron, "at least as the Troich amble." The sprytes quickly downed the fruits Tlarg had set out, then refilled their kuis, and tidied up. The dwarf finished wrapping up packets of foodstuffs, and tucked them into a lumpy dirt-stained rucksack. A stoppered water sack already lay on the bench. Once the sprytes had stepped through the entryway, he dropped the cover, and made a quick downward gesture with two hooked fingers, murmuring what Danai guessed to be a guardian spell to prevent unwelcome visitors.

Setting a steady pace that sometimes forced the sprytes into a trot, Tlarg tromped into the hills. The path, smooth-worn by countless boots, twisted its way like a carelessly tossed vine, with the glow-stones, as Tlarg called them, revealing dark side-arches that the dwarf explained led to old private workings.

At times, only the soft thud of feet and sharper clump of boots interrupted the quiet. "Tlarg," Aaron asked during the first rest, "how do thee keep any sense of direction, with no sun or shadows to guide thine eyes?"

"Can thee not smell the differences?" the dwarf asked in surprise.

"Smell?"

"Aye, smell. 'Tis common knowing that each turning point of the land, be it west or east, north or south, is possessed of its own smell. Eh, I see thee knows nothing of what I speak. Well enough, now is a good time as any for some teachings. Now breathe—no lad, through thy nose! Breathe deeply."

The sprytes obeyed, their noses twitching like rabbits'. "Smells like dirt to me," Joson blurted.

Tlarg laughed hugely. "Well, aye, there is that for sure. Expect thee aught else when under earth? Nay, I will guide thy nose. Smell for metal. Has a sharp, sourish scent, different from dirt. Here, sniff this—it will start ye on the right road." He held forth his blade, pulled easily from its thigh sheath. Each spryte sniffed gingerly. "Now smell again the air; hold thy mouth slightly open as well. Our folk call it 'tasting the air.'"

"I smell it!" Joson fairly hopped on one foot with excitement. "It's faint, almost like, like..." he grappled for the word, "like the taste of winter water scooped from the mountain streambed."

"Good, good," Tlarg beamed. "Are smelling the north, the direction in which we march."

"What smells are the other directions?" Danai asked.

"I will 'smell them' to thee until thy own nose recognizes the scents. West be a burnt smell, much like last season's burned wood after a rain. East smells of grass fresh-plucked, clean yet faintly sweet, like berries nearly ripe. South is of hot sun on old flowers, almost too sweet. The smells, they shift and blend as one marches the tunnels. See ye. All turnabout and walk a few steps from where we came."

"Oh!" exclaimed Tatia, who had been mostly quiet. "I smell kingcup and lily bells."

"Good! Now all turn very slowly, and smell as ye turn."

As she concentrated, Danai marveled at the shifting patterns of odors that filtered up her nostrils. She saw that the dwarf was right about smells being more pronounced if she held her mouth ajar. Flowers, grass, metal, fire. "Does this work above ground as well?" she asked.

"Aye," nodded the dwarf, re-shouldering his sacks. "But there on the outside, it is harder, with so many other scents hurrying about on the back of the breeze." He winked at her. "Happens our tunnels are not known for their flowers and grass."

Direction sniffing kept them busy on the next leg of the march, and the sprytes competed for Tlarg's approval. At what the dwarf said was mid-day, they halted by a sluggish underground creek. The sprytes were thankful for the break, and there was much rubbing of tender feet and tight leg muscles. As they ate, at Danai's request, he shared with them a bit of Troich lore.

"Hearken ye then, to the true tale of the *Tuil Mor*. Troich have been here perhaps longer than most other folks," the dwarf began, settling himself more comfortably on a humped stone. "The Mother called us forth at the dawn of the world to help shape her creation. The Troich-*eldrich*, the elder dwarves, were larger than us nowadays, and worked unflinching in the sunshine. We lived mostly above the earth then. Some say the Mother made us smaller when our work for her was done, others..." Tlarg frowned, then continued.

"The Troich-eldrich worked with the Mother for many upon many seasons. For a time, she gave them the power to call forth forces to carve the mountains, scrape basins out to cradle lakes, to chisel and crack the rock face, to mound and shape the earth. Forces of great power they were—wind, lightening, storms, rain—but always under the final command of the Mother. Hamorg was the *Maighstir*—master in thy tongue—and each morn, he reviewed the fruits of the previous day's labors and planned that day's work with the Mother.

"She saved our realm of Lughadon for the last, sparing no detail in crafting a place beyond beauty. Soft were the swelling green hills, noble the climbing mountains, bright the flowers that danced among the meadows. No water compared for sweetness, no breeze carried such fragrances, no soil brought forth so much bounty." Tlarg paused, his eyes seeing something beyond the tunnel walls.

"And so the seasons passed and passed, and once our work was complete, the Mother blessed us for our labors, and let us free to delight in the land we had helped craft. But as often happens when there is too much good and life is easy, some Troich grew restless and desired to create change for change's sake."

"Morathag, who traced his lineage back to Hamorg, felt beauty was not enough to live by and called a *Comhairle*—a gathering of elders representing each clan, for our folk gathered in groups much like thy vales. Morathag bespoke a vision from the Mother commanding he lead the folk under earth for a great water was forthcoming. Yet none would at first believe his prophesy. He ranted on the crest of Shamargadon—a great chambered cairn high-risen above a golden plain—and swore by all we honored that his was not a dream but a true vision."

"The folk doubted, wavered, wondered. Was he not in the right line of descent from Hamorg? And a storm arose even as they debated, and lightening flared, and wind wailed, and a strange sickly green fire flickered down from the clouds and darted among the grasses. Morathag cried out that it was even as the Mother had foretold him, warning that the waters would come soon after. 'To earth,' he cried."

"And a panic devoured us, and we scrambled down inside the great cairn, and we pleaded with the Mother to grant us life, and we vowed to do her all honor, even as Morathag directed. And we named him Maighstir, and swore to obey him as high Chief Tain."

"He ordered us to dig, and delve under the meadows, probing ever farther up into the hills, seeking out the beautiful gifts of the Mother—gold, silver, and gems. And our smythes wrought these into things of great beauty. Goblets carved from a single gem, crowns twisted with carnelian, topaz, and sapphires, blades runed with cunning scrollery and hilted in gems."

"For many seasons we did as ordered, creating a new realm within the darkness. Morathag permitted only his chosen few to leave, and forbade our digging more than a few exits, ever cautioning of the impending waters, even as he built a marvelous dwelling atop Shamargadon. But most found that out only later, for we were kept away from the cairn in our tunnels, and stepped out only to hunt and food-forage. There were murmurs of how the mead flowed, and gems were gifted, and of the revelry as he hosted gatherings among many folk. And Morathag crafted a craving among these folk for wealth and boughten beauty. And they in turn took up pursuits so that they would have barter and desirable commerce for Morathag."

"Often I wonder that none of these folk seemed to question from whence came the many treasures of Morathag, nor asked about where his kinfolk lived. Yet he was ever a great speaker and most likely told them a pretty tale. And all the while, as she does always, the Mother was watching. Watching her beautiful world warp into one where folk celebrated and fought for the joys of ownership, instead of savoring the gifts of life given."

"Seldom does the Mother speak. Hence many feel a need to put words into her mouth, even as did Morathag. But there comes a time she will speak. It may be a creature she raises above all others, often marked in a way not at first understood. Or she will call the great

Powers forth to remind all who indeed created this realm, who gifted them life."

"Be wary of thy untruths for they will haunt thee in the days to come. Such is a saying among my folk. And so did Morathag's much-heralded vision finally come to pass. Came a spring of rain. Seeping rain. Creeping rain. Pushing the great waters that surrounded Lughadon before it, slithering down the mountains' slopes to pool, swelling lakes, covering shrubs and small plants, gurgling up the sides of trees until their roots floated free, and they toppled. And soon the lakes joined hands with the great waters, and the land began to drown. On the flatlands south, our tunnels collapsed. Only the lucky ones escaped into the high mountains, pursued by the hungry waters. Well do I remember the sucking sounds made as the water gargled up those tunnels, ever closer to those of us huddled in unheeded prayer in our highest tunevich. Others likewise escaped into the highest reaches, but many died. Many, many died." Tlarg halted. Behind him the water gurgled and gulped, echoing a tragedy past.

"And Morathag?" Danai whispered after some moments had elapsed. "What happened to him?"

The dwarf started, then a slow grim smile oozed across his face. "One who preaches false visions must be prepared for when they come true. Morathag perhaps did not believe the truth when he saw it. He perched upon Shamargadon, like a bird of ill-omen, fleeing to the highest tower, and waited. Waited until long after it was too late to come down, for the tunnels were flooded. And under the hungry wash of waters, the cairn dissolved and collapsed into itself, swallowing Morathag, all his fripperies, and his toadying court. None have ever returned willingly to that cursed spot, though some say that he and his dwelling remain entombed within. It is known as Marbh Cnoc, the dead hill, and lies south of thy Goldyn Vale."

"How long did the waters stay?" Joson asked.

"Long enough that my beard half-changed from black to silver. Long enough that we invited other folk into our tunnels, and we helped each other to survive, sharing skills and knowledge. It was then that I first met the Fey folk. Long enough that when the waters finally retreated, they left behind a land so buried in mud and barren of living things, it was a place unknown." He shook his head sadly. "Lughadon was gradually reborn in the seasons after the Tuil Mor, the great flood, but only as a memory, a paler shadow of the glory it once had been. The Troich created a new home among the hills and mountains, with the wisdom to carve doorways out to the Mother's world and stay in contact with the other folk. And they vowed never again to grant any the title of Maighstir, nor to give any complete power as we had Morathag. Now, it is the Comhairle who must choose by vote, and every Troich may speak his piece. None are higher or lower than the other, and greatness is earned with deeds, not words."

Tlarg heaved himself up. "Come. We are near Dumarg's tune-vich, and I think it likely he will let us bide this night." Leaping lightly across the glowstones moored in the streambed, he strode onward. The sprytes scrambled to catch up, slipping and splashing through the water, shouting for him to wait.

* * * * *

Chapter Five

"**N**ear?" muttered Tatia later as the long march continued. "I'd hate to see what he considers far!" Their legs burned, their hot feet throbbed from the relentless pounding on stone and hard-packed dirt. Conversation flagged, and each focused on plodding forward. Only Tlarg seemed as fresh as when they started.

"Hey, is that real light up ahead?" panted Joson, swiping away a mustache of sweat. The others peered forward hopefully.

"Aye, that it be. Good eyes young Joson," Tlarg replied, emerging from some deep thought. "Dumarg is home it seems." He hurried ahead, shouting. "Hail Dumarg! Hail!" The echoes bounced off the tunnel walls.

A bristly-bearded shadow poked out from the light. "Who calls?" it bellowed in a voice higher than Tlarg's burly rumble.

"Thee are going deaf if thee cannot tell by thine old mine-mate's voice!"

"Nay, I knew it was thee all the time!"

"Hah! Then why ask?" Tlarg dropped his load, and the two dwarves hugged each other with much backslapping and smiles.

"And who be thy companions? By the Mother, Fey folk! Long has it been since I have seen the likes of ye!" Dumarg exclaimed, bending forward slightly to stare at the disheveled sprytes. "But where are thy wings?"

"Lout," Tlarg snorted. "Has it been so long that thee has forgotten that nowadays they must earn those wings? These be sprytes on journey to Meall Clarsair." He shifted to a more formal tone. "We ask the favor of thy hearth and hospitality this eventide, in the Mother's name. May we enter?"

"Welcome, thrice welcome! Enter and refresh thyselves." Dumarg bowed and stepped aside.

Wearily, the sprytes entered, forgetting courtesy in their exhaustion.

Dumarg twitched an eyebrow in askance at his comrade for such a breach, but Tlarg just smiled and shook his head. The four hesitated at the threshold, unsure where to sit, and looked up at Dumarg.

"First, a wash," their host cried, taking the situation in hand. "Back in that corner, near my grinding stone, shall ye find fresh water. Drying cloths I shall bring ye. Ye look like vagabond crows after a dust bath! Tlarg here has overworked ye this day. And thee, dear friend, share with me the meanwhile how thee came to be entangled with sprytes."

As they washed, the sprytes heard a pleasant sizzling sound, and the rich smells of cooking permeated the cave. Danai made her way stiffly over to where the two dwarves stood chatting by the hearth, then stood awkwardly, hesitant to interrupt.

"Aye, maiden?" Dumarg turned from stirring the skillet. Shorter and more slender than Tlarg, his hair and beard, which was tucked into his belt, were chestunut. Hazel eyes sparkled at her in the firelight. She noticed a finely-wrought torque of gold lay among the sand-colored folds of his tunic, and a topaz ring flashed gem-fire on his left hand.

"Good Dumarg, would thee forgive our lack of courtesy? We can only plead that we are unused to such lengthy travel, being not as sturdy as Tlarg, and forgot the rules of hospitality." The others crowded behind her, echoing the apology.

"Pish, tish. Ye are younglings, and besides, now ye have made up for thy oversight. And what am I cooking?" he smiled seeing them looking up at the steaming skillet, inhaling the rich fruity smells it gave off. "I have taken dried oats, and ground black acorns harvested while yet on the tree, and dried blackberries, and added dashes of other flavors. And then lightly fried them first in oil from the flowers of the sun, then added blackberry juice and a smidge of water. A hearty porridge, fit for travelers! There be no meat—I honor thy folk's ways. Seat ye over there on the hearth's edge, and I will serve ye."

Danai could not remember food ever tasting so good, and smiled at Aaron as he asked for a third helping. Even Tlarg served himself yet a fourth time, leaving little.

"And perchance a bit of a sweet, now that ye have taken the edge off thy hunger?" Dumarg returned from the sideboard bearing a long honey-glazed fruit roll and a sharp blade. He sliced it, then quartered two pieces into a manageable size for the sprytes.

Joson eagerly bit into a piece. "Mmmm, where did you, I mean thee find such ripe blackberries so early in the season?"

"In Srath Orach, the vale of the sun."

"Where is that?"

"It is a special garden of our folk, one started long ago from the seeds we saved after the Tuil Mor. We believe it to be blessed by the Mother, for even in winter, it often is sheltered and warm. Many are the fruits and plants that we grow the seasons round for our use. It is free to all Troich, yet we must work to keep it alive and growing."

"Thee are very lucky," commented Aaron, licking his fingers for a last taste of the sweet glaze, and pretending not to see Joson reach for yet another slice.

Dumarg shook his head, a twinkle sparking his eyes. "Youngling, when thee has lived as long as one such as I, thee will learn that luck, such as it is, almost always takes hard work."

Morrowmorn, Dumarg sent them along with good wishes—and an extra fruit roll to Joson's great delight. Stiff legs soon limbered as the tunnels began to twist upwards with a sharper slope. Danai's nose told her they were headed northwest, and she asked Tlarg how much further.

"Three more days, maiden, and we will reach the valley of the Well, four if we stop to see sights along the way. And tonight we will stay with Shamarig. A bard he is, and a tale teller, and there may even be tidings from the outside. And on the way, I will show ye a wonder of our folk."

Some time after mid-meal, Joson pointed. "Tlarg, is that sunlight I see far ahead?" He was peering so hard, he tripped over a glowstone.

"Unusually good eyes thee have, Joson!" Tlarg chuckled as he leaned over to help the spryte up. "But thy feet need some aid. What thee sees comes from the *Clahaich*, or the Delving in the common tongue." His stride lengthened, forcing the sprytes into a trot. "Many are the tunevich we Troich have dug in search of gems and such. But none are as this. Only here has every gem been unearthed. Down have we dug and down, until it be many levels deep, filled with hollows and halls. Many of our folk dwell here, for after Tuil Mor, the remainders of our clans came together to survive. Some have since left to found other outlying tunevich, but it is here where we hold our gatherings, be they for celebration or for council."

"But the bright sunlight?" Danai asked, puzzled.

"Happen we thought that such beauty should be open to Lugh and the Mother, so we have worked the stone to softly let in light without the wet. It but seems bright to ye after a long march in the tunnel dimness. Ye shall soon see!"

They approached a tall portal flanked by two pillars of elaborately carved glowstone through which the sunlight shone softly. Beyond it they could see a similar portal leading off to another tunnel; the portals appeared to be a cross path of sorts. Tlarg signaled them to wait and stepped through. After a quick glance to his right, he beckoned them to continue.

Entering, they saw matching portals on their left and right. After a few strides they were beyond the pillars, turning right where Tlarg pointed into the Clahaich—and they jerked to a halt in wide-eyed amazement.

A large cavern arched high above them. At its apex a perfect circle perhaps sixteen feylengths wide had been carved, through which a waterfall of sunlight shimmered as it passed through a translucent covering. The walls and roof were filigreed with a swirling design of leaves, flowers, fruits and vines—created from gemstones of every imaginable hue. The air seemed a veritable tapestry of color coaxed forth by the sunlight, weaving to form different shades as the sun advanced across the opening. Ruby and topaz burst into marigold, sapphire and tourmaline filtered to emerald. A soft ping-tzing could be heard as the sunbeams warmed the gems, expanding them slowly in their niches. The air seemed almost flavored with color.

Directly beneath the center of the apex, throned on a simple tear-shaped pedestal of burnished red gold, was a huge emerald, faceted to trap the dancing sunbeams within its heart. It glowed with rippling fire, seeming to pulse with light, at times throbbing to brightness that cast a veil of golden-green light through the cavern, at times a green ember. But never, ever still.

Tlarg tapped his heart three times with his fist, then knelt before the stone, motioning the sprytes to do likewise. "Behold the heart of Lughadon, the *Anam* of our folk," he whispered reverently. "It is said that when the Troich-eldrich completed their tasks, the Mother bestowed upon them the Anam in thanks. It was somehow rescued in the Tuil Mor, and carried to Srath Orach. There are times when the sun sits directly overhead, and the eye of Lugh rests above the western horizon that one can see...memories of the first Lughadon. Not often. But sometimes. Perhaps that is why we Troich so enjoy our work—because in these lovely stones, be they uncut or crafted, we see a little of our beloved Lughadon as it was in the ancient days."

Mesmerized by the Anam's throbbing heart, Danai had the sensation that the stone was swelling to engulf the cave. She beheld a convulsing light—or was it flame? Behind the light—or was it within?—she sensed a hint of something, as one does when slipping into the world of dreams and the door begins to open. The light pulsated, then coalesced, and before her stood a monstrous Feyree, swathed in twisting scarlet flames, skin seared a scorching cracked black, wearing a face half-remembered, fingers grasping, shouting silently at her.

She screamed, staggering back against Tlarg's leg.

Tlarg gargled with surprised fear, and from elsewhere came other startled shouts and cries. The image collapsed upon itself. The Anam subsided into dullness.

"May the Mother and Lugh preserve us!"

"What horror was that?"

Cries burst out from the few Troich that had been seated near the Anam and witnessed the blazing apparition. They milled about the Clahaich, pale under their dusky skins. Some stared sideways at the Anam, making gestures to ward off unknown evil. The rank smell of sweaty fear permeated the air.

Their shouts had attracted other dwarves, who now spilled in through the portal until the cavern filled, while others clumped at the entry peering over shoulders. One black-bearded dwarf, blue-clad with a triangular bundle slung across his back, hurried over to Tlarg. "Brother of mine! Thee are as white as new-dropped snow. Sit thee down, and let us calm ourselves. Do ye all likewise!" This last he directed at the seething throng that seemed to be growing by the moment. The sprytes huddled close to Tlarg's knees, balancing on his boot tops to avoid being crushed. The blue dwarf's tone seemed to settle the crowd, and most slowly sat down on the smooth floor, some casting nervous glances at the Anam.

"Shamarig, Shamarig," gasped out Tlarg, who remained standing, his eyes still fastened on the Anam. "A burning creature, yet it did not burn, although its skin was black-charred, its mouth and eyes naught more than flame slashes. A terrible thing, a nightmare thing!"

"Mayhap a message," replied Shamarig calmly. Tlarg nodded, as did others.

"From what?" cried one dwarf shouldering his way through the portal.

Shamarig turned towards the speaker, his lean figure nearly a head higher than most of the surrounding dwarves. "The Anam is the gift of the Mother. Can we not assume it be from her?"

"Aye, but what says she?" exclaimed another from behind the Anam.

"I would not pretend to know," Shamarig said slowly. "That is for wiser heads than mine."

"Perchance it was but a trick of light?"

"It was no trick," Danai blurted out, still trembling. "It was a sending, as he says!" Astonished, the dwarves searched for the disembodied voice; many started as they took heed of the huddled sprytes' presence.

"Aye, without question," Shamarig agreed. "But an incomplete one. A warning of some sort, of that I am most sure, but beyond such, I know not."

"We must call a Comhairle!" exclaimed several voices. "Aye, aye, a Comhairle," bellowed others, their shouts colliding into a loud rumble that set the gems vibrating with a discordant twang.

"Send the message out to the Eldrich from all the clans," ordered Shamarig, pointing at several dwarves. "Seythnak, Moishnag, Amnarolg, choose the messengers as ye will. We gather here at mid-day four days hence. Inform them it is by order of the Mother, and it is the *Ard-Clarsair* Shamarig who summons them to Comhairle."

Satisfied at the actions taken, the crowd dispelled, some singly, most in groups, discussing and debating the sending. In a few moments, the Clahaich was empty.

"Tlarg, we don't have to stay for the Comhairle, do we?" Joson gently tugged on the still visibly upset dwarf's tunic hem.

He glanced down, seeming surprised to see them. "Nay, nay, I will fill my troth and get ye to the valley. I saw the horror; I can speak well enough for us all." He shuddered.

"Come, bide with me this eve," urged Shamarig, gently taking Tlarg's arm and leading the way out of the chamber. The sprytes hurried after, nearly falling over themselves in their eagerness to escape. None risked a glance back at the Anam.

* * * * *

Shamarig's cave gave the sprytes the feeling of a place long-used to company, yet also where one could relax hearthside in comfortable silence. Carefully placing his bundle in a well-worn nook, he turned to provide for the comfort of his guests. "Mead for all," he advised, pulling down a pale green clay jug and assorted-sized drinking mugs from a shelf.

"We are on journey sir," protested Joson. "And without the Mentors' presence, I'm not sure it is permitted."

Tlarg and Shamarig snorted in tandem. "Nay, lad," insisted their guide. "If it be an Elder thee needs, I would wager I am many times the age of most of thy Mentors. And after that burning horror, can thee really say that a sup of mead would truly be amiss?" Joson shook his head, and reached for the proffered mug.

Danai swigged deeply of the sweet-scented drink, eager to dull the yet-vivid vision. The tangy liquid burned her throat, and she coughed and spluttered, tears clouding her sight. Between coughs, she heard the guffaws of her podmates and the dwarves. "Thee have not much experience with such drink, I warrant," chuckled Shamarig, to Danai's further embarrassment. "I beg thee to not insult my good mead by gulping it as if it were water."

"I'm convinced," Danai choked, wiping her eyes clear as a reassuring warmth radiated from her belly outwards. She settled on the soft rug before the hearth, her back to the fire, afraid of what might reappear in the dancing flames. Her podmates chatted with Shamarig. Tlarg watched her, but said nothing.

Bustling about the shelf and sideboard, Shamarig assembled an assortment of foodstuffs to tempt his guests' palates. Shortly a repast of seeds, golden honey and coarse brown bread, fresh fruits and new-harvested greens lay on trenchers before them. None of the sprytes had ever seen bread before, but Joson fearlessly took a piece slathered with honey and pronounced it excellent. For a time, the group applied themselves to the business of eating, and the cave was comfortably quiet except for the munching of food and an occasional hiss and pop of an ember on the hearth.

"And now," said Shamarig, after the trenchers had been cleared, another round of mead poured, and the fire replenished, "let us hear of thy journey."

Joson, sensing Danai's reluctance, stood up to speak, and Danai was thankful for her podmate's kindness. She had no desire to do more than sip at the mead and only half-listened to the tale, her mind cautiously probing around the edges of the vision like a tongue poking a sore tooth. What in the name of the Blessed One could it herald? Her thoughts were tugged back by Aaron's question.

"Please Shamarig, what is a—that word thee used when thee called the Comhairle?"

"An Ard-Clarsair," the dwarf replied, rising and retrieving his bundle, which he carried gently back to the hearth. Almost reverently it seemed, he unhasped the acorn-brown hide case, worn to a smooth sheen, and withdrew a delicate harp. "In thy tongue, thee would name me a Bard or perhaps a Skald, or more likely an Orpheii, for I tell tales as well as sing songs and chants. And because I have won the *Eisteddfod* festival, I am called the Ard-Clarsair—the High Harpist of our folk."

"Eisteddfod?" Aaron prompted.

"A great gathering of the Troich with much jesting, gossip, and, I think, a prideful showing of crafted wares. More to the point, it is likewise where we compete with music, poetry and stories. A select bench of elders judges each performance and determines the winners. It is not often one wins in more than one style."

"And he has done so, winning them all not once, but thirty times," Tlarg added, beaming with pride and delight. "No mean feat as the Eisteddfod happens but once every ten winters. What my too shy younger brother fails to add, humble Troich that he be, is that there are several rungs within each trial. Music be not simply the playing of one song, but five—dancing, mourning, celebration, talk-song, and feasting—and the judges watch to see how well the performer can play not only their instrument, but those who listen. For my brother to have earned the title of Ard-Clarsair, he had to win all. It is no mean skill that Shamarig has."

"How long is he allowed to be Ard-Clarsair?" Tatia asked.

"Until a new one arises who can best him in the Eisteddfod."

"But what if he doesn't win the next one?"

"No matter," shrugged Tlarg. "None can unseat him lest they win. It be our way of ensuring that there is always an Ard-Clarsair, for he is the speaker of our folk."

"Brother, brother," Shamarig chided, shaking his head. "I think sometimes thee are more proud than I of this thing."

"And why not? I am a mere crafter of bright things. Many are there of my like among us. But thee! I warrant thee could move stones to tears, and even the creatures of the wild halt to attend thy musical ramblings." He winked at Danai. "Yet no Troich-maid has won his heart." Shamarig blushed under his dusky cheeks, eliciting a loud guffaw and knee slap from Tlarg.

"See ye what comes of family," Shamarig growled, drawing forth the harp. "They think it nothing to speak of such matters. On to other things! Here be Clarsach, my queen, my voice." He stroked the dark red wood, high-sheened to brilliance by untold seasons of play. Strands of bright gold threaded between the harp's neck and sound box, anchored by elaborately carved tuning pins of a contrasting pale wood. At the pillar's crest was carved a delicate suggestion of a face, with half-closed slanted eyes that regarded Shamarig, a soft smile lightly curving the delicate lips. The two faces gazed upon each other, all else forgotten. Danai understood why Shamarig had found no dwarf-maid. His ladylove was Clarsach.

Long-callused fingers rippled across the harp strings, and a melody like running water trickled through the cave. The sprytes sat entranced. Tlarg settled himself more comfortably, his back against the wall, thankful his mug was yet fairly full of mead. A private playing by his brother was a rare event indeed, and one to be savored.

"And what shall I play for ye?" Shamarig's voice took on a different timbre, resonant, harmonizing with Clarsach's lighter notes. "Nay, ye know little if aught of our folk. Shall I tell ye a tale of the mountain to which ye journey, the Meall Clarsair, and how it came to bear its twisted peak?" He smiled at their eager nods.

"In the elder days, when the world had been shaped by the Troich-eldrich to her satisfaction, came the Mother once again to add new life to our wondrous land of Lughadon. From her sprang all creatures—the owl from her brow, the hart and hare from her feet, the nightingale from her breast, the squirrel from her hands. And when she was done giving life to them all, the day had waned. And she stood, awaiting the presence of great Lugh, he whom you call Lunasa.

"Mighty he arose, full swollen with majesty and light, his face lined with wisdom and seasons past counting. And the Mother began to dance in his radiance, her tiny feet springing and pirouetting, her emerald skirts aswirl in a shimmering rainbow mist, hands tracing patterns and shapes in the silvery light.

"And behold! The shapes gathered the light unto them and became solid. And forth first sprang the Ael, a maid and a lad, agile, lean, with sculpted ears and tip-tilted eyes, bodies as fluid as melting ice on a warm spring day. Lugh rose yet higher, and his light paled, yet still the Mother danced, and her laughter burst forth, swirling the radiant beams, taking shape as it flickered among the sparkling motes, until came forth the *Sidhiche*, thy folk. And the Ael and Sidhiche joined the Mother's dance with all the energy of the newly born. All that night the Mother danced, until her folk were imagined to life in Lugh's light.

"Yet let us now move forward to the time when the Troicheldrich had passed. And there came an Ael-maid to the cascading waters that descended a high cliff at the mountains' western edge. Aelvina she was called, and a great beauty among her folk. None other had such silver hair or skin, the fingerprints of Lugh, and her shimmering green eyes were like rain-washed grass in springtime. She was gentle of heart, and this sealed her doom.

"As Aelvina knelt to fill her vessel with the pure waters, she sensed eyes upon her. For the Ael are wise in woodcraft, and close to the creatures of the land, having been born but a short while after. Slowly she rose, slowly, slowly, no fear in her stance. Slowly she turned until she could gaze full wide upon the flower-gemmed vale in which she stood. And there, at the woods' edge, staring at her in unabashed admiration, she beheld a sapphire-eyed Troich lad. Curbarig. He knelt in mute homage.

"We Troich are not known for our looks, but Curbarig was handsome, even by the high standards of the Ael. Unusually tall he was, as tall as Aelvina, blackhaired, with pale hands callused not by mining but music. For he was the Ard-Clarsair. Unbidden, his hands strayed to his harp, and he brought forth sweet melodies to celebrate the Ael-maid's beauty. Such joy, such light, such harmony! The sun brightened, the flowers glowed, the very air was honey-sweet with music. And Aelvina, beauteous Aelvina, did what no Ael-maid had ever done. She fell in love with one not of her own.

"Lightly she danced, a dance of laughter, of love, twirling around Curbarig, casting a net of love about him. Not hard was Curbarig to woo, and his song shifted to express his wondering love. When he ceased, the very notes hung suspended in the sunbeams, singing to themselves with delight.

"Love knows naught but the moment. Aelvina and Curbarig met often in secret by the falls, and it was not long before she was with babe. Then great was the consternation of her folk, for she would not confess the father, and thus brought shame upon her family. Long were the days that Curbarig played sadly upon his harp by the falls, for Aelvina was hyell-bound, forbidden to leave the hollowed halls of her home.

"And when she gave birth, her father's wrath knew no bounds. For to any eyes, the Ael-babe was not one of pure blood. No Ael had hair the darkness of a raven's wing, nor rounded ears. He stormed from the birthing chambers, hands still wet with his daughter's blood, and sought the Ael-lord, petitioning for help to right this insult to his hyell.

"There is magic among the Ael, no matter how little they choose to use it, for the Ael-lord called forth his *draoidh*, and demanded a vision of the newborn's father. Thus bidden, the draoidh wove a globe of silver light, within which they beheld Curbarig, yet seated on a stone by the falls, ever-strumming his harp as he awaited his absent lady-love.

"If the father had been wrathful before, it was naught to now. A Troich! He recoiled, swearing terrible oaths. His servant cowered at such vows, and slipped in haste from the lord's audience chamber to return to the hyell, for he rightly feared for Aelvina's life and sought to warn her.

"Still aching with the agony of childbirth, Aelvina fled, carrying her son swathed in a coverlet of mossy green. Alainn, she had named him. She struggled along the familiar paths, ears straining for the beloved sounds of Curbarig's harp. And finally, as if through a veil, she heard them, and stumbled onwards.

"Curbarig sprang to his feet, his cry of joy shattered as he beheld the swaddled newborn and the terror in Aelvina's eyes. She panted out the tale, clinging to his shoulders, mindless of the tears coursing down both their cheeks. For Curbarig could see that Aelvina was dying. Her body, pushed too hard, too far, too soon, surrendered. Translucent became her skin and her emerald eyes dulled. Curbarig clasped her with all his strength, praying for his lady-love's life, but his grasp was not enough. And in a little while, Aelvina closed her eyes, her kiss fell from his lips, and she passed into the next world.

"No words are there for Curbarig's agony. He screamed his grief at the mountains, throat torn by pain and sorrow, cursing the father, the world, and all in it for taking away that which he valued beyond ought else. He even proffered his life in exchange, but the mute trees and mountains listened not, and at length he fell sobbing to his knees beside her still form. Under a cairn he buried her, gathering the purest white stones to place over her grave near the falls where they had known such joy. And against the stones he leaned his harp, for he knew the music within had died.

"Alainn was given into a foster mother's care. Curbarig had no eyes for his son, for he in part blamed the babe for the mother's death. Instead he sought out the *draoidh-eldrich* and told him all. He begged for and was granted spell of vengeance.

"In the high summer, Curbarig sent a challenge to Aelvina's father who yet smoldered with rage. He cared not that she was dead. Only for the insult forced upon his family. Gladly he agreed to meet in battle the Troich who had sullied his daughter. Upon the grassy vale near the cairn they stood, each accompanied by eight of their own, for it is well known that nine are the number needed to make a duel honorable. Then father and lover stood forth and stated their plaints, so that all could bear witness that right would prevail.

"Hot rage makes poor strategy. It is cold rage that drives one beyond his abilities. Aelvina's father burned with fury, lunging and slashing at Curbarig who danced easily away, dodging the blade, studying his opponent's strengths—and weaknesses. He darted in, drawing first blood, and laughed. For he meant to kill.

"The sun reddened the sky to match the bloodied grass. Both fighters were sore-wounded, but cared not, as do those in hard battle. And then Aelvina's father, perhaps sensing he would not win, drew forth a hidden dirq from his girdle, and flung it at Curbarig. Fast flew the silver blade stained with bloody light, gashing the

Troich's throat beyond hope. Cries of protest rent the air from all who witnessed such treachery.

"Curbarig dropped his blade, knowing he had received his death wound. Blood bubbled from his lips as he mouthed the spell. Spell? Nay, a curse. For as he spoke, Aelvina's father stiffened, his body twisting to the harsh words. Curbarig gestured, and the contorted body soared into the air, to land high above on the cliff top. Before the disbelieving eyes of Troich and Ael, the father swelled, twisting into a tortured, towering pinnacle of stone, taller than all nearby peaks, wrenching with agony as he yet struggled against his fate. Mantled in the blood of his body and the scathing glare of the setting sun, he gave a final scream, then froze into stone.

"A final sigh of content slipped from Curbarig as his friends gently lifted him. They buried him beside Aelvina's cairn as he had earlier requested. In his arms they laid his harp, and all stood in sorrow at his passing, grieving a loss brought on by blind misunderstanding. It was then that the Ael and Troich agreed to an alliance of friendship so that no such sorrow should again befall them. And as they clasped hands over the cairns, a wondrous event transpired.

"The cairns sank part way into the earth, and the stones reformed into a low rounded wall above both graves, now dappled with flowers of every hue, echoing with the sound of bubbling water threaded with music. In amazement, an Ael spoke out loud, asking 'what was this wonder?' And the new-made well answered in the mingled voices of Curbarig and Aelvina, a lilting rhyme telling of the gift of foresight it could bestow on those who asked. It is to this Truthing Well that ye journey, at the foot of Meall Clarsair—the Harpist's Mountain."

The lingering notes of Clarsach trembled in the dim firelight. Danai could still see the tear-wet faces of Troich and Ael, scent the soft fragrance of violets, hear the music of Curbarig and Aelvina's interwoven voices. Slowly, with a deep breath, she re-awoke to the cave about her, aware of tears dampening her cheeks.

Aaron stood up and bowed deeply towards Shamarig. "Never have I understood the power of tale-woven music until now. I believe thee to have a power greater than any sword, any spell, in thy fingers. Well have thy folk named thee Ard-Clarsair."

"Have thee given much thought to thy questions for the Well?" Shamarig asked as he returned Clarsach to her case and placed it back in the nook. The sprytes stared at each other in embarrassed surprise.

"Uh, no," Joson replied, coloring slightly. "I've been so worried about getting there in one piece that I haven't really thought about what I'm going to ask it."

Tatia piped up. "I want to know who my Chosen One is." She giggled.

Shamarig cocked a bushy eyebrow, then looked at Aaron. The spryte shrugged cheerfully. "I'm going to ask what my future holds."

The dwarf frowned. Sometimes he could perceive the shimmering light that emanated from all living things, and surrounded them until they died. It was a trait much cultivated by the *Slanaighear*— Troich-healers that could often diagnose an illness based on the colors of that aura. Aaron's aura had dimmed as he tossed off his reply, and Shamarig felt a shivery touch at the base of his skull. For a moment, he considered urging caution.

Danai, assuming he was waiting upon her response, said "My question is similar to Aaron's. I want to know what I should choose as my Calling."

"What a nice Feyree you are!" Tatia gave an irritated snort. "Makes us all look bad."

"Oh dry up Tatia." Aaron made a rude gesture. "At least she's not worried about who her lover is going to be. Like you're really going to stay with one fellow."

Tlarg and Shamarig exchanged rueful glances over the bickering sprytes' heads. Younglings! "Enough, enough," Tlarg intervened, standing and stretching. "Thy questions are thine own. Remember only that one question is allotted to each living creature—and one only. It can be used wisely or not. Now to rest all. We have a hard journey ahead, and I would fain hasten our departure that sooner I can return for Comhairle."

* * * * *

Chapter Six

On the morn, while preparations were underway, Danai found a moment to ask Shamarig a question that had been niggling at her. "What happened to Alainn?"

Surprised, the harpist halted his making of journey food packets and looked down at her. "Why?"

"I was thinking that, well..." Danai stammered, not quite sure how to express her thoughts. "Well, he was a youngling of love and light and music. Despite what happened, somehow it seems he would have become someone among the Troich."

He smiled. "A true thought. Alainn is my distant sire, father of my eleven forefathers. Even now, he is spoken of as the greatest of all the Troich Clarsairs. There was Ael magic in his music. Clarsach is his harp."

Her eyes flew to the covered instrument, snuggled in its shadowed niche. "Then the face is Aelvina's?"

Shamarig nodded. "As her son imagined her to be. None of the Troich had ever seen the Ael-maid, and although the alliance was established, commerce between the two folk has always remained uncommon. It is not known if Alainn garnered the image through converse with an Ael, but I think it unlikely."

"A harp so old must have its own magic. Does that magic affect thy abilities?"

The dwarf frowned briefly. "Not in the way thee may think. The harp allows me to express my skill in that it grants the most beauty of music of any instrument among our folk, but it cannot mask a flaw. That is why one of the music trials at the Eisteddfod is a song done without any instrument. To ensure our voices are our own." He gathered the food bundles and handed one down to her. "Thee asks more questions than I would expect from a youngling. Is such curiosity a way of thy folk?"

"No more or less than any other, I would guess," Danai replied after a moment's thought. "I tend to be a bit of a loner. Triasa—she's my aunt—says I'm just shy and will grow out of it. But I do have more time to think."

Tlarg, already loaded, stood beside the entry and stamped his boot with impatience. "Time to be on, time to be on! Have ye all refilled thy acorns with water, thy sacks with food? Good. Then let us away." He clasped his brother's wrists. "I will be back before Comhairle."

As they exited the cave, each spryte bowed low before Shamarig, thanking him for his hospitality. Danai was last, and unexpectedly the dwarf bent down and gently clasped her arm, his hand engulfing her to the elbow. "Thee are much like an Ael-maid," he murmured, a softness in his eyes. "Be wary maiden. There is a feeling in the Anam's sending that disturbs me greatly, and it was sent to thee, I suspect. Thee will have much need of thy folk's teachings. If ever thee feels a need for aid, cry thusly for my friends, the magpies." He imitated the birds' raucous squawk, startling the others. "Tell them to bring thy message, and I will do as I am able."

Aaron frowned as he saw Shamarig holding Danai's arm. He found himself irritated by such close contact and was glad when the dwarf released her.

Tlarg set a quick-march pace through the tunnels. "Sorry I am that we cannot stop to see some of the other marvels I mentioned," he said during a brief watering stop. "But I would hope ye will perchance come again to visit an old Troich and I shall have a chance to make amends?"

"How would we reach thee?" Joson asked.

The dwarf grinned through his beard. "Strange may it seem, but above earth, our closest comrades be the birds."

"The birds!" Aaron nearly stumbled in surprise. Airborne frolicking creatures did not seem the natural compliment to dirt-delving dwarves.

"Aye. A good tale that, and one to be saved for another visit with my brother. Needs not say that he tells it best. That squawk he gave was that of the magpie, and unless I miss my guess, he gave that knowledge to thee maiden if ever thee needs his aid." Danai nodded. "For me, shriek like the mocking azure jays. Those noisy upstarts remind me of my youth, and while I count all the winged creatures as acquaintances, among the jay folk I have special friends who will search me out with thy messages."

The tunnel, which ran fairly level, marched by many workings and caves. Dwarves would occasionally peer out to find the source of tramping boots, and Tlarg would give a cheery greeting. They stayed that night with Mandalak, and the sprytes were surprised at how closely the lady dwarves resembled their fellows, lacking only a beard.

The next day their path began to bore downwards through the mountain side with no off-tunnels, and the scent of metal, edged with fire, sharpened. The sprytes' leg muscles tightened as they braced against the steep descent.

"Phew," gasped Joson after some time. "Why so steep a trail Tlarg?"

"We are in the belly of a cliff near the Meall Clarsair, and never were found any gems of worth in its guts. Old diggings have long since been filled, and this route is simply to bring our folk to the Well, and the lands outside. Why go roundabout when the direct trail is quickest?"

"Well, at least it's helping you to lose weight Joson," Aaron half laughed, half gasped. "I swear the Mentors won't recognize you when we return. And won't the maids be impressed?"

Just when their legs felt as if they could not hike any further, the tunnel abruptly ended. A rock face greeted them, fretted with sunlight from a small rune-like carving that pierced the stone, set at the height of a dwarf's eyes. Tlarg peered through, then gently placed his hand on the rough-hewn wall and spoke a spell. The stone creaked open to reveal a narrow rocky ledge fringed with swaying tree branches, swathed in warm late-day sunshine.

"Tlarg, are all the tunnels sealed shut?" Danai asked, blinking at the brightness.

"Most are, where there be too easy an access." Tlarg shielded his eyes and stepped gingerly into the light. "At the higher reaches we often leave them open. For all that we are now creatures under earth, we still love the Mother's realm."

When their eyes had adjusted to the light, the sprytes beheld the vale of Shamarig's song.

On the far side a waterfall thundered down a weathered gray cliff, darkening its flanks with spray. A wide creek roiled away from the pile of broken stone at its base, weaving off on a course that flowed southeast from the valley's northern-most end. Rowan and holly dotted the vale's hem with bursts of ivory and gold blossoms, and the meadow was filled with flowers of every hue. Purple milkwort, yellow primrose, and pink wild thyme shared the grass with white and yellow daisies. Flashes of birds colored the air, while snatches of their melodies bounced from tree branch to meadow. A gentle breeze wafted the sweet fragrance of sun-warmed grass and flowers around them.

"There be the Well of Truth," pointed Tlarg, drawing their attention to what looked like a pile of white stones off to the near side of the falls. "And here must I bid ye farewell. Remember that eventide comes early to this vale, what with the high-cliffed mountains. Seek ye out a safe place—and sooner than when we first met." He chuckled.

Impulsively, Danai jumped forward to hug the dwarf's knee, startling a smile to his face. The other sprytes did likewise. "There's no way to say thanks," Danai said. "Thee saved our lives and more."

"Danai speaks for us all Tlarg," Aaron agreed. "Granted we are only small sprytes, not yet even winged, but if thee ever needs our help, thee knows from where each of us hails, and thee can send a message by thy jays."

Clasping their wrists and wishing them good tellings from the Well, Tlarg stepped back into the darkness. The stone swung shut with a faint click. Had they not known where to look, the small rune would have appeared as nothing more than the handiwork of wind and water.

"Let's go," Joson urged. "That grass down there is taller than us, and we need to reach the Well."

"And just how are we to get down?" Tatia knelt and peered over the edge. "Maybe dwarves can jump down from here, but I have no burning desire to break my neck."

"It's easy! We'll use spinners." Aaron whooped with glee, glad to be out in sunshine and open air. He ran over to one of the trees whose branches overspanned the ledge—a tall maple loaded down with wide-winged seed pods. "Grab one of these and down we'll go!" He seized a pod as large as himself and snapped it free, leaving the long stem intact. Then, giving a cheerful shout, he flung himself over the edge, the stem wrapped tightly around both hands. The upward rush of air caught the pod's wings, and it began to spin rapidly, flinging Aaron's legs every which way. He landed with a soft thump in the long grass near the tree's roots. "It's fun," he yelled up through cupped hands. "Try it!"

"I don't think so," Tatia said. "But the tree is a good idea." Jumping lightly onto an oak branch, she dodged among the dark green leaves until reaching the fissured gray bark. Its many hand and toeholds made it easy to scramble down, and Joson followed close behind her. Neither noticed Danai take a deep breath, then walk over and snap off a seed pod.

"Lunasa guard me, I must be crazy," she breathed, then launched herself off the ledge. The world spun crazily about, and she clung to the stem for dear life. In a moment, the wild ride was over, her rump colliding with firm ground.

"Good for you Danai!" Aaron grinned, helping her to her feet. "You may feel dizzy for a few moments. Good thing it's been a while since we ate. For sure don't try to walk in a straight line."

"Dizzy isn't quite the way I'd put it," Danai said, trying to ignore her still-spinning stomach. The other two reached the oak's roots then hurried over to join them.

"You're both sun-touched," Tatia snapped. "Whatever gave you such a madcap idea?"

"Ah, the fellows do it all the time up by Bubble Falls," Aaron shrugged. "Couple of lads have broken an arm or leg if the stem gets away from them but it sure is fun!"

"If you say so." Joson looked dubiously at his friend. "But we had better get going. The Well is still a ways off."

The wind-brushed grasses sighed high over their heads as they struck out towards the falls, relying on its steady thunder as a guide. The breeze did not reach below the green-tasseled grass tops, and the humid air smelled of ripe grass and moist earth. Aaron wiped sweat away from his eyes. "I have a new appreciation of the need for wings. You're awful quiet Danai."

She flushed. "Just thinking about Curbarig and Aelvina. So what if they were of different folk? The whole thing just seems so sad and stupid. I mean three died because of her father's false pride. If folk are in love with each other, then let them alone," she added with some heat.

"Easier said than done," Joson disagreed, dodging around a large pebble. "Can you imagine how our elders would react if we came toddling home and announced we were seriously in love with a dwarf or Ael? I know my kinfolk would throw fits."

"I don't see how we could be involved with other folk anyway," Tatia said. "I mean, when you get down to the, um, physical issues, there's not much that could happen."

Joson looked pained, but Aaron just chuckled. "Always the realist in such matters, huh?"

"But seriously," Danai insisted, determined not to let the conversation turn banal. "What if it did happen? Why would it be so wrong? Love is love."

"Yes and no." Joson paused to catch his breath. "I know the bards and skalds sing tales of love as if it were the highest of achievements. Talk about it sometimes like it's an altered state or something. But the fact is, love doesn't work alone, unless you go off and live apart from your dell. You have to live among your folk, socialize, follow the rules if you're to eat and survive. An absolute disregard for the framework on which we build our lives can only lead to trouble." He shook his head sadly. "Even a love like theirs that achieved bard legend couldn't transcend those rules. Maybe for a brief, wonderful while, but reality has a nasty habit of taking the heavy hand in the end."

"Maybe. But sometimes it does transcend in that it redefines those rules. After that tragedy, at least the Ael and dwarves were willing to associate."

"In word, but not much in deed from what Shamarig told us. So what did really change?"

Ahead, Aaron scrambled up the side of a rough reddish stone whose top protruded above the grass, and peered around, shading his eyes for a better view. "Hey! We made good time. Looks like just a short march. We need to bear a little to the right though, or we'll pass the Well and wind up near the base of the falls. Can you see the cliff face from there if you look up?"

"I can," Joson shouted back.

"Good. Then take a bearing. See that long blackish streak, about midway? We need to aim for the very end of that." He almost tumbled down the rock face with excitement. "We're nearly there!" His enthusiasm bubbled through them, and they hurried through a thicket of daisy leaves. A dumbledore buzzed loudly over their heads for a moment, its wings providing a welcome fanning of air. Ahead, the light seemed to brighten. Pushing through a barrier of flower stems, they stepped into a ring of close-sheared grass that surrounded the Well.

Despite its proximity to the falls, the ring seemed shrouded by calming silence. The Well sat off-center, closer to the cliff face, its stones weathered to mellow ivory, flowers competing for toeholds among its nooks. Flutterbies danced along air currents, brilliant spots of color; nearby a robin trilled, another answered.

The Well reminded Danai of a waiting elder, seated on a stone, content to linger in the warm sunshine enjoying a moment when past and future dissolved into now. They had journeyed seven days to ask it their questions. She realized she feared what it might say, and she exhaled slowly past the knot in her stomach.

"Now what?" Tatia whispered, giving voice to the question uppermost in their minds. She was oddly pale, her pearl skin dulled almost to gray.

"I guess we'd better get it over with." Aaron's bright smile couldn't quite mask the quaver in his voice. "Come on!" He strode forward, shoulders flung back, eyes fixed on the Well.

How brave he is, Danai thought, hastening into step behind him. He might be the pod joker, but underneath that cynical exterior, she had seen much to admire.

The Well loomed, framed by the sky-reaching backdrop of the craggy gray cliff. They halted under a clump of violets, the deep purple blossoms nodding in the breeze, providing richly scented shadows.

"I'll go first." Aaron took a deep breath, closed his eyes for a moment, then approached the Well. They watched him as he suddenly knelt before it, almost disappearing in the grass, then stood and reached out slowly to touch the white stones. His lips moved. Then he stiffened, mouth slightly open, eyes staring, a golden statue. After a few moments he gulped for breath as if coming up from under water, then bowed. His face wore a puzzled expression as he walked back to their violet clump. They waited for him to speak.

"It's...it's...no, you're going to have to feel it for yourself. I can't describe it. And I've not got a clue what the Well meant." He paused, frowning. "It said, *'Aaron, laugh not, mock not, die not.'* It just doesn't make any sense. What has that got to do with my future?" He gestured curtly at Joson. "You'd better go ahead. Remember what Tlarg told us about finding a safe place early."

Joson proceeded, and likewise returned with a confused expression. "I asked if I was destined for anything great among our folk. The Well said, *'Joson, you will stand with the three to fight fire, and give near your all.'* And I thought Aaron's reply was strange."

"Try bizarre." Aaron shook his head. "It answers in *kryptics*."

Danai held back, and with a slight sneer, Tatia advanced, soon retracing her steps, a contented smile lighting her eyes. "Yes, I asked about my Chosen One. It said, *'Tatia, through the doings of another, as a child shall you find a life beyond your imaginings.'* That sounds pretty plain to me."

They all looked at Danai. Trembling, she urged her feet to move, finally reaching the spot where the others had stood. The Well engulfed her, shutting out the sight of everything else.

The silence deepened, until all she could hear was a ringing in her ears. She felt an overwhelming urge to kneel and did, honoring those from whom the Well had sprung, then arose, panting softly, afraid to touch it. Her arm felt as if it carried a great weight. She placed her palm on the sun-warmed stones.

The ringing vanished. The silence was absolute, waiting, waiting. For her to speak. "Will I be of any use to my folk?" But that's not what I meant to ask, she thought. The words seemed to vibrate in the air before her. She waited, cocooned in the silence.

A soft sigh eddied about her face, and she stiffened as a shimmering vibration emanated from the stones, the ground, the very air about her.

"Danai of silver.
You shall sacrifice your self to fire.
See all stamped by misled desire.
Rake ashes of lives.
Know winter of bitterness; survive.
Then triad the realm with folks' dreams."

The two voices, female intertwined with male, dissipated, replaced by the everyday muddle of meadow sounds. Shaking her head, Danai staggered back a step. "What do you mean?" she cried out. The Well sat in silence. She turned, making her way gradually back to her waiting podmates. Joson and Aaron reached out a comforting arm simultaneously. She repeated the kryptic verse. "It makes no sense. None at all. Did we waste our time?"

"I don't think so," Aaron answered. "We're supposed to repeat this stuff to the Mentors when we get back, so maybe we're not meant to understand it. At least not clearly." Joson nodded in agreement, but Tatia laughed them off.

"Well, I did."

"You think," Joson returned sourly. "Let's go find a bower site. Haven't you noticed how the shadows are already half way across the vale?" He pointed towards a fallen tree, partially visible on the ring's eastern edge, with clumps of thick-boled ferns hugging its sides. "That may be a good spot. Although I'm not too keen on fallen trees just now."

Taking a wide loop around the Well, they approached the tree with caution in case something else was already using it. Behind them the shadows continued their own march, initiating the eventide melody of cricket thrumming and bird warbles. Aaron thunked on the tree and was rewarded with a hollow boom. "Been down a while. Let's look for a squirrel nest hole, but stay together. Nice place for snakes, this. Make a quick snack of us if we look into their eyes."

Cool green light filtered through the canopy of ferns as they paced along the trunk's side, dodging around hillocks of decaying bark and wood fragments. "Hold on!" Aaron pointed at his feet, which were sinking into the mushy soil. "We had better go back. It's looking real muddy up ahead, and I don't fancy a mud-bath right now." There was a soft sucking noise as he yanked his feet free.

They had more luck in the other direction, finding a knothole that widened into a comfortable hollow. A rank smell told them it had been used by some creature, but the dried grasses were dusty and undisturbed. Aaron grinned. "Saves us from having to dig out a bower."

"Maybe," Tatia wrinkled her nose. "But I am not sleeping on those smelly grasses. Come on Danai. Let's gather some fresh ones." They left the fellows behind to clean out the debris, and returned with large armfuls of fresh grass shoots and a few sweet-scented flower petals. By the time all was complete, gloaming had cloaked the vale. The now-still air was redolent with flowers' sweet fragrance, and here and there a shimmer of nightwings flickered. Above, the first star glittered as the last fingers of sunlight dragged forth the night. They sat a little way from the tree's trunk.

"See how Pyre Tor flames," Joson said, craning his neck to look at the peak.

"Ugh. When you think about what it really is..." Danai shuddered.

"Was. The Ael died in that spellcasting. Served him right too. Don't feel sympathy for him, Danai," Aaron said.

Tatia was studying the Well thoughtfully; it glowed softly in the darkness. "Do you think the rest of the pod has been here already?"

"Now there's a good question!" Aaron glanced about. "I guess we wouldn't see any signs of them. This is not the sort of place you leave stuff lying around in. But you figure we took a bit of a shortcut, so maybe we're first."

"That's assuming everybody started from the same point." Joson yawned. "Remember, we got lead off in different directions. It's anyone's guess. The real question is what path we're taking back. Going underground, we don't have a trail to follow back. Got any ideas? And let's get back inside. Stargazing is fine—but not in this strange place."

Inside, they continued to discuss their return journey. "We pretty much traveled west-northwest," Aaron said. "So we can head in reverse. I thought I saw a bit of a trail when I was on that high rock."

"We could summon the jays and go back with Tlarg," Danai ventured.

"Comhairle, remember?" Joson shook his head. "But calling the birds is a good idea. They may be able to give us directions." He chuckled. "If I've learned nothing else from this journey, it's to always look for landmarks. You've got to know where to begin and where to end. What happens in the middle is the adventure."

* * * * *

D anai rolled over, trying to get comfortable, wishing she could fall asleep like the others. As she lay there, she noticed the entry seemed to be gradually brightening, until it became a rough-edged silvery circle. The light beckoned, and she rose and slipped out of the hollow, unaware of Aaron's golden gaze.

Outside, a cool breeze lapped against her cheeks. Comforting night sounds dappled the air. A distant owl hooted. Cricket song tangled with bullfrog croaks. The rumble of the falls had softened. She found the lack of silence reassuring; any hunter's presence would have cast a pall of quiet. Above, Lunasa showed only as a thin crescent. Yet before her, the Well was shimmering with its own light, waves of silver and pearl iridescence lapping across the stones, seeming to ebb and flow to a silent music. Curious, she took a step forward.

"It's beautiful, isn't it?" Aaron perched on the entry's rim, smiling down. "Come on, let's go take a look." He leaped lightly to the ground, caught her hand, and pulled her towards the Well. As they walked through the ring, Danai felt a shiver of energy course through her feet, spiraling up her spine and spreading with the warmth of goldenvine dew. A thrum of harp music vibrated inside her mind, a sense of joyful eagerness. And something more.

Aaron tightened his grip.

"Aaron, wait," she gasped softly. "Not yet. Please."

He halted, pivoted, and closed the gap between them. "Why not?" he whispered, staring into her glowing emerald eyes, a smile tugging at the corner of his mouth. "You're so exciting, so different from any of the maids I've ever been with. I've been wondering what it would be like to kiss you ever since that moment you dug into the foxfire. Now I'll find out." He lowered his lips to hers, his arms sliding about her waist.

Danai closed her eyes, savoring the sweetness of her first real kiss, the fullness of Aaron's lips, the firm strength of his body. The insistent energy coursing through her intensified, and her legs felt as if they were melting. As the kiss ended, she opened her eyes, a small smile quirking the corner of her mouth.

"Disappointed?" he murmured.

"Oh no!" She giggled, surprising herself. "I've always wondered what it was really like, and it's much better than I imagined."

"You're not telling me this is the first time you've been kissed," demanded Aaron in astonishment, receiving his answer from her suddenly downcast eyes. His arms tightened, and he kissed her again. About them a swirling tracery of light gathered, but they were only aware of each other.

Danai finally pulled away, feeling giddy and strangely heated. "Aaron, look at the Well!" Even as she spoke, a swelling opalescent bubble engulfed them, expanding to the ring's edge. It played across their bodies, flickers of light dancing across their faces, tugging them slowly, irrevocably closer to the Well. Danai knew she should feel fear, but felt only a sense of anticipation. Aaron's face reflected a matching eagerness. The light pulsed through them in tingling bursts of energy, making it hard to breathe.

At the foot of the Well, they turned towards each other. Danai felt more than herself, as if another were filling her body with an unbearable brightness of desire, of need, of joy, of long-denied love. She reached for Aaron, murmuring his name. He opened his arms in wide embrace, then gathered her to himself, engulfed with an unfamiliar intensity of feeling fueled by well-known desire.

"Danai?" he whispered raggedly.

"Aaron," she assented.

* * * * *

Lunasa had traveled beyond the vale's western rim when Danai's eyes opened, aware of her body as never before. The duality she had sensed in the tumult of passion had subsided, and she was left to indulge in the warm aftermath of her first coupling. Aaron stirred, and she reached out to touch him, then hesitated, loathe to end the moment.

A deep note thrummed from the now-dimly glowing Well. Aaron's eyes opened, and he rolled over to face her, propping his head on his hand. There was a surprising shyness to his smile. "It's never been like that. No honest, I'm not just saying that. Look, yes, I've been with my share of maidens, but this was something different. It was more than just a physical thing. I...I felt as if I were a part of your heart, your spirit. As if I'd known you forever, yet had met you for the first time. I know, I know. It sounds sun-touched." He reached out to stroke her cheek. "Am I making any sense?"

"Yes and no, I guess. You are the first, so I have nothing to compare." She blushed at his surprise. "But did I feel one with you? Yes. As if we were more than ourselves yet as new as the dawn." She stretched languorously. "I am new at this, you know. Is it reasonable to request seconds?" He chuckled and reached for her.

* * * * *

The hollow seemed musty after the freshness of the vale. They crept in, returning to their original sleeping places. Danai would have preferred to cuddle next to him, but reality was intruding. Already a niggle at the back of her mind whispered they had broken a major Order of the Rites—no coupling— and it dispelled the lingering sense of pleasure. And she had frowned upon Tatia for lusting after Aaron! How was she herself any better? Would the Mentors know? Worse yet, what about Triasa? Sleep was once again long in coming, and her dreams were riddled with a ring of Mentors screeching as she and Aaron mated under the glaring face of Lunasa.

* * * * *

Chapter Seven

Pale sunlight flickered outside, tickling Joson's eyes open. He yawned and sat up, running fingers through frowsy hair. Glancing beyond Tatia's supine form, his eyes lingered on Danai, a wistful expression flitting across his face. Her silvery bodyglow dimmed as the light brightened. He gazed a few more moments, then with a soft sigh, rose. "Arise, arise, ye bower slugs," he cried. "C'mon, it's dawnshine or thereabouts, and we have yet another mystery to solve! How to get back to the Dell."

"Well, we're all bright and cheery this morn," Tatia griped, sitting up and reaching for a kuis. "We don't even know how to get back home, we're going to need to forage again, and I'm just tired of it all. Ugh, my mouth tastes like I chewed on old nuts all night."

"Are you always this fun to be around?" muttered Aaron.

Tatia gave him a cloying smile. "Not when I'm having a good time." Her smile vanished as Aaron ambled over to Danai, knelt and gently shook her shoulder.

"Hey bower slug! So you always wake up at dawnshine, huh?"

"I'm awake, I'm awake," she mumbled.

"Then let's see you sit up and prove it."

"You think you're a Mentor or something?"

"Ha, ha. Joson's right. We need to get a move on, and beyond knowing the Dell is somewhere southeast, I for one haven't a clue."

She sat up and yawned. "So we'll ask the birds."

Joson slapped his forehead with mock surprise. "By the Mother, so we said. They go everywhere, and we've all had basic Charmer training. Although I admit I didn't have much luck at it. How about you others?"

To everyone's surprise, Tatia stood up. "I got along pretty well with the sparrows. What are you looking at me like that for Aaron? I get along with a lot of things, don't you know?"

He ignored the hint, instead gesturing towards the entry. "Howsabout we have mornmeal, then go to the Well's ring and see if we can call down a sparrow or two?"

"You and Joson and food," Tatia scoffed. "Have you already forgotten that the best time to bespeak birds is at dawn?" Shaking bits of grass from her hair, she seized her rucksack and hastened outside. With a startled scramble, the others followed, Joson lamenting over postponing a meal.

"Wait up!" Aaron shouted as she charged ahead of them. "Did you even check around to see if it was safe?" She ignored him and kept going. They entered the ring, their tunics soon dew-sodden and chill. Tatia headed for the Well, and once there, searched the surrounding trees for those filled with sparrow song. She tossed her head back, trilled three notes, two long, one short. A pause. Another trill, followed by a query chirp. Nothing happened.

"It's noisy," Joson said. "Maybe if we trill together, we'll be easier to hear."

"Good idea," Tatia said. "One, two and three!" The effect of four young voices trilling produced what Danai privately felt had to be the realm's largest sparrow call. There was a flicker of several brown wings and a pair of sparrows plumped down before them, the backwash of their wings nearly knocking Tatia over. Danai swallowed. The birds always seemed so large, and she could not forget how lethal those beaks could be. One jab. For the hunter birds, a Feyree was but a quick morsel. Charmers ran the risk of becoming a meal when they summoned the wood folk.

The male sparrow cocked a dew drop black eye at them and query chirped. Taking a deep breath, Tatia replied in twitters and trills, even adding springy hops to emphasize her points. His mate bobbed twice, and hopped sunwise until her bill pointed southeast, and chirped. "They say the Dell is in that direction," Tatia translated. Danai forbore to mention she understood the sparrows. "They can't tell me how long we'll need, but did give some trail marks. She says we'll have to pass through three valleys."

"Could they give us a lift?" Joson asked with sudden inspiration.

"Fog brain! There's just two of them. How could they carry four of us?"

"Well, they may have some friends. Just ask, will you?"

Tatia chirped, and the female sparrow warbled briefly. "They can't. It's nesting time, and the young ones aren't yet ready to fly. In fact, they both need to get back to their family." They all bowed and chirped a thank you, then ducked to dodge the burst of air as the sparrows launched skyward.

"Three valleys, huh?" Aaron made a face. "After all this hiking, we're sure going to appreciate our wings."

"Well, I for one am ready to head back." Danai scooped up the rucksack she had dropped.

"We'll need more than our dirqs," Joson said. They turned startled eyes on him. "We're passing through unknown woods. This is a survival test, too, remember? I suggest we make two spears and two clubs."

"From what, grass stems?" Tatia jeered.

"No dim wit. We'll find twigs at the edge of the woods."

Aaron nodded approval. "He's right. Had it not been for Tlarg, we would probably have made weapons by second day on the ridge. Hunters just don't work at night, you know."

"So let's march." Joson started southeast, taking a bearing on a tall silverbarked aspen.

As the others followed, Danai lingered, gazing back at the Well. Sunlight had not yet touched the stones, but she was sure she detected a faint glow. "Wait! We almost forgot to find the trefoil to prove we've been here."

"Toads! Good thing you remembered." Aaron turned about. "Anybody remember seeing them yesterday?"

"They like sunlight," Danai suggested. "Maybe on the west side of the Well?"

"We'll go get them then." Aaron grabbed her elbow, and hurried her along. "Thirds?" he whispered, with a wicked grin.

The Well was silent as they prowled its perimeter. Directly behind, they found a large trefoil clump, the tightly furled yellow flowers awaiting a sunbeam's touch. The dark green three-leafed clusters bore an unusual golden band around their edges. "My guess it's the leaves we need to bring," Danai reached up.

"Let me help," Aaron offered, grabbing her around the waist and lifting her. He snatched a kiss as her feet returned to the ground. Both heard a faint harp thrum.

"Aaron! Stop. The others."

"Unless they can see through rock, we're fine." He reluctantly let go, and they hurried back to Joson and Tatia.

"I'll roll it up and keep it in my ruck," Danai suggested. "Lead on Joson." She glanced back and smiled at the Well as they left the ring and entered the high grasses.

They reached the aspen as the first direct sunbeams spilled over the cliffs' edge. Finding twigs for spears and cudgels proved simple. As the lads edged the spear points, Tatia and Danai foraged, gathering young charlock and hawthorn leaves. Mornmeal was a short affair; they were eager to get back to the Dell.

As they entered the woods, Danai inhaled deeply, mouth open. It was difficult, but she could detect the scent of old flowers and cut grass.

"How will we know we're still headed in the right direction?" Tatia asked.

"Can't you smell it?" Danai glanced at her in surprise. "The directions smell heavier than the regular forest scents. Try it." Only Joson seemed able to capture the elusive underscents. Aaron seemed frustrated, while Tatia looked bored after a few casual sniffs.

"Fine, you two lead then." Aaron dropped behind Danai with a wink. "I'm sure the view will be better back here anyway." Danai blushed. Joson and Tatia frowned.

A short while later, Joson pointed ahead. "Look! A cairn marker. Maybe there's a real trail." He was right. A well-trammeled trail plodded in a southeasterly direction through the woods. They could see cairns spaced at regular intervals ahead as it snaked among the tree trunks. "Probably came in a little closer to the river back there in the vale which is why we didn't see it."

By mid-day, the woods had given way to dark-needled pines, their branches woven into a dense canopy through which little sunlight penetrated. Seasons of dead twigs and dead leaves seemed to swallow sound, and their feet kicked up tawny puffs of dust. Somewhere a jay screeched once. Another answered farther away. The air felt heavy.

"What really bothers me," remarked Aaron as they trudged along, "is that this Rite is supposed to be one of the simpler ones. I have to wonder what the Mentors think is hard."

"We'll find out," Tatia grumped, extinguishing conversation.

In a small clearing, Joson called a determined halt for midmeal. Nobody argued. The food and water refreshed them, and they fell to discussing the rest of the day's journey.

"We really can't determine how high the mountains are down in these woods, and when the shadows will come," Joson said, glancing up at the nowovercast sky. "We probably should look for a bower site earlier than later."

"But not yet," Danai protested. "After all, we're near Mid-Summer's Eve, and daylight is longer than night. We should have plenty more time for marching."

"No disagreement. But it's just a sort of 'be aware' thing I've developed. You know? I wonder where the other sprytes are?"

"From the looks of this trail, we wouldn't be able to tell much of who or what has been on it," Aaron remarked from his comfortable sprawl against a tree root. "It's so old, and so pounded down—well, maybe after a rain, there might be tracks. But not now, when it's so dry. At least we can't lose it." He stood up and dusted off his rump. "Let's go."

* * * *

"I spoke too soon."

The four gazed in dismay at a wide river of gray-white stone that gashed through the woods. Carved by untold seasons of water, it was ridged and runneled by hollows and hills, and flowed as far as they could see in either direction. The cairns had disappeared.

The light dimmed, and looking up, they saw clouds billowing and frothing over the mountains, darkening to gray. Somewhere far behind, thunder muttered.

"Let's try to get across before the storm breaks." Aaron hurried forward.

"But Aaron," Joson bellowed after the sprinting spryte. "The trail!"

"I figure we can go straight across—aim for that big oak there." He disappeared over a ridge.

"Joson, the trail has to be somewhere over there." Danai started forward, walking with caution through the rough rock, Tatia close behind. She could not believe that Aaron had just charged across without waiting for them. "It's probably easy to see from dwarf or Ael height, or if we were winged. But I doubt they planned the trail for sprytes."

Storm quiet enveloped the forest as wiser wood folk scurried for shelter. Then thunder rumbled again, heralding a vanguard of seething green-gray clouds that galloped across the sky, racing southwards towards the lowlands. The sprytes were mid-way across when the wind took a deep breath, then shoved them to their knees with a chilling gust. As they staggered back to their feet, the storm-darkness was slashed by a blue lightstrike that pierced the trees ahead of them. Fire exploded, shattering a tall pine into burning chunks and branches, but those sounds were drowned in the crack and roar of thunder. The wind ripped the rain from the clouds, and in a moment they were cocooned in a pounding deluge.

Danai heard Tatia's terrified wail behind her. "Grab hands," she screamed, seizing their hands as her words were sucked away by the shrieking wind. She took a few steps, feeling her feet slip in the hurrying layer of water that slithered over the naked rock. She could feel it sucking at her feet, making her stumble. Another blast of sound, and the rain fell harder, the thick fat drops nearly knocking her down. They were trapped in a skin-tight bubble of wet that pummeled, pulled, threatened to melt them under its onslaught.

Tatia teetered a moment then fell, her feet yanked out from under by the deepening water. Her hand jerked from Danai's. The surging waters tumbled her along like a pearly petal until she was brought up headfirst against a black stone bulge. She lay unmoving, her face submerged in the hungry waters.

Clutching hands, Joson and Danai lurched and skidded towards the still form. Oh Lunasa, let her be all right, Danai thought, all dislike cast aside. "Joson, grab my waist," she shouted, her mouth next to his ear. "Brace yourself. Don't kneel or the stream will pull us under." She leaned into his arms, grabbing at Tatia's shoulder, but the tunic tore away. In desperation, she seized at the short crop of hair, yanking her podmate's face free of the water. She kept hauling, dread giving her strength to bodily lift Tatia enough that she could seize her under the arms.

"Danai, push...her...forward, against that...rock." Joson's voice came in snatches above the clamor of rain, wind and rushing water. "Water's...deeper. Can't move...drown. Lean her on...I'll lean on you...maybe...make it."

The water gurgled above their knees, their waists, up their torsos. Danai desperately wanted to check Tatia's breathing, but could only keep the limp, cold form wedged against the rock. Thank the Mother for Joson! She knew that alone, she and Tatia would have been swept away. She felt Joson slip slightly, his chin digging into her shoulder.

"I don't...know how much...longer I can...do this!"

"No choice. We don't, we die!" She felt his arms tighten around her. Her teeth chattered as her legs numbed under the water's chill onslaught. She closed her eyes and prayed.

"Danai, look!"

His shouting seemed loud; she realized the wind was slacking off. "What?" Her eyes unclenched.

"I can start to see the woods—see that burning tree? The rain is letting up! Look, the water's dropping back down a bit. Let's go!"

"No, wait. It could be deeper in other spots. We have to let it run off some more. And the storm could start up again. At least here we're safe." She adjusted her grip on Tatia. "Can you reach around me and touch her face. See if she's breathing?"

Joson complied. "I don't feel anything."

"Try again, please try again."

"Danai, I don't. I'm sorry."

The rain eased, the rushing waters about them gradually thinning to a transparent sheath filming the river of stone. The storm galloped southwards, trailing a long cloak of dark clouds, already thundering its challenge to the next valley. The westering sunlight sliced through, igniting the clouds, golden spears shimmering on wet leaves as the wind sighed away, leaving behind the chatter of dripping water.

Her limbs cramped with cold, Danai pulled one of Tatia's arms over her neck. Wordlessly, Joson did the same. Working their way carefully across the slippery stone, they steered left of the still-smoldering tree, gently dragging Tatia's body between them. Near the forest's edge, they found a pedestal of black rock, its top worn flat. They lifted her body and arranged it as if on a bier. "It's better than lying her in the mud," Joson said bitterly.

"I'm going to listen again. She can't be dead. It doesn't make any sense."

"Stop it Danai. Don't do this. She's not breathing. That's that." He reached to pull her away.

"But the Truthing Well said she would meet her Chosen One. If she's dead, that means the Well lied. It can't lie. It's supposed to know the future!"

"It said a 'life beyond your imaginings.' Tatia took that to mean her Chosen One would give her a wonderful life. Maybe the life the Well meant was death!"

She yanked away from his restraining hands, and poised her ear by Tatia's half-open mouth. Nothing. She moved to listen to the heart, but her shivering made it hard to hear anything.

"No! No! No!" Raging, she seized Tatia's body, shaking it so hard the head and limbs flopped. Shocked, Joson remained rooted for a moment, then grabbed Tatia, struggling for the body. The contest lasted a few brief moments, then Joson's greater strength prevailed. He hauled hard, lost his balance, and Tatia spilled on top of him. Danai began to sob.

Tatia coughed. A horrible choking gag.

"Lean her over at the waist," Danai cried. Tatia spewed water and vomit, heaving repeatedly, gasps punctuated with chest-tearing coughs, suspended by Joson's arms. At last the hacking abated.

"Tatia? Tatia?" Danai knelt next to her, gently touching her cold cheek. Her breath came in jagged raspy pants.

"Let's sit her down against this rock." The position seemed to help. Gradually Tatia's breathing settled to a hoarse but steady rasp. Danai felt her clammy brow, and encountered a large lump just above the left ear.

"In the name of the Twins, where is that dolt?" Startled, Danai looked up from her inspection. Joson was glaring about the area, his eyes flashing violet. "I don't see Aaron anywhere, and we can't go searching for him. We've got to set up bower now, and get her comfortable. Don't argue. We don't have time. I'll hunt around, you stay with her. I'll stay in sight, I promise. That burning tree is hard to miss, even at gloaming." He hastened towards the tree, guessing the shattered trunk might offer shelter. Large slabs lay about, some still orange with embers, wisps of smoke trailing upwards. His search was rewarded when he found a long piece with a large hole, probably from a rotted out branch; it was lined with feathers, and bits of leaves and grass. There was plenty of room for the three of them. He ran back to Danai. "I've found a spot. Here, I'll carry her. Grab the rucks."

While Danai made Tatia as comfortable as she could inside the dry hollow, tucking feathers about her, Joson took their kuis and refilled them from raindrops that still dangled from larger leaves. Gloaming was already gathering; it was too late to forage, but they still had miyacan, however soggy. He climbed inside the hollow. He could see Danai's silvery shimmer, but Tatia's pearly glow was almost non-existent. He knew what that meant.

"I think her body is shutting down." Danai wished they had covered basic Healer lore in survival training, briefly wondering why not, given they were to be tossed into the clutches of the wild.

"So what do we do? Her bodyglow's dimming Danai."

"I know. I know. Keep her warm, try and get something into her if she wakes up."

"Warm? With what? I'm chilled to the bone myself, and all our tunics are sopping wet."

"I'll use fire magic."

He started. "Excuse me?"

"We've been taught the basics. I think this situation warrants using it."

"If we're allowed to use it, then why did the Mentors tell us we could only do so in their presence?"

"Joson, Tatia's dying. Triasa would know what to do, but I'm guessing. I know she'd be wrapped in covers to keep warm. We don't have any. Fire's the only choice. I can use it to heat water to warm her. Would you really sacrifice her for those rules?"

"No," he replied slowly. "I guess I'm just worried that those rules probably have reasons behind them. Rules usually do."

Danai clenched her fists at his stubbornness, then let her breath out slowly. "You're right. But what else can we do? Besides, my Mentors didn't say anything like that. They just taught us the correct arrangements and spellcasting gestures."

"We could try to get some embers from the tree."

"We have nothing to grab them with, or carry them in, and the pieces I saw were all too large anyway. Fire magic will be faster and easier." Danai felt an odd eagerness to try her hand at the spell, as if something were nudging her along.

"I hate quandaries." Joson grimaced in disgust. "This just doesn't feel right, but I'll get the stuff together so you can spellcast. There are plenty of lightstrike-blasted chips and twigs about. I'll gather them, and set it up just in front of the entry. I'll call when ready."

As he moved about, Joson had an uncomfortable sense of being watched. Probably just a hunter he thought, staring into the darkness for eyes. First thing tomorrow they would need to replace their lost weapons, he decided, picking up a knobbed branch that he could shape as a cudgel.

He gathered several armloads, piling most of them on the side, arranging the others as they had been trained. "Danai, ready when you are."

She came out, and inspected his preparations. He had stacked the wood so that it formed a small triangle, with small chips about the base. A carefully shaped circle made of bits of broken twigs representing Lunasa was placed a palm's length out around the pile.

"I've gathered enough so that we should have plenty to last the night. Are you sure you don't want me to do this instead?"

She shook her head, too excited to speak, then sat cross-legged such that she faced west. In her mind she beheld Mentor Melarna seated in just the same position before an enthralled cluster of nine sprytes. Beside her stood Mentor Alamai, who had just finished instructing them in the proper placement of the wood. The group was surrounded at some distance by seven evenly-spaced Mentors, each clasping a Lunasaberry-topped oak staff. The thought flitted through her mind that they might have been more than spectators, but she banished it. She remembered how it grew chill, despite the warmth of the day, as the Mentor's hands slowly wove the spell so that they could observe each gesture. There was a puff of smoke, the flicker of flame. Followed by their own clumsy attempts, and Damon's misdirected spellcast that singed Mentor Alamai's robe. The sprytes had practiced all day, the Mentors never stepping out from their circle. Pook had been praised for his quickness. She remembered feeling jealous that Pook always seemed to excel in magic training. Pushing aside a flicker of doubt, she inhaled deeply, summoning her energies. Another breath. And another. Her heartbeat quieted. She felt her energies centering, just beneath her ribs. She raised her hands, cupped palms facing the wood, fingers slightly arched, then rippled them in an increasingly rapid up-down motion, emulating the flickering of flames. A chill breath of wind shivered her arm hairs, there was the scent of rotten eggs. The wood chips began to smolder, flickered, died, then burst into flames that ran up the pyre. In moments, it was blazing.

As Joson fed the flames with thicker pieces of wood, Danai sat absorbing the fire's energy, a fair exchange for what she had given to create it. She stared deeply into the dancing gold and orange, a sense of pride filling her. The sensation was soon replaced by one less pleasant—as if something was watching. She glanced about, thought she saw a glimmer of red light beyond their chunk of trunk; it vanished. Just a leftover ember from the lightstrike she decided, or perhaps a drop of water reflecting the firelight.

"Now what?" Joson had sidled up as close as he could to the flames, trying to dry his tunic.

"We have to warm some water."

"With what?" He felt tired, irritable, unable to shake that being-watched feeling. This was a different Danai than the one he thought he knew. Telling him what to do. Flirting with Aaron. Taking charge of things. Right now, he wished she'd just be her old self.

"Joson, stop it." Her eyes blazed bright green with exasperation. "Think. This is where our survival skills are supposed to kick in. We need a container of some sort. What about a kuis?"

"Um. It may burn, being so dry, but if we hold it just above the flames, and wet the shell first, it could work."

"Good idea." She felt bad about snapping at him and smiled. "But as much as I'd like to dry off, I don't fancy toasted arms. What if we balance it near the fire, and slowly rotate it? Might take a bit longer, but we won't get burned."

He nodded, reached for a kuis, and sloshed water from another over its sides, then began to test the idea. Periodically he stuck his finger in. "It's working," he said on the fourth check.

Danai hugged the warm kuis as they both crawled back into the hollow, ripples of flames and shadows dancing up its walls. Joson propped Tatia up in his arms, then gently pried open her mouth. "She's so cold," he whispered. Danai scooped out a handful of the warm water, poured a tiny drip into the open mouth, waiting like a baby bird's, then stroked Tatia's throat. She was rewarded by a feeble swallow. Patiently, they fed her three handfuls. Then Danai sealed the kuis and placed it on Tatia's stomach, wrapping the spryte's arms around it before Joson leaned her back against the wall. They tucked feathers all around her, then covered her with a fresh aspen leaf, hoping to entrap the warmth.

"We need to tend to ourselves now." Joson tugged at Danai's arm. "Sorry to be blunt, but if we get sick or hurt, it's not going to matter much about her." Outside, they worked on drying themselves, huddling close to the fire's friendly warmth, nibbling half-heartedly on miyacan scraps. About them, the forest mumbled softly with the sounds of a warm summer's night. Lunasa, only a faint crescent, was hidden by the trees, and the humid darkness pushed against their fire's tiny orange orb.

"Do you think she'll wake up?" Joson looked up from the knobbed twig he was shaping with his dirq to replace the cudgel Danai had lost in the flood. Thin white wood flakes sprinkled the ground around him like petals.

"I wish I knew." She chewed her lip. "I feel so helpless, you know?"

"Mmm. What about Aaron?"

She looked up from the dueling flames, surprised. She hadn't thought about him at all since Joson's outburst. "We need to try and find him. He's probably holed up somewhere awaiting dawnshine."

"If he got across in time." Joson watched her face closely.

"He was running so fast, the idiot, I'm sure he did..." Danai's voice trailed off as she stared into the flames. They flared, then coalesced. A vivid image of Aaron's face, wide-mouthed, with anguished golden eyes, oddly tangled among grasping twigs, seared her vision. She gasped, recoiled. Aaron couldn't be dead! He had to have made it across.

"Danai? Danai, what's the matter?"

"Nothing. I thought I saw something in the fire, but it's just a tired mind playing tricks on me."

"Look, I'll take the first watch, and keep the fire burning. No, I won't sit outside—you think I have webs for brains?" He smiled at Danai's worried expression. "I'll just perch inside the entry, and hop out to restoke it. I'm not going to be dinner for some hunter. At least the fire will make their eyes really shine. I'll wake you when it's your turn."

Inside it was warmer, and touching Tatia's hand, Danai was re-lieved to feel that the extreme chill was gone. She removed the cooled kuis and handed it back out to Joson. Carefully adjusting Tatia until she lay prone, she tucked in the newly heated kuis at her middle. Then she lay down behind the unconscious spryte, cuddling her to share her own warmth, pulling the leaf over them both. With a soft sigh, she stumbled into a dreamless sleep.

An insistent gentle tapping on her shoulder dragged her awake. She groaned; stressed muscles had stiffened, and the arm under Tatia had gone numb. Joson helped her to sit up, and she leaned into his chest for a moment, eyes half-closed, thankful for the comforting safety of his arms which tightened about her. "I began to nod off," he murmured. "I wanted you to get as much sleep as you could."

She yawned wide. "Where's your cudgel?"

"At the entry. I've been shaping it. Fire is still going, but I've banked it. Dawnshine isn't far off."

"Joson! You were supposed to wake me a lot sooner."

"Well, yeah, but." He grinned like a chipmunk. "I just didn't, I guess. Hey!"

She tapped her finger on the tip of his nose, then lifted her face to his. "Thank you," she said simply, before giving him a gentle kiss on the cheek. "I'll wake you after the sun rises. You need some sleep."

The fire was smoldering, a small heap of dark glowing orange freckled with gold, barely pushing away the darkness. She sniffed the pungent fragrance of damp pine, moist earth, and the acrid scent of charred wood. Somewhere a bird cried out in its dreams, the call piercing the heavy indigo-blue stillness that cloaks the land in the time before dawnshine. In the distant east she knew that the faintest glow was running its fingertip along the rim of Lampion, but here it was yet dark. She was eager for sunlight. But then what? If Tatia had not awoken, could they carry her all the way back to the Dell—maybe using a hauler? Or would it be better for one to stay, one to go? And what about Aaron? Where had he disappeared to? How much she wished he were here to lean against and talk with. Her thoughts scampered about, colliding with each other, breeding new ones.

She thought back to Joson's remark about the Rite. To her, this whole journey had been dangerous—and it wasn't over. Yet the Mentors couldn't intentionally want to kill off the sprytes. Or could they? Triasa had cautioned her that only panic could kill. But she had never said sprytes couldn't die. Danai culled her memory, searching for mentions of lost sprytes. She couldn't recall any from Goldyn Vale, but what about other dells? She shuddered, clasping her arms tightly about her knees. How naïve they really were, when she came to consider it all. Sheltered in their dells, food readily available, daily living moving along in a reliable jumble of chores, feasts, dances, births, birdsong...all the things they took for granted, that became so boring that one couldn't wait to earn their wings and become a full-fledged Feyree!

Wings. It seemed the be-all and end-all. To have those wings, flit about, no longer be ground-bound. Other Feyree had passed these Rites. Had they endured the same things? "Maybe if they spoke about it more and swathed it less in mystery, some of us might be better prepared," Danai muttered to the furry shadows. "And yet in our eagerness, would we really listen?"

Her thoughts marched along into another trail. Sheltered. Co-cooned really. Protected from the harsher realities of the realm outside their dells. What they were experiencing now was normal, the same that any Feyree would encounter when they stepped outside the truce zones. Looked at from that angle, the real issue was not so much that things were happening to them, but rather how they reacted that would determine the outcome. And not just reacting. Planning. They hadn't done much of that, she had to admit. More of a follow-the-leader and hope it all turns out fine. She felt a blush crawling over her cheeks. We think we're so smart.

It seemed lighter. She peeked out, glancing over at the stone river; her breath caught. It shimmered, catching the first tracery of dawn along its frozen waves, bouncing them back towards a sky filled with fading stars. A cool breeze, laden with the clean scent of mountain snows and rain-washed forest swept down the distant cliffs into the valley, stirring the birds awake. The stone river blushed rose, then gold, then blazed to silver-white as the sun surged over the unseen horizon, coloring the sky a brilliant blue.

A faint 'click-tick' attracted her gaze to three deer, poised beyond the stone river's edge. She marveled at their extreme caution, given their tremendous size. Two were the copper brown of elders, but the other still bore the spotted badge of a fawn. Danai smiled as she watched the youngling nudge what was presumably its mother, eager to be off. Mother did not budge, scenting the air, glancing at her likewise-sniffing companion. Deer were not among those the Charmers often spoke to, but Danai had heard they were not a vocal folk, instead able to communicate by looks and through thoughts. Triasa had once told her that was why they rarely spoke, except in the extremes of rage, joy or fear; they no longer had the need. A quick clatter of hooves, a bounding gallop across the stone, and they vanished into the trees just south of the bower site.

After the sun had fully risen and topped the trees, Danai retreated back into the hollow, and woke Joson. Tatia felt properly warm now, and she scooped up the kuis that had rolled free during sleep. Outside, the two stretched, taking deep breaths of the new day.

"Hey there!" Aaron bounded towards them, his face awash with delight, arms flung wide. "By the Mother, I prayed to find you and she granted my wish. I was so worried! Where's Tatia? Still asleep?" Words tumbled from him as he engulfed first Danai, then Joson in a breath-stealing hug. If Joson noticed Danai's hug lasted a tad longer, he said nothing, too relieved that his friend had returned.

"Tatia's unconscious, Aaron," Danai said, then explained the events.

Aaron gave a low whistle, shaking his head. "Can I see her?"

Inside the bower, he gazed at the quietly-breathing spryte. "Maybe we should carry her outside? The fresh air and sun might help."

"I'm not sure." Danai was dubious. "I guess it can't hurt."

Joson carried Tatia to the entry, carefully handing her limp body off to Aaron. Outside, they propped her against the trunk, tucking leaves and grass behind until she was cushioned. Joson meanwhile busied himself pulling out their journey food, and replenishing the kuis from dew. "We'll have to forage," he remarked, calling them over for mornmeal. "I suggest we stay put this day, restock our food and water, and give ourselves a chance to figure out what we're going to do and how. What say you?" They agreed, mouths too full to reply.

Joson shuffled his hands a moment, then blurted "Aaron, what in name of the Twins possessed you to bolt without waiting for us?" His voice was taught with long-simmering anger. "Had we not tried to follow you, none of this would have happened!"

Aaron bristled. "So what said you had to follow me?"

"Oh come on. Don't be dense. We're a team. We stay together. And if you want to be particular, you actually told us to try and get across before the storm broke. Or don't you remember?"

Aaron glanced at Danai, seeking support, but she couldn't give it. Joson was right, and they all knew it. Aaron ducked his head in apology. "Look, I'm really sorry. You're right. But I just want to get back to the Dell so bad, and I didn't expect the storm to break that fast. I didn't think."

Joson nodded his head hard. "I'll say you didn't."

"Aaahannnnn?"

The three jumped at Tatia's mumbled groan. Danai hurried to her side, the others on her heels, knelt down, and scooped up the spryte's hand. "Tatia? Tatia? It's me. Danai. Can you hear me?" She gave the hand a few small shakes.

Gradually, as if lifting a tremendous weight, Tatia's head came up, and her eyelids dragged open, an odd blank expression filling her violet eyes. She studied her stone-chafed and bruised arms, then the tightly-held hand, then Danai's face. "Who are you?"

* * * * *

Chapter Eight

Tatia's serenely innocent eyes gazed expectantly at each of their aghast faces. "I'm Danai. You don't remember me?" Tatia shook her head with the slowness of someone remembering how to.

"C'mon Tatia, you know me." Aaron gave her a roguish smile and wink.

"No...You say...my name is...Tatia?"

Aaron gulped and nodded. "Do you remember anything about the Rite we're on, the clawcat, Tlarg?"

She shook her head again. "What's a Rite?"

Danai was struck by the absolute lack of fear in Tatia's eyes. They were instead filled with the puzzled curiosity of a toddling spryte, unaware of all it did not know, not yet afraid of anything. "We're your friends," she soothed. "You hit your head yesterday when you fell down. Remember the terrible rainstorm and falling?"

"No. What's a rainstorm?" Tatia's tongue stumbled over the word.

"By the Mother," Joson hissed under his breath. "She's a talking babe, as blank as a teaching slate."

"Are you hungry Tatia? Food?" Danai pretended to eat. An ember of recall flared briefly in Tatia's eyes, and she nodded. "Joson, get her some miyacan and water." They watched as the spryte gulped the water, clutching the kuis with both hands like a youngling, then gobbled the food, smearing a goodly amount on her cheeks.

She beamed at them. "More?"

"Not now dearling," Danai adopted a mother-like tone. "We have things to do."

"Can I help?"

"Of course. Can you stand up?"

With Aaron's help, Tatia wobbled to her feet. She grimaced. "My legs are sore."

"Walk slowly to the end of this log and back, like a good youngling. That will help." Danai watched Tatia toddle off, then turned at the joint explosion of breaths behind her.

"What are we going to do with her?" Aaron watched as Tatia paused, mesmerized by a warbling robin.

"We have any choice?" Danai sighed. Yet another problem. "Treat her like a youngling, try and stir up some memories—maybe her loss is temporary—and get her home to the Healers as soon as we can. And for the Mother's sake, don't let her out of our sight. She's an easy meal for any hunter."

Joson shook his head, a wry smile crossing his face. "All this for a pair of wings. It's a good thing we don't know the future, isn't it? Or we'd choose to stay ground-bound for life! Danai, you'll stay with her? C'mon Aaron, grab your ruck; let's go berrying. We'll be back by mid-day."

She watched them lope off, wary of their surroundings. How much we've already changed, she thought, then felt a tug on her arm and turned to gaze into Tatia's hopeful eyes. "We going with them?"

"No sweeting, you and I are going to go look for water. See that kuis? Yes, that acorn there by the woodpile. Get that, I'll carry these two, and we'll go see what we can find." She put the kuis into Tatia's rucksack, and showed her how to carry it. Soon they were walking in the direction the deer had gone, once Danai had taken her bearings. She wouldn't ever forget to do that again, she thought.

The woods smelled sweet, the moist soil pleasantly cool beneath their feet, dappled with sunlight and tree shadow. Danai halted, listening. Among all the bird talk, she could discern the gurgle and burble of running water. As they walked towards the sound, she avoided thickets where anything might hide in wait. Tatia gasped then clapped her hands as a brilliant lavender-blue flutterby flapped overhead, the wing-puffs of air rustling their hair. "What's that?"

Danai answered, and continued teaching, pointing out objects and making Tatia repeat them, pleased with her quickness of recall, hopeful at what it might imply.

A brightness up ahead alerted her to a clearing. Ordering Tatia to stay put, Danai scrambled up a rough-barked walnut tree to peer above the green-gold grasses. The clearing was bursting with activity. Deer grazed, birds dove about, and already the insects were commencing their creaks and clicks, signaling a humid day. Finding water or foraging in the meadow wasn't an option—too much risk of being stepped or dined upon. But the gentle slope of the clearing gave her an idea.

"We're going to walk a bit more, dearling," she explained as they set off around the edge of the meadow, walking upslope towards where Danai hoped the stream she heard was flowing. The mutter of water grew louder, and soon they came upon a rock-strewn rivulet that slipped through the forest and crept away among the meadow's grass-stems. Mounds of twigs and crumpled leaves told a tale of how the small creek had swollen to a raging torrent from yesterday's deluge. They knelt to scoop a handful to drink, and Danai grimaced at the taste of torn greenery and stirred dirt. "Journeyers can't be choosers," she quoted the old saying aloud, before showing Tatia how to properly fill the kuis.

On their return, Tatia sidled up to a lone daisy drooping by the meadow's edge, and stood on tip toes with her hands on the creamy white petals, taking happy sniffs of the golden center. Danai had to smile. Tatia was actually kind of fun this way, and after all, it wasn't her fault. They would get her home some how. Home. It seemed so far away. She sighed.

The fellows had not yet returned. Danai added several twigs to keep the fire alive, then they spent time gathering more twigs and searching for edible greens. She could not shake the prickling sensation of watching eyes, but constant scans of the area revealed nothing. Just nerves she decided. But she was glad to hear the cheerful shout of Aaron, the two appearing over a ridge in the stone river, their rucksacks burgeoning with success.

"Squirrel here just had to have a second mornmeal," snorted Aaron, thumbing at the tell-tale dark red stain around Joson's grinning mouth as they set down their loads.

"Squirrel?"

"His lirupai's nickname for him. How'd you think he got so big and tall? Fasting?"

"I'm a growing spryte," Joson protested. "When we get our wings, think of all the energy it's going to take to make them expand and fill up. I don't want wobbly wings, you know."

"Whatever you say, Squirrel."

Joson laughed, opening his rucksack to reveal plump sweet-smelling red berries.

"Tartberries!" Danai was delighted. "Where did you find them? It's early for those."

"Sunny spot a bit above here. It was already warm—the stone reflects on it, and probably is baking them to ripeness. Hey Tatia, wait up!" His warning came too late. Tatia buried her face into the tartberry he had handed her, gobbling the sweet-tart scarlet pulp, unconcerned about the juices leaking down her tunic. "Oh well. At least she's enjoying it."

The rest of the day was spent teaching Tatia new words, basking in the warm sun to relax sore muscles, and planning their next steps. Danai wove four rough baskets from slender bark strips to carry the tartberries they planned to gather the next day without squashing them. Aaron entertained Tatia with bubbles of Feyree dust, while Joson put the finishing touches on the cudgel and a new spear.

Eventide brought a magnificent sunset; slender strands of clouds that were every shade of ruby and bronze lanced with gold rumpling the horizon above the trees. Tomorrow would be *noiray*, the dark eve when Lunasa turned his face from Lampion to regard his other realms, but tonight a thin crescent still gleamed. They twigged their embered fire to a cheery blaze as gloaming advanced, and fell to discussing the Well's prophecies. Tatia seemed restless, and kept gazing over her shoulder into the darkness just beyond the edge of the log.

"I wish she wouldn't do that," Aaron said. "She's making me nervous."

"Something there," Tatia announced a few moments later.

"By the Mother," swore Aaron as he and Joson seized their spears, springing to their feet. Danai grabbed Tatia's wrist, and they all placed the log at their backs, peering into the dark.

Tatia strained against Danai's grip. "There. Now she's gone." She sniffed. "She was shiny. Pretty. Like the fire. Why did you scare her away?"

They stared wide-eyed at each other. "She?" Aaron asked.

"Hello?" Joson's voice cracked. He swallowed, a sense of presence stiffening his neck hairs. The others felt it too, as if a warm hand had lightly ruffled the air about them. There came a soft hiss of laughter, like the drop of water on hot stone.

"Everyone in the bower," Joson ordered.

Danai shoved a protesting Tatia in ahead of her, her hands slippery with fear. Aaron was next, then he grabbed Joson's arm and hauled him in. They stepped back, and as one lowered their spears at the entry which began to brighten with a flickering light.

The hiss, longer, angry-sounding, was repeated. What might have been a female face appeared, only it was carved from living fire. Glowing scarlet eyes pricked with orange embers, surrounded by long shifting tresses of blue white flame stared at them. A shimmering finger beckoned. "Fi-re," it crackled.

"In the name of the Mother and Lunasa the most high, be gone," Joson rasped, brandishing his spear. The swirling face frowned, eyes narrowing. An arm quested in, illuminating the bower with a ruddy glow.

"Get thee gone," Aaron bellowed, darting forward. His spear passed through the arm, charring slightly. With a snarl, the she-thing recoiled. The entry dimmed.

"She's gone," Danai gasped.

"I doubt it." Joson's eyes never left the entry. "She wanted something from us, and now she's mad. It's going to be a long night."

"We're safe here at least," Aaron growled, inspecting his spear for damage.

It was striated with burn marks. "We'll take turns and stay on watch. Maybe dawnshine will make whatever it is go look elsewhere."

"Maybe. We can only hope." Joson had his doubts.

"I don't think I can sleep anyway with whatever that thing could possibly be out there," Danai muttered, as she tried to calm Tatia, urging her to stay still and stop crawling towards the entry. "What in the name of the Twins do you think it was?"

"Fire daemon."

Danai and Joson stared at Aaron. She swallowed. "A what?"

"A fire daemon. Let me guess. You didn't build that fire from burning wood bits off the lightstrike hit, did you? One of you used fire magic. Toads! Didn't your Mentor tell you not to ever do that?"

"We couldn't get close enough to get an ember," Danai protested. "And tell us what? Sandagon and Tyra were having trouble with the basic spellcast, so Mentors Melarna and Alamai spent a lot of time with them."

"I can't believe you actually weren't told!"

"Aaron, get to the point, will you?" Joson gestured curtly with his spear.

"Mentor Shanaron and Sombron told us we're not supposed to use fire magic until fully-fledged and trained because it attracts the fire daemiani. They're not from Lampion; they're not even from our lands. They're in another, oh what's that word...daemension. Yes, that's it. And they can only cross over to ours when fire magic is used without proper guardian spells. That's part of the reason the Mentors encircle us with the sacred staffs—to keep the gate or whatever it is closed."

"Mentor Quenton didn't say anything like that to us," Joson frowned.

"Did he say don't use it just yet?"

"Well, yes, but he didn't explain why. He did say it would be dangerous though."

"Great. I thought all the Mentors taught things the same way. Guess not. I wonder how many other sprytes decided to ignore orders."

"That's not fair Aaron. This was a special circumstance. How else could we have helped Tatia?"

Aaron shook his head. "Danai, there was a burning tree. Even I could see it from way up where I was bowered. You could have stuck a long twig on an ember or something."

Danai bit back her retort, a cold feeling aching her stomach. Tatia whined, the sound scraping their ears like metal on stone. They waited, straining to hear any hint of noise outside. "No normal night chatter," Aaron whispered. "Definitely not safe out there right now."

Time passed. Finally, a sulky Tatia pillowed her head on her arm and dozed off. The darkness outside deepened as their small fire starved to extinction. Except for the occasional popping ember, all was silent. As if everything were waiting, watching, Danai thought. She noticed that it seemed to be growing lighter outside. Dawnshine already?

Joson's head snapped up from a light doze as the unmistakable odor of burning wood began to trickle through the entry. He scrambled to his feet. "Is it my skin or does it feel hot in here to you?" He felt along the wooden walls. "It is hot! The log is burning. Get out! Out!"

They darted out, Joson and Aaron leading. A seething figure of fire stood near the far end of the log, its hands embroidering the wood with hungry flames. Seeing them, it gave a wild laugh, spewing fire, then flowed towards them, crisping the leaves and bits of wood in its path. "Fi-re. Fey-reeeee fi-re!" The voice skirled upwards in the smoke, and the trees moved uneasily on their roots.

"Make a run for the rocks! At least they won't burn!" Joson guarded their retreat as Aaron half-carried, half-dragged a protesting Tatia.

"She pretty! I want the pretty!" Tatia wailed into the rising wind.

Behind them, the fire daemon inhaled deeply and grew, illuminating the rocks and woods in shuddering bloody light. Already it was the height of the sapling birch beside it. With a smoldering crackle of a laugh, it wrapped its arms around the tree. A swirl of flame scorched the silver bark, sizzled the leaves, and ignited it into a torch. In moments, all that remained was a crumbling black skeleton, outlined by flame. The forest cowered. The daemon took a step towards them.

"Keep going," panted Aaron, his sharply etched shadow bobbing and weaving before him. "Run. It's our only chance."

"We're not going to escape."

There was a terrible finality to Joson's voice that chilled Danai's heart, despite the wall of heat pursuing them. "Don't give up, Joson. Not yet," she gasped. Her next words flowed out unbidden. "Oh Lunasa, Mother, hear me, I beg you to aid us please..."

The surging wind snatched away her words, as it whipped about the fire daemon, billowing it into a howling, spinning vortex of flame, head towering among the trees. It strode onto the rocks, laughing, its mouth a blue-black hollow of heat. Three, maybe four strides, and it would be all over. There was no room for thought. The scalding air strangled them with heat. They dropped their weapons, fell to their knees.

Far above, Lunasa seemed to glow, brighten, silvering the river of stone. There was a flash. A hurtling orb of brilliant white appeared, trailing blue and scarlet, blazing towards them.

The daemon raised a twisted fist of flames, struck, missed. A shower of sparks seared their skin. Screaming, they slapped the embers off. With a shriek of rage, the daemon lifted a foot.

The orb, a searing spear of light, plunged through the daemon's forehead, releasing an eruption of sparks, then struck the ground and exploded. The daemon's agonized screech trembled the ground. The giant flames wilted, condensed, collapsed. With a quenched gasp, it shrank to an ember, then winked out.

The wind died down. The sprytes wept, silent tears coursing their cheeks, thanking Lunasa and the Mother for their lives, while Tatia watched in puzzled wonderment.

They huddled where they were for the remainder of that interminable night. There was no conversation. A lingering intensity of terror silenced them. At last, a nightingale's welcome twitter heralded the coming of dawnshine. But not until the sun had fully risen and warmed their chilled bodies did they at last gather enough courage to return to their charred bower.

Danai skirted around the daemon's scorched steps, and was relieved to find their rucksacks and kuis safe where they had been piled. She seized them, handing one to each.

Joson shouldered his rucksack. "I vote we're out of here now." The others followed, Danai grabbing the basket with the remaining tartberries, and they hurried back to the stone river.

"The oak I dashed to is up there," Aaron pointed. "I'm pretty sure the trail picks up again nearby—I saw a cairn by its roots." A quick march brought them up to the ancient tree, and they were soon jogging along the well-worn path, eager to put as much trail between them and the stone river as possible.

* * * * *

The trail passed through a narrow moss-walled cleft, and it led them into another valley of the Wynndowns, which was thick-cloaked with pine. From time to time, the trail branched off, but they kept on the one headed east. There were few birds or wood folk to be seen, but plenty of boulders and downed trees, making for a toilsome walk. They made bower early inside an old rabbit hole, tucked deep underneath a birch's roots. It was noiray, and strange things could happen on the dark eve. Feyree as a rule preferred to stay snug in their bowers and the Guardians maintained a special vigilance. Tatia soon fell asleep as the others spoke quietly.

"Danai, I was thinking about the Anam," Aaron said. "Maybe the fire daemon was what it foretold."

"I hadn't thought about that." She shuddered. "But I think what I saw was male. That horror was female."

"You've got to be joking! I didn't think it had any gender but ugly."

"Perhaps you're right. I can only hope." She changed subjects. "Do you have any idea what the next Rite will be?"

"I heard Mentor Anoran mention something about the Ancient Ones," Aaron answered.

"I wonder what that's all about."

"I'd guess we're going to go look for something old."

Joson sniggered and Danai giggled before taking a moment to count on her fingers. "Do you realize that Mid-Summer's Eve is not far off? Do you think we'll be back in time?"

"I hardly think we'll be attending any celebrations." Joson settled himself more comfortably against a heap of grass he had gathered. "Would be nice though. I can just imagine all those trestles filled with food..." He licked his lips, his voice trailing off. His friends chuckled.

"I had a great time last year. All that dancing and laughter." Aaron smiled at some memory, but stopped at Danai's prim expression. "I like the bard songs best, especially the Birth of the Seasons."

"Why?" Joson asked.

"It makes me wonder why anybody would give up the beauty of warmth, food, and greenery year 'round just to prove they were stronger than Lunasa. His two sons and two daughters had more power than all the Feyree—and probably all other folk—have put together. Think of how each one wanted to prove why they were the most powerful. First with beauty and then, when Lunasa refused to concede that any one of them was superior to the others, they tried to force him with strength. As punishment, he refused to rescind the resulting seasons. So now we get to shiver, bake, and all the other weathers the four seasons care to give us. Dumb, you ask me."

"I bet we can add some new tales after all we've heard and seen." Danai yawned. "Joson, wake me when it's my turn for watch."

The next day dawned dull and overcast. They began to climb uphill, the pines retreating before the boulder-strewn slopes. The humid air coaxed trickles of perspiration down their necks. During one rest stop, Danai stood gazing north, where the Anlyn Hills folded into the Rymple Mountains. She had never been over the Rymples, although she knew of Kristal Glen which was situated just northwest of them.

They continued to trudge along, wishing the journey was over. Tatia complained of sore feet and begged for a tartberry.

"Who would have thought this would take so long?" Danai grumbled. "It's not fair that we can't really rest."

"Who said life is fair?" Joson shrugged. "Ups and downs are just life, I guess. The Rites just put us in the way of a lot of steeper ups and downs so we learn to survive. Even if it kills us."

"Joson, don't joke," Aaron grimaced. "They nearly have. Didn't you wonder if any of the sprytes haven't made it?"

"I know they sometimes don't."

"What?" He had their full attention.

"Two Krisalys' ago, nine sprytes were sent off from Firebaugh, Pook's glen. He said he was so jealous when they left. Two were close friends of his—twins in fact." Joson paused. "One of the twins didn't come back. He tried to get the brother to tell him, but couldn't get much beyond the fellow saying it was something that happened during the Rites. He disappeared from the glen shortly afterwards and hasn't been seen or heard from since."

They were quiet for some time after that.

As the sun began to wester, they crested the hill and stood staring, as Aaron dryly observed, into yet another valley. It was more meadow than forest, meaning they would have to work their way through the thick grasses and flower stems. The cairns vanished, swallowed by the tall grass. Aaron suggested going around, but after a good look at the valley's length, they agreed that it would probably take even longer.

They had halted by a large knobby rock, tucked into a cradle of stone. They could see its shadow visibly moving, reaching like a long finger pointing into the meadow. "This place is a little too exposed for me," Joson said. "Any ideas for a bower site? I'm not good at digging through stone."

"Look!" Aaron pointed. "A rabbit!"

"I've got an idea. Stay here." Danai took several steps away from the rock until she could tell the fawn-colored rabbit had spotted her. It sat up, brown nose twitching. She bowed then called out a greeting, remembering Triasa's training. After a few moments, it sank back to all fours, and nodded at her to approach.

"May sweet flowers always be there for thee," she began courteously. "I am Danai of the Feyree."

"May soft grasses line thy trails," the rabbit replied. "I am called Lapinya. It is not often we see fey folk in this valley. What do yeu here?"

"We are on journey back to the Great Dell of our folk. Night comes, and we seek shelter. Is there a burrow or hole nearby where we might shelter this eventide?"

Lapinya washed her face a few strokes. "None that are not already filled with other folk."

"We would not wish to intrude. Perhaps there is some other place thee would kindly suggest?"

"None that I know. But wait a little while, and I shall ask my mate." Lapinya sprang over Danai, and disappeared into a small patch of grass several long hops away. A thin breeze trickled over the rocks as the shadows gathered. In a few more moments, Danai decided, she would return to her podmates, and they would have to fare as well as possible. She heard a click of toenails on stone, and the rabbit reappeared.

"My mate says there are no open burrows. But close by our hole is an old bramble in which our young often play. Ye are welcome to rest there for the night."

Danai smiled and bowed. "Thee are beyond kind, Lapinya. Let me get my friends, and we will follow thee to the bramble bush."

Lapinya's mate Yenoc was waiting to welcome them. "It is a safe place," he reassured them. "Just stay within its thorny ramblings, and nothing should bother ye."

"I've heard that before," Aaron whispered as the two rabbits disappeared into their burrow. They gazed through the leafy arch. A dimly lit corridor twisted away into gathering shadows, thick trunks of contorted wood standing like pillars along the path. Thorns of every shape and size pierced the air; many held shreds of fur that twitched in the breeze. "Well, we'd better head in. Not too far, if you don't mind. Maybe nothing would bother a rabbit, but I'm not so sure about sprytes."

They approached a gray-brown trunk behind which the supple bramble canes had formed a small hollow, just big enough for the four of them to stretch out. The thick dust set Tatia sneezing, and Joson coughing. "I simply can't wait to curl up in my bower and hide under a soft, clean coverlet," Danai admitted, uncapping a kuis for Joson. "We have, what, another three lumnas to go before our wings? I'd suggest getting some leaves to lay down, but the bramble leaves have sharp edges and pointy hairs and are not at all comfortable. We'll have to make do. Who's taking first watch?"

* * * * *

Aswirl of red and sliver twisted and reformed in a rift of fire. A silver-draped lady summoned her, and together they approached the blazing gash. Flames seethed along its edges, like blood from a wound, as the gash widened. Danai could see something through it. Short squat structures crouched on barren sloped hills, with a few trees scattered about. A brownish haze stained the sky, and the acrid smell of smoke choked her. There were figures moving about, some of fire, others looking much like her podmates. She thought she saw a dwarf. The silver companion motioned her forward, and the flames stretched out to engulf her. "No!" Danai jerked awake.

"Bad dream?" Joson looked over from his watch. She nodded. "No surprise, all the things we've seen."

"Do you mind if I take over watch?" She stepped lightly over Tatia and Aaron. "I really don't want to go back to sleep." He nodded and handed over his spear.

* * * * *

The rabbits were already out and about when they left the bramble, gray with dust. After polite greetings and thanks, they headed towards the stream that Lapinya had pointed out. "It wanders the field to the other side," she explained. "Perhaps it will be easier for ones of such small height. Be wary. There are fish that hunt those waters, and others that hunt the fish. Make sure you do not become their food."

When they reached the stream, each took a dip in a small back eddy, glad to rinse the dust and sweat away. The refreshed feeling lasted only briefly. The sodden stream banks made for sloppy going, and it required careful study to avoid stepping into deeper pockets of rank-smelling mud that sucked at their feet. It was a windless day, and the sticky heat of high summer added to their discomfort. They had traversed more than half the meadow when they stopped for midmeal.

"I wonder how much farther?" Aaron asked as he handed Tatia the last tartberry.

"We could ask the birds," Danai suggested.

"By the by, I didn't know you spoke rabbit," Joson remarked around a bite of early blackberry. He had found some as they passed along the brambles, and they had refilled the basket. They were not as sweet as they would be in late summer, yet they had a restorative tang to them.

"Triasa taught me during my fostering. I know the basic greetings for many of the wood folk; fortunately most speak the common tongue. She's helped a lot of rabbits because Goldyn Vale is at the edge of a very large meadow, so I had to learn to speak with them." She stood up and dusted her rump. "Shall we try it together? We're more likely to be heard."

"Ummm, just let me finish this berry," Joson protested. Aaron laughed and lobbed a bit of seed hull at him.

"Let's call for the magpies," Danai suggested. "I see a lot of them in the Dell." They gave the wild raucous screech, startling other birds into silence. "I guess there are none around," she said, after their third attempt.

"Look out!" Aaron jerked her aside as a rush of white and black plummeted to land where she had been standing.

"Greetings," it glarked. "My name be Wag-Tail, son of Long-Tail." It cocked its head, and they could see themselves reflected in its ebony eye. "What will ye?"

"I am Danai, this is Aaron, Joson and Tatia. We seek the Great Dell of Feyree. Do thee know aught of it?"

Wag-Tail gave a croaking chortle. "Know of it! Youngling, ye are perhaps two day's march as thy folk travel. I could as easily wing ye there before the night calls us back to our nests."

Danai felt a surge of hope. Should they? There was nothing in the Rite that said they couldn't enlist the help of others—in fact hadn't they done so with Tlarg? "Would thee? But there be four of us, only one of thee. That would not be good courtesy."

The magpie gave another chortle, followed by a rasping screech, and bounced a few times on its long ash gray legs. There was an answering squawk, a flurry of wings, and another magpie landed, introducing himself as Crook Beak, son of Long Shank. "Be there enough magpies now for thy liking, Danai of Feyree?" She smiled up at him and nodded. "Come then. Time flies on the wings of the Feathered Queen. I will take thee and the other maiden, Crook Beak the two lads."

He crouched and, with many apologies for tugging on his feathers, the two sprytes clambered up on his shoulders. At his instructions, Danai burrowed her hands deep into the blue-black feathers, first bracing her arms around Tatia's waist. "Now away!" The two magpies sprang through the warm sunbeams, nearly unseating their riders, their wings a blur of black and white as they caught an upswell of air to soar above the treetops. Leveling off, they coasted along with an occasional flap.

This is what it will be like when I get my wings, Danai exulted, staring about and spotting the ridge along which they had hiked so long ago. She glanced behind, and saw Pyre Tor, hazy in the distance. Ahead she saw the Wynndowns slumping into the forest. Beyond, the Great Dell nestled like a glowing golden gem. Wag-Tail began a slow lazy spiral over the meadow, and Danai noticed a strangely shaped black stone squatting among the grasses a short distance behind the barrier of red-flowered bushes beyond which the sprytes had not yet been permitted to go. Her attention was distracted by figures pointing up at them.

With a sudden chuckle, Wag-Tail folded his wings and dove towards the ground. Tatia shrieked, while Danai clutched his feathers for dear life. The ground rushed at them, and at the last possible moment, the bird flared his wings, and landed with nary a bump, Crook Beak a breath behind him. The sprytes tumbled off.

"I'm supposed to be the jokester around here," Aaron laughed at Crook Beak, wagging his finger at him. "But you win this round." The bird chuckled.

The sprytes clustered before the two birds and bowed. "If ever we can be of service, please call," Danai offered. "I know not of what aid we can render, but we will do our best."

Wag-Tail leaned forward, cocking his head to stare Danai in the eye. "Little maiden, I will remember thy pledge. It may be sooner than thee think that we meet again." With a parting squawk, the two vaulted skywards then melted into the woods.

Danai turned to face the Mentors and sprytes hurrying towards them, soothing Tatia who clung to her arm so tightly she pinched.

"It's all right sweeting, I promise." Joson and Aaron joined her, and in unison they stepped forward.

* * * * *

Chapter Nine

Pook sprinted ahead of the others, arms wide, his face a delighted grin. "Danai! Joson! You're back. Now there's only one group missing, and this Rite will be completed." He gave each a hug. "Aaron, Tatia, welcome. Tatia? What's the matter?"

Several Mentors arrived. Tatia cowered, whimpering. Danai spoke. "Mentor Illiai, it's your cowls. Please pull them back."

Puzzled, Mentor Illiai and the others complied. "This is most unusual, Danai. What is the matter with Tatia?"

Taking a deep breath, Danai briefly explained the incident, Joson and Aaron chiming in as needed. Mentor Illiai shook her head sadly, then gently extended a hand, palm up to Tatia. "Come with me darling," she cooed. "I am your friend. We shall have something nice to eat and get you a pretty new tunic. Would you like that?" Tatia clapped and gave a little skip, then grasped Mentor Illiai's outstretched hand and followed her.

Danai felt a strange ache of sadness as she watched Tatia being escorted away. "I wonder if she'll get back her memory," she asked nobody in particular.

Mentor Nacci answered. "The Healers will have to determine that. It could be temporary or for always. But she will be removed from the Rites. It is well you three brought her back—she would have otherwise died, babe that she has become."

"She nearly wasn't the only one," Aaron muttered under his breath.

"But what about her wings?"

Mentor Tamilyn answered with a small shrug. "If her wits do not return, then always will she be a spryte. There are yet six Rites, and gone are her abilities to learn the needed skills." His voice gentled. "I am sorry, but what sense would there be in giving wings to a babe? She won't ever know what she is missing, perhaps never recall what is lost. But she will be cared for always. Come. It is evenmeal, and," he wrinkled his nose at their bedraggled appearance, "I would suggest a dip in the Trykle before eating."

* * * * *

Shaking her head to rid her hair of the last droplets, Danai sat trailing her feet in the cool water. At the mention of food, Aaron and Joson had raced into the woods, jumped in, swirled around, then run back, waving as they passed Danai. She harrumphed to herself. Evenmeal could wait. She fingered her tattered tunic, doubting it would last another three lumnas.

As if in response to her thoughts, Triasa appeared, bearing a plum-colored bundle under her arm. She knelt to give her niece a breath-stealing hug. "I was worried, dear one. Almost all the others are back. We lost track of your group at the ridge, and feared the worst." She scooped up the bundle and gave it to Danai. "Here, put this on. That rag you're wearing isn't fit for scrubbing bowers."

Slipping the tunic over her head, Danai belted it, then picked up on her aunt's remark. "Keep track of?"

Triasa tucked Danai's hand into the crook of her elbow, and together they ambled back towards the Dell. "The birds. We arrange a relay with them for this Rite, and they report back on your whereabouts. Wag-Tail lost sight of you between eventide and dawnshine, and has been searching for you ever since. Even the owls couldn't tell where you'd vanished to."

"That explains why he was so glad to see us," Danai laughed. "But I thought you abandoned us for this Rite."

"We do, and we don't. It is really two Rites, but we combine the Rite of Abandonment with that of the Truthing Well. Imagine if we had said, 'now you will be abandoned.' Wouldn't that cause a bit of panic! The birds will intervene if they think a life is at high risk and summon us." A bleak note entered her voice. "It usually works."

"Usually?"

"You'll hear soon, but Sandagon was lost in a bog."

"No!" Danai halted. Sandagon was a podmate from her vale. Together they had hidden from a Teaching Skald one glorious early spring day, then spent the time teasing squirrels and gathering rainbow-hued cobwebs to bring to the Healers. "What do you mean 'lost'?"

"He's dead Danai. His group chose not to stop that night and became disoriented. There are many meadows among the valleys of the Wynndowns, some more water than dirt. He stepped into bogsand. They tried to save him and nearly lost Tania, but it was all over in moments. At dawnshine the birds spotted them, told them to wait, then flew back here. Mehrten flew out, told them to continue, and brought the body back. We held the mourning feast that day, so that he could be returned to his dell."

"Told them to go on! But why?"

"Because the Rite still needed to be finished, Danai. The sayings of the Well are of considerable importance in Krisalys. Sometimes, no matter how terrible, you just have to keep going."

"Joson was right, then. Sprytes can die during the Rites. But Auntie—"

"Shhh!" Triasa held up a warning finger. "Mistakes and panic will kill, Danai. Both have their roots in bad choices. And sometimes it's just plain bad luck." She flung out her arm, the gesture encompassing not only the Dell they were just entering but the whole realm. "Life can kill, my dearest niece. We're trying to teach you how to prevent that. Usually we succeed. But, to all our sorrow, not always. It is rare that anyone dies during the Rites."

Danai struggled to regain her composure. "And the other group that still isn't back?"

Her aunt snorted. "Plain bad sense of direction, that group. Headed due south. We finally had to send a bird to get them steered back towards Pyre Tor. Did you reach it?"

"Thanks to Tlarg, yes. And we have the trefoil for proof."

Now it was Triasa's turn to halt. "Tlarg? That's a dwarf name. Explain."

As they strolled towards the trestles, Danai summarized their journey, leaving out only her joining with Aaron and the fire daemon. The vision of the Anam and the dissonant verse sketched a frown on Triasa's face. "Those will both warrant the review of all the Mentors and the Dolmen. Strange events, those," she murmured, more to herself, then released her niece's arm. "Dearling, you need to eat. Join your friends. We will talk again."

Staring after her, Danai sensed a ripple of unspoken worry. She wished she had mentioned the fire daemon. It was almost as if something had nudged her to stay silent. Ah well, time enough to tell when she had to go before the Mentors and Dolmen on the morrow.

Her trencher fully laden, she joined her group, where Joson— already finished eating—was recounting their journey. Aaron was seated beside him, still nibbling. When Joson was about to speak his verse, Pook held up a hand. "Those are for the Mentors first. They told us earlier today we're not to discuss them beforehand."

Danai let Joson tell their story, content to relax and savor the freedom of doing so without setting a watch, or fearing the gathering shadows. Rhytha and Elanoria interrupted to ask about the gems they had seen. Pook seemed perturbed that his journey had lacked such excitement.

"Believe me," Aaron interrupted. "There's some excitements you don't want. Sorry, Jo'. Keep going—you're doing a bard's job of it."

As he described the flood of the stone river, Danai realized Joson was trying to catch her eye. She guessed he wanted her to approve telling about the fire daemon. She gave a single shake of her head. Aaron seemed surprised when Joson skipped the terrible night, but left well enough alone. "And now tell us of your journeys," he asked the others. The group talked until silenced by the Mentors for sleep.

* * * * *

The trill of a Mentor's reed pipe dragged Danai out of a dreamless sleep. She awoke feeling rested for the first time since they had left the Dell.

After mornmeal, Mentor Armerion summoned her journey-group and escorted them through the bushy barrier of weathersign, their scarlet flowers bobbing on the long branches. It was a sunny day; were it cloudy, the flowers would be curled tightly shut. Danai realized they were approaching the strange black stone she had seen yesterday, and it soon loomed before them, knotted about itself like the roots of an ancient tree, so black it consumed the light. A thin oval hollow was visible off center.

"This is the Skystone," Mentor Armerion explained. "Here the Dolmen resides, in this clearing beside the sacred stone, and inside is a cave in which he can speak with Lunasa and the Mother." A clot of hooded figures stood near the Skystone, and they positioned themselves into a half circle as the sprytes approached.

From out of the stone emerged the Dolmen, its sacred oak staff freshly crowned with Lunasaberries. The Mentors seated themselves, and Mentor Armerion seated the sprytes such that they were within the horns of the half circle before taking his place. The Dolmen pointed the staff at them, the carved leaves seeming to rustle off the wood in the fresh young breeze that was springing up. "Speak ye."

Joson and Aaron both looked at Danai, and after a moment's hesitation, she recounted the same tale she had told Triasa. None of the Mentors interrupted, and she could sense the intense concentration they emanated, as if they were listening to all that was not being said as well.

"Mentor Illiai." The Dolmen gestured at the Healer. "Tell what Tatia said yester gloaming."

Illiai rose in a fluid motion, bowed, then spoke in a flat voice as she stared at a point above the sprytes' heads. "Tatia told me of a 'fire pretty,' and 'a lady made of flames' when I probed her further. She told how you wouldn't let her play with this lady, but ran away on mean stones that hurt her feet into the dark until the lady was hit by a shiny ball."

The Dolmen's questing energy struck Danai like a blow between the eyes, and she rocked back. Aaron reached out to steady her.

"It was my fault," Joson held up his hand. "Tatia was injured after the storm, and so terribly cold. Danai said we needed fire to help her survive the night. So we used fire magic."

"We?" prompted the Dolmen. Joson hesitated.

"I," Danai choked out. "I decided to use the fire magic. I thought," she gulped. "I thought that because Tatia's life was at such risk, it was proper." Despite the warm air, she felt chilled by the Mentors' frosted stares.

Another familiar voice spoke, curt with anger. "Why don't you tell us exactly what occurred—and try not to leave anything out this time."

Afraid to look at her aunt's face, Danai described the harrowing night, no longer seeing the bright sun-filled clearing, but instead the stalking inferno that nearly consumed them until Lunasa had sent the silver firestar.

"This is the truth?" The three nodded. "Bard song and skald tales recount such happenings, but never to sprytes." The Dolmen spat the last word out. "Sprytes who ignore the rules, who summon Lunasa and the Mother's aid—and are answered!"

"That's not fair," Joson blurted. "Aaron wasn't even with us when we spellcast the fire magic."

"Silence," the Dolmen hissed. "Have ye not done enough? Releasing a fire daemon that near-killed ye, and then would have rampaged who knows where, perhaps to destroy who knows how much of Lampion before stopped?"

"I didn't know I would release it," Danai said quietly.

"Not know? Not know!" The Dolmen struck the staff to the ground, shattering a pebble. "Did thee not know the basics taught by the Mentors?"

"There never was a mention of fire daemiani!"

"Impossible!"

"Nor for me," Joson interrupted, riled at the torrent of abuse. Out of the corner of his eye, he saw several Mentors squirm.

The Dolmen swirled about, facing the Mentors. Its tone changed from anger to cold rage. "Speak these two the truth? Think before ye answer, for if they are lying, wingless will they remain for ever." The words plummeted like hailstones into the charged air. The sprytes gasped in disbelief. The Mentors sat motionless.

Then one stood, somewhat unsteadily, and pushed back her cowl. "It is the truth." Melarna bowed her head. "I taught Danai. I offer no excuse, save that I was distracted by a slow spryte, and failed in my duties." She was pale beneath her rose-hued skin.

"It is the truth." Quenton also stood, his amber head bowed. "Joson is my pupil. I prohibited usage, but I did not explain why."

"So, there are other sprytes who have the same lack of knowledge—most of them it seems." The Dolmen turned to another Mentor. "Oyon, see to it that all the sprytes are gathered at midmeal, and instructed as to this dangerous omission. Ye are dismissed." This last was to the sprytes at which it did not even glance, its unblinking eyes fixed on the two waiting Mentors.

The sprytes fled as quickly as courtesy would allow, ducking between the flower stalks, relieved to return to the central Dell. "Something awful is about to happen." Danai halted, and looked back.

"I know, but what?" Aaron bit his lip.

"I don't know, I don't know. Oh Jo', why didn't I listen to you? What was that?"

An ugly sound, like a violent ripping of cloth, shredded the air. A puff of breeze carried the stink of burned feathers to their noses. Then two brown-clad sparrows, uttering mournful chirps, sprang skywards, and quickly disappeared among the trees.

"It's not possible. The Dolmen can't have done that to them. What gives it the right?" Danai trembled, eyes straining to locate the two brown shadows.

Aaron grabbed her shoulders. "It's not your fault. You can't blame yourself."

"Then whose is it? I chose to use the fire magic. Joson tried to stop me, but I couldn't be bothered to listen."

"You don't even know that was Melarna and Quenton. It could just have been a coincidence."

"It was not." Triasa seemed to materialize behind them. There was no warmth in her eyes as she glanced at Danai. "You are not to speak of this to anyone. If you do, your wings are forfeit. That is an Order. The rest of the pod will be given a plausible reason for their abrupt departure." She paused, a trickle of pity briefly crossing her stony features. "Their punishment is for the duration of Krisalys. If they survive, the spell ends the day of that Rite, and they return to their birth forms. Wiser it can only be hoped." She retreated back behind the weathersign bushes.

"I need to sit down," Aaron grunted.

Danai wondered if she and Joson looked as ashen as Aaron as they joined him. "I feel uncommonly like being sick." Somewhere a sparrow called. Tears smudged her vision.

"This is wrong!" Aaron slammed his fist into the dirt. "So they made a mistake. Everybody makes them."

"I think they realized what was about to happen to them, although maybe not what form it would take." They stared in surprise at Joson. "Think how they looked, how dull their voices were. Almost as if they were going to be executed."

"Well for all intents they were," Aaron snapped. "Any owl, weasel or hawk can make a meal of them. What else did you think Triasa meant when she said 'if they survive'?" He glared at the hidden Skystone. "I'm beginning to wonder how many things about our folk we don't know. What type of creatures are we that we cast our folk to virtual death because they failed to teach us something?"

"To me, there's a piece missing in this whole kryptic," Joson said. "Those fire daemiani mean a whole lot more than we've been told. Obviously something so awful that the failure to follow the rules is..." He jerked his fist towards the forest, leaving his sentence unfinished.

"I feel as if I don't know anything anymore," Danai whispered sorrowfully. "Did you see the look my aunt gave me? It was because I didn't tell her about the fire daemon yesterday." Pain clutched her heart. "She doesn't trust me now. Another failure. Did you know Sandagon died in this stupid Rite of Abandonment?"

Joson's face contorted. Danai belatedly remembered he was Joson's half-brother. She reached out to clasp his hand. "Jo' I am so sorry! I forgot."

"All for a stupid pair of wings," Joson said bitterly, clenching his jaw. "I'm beginning to wonder if it's really worth it." He heaved himself up and stalked away towards the woods.

Aaron's eyes narrowed. "What do you mean, 'abandonment'?"

"Triasa explained that it's actually two Rites, but they don't tell us that so it won't cause a panic. I presume they say something when they review our verses." She bit her lip. It was unlikely her aunt would confide in her again anytime soon.

After midmeal and Oyon's mandate regarding fire magic, Aaron and Danai kept away from their podmates for the balance of the day, knowing that at some time in the next day or so, they would be called back to the Skystone. Joson simply said he wanted to be left alone and again retreated into the sanctuary of the woods. The two sat on a pebbled bank beside the Trykle, taking comfort in each other's companionship. Somehow the sun-dappled waters did not look as bright or cheerful, Danai thought. As one loses their innocence, does it taint the colors of beauty?

The fluting note of the Mentor's reed pipe summoned them to evenmeal. "I am not hungry." Danai pitched yet another fleck of sand into the shuffling waters, watched it drift a few paces, then sink.

"I know." Aaron lay staring at the sky, netted by tree branches. "But we're in enough trouble as it is. Being absent probably will only make it worse."

"This from the lad known for his jokes and pranks!" She tried to smile.

"Somehow, I don't feel like pranking anybody."

They rose, dusting the bits of forest duff from their tunics. Danai stared once again into the trees. "Where do you think they are?" she whispered.

"I don't know. I hope together, so they can help each other. The way I would always like to be with you."

Danai swung about to face him in surprise. "What?"

Aaron squirmed, an awkward half-smile on his face, and caught her hand. "I know this isn't the time or the place. But you're something special Danai. And I've seen how the other fellows look at you. You don't have to answer me now, but would you consider me for your Chosen One? At least for a while?" His voice was hesitant, eyes hopeful, watching the shifting currents of emotions cross her face.

"Aaron, I truly don't know what to say. I've never even thought about such a thing, really." She blushed. "I never thought the lads even noticed me."

"Huh! You're blind then. You mean you haven't noticed how Pook looks at you, among others? By the Twins, maiden, even Shamarig gave you the once over."

Danai spluttered. "Shamarig? Aaron, he's a dwarf!"

"So?"

"I think you're exaggerating."

"You just keep thinking that. Fine with me."

A shy smile lit her face. "Yes, I'd be willing to be your Chosen One."

Aaron hugged her, then stared down for a long moment into her glowing green eyes, his own sparkling as brightly as golden shafts of sunlight. "I guess we had better get back. But remember—we're handfasted." He didn't let go of her hand until just before they left the trees.

* * * * *

Morrowmorn, Danai was again summoned, this time alone, to the Skystone. She was made to recite the entire journey, and quickly became used to the interruptions and questions as she progressed. But it was the description of the image in the Anam that seemed to most agitate the Dolmen. "In the name of Lunasa, this be without doubt a sending." It addressed the Mentors. "What are thy thoughts about its meaning?"

"Solon?" Toron ventured.

The Dolmen frowned. "He died an age ago."

"The past never dies," Triasa pointed out. "It just reshapes itself. A warning?"

"About the fire daemon she would later release." The Dolmen nodded, satisfied with this interpretation.

Danai took a short breath for courage, then spoke unbidden. "The figure in the Anam was a fellow, not a lady. The daemon that stalked us was a lady."

"The sending was brief. In thy fear, thee could not have seen clearly. Continue thy tale."

It had been fellow, she was sure of it. Danai had to try again. "Ask the dwarves what they think." The Mentors started, and she was rewarded by a series of stares, some hard, others intrigued. Toron motioned her to continue. "They were going to call a Comhairle—an elders' gathering, it upset them so much. It was to have begun," she paused to count back on her fingers, "six days ago. They are wise in the ways of the Mother and claim to be the first of her folk. Why not ask them?" She felt a wash of hope as she caught approving glances from Triasa, Toron, and several others.

"Preposterous." Mentor Nporan shook his head, his jowls quivering with protest. "I have seen more seasons than most of you, and what commerce have we with these dwarves?" He gave an elderly sniff.

"That's not true," Danai shot back, made brave by a burst of irritation. "Tlarg said he has often made things for Feyree. And even if such is not known by all those here, he did help us, and we know how to contact him." She had all their attention. "They too speak with the birds. If we want to hear what the dwarves have to say, we need only send a messenger." The Dolmen was staring at her as if she had become some unknown and suspect creature, and it sent a shiver through her.

"I think Danai offers good counsel," Toron said. "Dolmen, I motion that contact is made."

The Dolmen frowned as it heard the chorus of 'ayes' supporting Toron's proposal. "It is not our way to consult other folk in such matters. We will speak with Lunasa after this and seek his guidance. But first, complete thy overlong tale. It be only half-done, and we suspect there are yet more oddities to follow."

She shortly came to the Truthing Well's verse.

"Danai of silver.
You shall sacrifice yourself to fire.
See all stamped by misled desire.
Rake ashes of lives.
Know winter of bitterness; survive.
Then triad the realm with folks' dreams."

Danai had suspected the Dolmen was perturbed by her presence, but there was no doubt of it now. Its face ruptured into ripples of emotion it struggled to control. "Fire, fire, fire. Seems like thee are entwined by this daemiani magic. Again a warning of fire." It approached, and Danai fought the desire to recoil from the scouring look in its bottomless eyes. "Spryte, this requires discussion not for thine ears. Nay, stand still. We gave no order to depart. Thee shall hear nothing. So." With a murmur of words, it tapped her chest with the staff.

A numbing burst of cold radiated from the staff's touch point, stiffening limbs, dimming eyes, and extinguishing hearing. From far away, Danai heard Triasa's protesting cry. She knew she was yet alive, but her body felt nothing. Her last thought was engulfed in a wave of darkness. I am a pillar of stone, like the Ael of Pyre Tor.

"Dolmen, what means this?" Triasa had sprang to her feet, appalled by the dull gray statue her niece had become. "Thee are over generous with thy magic these two days it seems."

"Halt thy ever-sharp tongue Triasa. The spryte's verse is laden with a message the likes of which has not ever been heard in our memory. When did thee ever hear a verse such as this?"

"The Well's verses are ever kryptics," Toron argued. "Would ye have thought that its message to Tatia, as Aaron told us, would herald her life as a babe-spryte? Aye, she found a life beyond imaginings, but would any of us have explained it as such?"

"Yet Aaron's made sense," Asagion said. "It was a simple warning about his mischievous antics. And as we told him, one he should heed for the upcoming Rite."

"It is Danai's verse we discuss," snapped the Dolmen, rapping its staff on the ground.

"It is a message from Lunasa or the Mother—silver is their sacred color," Triasa replied, still staring at her niece's frozen form.

"Agreed."

"And in some fashion she will confront fire that will nearly take her life, yet does not. But the rest of the verse?" She shook her head, looking at the other Mentors.

"It warned of the fire daemon she was to encounter," the Dolmen insisted. "As for the rest, did she not have hope and desire to help Tatia? And is not Tatia's life now ruined—in ashes?"

"And the other words?" Triasa wrestled with the unpleasant sensation the Dolmen was trying to jam the verses into too simple an explanation. The wrong one.

Impatient, the Dolmen dismissed her question. "Danai faced her death—her winter—during the fire daemon's attack, and in desperate hope she called upon Lunasa. The Well tried to warn of her folly, but she had not the knowledge to understand and continued on the path to disaster."

Triasa and Toron glanced at each other. It felt wrong. A sudden eddy of cold air swirled through the group, scattering puffs of seed flakes, broken bits of grass, and dust that set them coughing. Wiping dust-tears from its eyes, the Dolmen tapped Danai on her forehead and heart with its staff.

Like a frozen flower in sudden thaw, the silver flooded back into Danai's face, then limbs. Arms twitched, air was sucked, eyelids flickered. A cracked cry burst free as she toppled forward, legs yet too rigid to provide support. Ignoring the Dolmen's order to stay in place, Triasa ran to kneel at her niece's side. "Dearling, sweeting," she crooned, cradling the chill form. Danai's eyes began to focus.

"Auntie." She could scarcely whisper. "I'm so sorry. Please don't be angry at me."

"Shh, shh. Calm yourself. But fail not to tell all. There is much that is not understood, despite what others think." Triasa returned to her seat.

Danai sat up, her stomach roiled by nausea. "What does my verse mean?"

"It is our interpretation that it forewarned thee of the fire daemon." The Dolmen held up its hand as she opened her mouth to protest. "Silence. Rare be it the Well's message warns of something that will happen before thy return, but so it did with thee and Tatia. We have spent enough time on this. Did aught else of note happen after thee left the stone river?"

She shook her head, attempting to free her mind from icicles of frozen thought.

"Then return to thy fellows. Send Thran, who arrived last eventide with the final group, to us."

* * * * *

Morrowmorn, the sprytes awoke, groggy and surprised to see the sun full over the treetops. There had been no Mentor's reedpipe summons to mornmeal—in fact, no Mentors were to be seen. Most lay back, welcoming the respite and the chance for extra sleep.

Pook stretched, stood up, and gazed with a half-smile at his still-dozing friends. It was too warm to snooze in the sun, he decided, and he ambled off to seek cooler shade in the woods. The enticing burble of the Trykle lured him to wade along its bank for a few feylengths, before climbing out to wander alongside. For a bit he practiced the woodcraft of silent motion, knowing that like anything, it took repetition. He'd often wondered how Feyree could be there one moment, invisible the next, and had concluded it must be magic. Mentor Marcelon had taught them it was otherwise—the proper placement of the foot, the quick fluid step behind a wide grass blade or sapling—any object that blocked vision—all carefully controlled movements that gave the illusion of disappearing.

"Be alert always when ye are in an unfamiliar place," Marcelon had stressed. "Hiding is far safer than flight. There is little ye can outrun, much ye cannot outfly. Choose wisely where ye pause for rest. Ye never know what eyes are watching, what nose is smelling."

"Mentor, why not just use magic? Surely there are spells to make one invisible." Pook could not grasp the apparent reticence to use such a wonderful resource. It irked him that the sprytes were being forced to learn such banal skills, when he was sure there was a simple spell that would easily take care of things. "I mean we're learning ways to protect ourselves and survive with woodcraft and basic magic. Why not use a higher spell to transform an enemy or cast an illusion? Why must we hide?"

Marcelon's lips tightened into a thin band across his gaunt face. "Answer?"

Eager for approval, Tania had blurted out, "Only use magic when truly necessary. Trust in your self first."

"But why?" Pook argued.

"It is the Law, and it is our way," snapped Marcelon, a flush browning his amber skin. "You do not question the Laws."

"Oh, but I do," Pook whispered as he stopped beside a quiet eddy. The slow-flowing waters tossed bits of sunlight into the air, and an almost hot breeze ruffled his hair. It was warm, he thought. Surprisingly so in the shade. He knelt and scooped handfuls of cool water, savoring the mingled flavors of moss, stone, and moist earth. He found himself thinking of Danai. She had seemed so withdrawn yesterday, staring without seeing, wandering towards the woods to listen to the sparrows chatter. He had tried several times to engage her in conversation, but she had shied away. It had annoyed him to see her later with Aaron. As if that jokester could be anything special to a maid as smart as Danai! He hated her being so distant and sat there yanking at the tender moss, tossing strands into the water.

"Poor moss. As if it could protect itself from a strong spryte like you," whispered a bodiless voice from just across the stream.

Pook jumped up, lost his balance on the slippery moss, and toppled backwards, landing with a muffled thump on his backside. The voice tittered with the sound of dry rasping leaves.

"Show yourself!" Pook scrambled to his feet.

"Give me a good reason to."

"Common courtesy."

"Sure. Of course."

"Then I'll just have to assume you're afraid."

"Never met a daemon who was."

Pook felt the fine hairs on his neck rise as he stared at the spot the voice seemed to hang. The faintest quiver twitched the air, like slow-running water distorts the look of the streambed below. An invisible daemon? "I've never met a daemon before."

"You're joking me."

"No. Seriously. I've heard about you, but never believed—"

"That we existed?"

"Oh, no! That I would ever meet one." Pook felt it would be unwise to add that he had long presumed they were just another myth—at least until now.

"Make you a bargain. You do a little spellcasting for me, I'll show myself. Seeing a daemon! Something to impress your friends." The voice had a rich throaty timbre.

"Um, what kind of spell?"

"Fire magic." The voice dropped to sibilant whisper, lisping through the silence.

"Don't know that yet," Pook lied. Something felt wrong. But to be able to actually boast that he had seen a fire daemon! None of the others could top that.

"Spare me. All sprytes learn that spell as one of their earliest Teachings."

Pook stalled. "And how do you know that?"

"Oh, we watch. Why not? It makes an interesting change."

"You watch us?"

"Whenever we feel like coming to the barrier," the voice explained. "Especially during your Rites. You seem to have a real knack for magic you know."

"Oh please." Pook swallowed a bulge of pride. "I'm the fumblefingers of my pod. Besides, how do you know about me anyway?"

"I enjoy watching you, Pook." The air shimmered, seemed to coalesce, revealing embers or eyes—he wasn't sure which—that glowed underneath a mane of blue fire, rippling, waving in an unseen breeze. A flickering arm appeared, golden-white. She beckoned. He hesitated, unable to tear his eyes away, took a step forward.

"Make fire, Pook," she hissed softly, glittering eyes rich with promises. "Make fire, and I'll teach you more, oh so much more that you can do with it." The rest of her appeared, sumptuous curves barely contained by a scarlet tunic of flame. She flung her arms wide, as if casting a net.

Mesmerized, he didn't notice the slight movement of her lips as he concentrated on the spell. His hands began to weave the air, forming the symbols. He took yet another step towards her. Even from across the stream, he could feel her radiant heat, caressing his face, drying his lips.

"The fire. Now."

He gathered himself to release his energy into her outstretched arms.

With an angry screech, a young crow slammed into Pook's back, knocking him into the stream. Gasping and cursing, he floundered back towards the bank, while the agitated bird, still giving its alarm caw, danced from one black claw to the other, preventing him from climbing out.

There was a disappointed hiss. "We are watching Pook. We will await you."

Five Mentors converged upon the scene, three uncloaked and flying, two on foot. "In Lunasa's name," shouted Conya, landing near the crow. "Can anyone quiet this creature? Who speaks its tongue?"

Triasa pulled back her cowl, and pursed her lips to emit a soft gargling cluck. The crow cocked his head, cawed twice, then strode over to her with its rolling gate. Anoran and Memnon landed in the stream and helped Pook out of the water, where he stood pulling bits of waterweed from his hair. "What happened?" Anoran asked.

"Nothing really. This snail brain of a bird attacked me for no reason."

"That makes no sense," Nacci snapped, her cowl flung back, hands on her hips.

"No, it doesn't," Triasa agreed, turning to stare at Pook. "Particularly given it's untrue."

Pook peered through his sodden hair into Triasa's glowing sapphire eyes. "Mentor Triasa, I don't know what you mean. I was just standing here, doing nothing when—"

"Nothing? Cawc says you were talking to something hot, making strange movements with your claws." She frowned. The bird did not yet have the vocabulary to explain what it had seen, only that he knew it was burning danger. But what?

"I am not lying!" Pook shoved away from the two Mentors, his breath coming in angry, shallow gasps. "I don't remember talking to anything at all. You can believe me or the bird."

The Mentors glanced at each other. Pook was not known as a troublemaker in any way. Smart, yes. Unusually skilled at spellcasting and inquisitive, yes. But not a liar. "Return to the Dell," Triasa ordered. She was inclined to believe the bird.

* * * * *

The glaring sunlight momentarily blinded Pook as he plunged out of the cool woods into the humid Dell. He staggered a few steps then halted, disoriented. And inexplicably perturbed. What had happened back by the stream? It was all a muddle.

"Hey Pook! Over here!" Damon waved from under a shady clump of daisies. As Pook approached, Damon muttered to the others. "What's the matter with him? He's almost gone violet, he's so angry, and look at his eyes!"

"I wonder if it had anything to do with that awful screeching we heard a short bit ago," Elanoria asked, sitting up and dusting freckles of golden pollen from her arms.

Danai studied their friend. His normally springy pace was plodding, shoulders hunched forward, eyes focused on each step as if unsure where to place his feet. Despite the angry bodyglow that shimmered even in the sunlight, he seemed strangely shadowed. She shivered.

"You look beat!" Damon stood up. "Can I get you anything? Some water?"

"Not thirsty," Pook groused, looking down.

"Are you all right?" Elanoria asked solicitously, touching his hand.

"Get off me!" Pook jerked away. "Just leave me alone, can't you?" He sprinted through the shocked group and disappeared into a patch of clover.

"What in the name of the Twins has got into him?" a wide-eyed Rhytha asked.

"Did you see his eyes?" Danai looked at Joson. "When Ela touched him, they looked as if they were on fire, whirling with orange embers. Or I think I saw that. Did any of you?"

Joson and Damon nodded. "Creepy, if you ask me." Damon shook his head. "No, Danai, sit back down. Don't go after him. Sometimes a fellow just has to be alone."

Too restless to remain still, Danai instead headed off in the direction from which Pook had come. There was more than one way to discover things, she decided. Inside the forest, she paused to watch the agitated dance of the rain gnats which soared and plunged in mad arcs through yellow sunbeams, warning of rain. She heard a magpie squawk, a jay rasp, and felt a surge of happiness. I love this realm, she thought. I hope it never changes.

A flap and clap of wings, and a burst of air shoved her forward. She spun around to encounter two white-ringed black eyes. "Wag-Tail! However did you find me here?"

"We see everything," he chided, preening smooth a white-tipped wing feather. "Well, most everything," he amended as he saw her cock an eyebrow. "Sprytes who vanish are not common." He ruffled his neck feathers, clearly still annoyed by the incident.

"I am so sorry about that. Of course, we didn't know thee were watching us. A gem-dwarf, Tlarg led us through the hills to the Well."

"Lucky thee were. It is not often these days they speak with fey folk."

"Wag-Tail, could thee get a message to him for us?"

"I know not this Tlarg."

"Perhaps his brother, Shamarig?"

Wag-Tail bobbed and hopped with excitement. "Know thee Shamarig? He is a great songster! Often has he played for us in the early dawns by the garden arch."

"Where is that?"

"Up, up above his nest, high in the mountains, in a garden always green."

"Oh, the Srath Orach. Another dwarf told us about that. Yes, I know him."

"Great is the respect given to him by the bird folk." Wag-Tail preened a breast feather. "He calls me Troich-friend, a great honor."

"Being so named by such a dwarf is indeed high praise. Could thee please deliver a message that Danai and her friends returned safely to the Dell? He and Tlarg were most kind, and I would like them to know."

"With all gladness will I do so maiden." Wag-Tail bobbed. "It is overlong since I have seen good Shamarig."

"Another question. Earlier I heard a crow cawing nearby here. Does thee know something about it?" The magpie avoided her eyes, bowing down to inspect a claw. She waited.

He finally answered, rattling his pinions. "Know I aught of the one that the spryte nearly summoned? By tales only, but it be enough."

"What are you talking about?"

"He played with spells, maiden. And not at his own bidding. There was a presence of something else. Or so says Cawc. But Cawc is only a season out of the shell, and cannot tell what he saw, only that it was not good. My guess it was a creature from the other side."

"Other side?" What had Pook been doing, Danai wondered.

"It be not something of which I can yet speak, maiden. Yon hooded ones will tell thee. Until then, my knowledge I must hold." Glancing about, Wag-Tail tipped forward until she could see her face distorted in his eye. "Be wary of that one maiden. He has tasted something forbidden. Be most wary." He stepped past her a few strides, then vaulted skywards. "I shall carry thy message on the morrow," he called back. "Nest well, maiden."

"A fair wind under thy wings," she cried back as he disappeared through the branches. She turned at the call of the reed pipe from the Dell. Odd time to summon us, she thought. Odd day overall. What had Pook been up to? She hastened to join the gathering sprytes.

* * * *

Chapter Ten

The cowled Mentor who had summoned them waited a little off to the side until all had gathered, then motioned them to sit. The other Mentors appeared, circled the group thrice, then halted. The Dolmen uncowled, stepped forward.

"This be the Night of Wraiths," it intoned. "Each of ye shall be taken to the Great Bog Marsh, left alone, separated from all but thyselves. None shall be there to succor ye, so mark well thy movements lest the bog swallow thy wandering feet, and ye perish. Ye have heard tell of the bogs—but few of ye know of their true dangers first hand, except for those who bore sad witness to the fate of thy podmate Sandagon. The bogs may be pretty to behold, but treacherous is the land which they cloak. Follow thy head, not thy heart. Beware thyselves."

Danai glanced at Aaron, then Joson out of the corner of her eyes; both had paled. Wraiths! Shadow creatures of ages past. Nightmares used to keep curious younglings in their bowers. Fragments of skald tales groped from her memory. Image wraiths who assumed your features as you gazed into their pools, dragging you to your death if you came within grasp. Reed wraiths who moaned and whistled in the wind, wailing for their lost lives. Even the wraiths of vanquished daemiani were said to dwell in the bogs. No folk with any sense ventured into the realm of the unpassed dead at night. And they were being dumped there alone?

An unusual flock of birds appeared, swooping above their heads in an intricate dance, each dive bringing them closer to the pod. Jays, ravens, sparrows, chickadees, magpies...the sky was streaked with flying colors. With a rush of pinions that gusted back many a Mentor's cowl they landed, one for each spryte. Danai searched hopefully for Wag-Tail, but saw Triasa motion Pook towards him.

Melitsa stood by a jay, shouting for Danai. "This is Tumblor," Melitsa formally introduced the bird. "She will take you to the Bog, then retrieve you at dawnshine. May Lunasa guard you in this trial." Tumblor tipped her blue crest down in salute, then crouched so Danai could clamber up. The babble of Mentor shouts, bird squawks, and spryte farewells was deafening. When every spryte was birdback, the entire flock launched, flapping aloft towards the sun.

"Good luck Danai!"

She twisted, searching for the source of Aaron's voice. He was waving from a crow's back, a jaunty smile on his face. "See you tomorrow! Watch out for toads!"

Tumblor banked south as they rose above the tree tops, and the small cloud of birds followed the Dunakey River, the great river of Lampion, which flowed down into the southern marshlands. Flapping occasionally, she coasted along on currents of air that were as familiar to her as the pathways of the Dell were to Danai.

"I'm not holding on too tight, am I?" Danai squawked in her best blue jay. She hadn't used it much, but Tumblor screeched back appreciatively, then replied in the common tongue.

"Nay, maiden. Short of tugging out my feathers, there is not much thee can do to harm them. Our feathers are stronger than many realize, but thanks to thee for asking."

The land gradually leveled out beneath them, and Danai gawked at the twisting copper-hued river that carved its way down from the craggy Rymple Mountains through the lush woods and meadows of Lampion. Far ahead she glimpsed a golden-green haze. "Tumblor, where does the Dunakey begin and end?" She had to shout near the bird's ear, and even then the wind snatched the words away.

"Above the Creag Roinn where spill the five falls, carved by the Mother of all birds when she scratched with her claw for the first born. Down they roar to the Cauldron of Cold. Joined by other waters, they become the great river. See thee the bluish veil yet far ahead? Nay? Ever were other folk's eyes not as birds. Even so, those be the salt waters, where the river loses itself forever. Once my mother told me that clouds are rivers trying to return home. Perhaps it is true, for the clouds weep when they cannot fly over the mountains, and must once again begin their journey."

The golden haze shaped itself into a grass-choked marshland—the Great Bog. The flock scattered and Tumblor began spiraling downwards. Beneath, Danai saw a sprawling patchwork of murky water, stippled with tall catkins, warped scrub bushes, and scraps of mud in different shapes and sizes. As they drew closer, she noticed ripples of skitter bugs darting along the water's surface, frequently interrupted by the surge of a hunting fish. "How far are we from the Dell?"

"At least ten days journey by thy wingless feet." Tumblor dropped below the tall wind-brushed grasses, then back-flapped to alight on a small hummock in the middle of a creeping eddy. Danai coughed at the stink of rotting plants. A whole night of this? Carefully she dismounted, cringing as her feet sank into a surface coating of slimy muck. "I really have to stay here?"

Tumblor bobbed once. "On the morrow's dawn I will return. Safe nesting!" With a squawk she leaped skywards, the fading rays of the sinking sun stroking her blue feathers with scarlet.

"All this for a pair of wings," Danai muttered, trying to ignore the shadows of old nightmares gathering around her memory. The smear of an islet was principally mud, pimpled with small bulges where grass had avoided being drowned. She searched among them for somewhere to sit, and at last perched on the largest knob. The gritty whine of mosquitoes frayed her nerves, and she started at every crack and splash. It was going to be a long night. She adjusted her dirq, and glanced about for a more substantial weapon, but the muddy hummock offered nothing else. The air cooled. A sticky gray mist oozed from the water's surface, swelling up to blot out the newborn stars overhead. It crested over the hummock's edges, crawling towards her. She stared, mesmerized.

Somewhere a duck quacked twice, snapping her alert. It seemed a signal. Crickets and frogs began to thrum, puncturing the mist with their repetitive chorus. Danai hugged her knees and tried to think of sunny revels, flower gatherings, and how much she enjoyed helping Triasa with the wood folk. Slowly the eventide noises ebbed into the heavy silence of deep night, interrupted only by the gloop and gurgle of water. She heard the slightest of rustles in the grasses off to her left and tensed. There was no wind.

Easing off the knob she lay flat in the mud, peering around its base. A flicker of red—perhaps eyes?—paused, then disappeared. She waited, the mud oozing through her tunic, until the rustle had long-passed before getting back onto the grass knob. Her nose wrinkled at the mud's stench. *And I thought the air smelled bad.* She dozed after a time, her head slumped on her knees.

A terrible scream shredded the air, was cut short. "Blessed Mother what was that?" Danai whispered, leaping to her feet. Now she knew how a trapped creature felt. The terrible sense of impending danger, unable to escape, to give vent to the panting terror that left one wide-eyed and trembling. The engulfing mist thickened, coalesced behind her. A long filament necklaced her throat.

And tightened.

She clawed at it, her fingers pulling through what felt like mushy pond scum. "Let me go," she choked.

The filament uncoiled. The shadow drifted around to face her, a seething swirl with two holes where eyes might be that glowed like old foxfire.

"In the name of the Mother, who or what are you?" she whispered.

The shape contemplated. It raised what she guessed was an arm of sorts, then unfurled it. A flicker of dancing blue light, the color of old ice, appeared in its hand—a wisp. The sign of a wraith. Skalds would tell of how on a clear night, one could see the wraiths drifting over the bogs, their meandering made visible by these bobbing wisps.

Her knees nearly gave way. This was her death. The wraith would strangle or drown her. Tumblor would find her corpse floating in the stagnant waters. Could she try to outrun it? Drowning might be preferable.

"Better it be asked, who are you?" The deep voice was sonorous, like a muffled breeze inside a stone cave.

She squeaked out a reply. "Danai of the Feyree."

Something resembling a laugh came from its smudge of a mouth, and the wisp flared brightly. "A high voice have you. A spryte, yes?"

She nodded. The wraith ebbed and flowed in place, apparently mulling things over. It drifted a bit closer. The blood pounded inside Danai's head, and a shrill ringing filled her ears.

"Call me Ombre." It rolled the 'r' like a buzzerbug on a humid summer's day.

"Ombrrrrrre," repeated Danai. Now what should she say? It seemed to be waiting for her to make the next move. "Why are you here?"

"Long has it been since a creature of two legs was stranded in this one's patch of marsh. This one thought to learn more."

"But you recognized me as a spryte."

"This one has met sprytes before."

"Why did you try to strangle me?"

"Strangle?"

"Your arm around my throat."

"This one can only touch if one first retouches oneself. Were one to brush Dan-a-ya-ee's shoulder, it would have only felt like colder mist. But when one's vapors connect in loops, then one can make Dan-a-ya-ee feel contact."

"Are you here to kill me?"

Ombre's wisp flared violet. "This one is saddened to hear Dan-a-ya-ee say such a thing. Why should this be?"

"Well aren't all wraiths dangerous and evil?"

The glowing eyes dimmed. Ombre swayed forward slightly. "As much as all sprytes are."

Danai was nonplussed. Could a wraith be other than as she had been taught? "What were you in life?"

"Ahhhh," Ombre sighed. "A question long unasked. Fear makes frog wiggles of most creatures. They flee a perception, seeing not the reality. Some to grow the number of wraiths in this watery land."

"You drowned?"

"Returning from a journey through the southlands, this one became lost of an eventide when the cold froze the water's skin solid. Paths there are through here, though difficult and ever-changing. This one placed a foot unwisely, broke through, and the sucking waters dragged one beyond the air's reach. Never misjudge these waters, Dan-a-ya-ee. Still they may seem, but many are the currents that tug them without surcease towards the salt waters. Like life to death."

"But if you drowned, why are you here?"

"This one's body is long rotted. But one's spirit could not bear to leave this realm. Thinking to return home, even if it were only as a shadow, one clung to the Veil that girdles this realm from the land of shadows and thins only to admit the newly dead. When the Veil regathered, this one's spirit remained on this side. Little did one know that one could never leave the marsh. This one sought to escape the clinging waters and return to the happy hyells of the Ael, but discovered the boundaries of these wet lands are this one's own. And so this one flits over soggy mud, twines about bulbous catkins, trapped outside the Veil." The wraith condensed into thoughtful silence, the wisp dulling to the faintest ember.

"Are all of you trapped spirits?" she ventured after the silence grew too long.

Ombre roused himself, the wisp flaring. "After a fashion, but for different reasons. Some are here by foolish choices, as with oneself. Others are those who were outcast here to die, or chose to end their lives. And others," he paused, seemed to glance around, then muttered, "others are placed here as punishment for evil deeds. And they in turn wreak their rage on the unwise, the unwary, the unfortunate. Those are the terrible tales told among the many folk on the outside."

"Do you know much about the Feyree?"

"There was a time when the Ael had much commerce with you small folk. Even in this one's time, there were comings and goings, and it was common to find Ael, Troich and Feyree living among each other."

"It's not that way now." Danai frowned. "I did not even know of the Troich or Ael and thought them skald-myths until I met a dwarf."

"Have you also met the Ael?" There was a hopeful eagerness in Ombre's voice; the wisp flared sky blue.

"Not yet." Ombre's shape slumped, and she surprised herself by feeling sorry for him. "But I heard the tale of Aelvina and Curbarig, and one of my podmates met Rynok of your folk."

"One has never heard that tale. Is it new?"

"Shamarig—he's a dwarf bard—said it was long ago. Are you even older than that?"

"Perhaps. Perhaps it was not an Ael-tale. One has lost track of how long it has been. Time fades with immortality. Even an immortality such as this." Ombre paused, as if recollecting long unused memories. "But even in this one's time, changes came about. Your folk became restless. Many spoke about seeking more exciting things, visiting other realms, discovering other folk. A few muttered about the forbidden arts, which the Great Mother had banished when she formed our world. Banished to those realms from which evil wraiths come.

"Yet many were the fey folk who chose to stay among us. Lovers of the land, they had homes in trees and lakes, and became wise in the ways of the Great Mother. The Ael would often visit with them. After the Battle of the Forbidden Arts, where so many Feyree perished, the whereabouts of these other fey were mostly forgotten."

Neither noticed that off to the left another clot of mist was drifting towards them, pierced by glowing red eyes. "Your folk followed one with a tongue of gold, who could create stories and stir hopes as only the greatest of loremasters can. He promised them a better realm, filled with things to make their lives easier, richer, better. And so they flocked to him, lured by his honeyed promises, fueled by their own desires."

"Do you know what his name was?" Danai suspected she already knew.

"Solon. Master of the Forbidden Arts."

"Well done, Ael." A flinty voice sliced in. "Finding this tasty tidbit for my delight."

Danai and Ombre slewed around to confront a wraith that seemed blacker than the darkness, a glittering orange wisp floating by its side.

"Get thee gone, daemon-wraith!" Ombre sank into a crouch, focused on the thick miasma roiling and coiling before him. A miasma that began to laugh with the gritty sound of tumbling gravel.

Danai retreated a few steps. Her foot sank into the mud at the hummock's edge. Her toe brushed against something hard.

"You puny drowned Ael. Do you think something as worthless as you can deny me?" The daemon-wraith roared. "I am of the great time daemiani, keepers of the forbidden arts, makers of the great one you just named."

"You are naught but a foul wraith, cursed by the Great Mother to wallow in this miserable hole until she sees fit to renew the world."

Danai wriggled her foot deeper, trying to get her toe under the object, and lift it to the surface.

"You dare to tell me what I am not? I can extinguish you with a mere swipe of my hand!"

"Hand?" Now it was Ombre's turn to laugh. "Mist. You are but fog. Or have you forgotten that small fact?"

A branch slurped free, precariously balanced on her foot. Careful not to attract attention from the arguing wraiths, she reached down, then held it behind her back.

"Smothering requires no hands," snarled the daemon-wraith. "Ask that cowardly spryte who lies some ways over, face down in the mud. He ran, fell, and I did not let him get up. The mud served my purpose equally well." It gave a satisfied hollow laugh.

A surge of rage overcame the clutch of fear in Danai's chest. Another death!

"Get out of my way, you puling Ael." The daemon-wraith drifted a feylength closer to Danai, its embered eyes twirling orange and red in a dizzying pattern that clouded her thoughts. "She is mine."

"You shall not harm her!" Ombre lunged for the daemon-wraith's wisp, flinging looped mist tendrils towards it. They struggled, two pillars of dark fog ebbing, flowing, pummeling each other, their blazing wisps bands of color smearing through the air.

No, Danai suddenly realized. Ombre is not hitting him. He's trying to smother the daemon wraith's wisp. And Ombre is losing.

Ombre collapsed, unable to further defend himself, attempting to shelter his now-vulnerable wisp. The daemon-wraith loomed over the slumped shadow, bellowing with victory.

"Let him alone!" Danai lunged forward, swinging the stick down through the swirling black murk. It struck ground, jarring her arms.

The daemon-wraith recoiled, then surged forward to engulf her, an elongated mist loop cinching around her waist and lifting her off the mud. She yanked her left arm free, but the slimy stick slipped from her other hand. Gobbling with laughter, the daemon-wraith cast another loop about her throat, tightening it slowly. She glimpsed Ombre trying to rise, gesturing towards her waist. She struggled for air, sparks exploding through her vision, and glanced down.

The wisp blazed orange by her hip, flaring ever brighter as the chortling daemon-wraith choked her life away. Her arms felt as heavy as stone, her hands numb. As if pushing through deep water, she swatted at the wisp, hard enough to knock it clear of the wraith's form. It fell in a brief arc of light, and landed sizzling in the mud.

Flinging Danai aside so that she went sprawling, the daemon-wraith lunged towards the flickering wisp. It guttered, flared up, then extinguished into blackness. With a wail of agony, the wraith exploded, fragments of hardened black fog hurtling in all directions. There was a soft splash as a last piece plunged into the water. Then silence.

Danai got to her feet unsteadily, tingling sensations prickling her arms.

"So it is true." Ombre's voice held a note of wonder.

"What?"

"We can be destroyed."

"Is it dead?"

"Yes and no," Ombre answered slowly, still staring at where the dead wisp lay. "In this realm yes, but is said a wraith extinguished does not go to the land of shadows, but into an oblivion where it must wait until the realms are renewed, unable to move or speak. This one did not truly believe, having so long been tethered here."

"You saved my life, you know." Danai walked over to Ombre and smiled up into his glowing eyes.

"You saved this one's existence. Now this one realizes how precious that is, even if it must be done here in these marshes. It is not as this one would have desired, but so it must be. Perhaps someday, the Veil will be opened once again, and this one can accept the gift of the next realm without regretting this place." He paused. "There is much beauty hereabouts. Perhaps one should take more time to explore it and cease mourning what might have been."

"I think you are very wise." A bird trilled and they both started. Above them the first fingers of dawnshine were trailing across the unseen sky, gradually shading the mist from gray to pearl, piercing it with shivering rainbows. Ombre began to fade, his wisp growing translucent.

"This one must go now. The day is not for us, and this one's barrow, on which you stand, awaits. May the Great Mother guard you in all that you do." His voice was fading.

She formally bowed to his indistinct shade. "Ombre, I promise you that if ever I find a way to open the Veil of Shadows, I will return to aid you across."

"Be that as it may, Feyree maiden Da-na-a-yee. Be that as it may."

She blinked. Ombre was gone.

About her the marsh grew luminescent. A water-beaded web shimmered between two catkins, trapping light in globes of moisture. She heard a faint 'cloop' as a nearby fish broke water to gulp an unwary skitterbug. Another bird broke out in a warble; more joined. The mist was thinning, rising up to ride away on the young breeze. She looked about, wishing Ombre could enjoy the beauty of this strange watery place in day's light, then walked over to the spot where the daemon-wraith's wisp had expired. A lump of dull black stone that swallowed the light squatted in the mud. She bent over to scoop it up.

"Touch it not maiden." Tumblor had glided in soundlessly to land just behind her. "Yon death stone is evil." Seizing a twig in her beak, she poked the lump over to the water's edge. A final push, and it tumbled into the water, leaving behind an oily film. They both shuddered.

* * * * *

Chapter Eleven

"Glad I am to see thee well, albeit more mud than maiden," Tumblor remarked, giving Danai a quick once over. "Much can happen in this wet, dangerous land, yet there are those among my folk who would not live elsewhere. Yet thee seem not pleased to see me."

Danai tried to focus on Tumblor, but the bird seemed to be receding down a long shadow-filled tunnel. "I feel...queer." Her knees buckled, and she slumped to the mud. As the darkness closed in, she thought she heard Triasa's voice and called out. "Oh Auntie. Such nightmares I've had. Must I still seek my wings?"

Nudging at Danai, Tumblor danced with impatience, worried that a ground-bound spryte and her bird would make tasty morsels for those who stalked the dawn. Other burdened birds began to soar overhead, flapping northwards. She gave a loud rasping screech.

A magpie banked sharply, then plummeted towards the marsh, a blur of black and white. Caught without warning, Pook clasped Wag-Tail's neck feathers so tightly his knuckles showed lavender. They landed with a jolt. "Wag-Tail, what's wrong?" Pook asked, brushing the wind-tears aside. He spotted Danai. "Blessed Lunasa!" He spilled off Wag-Tail's back, and ran towards her. "Danai? Danai!" Kneeling, he cradled her body. "She so cold, so terribly cold," he said as both birds crowded close. He gently slapped her cheeks, calling her name, oblivious to the birds' darting looks at the surrounding grasses. Somewhere nearby, a water-bird gave a startled cry.

"Pook, needs we must fly her from here. No time to tarry, else likely we will not ever leave." Wag-Tail hopped in place with urgency. "Now lad, now. While there is yet time."

The spryte draped Danai over the bird's back like a large rucksack, then clambered up. Tumblor erupted in a barrage of screaming squawks and flapping wings, lunging towards the rustling rushes on the left. With an oath, Wag-Tail launched, wings pumping hard to lift the double burden. The jay gave a final screech, cursing their would-be attacker in no uncertain terms, then blazed by them, a vivid streak of blue.

The cool wind seemed to revive Danai, and she sighed, prying open her eyes with effort. Below, the marshlands scrolled by. "Don't move dearling," Pook shouted. "We're safe. Wag-Tail, she's awake!"

"Thanks be to the Feathered Queen," Wag-Tail clacked over his shoulder. "Stay still maiden until I can safely land, and then we will share our sprytes." They soon set down on a rock bulging above the grasses, allowing both birds to easily keep watch. The sprytes slipped off.

Danai was embarrassed. Fainting! Although come to think of it, she hadn't eaten anything since yesterday's mornmeal, and precious little at that.

Pook interrupted her thoughts. "So what happened to you?"

"Two wraiths."

"Two? And how did you rate two?" he jested, trying unsuccessfully to reap a smile from her.

"One was, uh, I guess you could say a normal wraith. Ombre. But the other was a time daemon, one who had served Solon. A daemon Pook! What have we to do with such horrors?"

Pook shifted uncomfortably, an ember of memory flaring in the recesses of his mind. "Fi-re," a sultry voice sighed from a great distance.

"Who is to say that all daemiani are evil?" He tried to ignore her dismayed expression. "Well, consider. We thought most stuff was just bard jabber, only to find out that a lot of it is real. How do we know that the tales they tell about daemiani aren't just so much marsh gas? There are good and bad Feyree. Why not daemiani?"

Danai grappled with his suggestion, thinking how she had come to the same conclusion about wraiths. But her heart told her otherwise.

Wag-Tail stamped over to Pook, clearly upset. "Speak not such foolish words youngling." He tipped forward until his eye was level with Pook's face. "All daemiani are evil. They have honeysuckle tongues and tales to lure any creature. But they live to be masters of this realm. Doubt not the Teachings of thy bards in this instance— they tell the sorrowful truth." He could see by Pook's tight-lipped expression that his message went unheeded and opened his beak to say something more, then thought better of it. "Up!"

Beside them, Danai was already climbing up on Tumblor's back. She burrowed down, thankful for the feathers' warmth in the damp air. "Heed Wag-Tail maiden." Tumblor broke into Danai's jumbled thoughts. "He is a wise and trusted messenger to both Troich and Ael, as well as other folk. Much has he been witness to that I, a mere fledgling of ten blossomings could never imagine. Says he that daemiani be evil, then honor his wisdom."

"Even had he not said so, there could be no doubt." Danai's voice was thick with remembered fear. "It said it had just killed another spryte before it came after me. Tell me it was a lie Tumblor. A terrible boast." The bird's silence was her answer.

She glanced down at the retreating marshes, now swathed in a faint veil of silvery gold. Far ahead swelled the Anlyn Hills, beyond them the jagged snowtipped Rymples. I feel as old as those mountains, she thought. I'm not looking forward to facing the Mentors, especially the Dolmen. I don't trust it. What will it try to say now?

They were the last two sprytes to arrive. Wag-Tail dropped Pook off, then without a farewell flew off into the trees. Pook stood a moment glaring after him, shrugged, then looked around for Danai.

Tumblor crouched to make dismounting easy. Danai turned to thank her. "I sorrow for thee maiden. A great burden do thee carry, perhaps one thee does not yet truly see. My nest rests in the birch thicket at the north end of the Dell, beyond the dark stone of cold fire where yon hooded ones often meet. If ever thee wishes to visit, thee will be most welcome. A fair wind to guide thee."

"My hands are ever at thy service," Danai answered correctly, then added, "You saved my life Tumblor, at great risk to your own. Thank you." She stood watching the jay flap away. I don't want to return to the pod, she realized. I just want to hide somewhere. What happens if a spryte chooses to leave the Rites before getting their wings?

"Danai?" Pook gently tapped her shoulder. "Come on. Didn't you hear the reed pipe? You look so sad. What's wrong?"

"Nothing." She forced a smile. "Just tired I guess. It was a very long night."

As they joined the pod gathering in the Mentors' Circle, she searched for Aaron. He was with their other friends, and Pook and she hurried over to sit with them. "How'd it go?" he whispered, giving her hand a quick squeeze.

"You don't want to know."

Startled, he opened his mouth, but the Mentor's hand-clap precluded his question. One by one, they stood to recount their ordeals. The sun lumbered over the tree tops, heating the already warm air to a sticky flower-scented blanket. Danai was amazed at how only nine of the pod had actually encountered a wraith, including a very muddy Elanoria, who haltingly described her flight through the river rushes. Aaron seemed to almost boast about his escape, going into such detail that the Dolmen finally gave a short downward jab with his hand to silence him into summary. Pook was terse, almost irritated, stating the bare facts of a damp night with nothing but his thoughts to wander through.

Then it was Danai's turn. She could already sense the Dolmen's smoldering hostility. It took all her energy to tell her tale. She tried to ignore the jaw drops and gasps of her podmates, felt the shimmer of agitation that swept through the Mentors' Circle, but stayed focused on an empty spot just above the Dolmen's cowl. Finally finished, she started to sit.

"Remain standing," the Dolmen rasped. "Again, thee have a night with a daemon. What about thee attracts them? A spryte who converses with wraiths and runs not, who fights for a wraith's non-existence?" The air about it seemed to crackle with threads of greenish light. The carved leaves of its staff shivered, then lay still.

"You warned us to be aware of our selves." A wave of anger overcame Danai's fear, and she forgot to speak formally. "My first thought was to run, but Ombre did not attack or really threaten me. And how could I not defend him when he was attempting to save me?" Her tongue seemed to free itself of all restraint, her skin blazed silver. "How dare you criticize me for doing what was right, you who send us into situations where someone can die for simply being there! Without Ombre, that daemon-wraith would not only have killed me as he did another of our pod, but been around to kill some other spryte at some future Rite. So why don't you tell everyone who it was this time?" She heard the sharp intakes of breath around her, saw the Dolmen stiffen. "I know because the daemon-wraith boasted about the murder. Who is it this time?"

"Another spryte dead?" Joson rose to his feet, fists clenched by his sides. "My half-brother Sandagon was not enough?"

Mentor Armerion stepped forward and slowly uncowled. "My first born son, Balanoran." His face was gray with grief. "He was found as you described. His body is being carried to his birth mother." He paused, then turned to face the Dolmen. "I ask permission to forgo my role as Mentor. It is no longer within my ability to teach these sprytes, for I seek my dear son's face where it can no longer be, and I cannot be of safe use."

"Armerion speaks justly." Melitsa stood. "I support his request."

"And I."

"And I."

Nearly all the Mentors stood for Armerion, including Toron and Triasa.

The Dolmen raised its staff. "It weakens the Circle, but thy request is granted."

With a curt formal bow to the Dolmen, Armerion stepped free of his cloak, leaving it a brown puddle on the trampled grass. He paused. "Let there be no mourning feast for my son. I would rather he be remembered as he was in life, a lad of joy and dreams." Unfolding copper wings, he sprang into the air, and flew into the watching woods.

"Mentors meet me at the Skystone. Sprytes, ye are dismissed." The Dolmen stalked off.

* * * * *

Never before had Triasa seen the Dolmen so agitated. It was always so unemotional. No. That wasn't true, she corrected herself. Its emotions were incredibly controlled, enabling it to concentrate with such intensity that it could send an individual or creature reeling from the impact. As it did with magic. The way a dew drop could focus sunlight to burn small holes through a leaf. And if it ever let go that control? She shuddered at the thought.

The Mentors seated themselves in a half-circle before the pacing Dolmen. "Daemiani!" It glared at Triasa. "Twice thy niece has dodged the death they intended her. And why? We have consulted the Scrolls of Atonement, spoken with the Guild Masters. Nothing! Nothing that explains, much the less foretells, these strange happenings."

"Most High." Triasa kept her voice mild. "Thee knows it is not the first time that deaths have occurred from daemiani at the Wraith Rite, although long has it been. We had thought we had found a safe part of the marshlands; who could have known a daemon-wraith claimed it? The Rites open the gateways of life, and we can only hope that the skills the pod learns will preserve them. As they preserved my niece."

"She speaks truly." Toron agreed. "Recall that sad death of Talima at the hands of a shadow wraith, or those that wild creatures have seized on the sojourn to the Well or to tame the beast." His voice deepened with sorrow. "Too often, it seems to me, we lose one of our own—but never more so than this Krisalys. Times are I wonder if the Twins meant the Rites to become as such." Some Mentors gasped at such heresy, but others nodded.

"Thee questions the will of the Twins?"

Toron stared calmly into the Dolmen's angry face. "I do not question. I wonder. Traditions must begin somewhere, and they are then adjusted as time progresses in response to changing reality—or someone's vanity. The reasons are often lost to time. But when they become chiseled in stone, unchanging, nay, unresponsive to the needs of the folk, is it not right to wonder that they may in truth do more damage than good?"

The oak staff whined in the Dolmen's grip, the crackle of latent magic lacing the air with a sour scent. "The Twins' Laws were perfect when created. They preserve us from ourselves. Would thee return to the time of Solon?"

"Never. Yet an age has passed since that time, and much of what the Twins gave us was through the spoken word, not just the Scrolls. And as such, the Laws are always subject to the interpretation of the speaker. Where says it that the sprytes must risk their lives for their wings? Where do the Scrolls even speak of the need for Rites?"

"They do not," Mehrten answered. A Tier Six Skald loremaster, he was well-versed in the Teachings, one of the few permitted to study the Scrolls in their sacred chamber at Revelstoke. "The Rites were created by the second Dolmen. It sought to ensure that all Teachings were consistent by gathering the pod in one place."

"Ah. And given a Dolmen holds its post until death, or its own choice to step down, how long was that from when the Twins bestowed the Scrolls?"

"Our Dolmen is the fifth in line. It has been near a thousand winters," Mehrten said.

"It is not thy place to question the Rites!" The Dolmen struck its staff to ground. "Silence we say!" Seasons of habit subdued Toron's protest. "We shall call upon the Mother for counsel. Join thy energies with ours." The Mentors bowed their heads, palms extended towards the Dolmen, who commenced a sonorous chant, punctuated by curving gestures of its staff towards the sky. After a time it grew silent. They waited.

"The Mother speaks through us. We say that the spryte Danai shall bring change to the folk. We behold shadows gathering about her, the smell of bitter smoke, the sounds of tears. She heralds a curse that must be halted—while we still have the power."

Far off, a magpie gave an angry shriek, splintering the Mentors' mesmerized silence. The Dolmen smiled. "The Mother has spoken."

Ignoring the clutch of terror around her heart, Triasa stood. "Most High, remember that Lunasa intervened and saved her life from the fire daemon. That is not the sign of being cursed, but of honor. I beseech thee to let her continue. Time enough to make judgments as the Rites proceed." Other Mentors spoke out.

"Most High, she is but a spryte."

"Lunasa did save her life. And are not the Mother and Lunasa consorts?"

"She has done no wrong."

The Dolmen seemed taken aback that its pronouncement on Danai was being questioned. Its eyelids drooped in momentary thought, then a thin smile gashed its face. "Very well. We shall acknowledge the voices of the Mentors and see what other troubles Danai brings to us. But remember this. It is our duty to protect the folk at all and any cost. In the end, we have the right to do as we see fit, for the good of the folk, always with the blessing of Lunasa." It spun about and stalked into the Skystone.

Triasa shuddered. Her eyes met Toron's taut expression. The Dolmen was right. At least in one respect. Something was out of harmony with these Rites. She had a premonition that not only did the Dolmen not understand what it might be, but that whatever it was could be of far greater import than any of them could conceive.

* * * * *

It was the most subdued Mid-Summer's Eve feast Danai had ever attended. The Mentors had reappeared from their meeting at the Skystone and moved about the Dell in small clots, keeping away from the sprytes. Not until late-day did they seem to revive, and then the sprytes were sent hustling to gather fresh foodstuffs for the feast, set up the trestle tables near the Shehn's roots, and arrange the fragrant blossoms they had cut and hauled into the semblance of a circle. As Lunasa rose above the oak's branches, the Dolmen had joined them; its presence did not serve to enliven things. While the sprytes enjoyed a chance to indulge in gold-envine, sweet cakes, and honeycomb—something most had not had in nearly three lumnas—conversation lulled. There was no music, no dancing, no tale-telling, and certainly no couples weaving unsteadily into the woods.

At the conclusion of the meal, the Dolmen stood up, motioning for silence. "Tomorrow is the Rite of the Winged. Ye will be sent out in pairs, each accompanied by a Mentor. Ye are to each find a winged creature—it must be of the Shribizik folk, the many-legged ones. Capture and ride it until signaled by the Mentor that ye have fulfilled the Rite."

"Where in the name of the Blessed One do they come up with these Rites?" groused Elanoria as they settled in for the night. "And just how do you convince a dragonfly or flutterby to just land, and let me ride you, thank you kindly my lord or lady."

"No dragonflies for me, thanks," yawned Aaron. "They'll toss you off in a moment. All those bends and kinks in their bodies, they buck, or have a nasty habit of stopping dead, and you go right over their heads. Good thing they tend to fly low, so it's not too far to fall. Me, I'll stick with a flutterby, dumbledore or another of the fuzzy ones."

"Dumbledores have stingers," objected Damon.

"So do yellow-banded buzzers," Joson added. "You really want to avoid those manylegs. They can bend themselves nearly in half, and will try and stick you in the leg. If you don't get a Healer's help, it can make you pretty sick."

"I think I'll try for a woodfly," Rhytha remarked. "They're fast, but you can coax them with sweets. I saved a bit of honeycomb after the Dolmen told us about the Rite."

"Smart girl. Hide it from Joson," Aaron suggested, poking his podmate's waistline.

"Ugh! I can't imagine riding a woodfly." Elanoria grimaced at the thought. "They dive around looking for things to eat—we won't discuss what—and only after they're full do they slow down. And they're so hairy!"

"What about you Danai?" Aaron smiled at her.

"Haven't a clue," she yawned hugely, her head pillowed on an unopened birch catkin. "I'll just see what flaps up. Catch and ride a manyleg. You're right Ela—how did they come up with these Rites?"

* * * * *

Dawnshine was cool and overcast. Heavy clouds were hurrying towards the west, their bellies gorged with rain. "Good weather for hunting manylegs," Aaron observed as the group headed for the Mentors' Circle. "They don't fly about as much in this—wet wings and all that."

To Danai's unspoken delight, she was paired with Aaron. Mentor Salomai escorted them inside the woods, then halted. Pushing back her cowl, she shook free curly red hair that contrasted sharply with taupe skin and yellow eyes. "Where do you wish to go?"

Danai was taken aback. She had assumed the Mentor would take them to where ever, and they would proceed with the Rite. She could already imagine Elanoria's reaction—"Oh, sure, now I have to find one of these hairy things too?"

"Let's go to Shallyr Mere," Aaron proposed. "It's not too far from here, and there are a lot of flowers and damp spots that attract manylegs. Soft places to fall off too." Salomai stifled a smile, although she could not hide the twinkle in her eyes, and gave a quick nod of approval.

Aaron leading, they tramped along the Trykle's bank. At mid-day, they stopped for a bite, nibbling on fresh deep red elderberries, and cooled their feet in the slow-moving waters. "Look!" Aaron pointed at the base of a small stone protruding from the creek. "Feyree dust. Must have washed down when we took our bath way back when."

"Fool's gold." Salomai chuckled. "There are many who think it valuable. The crows like it for their nests. I've seen some rookeries where the highest ranking crow is the one with the most dust in his nest. If ever you want to earn a crow's friendship, offer to line its nest with Feyree dust." She rose. "Come, let us off. Shallyr Mere is not far."

They emerged from the forest at the top of a small hill that overlooked a clearing. At the center lay a shallow pond. Bronze bulrushes spiked its grassy shoreline, motionless in the humid air. Pale cream water lilies crouched on their dark green pads, golden centers glowing despite the lack of sunlight. A buzzerbug whined somewhere in a tree across the mere, and the air vibrated with the flash of wings and buzz of flying manylegs.

"Look at the size of that one!" Aaron leaned into Danai and pointed. Easily twice as long as a Feyree, a crimson dragonfly with iridescent blue wings flickered over the green-black water. Behind it followed a woodfly, intent on something in the air ahead. A sudden "cloop" and it was gone.

"Oh fish feathers!" Aaron pointed at a lily pad. "I forgot about the frogs and toads at this time of year. I've been hunting here with some of the other fellows, but it's in the spring when most of them are just small wiggles in the water. We'll have to be extra careful. Stay away from the lilies. And watch for eyes."

"Ugh. Wonderful. Frog food. Just what I've always wanted to be." Danai forced herself to smile. The mere reminded her of the marsh on a very small scale, and she wondered if any wraiths dwelt there. Her attention was diverted by a large purple flutterby, gold speckles dusting its black-edged wings. It was perched on a tall spire of indigo lupine, nursing the slender long-necked flowers rich with nectar. Occasionally it fanned its wings to feel the air. "I'd like to try for that one. I guess I'll need a binding of some sort." She glanced about. Several clumps of wiry dark green reekgrass caught her attention. Unsheathing her dirq, she walked over and hacked free a fibrous stalk.

"Phew!" Aaron backed away. "Couldn't you have picked something that smelled better? At least stand down wind! What are you going to do? Knock it out with the stink?"

"Maybe I am," Danai replied primly, studying the lay of the land about the flutterby, who obligingly remained in place, crawling from blossom to blossom. The surrounding paler grasses contrasted starkly against the lupine's bushy dark green. A small breeze ruffled their hair.

Salomai sniffed the air. "Rain is not far off."

"May we work together, or must we do it alone?" Danai asked.

"Aaron may serve as protector, but you must do the catching and riding. He may not assist in any way."

"I like the idea of catching and riding," Aaron grinned, once they were out of earshot.

"Shhh, the flutterby may hear us."

They slipped quietly through the grass stem tunnels, the moist air pungent with rotting plants, the shifting green light making them feel as if they were under water. Ahead, the bulge of the lupine bush loomed like a solid shadow. They edged closer, peering up through the twitching blades of grass—the wind was puffing more often. The flutterby still suckled. "I'm going to climb up with the breeze," Danai murmured. Aaron nodded.

She eased among the wide leaves, waiting for the next gust. After a few moments, she heard a tell-tale rustle begin at the far end of the clearing, the trees sighing as the wind stroked their leaves. When the grasses began to rustle several feylengths away, she gathered herself, then climbed quickly as the plant began to rock, until she was lodged on a stem just above the flutterby. The swell of purple-blue blossoms not only hid her, but provided a welcome sweetness after the fustiness below.

At the next wind gust, she eased out along the leaf stem, and studied the flutterby. I don't want to hurt its wings when I land on it; that would be cruel. But how do I get it to stay put a few moments? She noticed it was leaning forward, wings spanned for balance, cleaning its soft black feelers free of pollen with its forelegs. It obviously didn't want anything stuck to the fine fuzz, she realized. Not anything. She smiled.

Concentrating, she sighed the spell into the next gust. Then, after the breeze passed, she slowly trickled the silver Feyree dust from her fingers, watching it tangle in the flutterby's feelers. It began to clean. She released yet more, directing the particles onto its head and back. The cleaning became more intense. Holding the reekgrass in one hand, she jumped.

Landing with a soft thump, she slid slightly off to one side. The flutterby reared, it wings clouting her on both sides of her head, but pushing her firmly onto its back. She slid the reekgrass around its neck, then dropped it, worried it would cut into the creature's neck. She wrapped her arms around instead. With a shrill whine, it hurtled off the flower, blown upwards by the strengthening breeze.

She gripped with her knees, afraid to brace her feet lest she damage the delicate wings. The flutterby rode the tousled air currents to the treetops, darting left and right as it tried to shed the clinging spryte. Then it dove for the mere, the wind of its descent pushing against Danai so hard she was nearly shoved off over its rump. It veered among the catkins, bucking, then dropped near the mere's edge, just above a large cluster of lily pads. I've been on long enough, Danai decided as her head snapped back after another toss. Her knees ached from gripping the fuzzy body, her arms felt overstretched from clutching on. She let go.

She twisted about in an attempt to land feet first. Grass rushed by her face, snatching her tunic up above her head. With a soft jolt, she landed knee deep in smelly mud. After tugging her tunic back into decency, she stared about. A large bulbous toad sat hunched among the roots perhaps five fey lengths before her.

* * * * *

Chapter Twelve

Danai knew it had seen her, but it seemed indifferent. I hope it's eaten already, she thought, as she wrestled with her right leg, finally pulling it free of the clinging mud. The toad's eyelids rose half way. She hauled on her other leg; her foot felt caught beneath some root. She kept glancing at the toad. There, her foot was free!

The toad's tongue lashed out, a blur of sickly pink that parted the air with a soft swoosh, and wrapped around her right leg. She fell back as the toad began to pull, dragging her towards its gaping mouth. Screaming, she clutched at passing roots with desperate effort. But the tongue was winning, the inexorable pull breaking her grip. Clawing at the mud, her raking fingers felt the coarse bark of a broken twig. She seized it, then rolled over, twisting the tongue upon itself.

Above her, the cavernous mouth loomed. The toad panted with eagerness, the sour stench stifling her. Its cold slimy lip pressed against her foot. Jerking into a sitting position, she plunged the jagged end of the stick past the tongue, deep into the creature's throat. The jaws clapped shut about the stick and her foot, then jerked open as the toad convulsed, choking. The tongue released her, then slapped about the ground like some headless snake, roiling and coiling, gathering dirt and debris. Danai scrambled away.

"In the name of Lunasa!" bellowed Aaron, bursting out from behind the toad with Salomai a half step behind. He was armed with a long stick. The Mentor had her dirq drawn. The toad in its agony took no notice. Aaron raised the stick over his head, then hesitated as he saw Danai, mud-streaked and kneeling against a bulrush stalk among the watery shadows. Salomai stepped past him, glanced at the dying toad dispassionately, then drove her dirq into the soft spot at the base of its skull. It jerked, then lay still. Above them the first patter of raindrops brushed the grasses.

Danai watched them approach through a spark-shot black haze. Her stomach heaved. She closed her eyes. Her leg was scraped raw by the sticky tongue, tender even to the air's touch. As if from far away, she heard the rain. A fat drop fell onto her head, deluging her in a shower of cool water. She gasped, vision clearing.

"Danai? Danai!" Aaron was next to her, his arm about her shoulders, helping her to stand. Salomai hurried towards them.

"We must leave this area with all speed," she urged. "That is not the only toad hereabouts, and its death throws were surely audible to others. Can you walk? Good. Let us go."

Limping along, leaning on Aaron for support, Danai felt the ground beneath change from mud to dirt, and they soon emerged into the clearing. Rain splattered down. In the distance, thunder grumbled. Salomai lead them under a protecting thicket of ferns, the light green fronds glowing weirdly in the storm's shadowy twilight. Before them, Shallyr Mere became raindrop-pocked. The lilies had furled, their broad pads sinking just below the surface.

Salomai inspected Danai's leg which glared an angry scarlet. "That toad got some good of you." She reached into her rucksack to extract a woven pouch. "Took off several layers of skin. We've got to prevent any infection from forming here. Toad spit is only good for toads." She sprinkled marigold powder over the leg, and Danai felt a soothing relief as the burning lessened. Salomai glanced over at Aaron. "What about your Rite? It must be completed. What do you wish to do?"

"Danai is all right?"

Salomai looked with some surprise at the urgency in his voice. Her eyes softened as she saw how the young spryte gazed upon the maid. So, she thought. "Yes. Slightly damaged, but otherwise all right. Would you agree Danai?"

She nodded, finally grasping that she had passed another Rite.

Aaron released a pent-up whoosh of breath, regarded her a moment longer, then turned to study the mere through the steady waterfall of rain. "I should be able to catch something close to the ground right now. They don't like to fly in this at all. Only when startled."

"Trust me." Danai's tone was pardonably sharp. "They will fly, rain or no rain, when you land on their back. I'm not sure what hurts more—my leg or my neck."

Aaron continued to scan the shoreline, a slow smile curving his lips. "There. See? A dumbledore. There, by the yellow loosestrife. It's just under the petals, flicking off the drops. It's near enough that you can both keep an eye on me—just in case I run into some ugly runt of a toad." He grinned at Danai's glare, then slipped out into the rain, soon to be lost in the tossing grasses.

The steady thrum of rain muted all sound. Aaron smiled. I could easily run up behind the dumbledore, and he probably wouldn't hear me. The bright yellow flowers served as an easy guide through the grass, and he swung about in a wide arc until down wind from the manyleg, then crept up behind. The rain increased, but the fading thunder told him the storm was passing on. He started to climb. The stem was slipperier than expected, but the wide leaves provided secure hand and footholds. He got into position. Beneath, the dumble-dore sat grooming its feelers, facing into the wind for quick liftoff. Its furry golden back, dappled by pats of rain, was directly under-neath. He leaped.

For a moment the dumbledore sat still. Then, with a vicious buzz, it soared into the air. The sodden wind seized them, whirling them about like leaves. Frantically fanning its wings, the dumbledore struggled for stability, flipped over, tumbled down and recovered for a moment, before being batted into a new direction by a fresh gust. Aaron clung to the wing roots, feeling their furious flapping. Sky, shore, water flashed by in one mad-colored blur.

The flapping grew slower, the dumbledore's angry buzz changing to a shrill whine. Aaron realized the rain was soaking through its delicate wings and that their combined weight was insupportable. "Take us down," he shouted near its head. "I'll jump off, I promise."

Folding its wings, they plummeted towards the mere. The muddy surface hurtled towards them. "Here goes!" Aaron yelled. Releasing his grip, he somersaulted off the dumbledore's back. The brown waters splashed around him, and closed overhead.

"Aaron!" Danai pushed to her feet, trying to hobble down the small slope towards the mere. Salomai seized her arm. "A moment will make no difference in the outcome," she said.

"He could drown," Danai shot back.

"If he is to die, he will be dead before you can get there," Salomai answered, her eyes never leaving the splash point.

"He can't die. I love him." She gave a throaty sob, the twisting pain in her heart erasing the throbbing of her body.

"He hasn't. Look."

A golden head popped out of the water. With a strong stroke, Aaron swam to the mere's edge, clambered out, and jogged towards them.

"Action for action's sake is not always the best choice," Salomai remarked. "If you cannot change the outcome, it is often better to wait and see where you can make a difference, rather than expend your energy in a direction where it will be of no use."

"That was fun! Did I pass?" Aaron scampered out of the grass, and stood hopefully in front of Salomai. Danai had to resist the urge to hug and kiss him in front of the Mentor. He'd been nearly killed, yet here he stood grinning like an absolute fool! Later, she decided.

"Yes. But a question. I saw you speaking to the manyleg. Can you speak with such?"

Aaron looked uncomfortable. "I guess. Some of the fellows have come out here to ride the manylegs—kind of a dare, you know. I was trying to stay on a dragonfly one time, and it was just diving and bucking so wildly I was afraid it would snap in two. So I shouted near its head to take me down and it did. Same thing worked on a woodfly and flutterby, so while I can't understand them, they seem to understand me."

Salomai chuckled. "Has no one ever told you the manylegs' legend about us?"

Danai raised an eyebrow. "But you said we can't understand them."

"You may not," Salomai corrected her, "but there are others who can. And the manylegs' queen has made it her business to learn the common tongue."

"So about this legend?" Aaron sat down. "Since it's still raining and all."

"Manylegs insist they are the eldest of all the Mother's folk—they call her Mzangya—created at dawn on the very first of all days. Brought into being from the first rays of sun and the first breeze, they say Mzangya gathered dewdrops of all sizes and cast them about her head. The sun filled each drop with one or more different colors, and wings appeared wherever the breeze stroked their sides. They flew about Mzangya's head like a dancing crown of rainbows, and so delighted her with their colors that she next created flowers to bring yet more color to the realm—and so that there would be food for manylegs."

"I thought the dwarves were the first folk," Danai said, remembering Tlarg's tale.

"I thought it was the Ael," Aaron added.

Salomai studied the falling rain a moment before answering. "Who is to say what truly occurred on that day the Mother gave birth to Lampion? Mayhap all things came forth together, so that all things were created equal, and none could claim precedence. The Mother loves all her folk, but like younglings, perhaps we all want to be the one she loves most."

The rain was easing, the drumming changing back to a delicate patter on the leaves. Salomai stood, stretched, and sniffed the air. "The winds are coming to clear this storm. It is time we returned. Did you know that the manylegs actually claim kinship to the Feyree?" She laughed at their startled looks, leading the way back towards the Dell. "According to another of their legends, there was a day when the Mother had come to the lower hills escorted, of course, by a guard of manylegs. She paused to rest by a lake, the birds gathering to sing their sweetest melodies for her. She passed into dreaming, and from her dreams into being walked forth the Ael and the dwarves.

"The manylegs and birds delighted in these newest creatures and praised the Mother for her art. But amid all the good cheer, a dragonfly approached, bowed and asked a boon. "Lady most high, what about a folk with wings?" And the Mother laughed with delight at the idea, then tapped the dragonfly on its brow, and before all, he changed into the first Feyree. And to this day, our wings appear like those of the dragonfly clan, and like them, we are born with only wing bumps."

"Do you believe that?" Aaron asked. He kept trying to catch Danai's hand, but she shook her head, pointing at the Mentor's back.

"It is not a case of whether I believe or disbelieve." Salomai sidestepped a pinecone. The Trykle gurgled beside them, swollen by rain. "I respect their legends, but prefer those of our folk. Judging other's beliefs is a dangerous habit."

"Are you a Weathercaster?" Danai asked. Bits of blue sky were peering among the branches. Her leg felt better.

"Yes, it is my Calling, but not all that I do."

"Can a Feyree have more than one Calling? Those in my vale don't."

"Yes and no. In the Dream Council, a Rite forthcoming, you will discover that to which you are best suited. We all have talents, though we at first do not always realize it. But some talents, such as weathercasting, while important, are not enough to serve the folk throughout the day. So we choose other crafts in which we have some interest or skill, and while it may not be given to us to rise beyond the Second or Third Tier of a Crafthall, we are still busy."

"You're from Rymple Dell, aren't you?" Salomai nodded to Aaron's question. "What else do you do?"

"I am a Gatherer." She smiled, more to herself. "I cannot bear being inside day after day. I crave the smell and feel of this lovely realm—perhaps because of my weather talent—and so gathering allows me to roam the forest and meadows seeking the harvest that tides us through the winter. Ah, look. There are others ahead. The Dell is near to us."

"Mentor Salomai, is it all right if Danai and I stop here and rinse off? That wasn't exactly clean water I fell into, and I stink of pond scum."

Salomai looked at Aaron for a long moment before nodding. "Take not overlong. Just before evenmeal, the Mentors are to announce the results of this Rite." She strode off.

As soon as she was out of sight, Aaron gave a cursory glance about before grabbing Danai in a big hug. She laughed, the pain in her leg forgotten. "Feel like skipping evenmeal?" His voice was husky with eagerness.

"I would if we could. But you heard Salomai. Being late would get us in trouble and be awkward to explain, don't you think? But a dip would feel wonderful."

Aaron released her with a mock scowl creasing his face. "I don't know if I can wait the entire Rites. They sure make it hard on a fellow. I hope we get sent off on another journey." She laughed, caught his hand, and together they dove into the water.

* * * * *

After evenmeal, Danai's group, of which Aaron had become a permanent member, lay sprawled about recounting their manylegs rides. Rhytha's woodfly had tossed her into a bramble bush; she twitched as she spoke, the small punctures stinging despite the Healers' soothing salve. Damon had jumped a dragonfly only to discover he was interrupting a mating dance, and had to hurriedly dismount as the disgruntled male attacked him. Pook and Elanoria's dumbledore rides proved relatively uneventful, if, as Ela duly noted, being dumped off in a mud puddle didn't matter. Joson had trouble finding a manylegs that would support his weight, but had finally found an unusually large dragonfly.

After a lull in the conversation, Pook sat up and glanced about. "Rumor has it that tomorrow's Rite is going to be dangerous." He kept his voice low, keenly aware of the nearby Mentors.

"What?" Startled out of calmness, the sprytes' voices were loud.

"Shhhh! Oh, frog feathers, you've attracted the Mentors' notice. Now I'm going to have to wait until they lose interest." He lay back, returning to his gaze to the star-strewn skies. Fuming, his friends settled, mentally reminding themselves that this was Pook's favorite ploy, and they had once again played into his hands. But they were glad his strange mood seemed to have dissipated, passing like a cloud's shadow.

When the sky was more stars than darkness, Pook continued. "Does anyone know yet what we're supposed to be doing? No, I didn't think so. Well it's a search for Dryads and Nyads." He ignored Elanoria's gasp. "It turns out they're actually ancient Feyree who for some reason chose to become part of trees or water after some great war, but I don't know which one."

"I think I do." At their surprised looks, Danai reminded them of the Hunted Rite's tale of Solon. Their eyes, glowing softly like a necklace of many-colored gems, flickered with dismay.

"I'd forgotten about that. It's hard to believe our folk would actually...slaughter each other." Damon said the words with difficulty. He abhorred violence, and was in fact the only spryte who had successfully passed the entire Hunted Rite.

Pook pulled their discussion back to the more immediate problem. "From what I've heard, we're going out in groups again, and a Mentor will escort us to meet the Hidden Ones."

"How did you manage to find this all out, Pook?" Elanoria smiled at him from under lowered lashes.

Joson frowned. "Yes, how?"

"Oh, just in the right place at the right time, you know." Pook brushed aside the question.

"And why disturb the Hidden Ones?" Joson's stomach clenched. He was suddenly tired of the Rites. "Our Skalds have spoken of them—they're known to be unpredictable, even violent."

"But terribly wise," added Danai. "At least that's what Triasa told me. She gave the same cautions as you did Joson, but also said their wisdom comes from being rooted in the ancient ways. At some point they left their dells, and are closer to the Mother and the wood folk than Feyree. Perhaps the Rite is a chance to hear their wisdom?"

Elanoria shook her head. "More likely to get our wits scared out of us yet again. I, for one, will never be going back to the Great Bog."

"Never is a long time, Ela," Pook said. "Maybe Danai's onto something. We are learning a lot. We've been introduced—not always by choice—to all sorts of creatures and folk that we pretty much thought were bower-tales. It's a big place out there." He sighed. "Sometimes I wonder that if I had known what the Rites would entail, would I have left the Circle when the Dolmen gave us the chance? And all for wings that it could probably give us without any of this risk."

There was an uncomfortable silence. Pook had given voice to a thought often uppermost in their minds. And yet there was something almost seductive about learning all these forbidden things—forbidden to sprytes anyway—that kept them going despite the worst moments.

"Oh, bother," Joson said. "What will be will be. We'll find out tomorrow." He rolled over onto his side, crooked his arm beneath his head, and gave a deliberate snore. The tension broke, and with a smattering of chuckles, his friends settled for rest.

* * * * *

The trail to Silver Lake seemed barred with gnarled roots and looming stones. Not a trail that invited visitors, Danai thought, as her group followed Mentor Toron's tall figure. The nine sprytes were strung out, Danai in the middle along with Pook. In an effort to calm her nerves, she thought back on the Dolmen's instructions at mornmeal.

"Be cautious. Be courteous. Obey to the highest degree the Orders of thy Mentor. These are our kinfolk, but they are so long-lived, that in truth it is only we who claim the relationship." It paused, and Danai would have sworn that she saw a trace of emotion—worry?—in its eyes as it glared at Aaron, Ujerion and Dlargon, who gazed innocently back. "We say again. Obey all and any Orders. No room for foolishness or game-playing is there in this Rite."

She smiled at the memory of Aaron's jaunty salute as his group headed north, a warm feeling replacing her nervousness. To be his Chosen One...a trailing root grabbed her foot, and she was yanked back into the now. They were heading west up into the Wynndowns. As the sun stood overhead, the group crested a slope, and Toron halted and seemed to be inspecting the terrain.

Before them towered a host of gray-trunked aspens, their leaves twitching silver even on this windless day. Some distance beyond, Danai saw a ripple of what she thought was water, but it had an unnatural radiance, as if it had captured Lunasa's rays. She also noticed a lack of bird chatter. Earlier they had been chirping and darting about everywhere. She tensed; the waiting silence was too much like storm-quiet.

Toron spoke, his deep voice pitched just above a whisper. "Through these trees you can glimpse Silver Lake. The nyad Lady Argentyne dwells within. She tolerates no discourtesy, and at times will not even tolerate our presence. Yet if the mood suits her, she will on occasion appear to share a tale. Be silent unless spoken to. If that happens, before you reply, bow first. Address her as 'my Lady Argentyne.' And make no abrupt motions or loud sounds. Understood?"

Danai waved her hand to catch Toron's attention. "Mentor Toron, is it possible the Lady will refuse to show herself? If so, what do you wish us to do?"

"A good question. It can and has happened. I will signal you by bowing towards the lake. Do likewise, then follow me. But do not speak until I have given permission. That is an Order." His tone brooked no further questions.

The aspens seemed to oversee their passage. Danai had the odd sensation she could feel their energy waves slipping past her towards the lake, as if conveying a message. The silence deepened. They emerged on a sandy shore of a lake nestled against a brilliant white cliff flanked by outcroppings of dark gray stone. The sand itself was a-glitter with silvery light, the sun's rays leaping and flashing in so many directions it was near-blinding. Vibrant purple foxglove and pink willow herb girdled the shore's edge. The lake seemed to be waiting for them to make the first move.

"My Lady Argentyne," Toron called, his voice deep with respect. "I am Mentor Toron of Goldyn Vale. I bring with me nine sprytes who seek their wings. My Lady, would you grace us with your presence and your counsel?"

A breeze ruffled the waters, pushing a lap of wavelets against the shore. They waited. The shadows lengthened. Danai wondered why Toron did not call again, expecting him to bow at any moment. A soft hiss from Pook jerked her eyes towards the lake.

The breeze coiled itself into a swirling pillar, tugging the waters upward. They coalesced into a wavering shape of silver so bright it bordered on white. A face materialized, cowled with a mantle of darker silver. The piercing silver eyes slid across the sprytes' open-mouthed faces to settle on Toron. Slowly, escorted by the whirlwind, the figure approached.

A bow-wave of intense emotions engulfed them, and Danai found herself wanting to scurry away, her mind reeling from over-stimulation of the senses. Every bit of her body was tingling as if brushed by rough cloth. She could hear the crack-pzing of sun-heated stone far across the lake through the wind's roar, struggled to breathe while scenting an unknown sweetness. She glanced at Toron, wishing they could flee. He inclined his dark head and waited for the nyad to make landfall.

The windswirl split open and the nyad stepped forth. Her long robe shushed across the sand as she drew near, still emitting bursts of disturbing energy. She pushed back her cowl, and a cascade of translucent hair tumbled free to frame an ageless face. It was not a face of beauty, yet a feeling of peace seemed to permeate her countenance with an indescribable radiance.

"Mentor Toron." The lady's voice vibrated the air with the clear tone of a well-plucked harp string.

"My Lady Argentyne." He bowed deeply. The sprytes followed. The nyad reached out and gently stroked Toron's shoulder, a soft smile gracing her lips.

He stiffened. Their eyes locked. Then he covered her hand with his. A wordless communion transpired, and Danai saw his blue eyes flicker silver. Nodding, the nyad dropped her hand, then turned to peruse the sprytes. After a few moments, she again nodded. "Be seated."

With one accord, they knelt, staring at her with awe. "Toron informs me that ye are on the Rite of Search, and that perhaps my knowledge may be of use. Shall I tell a tale?" She smiled at their eager faces, and with a fluid motion, settled on the sand before them. "It shall be a new tale, one not even Toron has heard, though many from me has he listened to across the seasons." She glanced at the handsome Guardian, a small smile again twitching her lips.

"In times long-gone, when all were one, we lived in peace with ourselves and our realm. Dancing and laughter ruled the dells that nestled within a day's flight of each other, not yet scattered across the lands. The gatherings and feast days were places to meet, exchange tales and gossip, and perhaps even couple. On occasion a maid and lad would mate for life, and it was announced at Mid-Summer's Eve, so that all might share in the joy of such a Union. Know you that in those bygone days, there were no such things as Rites. A young spryte simply had their wings released when the time was ripe."

Pook brushed Danai's foot with his toe.

"But as it happens, because things were easy, and there were no great challenges, a restlessness began to gnaw at some of the younger fey folk. Restlessness is the messenger of trouble, and like a worm, trouble began to gnaw into the peace. Trouble found a leader in a handsome Feyree named Solon. Bright as gold was he, and young maids would daydream of a Union. But for Solon, maids served one purpose, a release of physical needs. He regarded them as inferior and excluded them from his councils. Perhaps, had some been included, it would not have happened.

"When the Lady Eliasa and Lord Lothonio were discovered murdered, their bodies sprawled in their private chambers at Revelstoke, panic ramped through the dells. Such a thing had never happened. And into that morass of confusion stepped Solon, flanked by an army of aye-sayers who clamored for his election, and awarded him rulership before the folk grasped what had occurred. And because he was so handsome, so well-spoken, and so full of promises, and had already been made ruler, the folk accepted his counsel to forsake finding the murderer. After all, dead was dead, correct?

"They sought to return to the patterns of their existence, but a stain seemed to have spread across their lives, a stain that dancing and reveling, eating and coupling could not erase. And that stain was Solon.

"For he was not content to advise, but instead sought to order, to direct, and finally, to control. It was as if a series of small fires had been set that could not be put out—nobody thought to try—and by the time they realized what they had done, it had grown to an inferno, incinerating all it touched. Only then did the folk finally awake to the foul toad they had permitted to nest, and they began to fight back.

"Somehow, somewhere, Solon had discovered the Forbidden Magics. Likely a renegade loremaster revealed their existence. It is told that he consulted with the time daemiani of Horloje to whom he promised the right to reside in Lampion should they help him force the folk to submit. The Mother knows that daemiani create chaos when completely freed. But magic is power, and Solon was drunk with power. He would do anything, sacrifice anyone, just for a quaff of this briny potion. Of course, he taught much of this magic to those folk who supported him, so they could 'subdue the dissidents' as he referred to those who dared to rebel.

"And in turn these 'dissidents' likewise learned many spells from the loremasters who took their cause. They attacked in small bands, never bowering anywhere long, always on the move, always in pursuit of that one goal—to destroy the tyrant who was destroying their beloved realm. Many, many died. Both sides bled almost to the death in the struggle, and I do not know if I would have been here to tell this tale had Solon not made a simple error.

"The time daemiani were very clever—as are all their kind. They are the few among the daemiani who can actually work with magic, and much did they teach Solon of their magics. But perhaps so familiar were they with their spells that they forgot to tell him there were those that could not be used on one's self—only on others—without sacrificing all.

"During the Battle of Sagad, Solon made his mistake. His forces, and those of the rebels, battled on the once-sacred plain. Blood flowed like mead, pouring into the mouths of those already dead that lay strewn about the crushed grasses, some alone, others heaped like crumpled leaves. The air crackled with skin-crisping spells, ones that blinded, others that tore bodies to pieces. Dirqs slashed, spears impaled. Maids, lads, even younglings killed each other.

"The struggle wrinkled back and forth across the storm-cloud-shrouded battle plain, and Solon, never patient, grew angry at the unexpected strength of his enemies, as he saw victory slipping from his grasp. He had been taught a hideous spell by the time daemiani, a spell of transformation, one that could call forth the daemon that lives deep within any Feyree, although there was no predicting what that daemon would be. It was all according to that Feyree's nature. All that was known was it would be violent.

"Daemiani can be killed. Perhaps Solon forgot that, so swollen with himself had he become. He wove a krisalys of transformation about himself. Like a whirlwind of red lightstrikes, it spun about, spitting sparks and flames. Then it peeled apart.

"Solon erupted forth as a fire daemon. Black smudges were his eyes and mouth. With a scalding laugh, he blazed a path through the warriors, burning friends and foes alike. The horror he had become inhaled the protesting wind and grew, scarlet flames reflecting off the swollen bellies of the lowering clouds. Reaching down to grasp and kill, he delighted in the agonized screams as he seared his victims. None would he release until they burned into a gray ash that he flung skywards with maddened laughter. Even those untouched nearby would collapse, clawing at their throats as Solon's burning body consumed all air.

"But it was when the despairing wail of a mother who had seen her spryte seized and torched rent the air that the Mother and Lunasa finally interceded. A scarlet firestar flashed across the sky, passing beyond the mountains to explode in a column of fire. A many-pronged lightstrike plunged into the ground before the Solon-daemon, driving him back a pace. A second and third strike followed, forcing him away from the watching warriors. And then, with the roar of a thousand floods, the rains poured fourth, gushing in torrents upon Solon, inundating his fires, smothering him, drowning him, collapsing him, until there remained a black twitching shell hunched over the scabbed earth.

"And still the rain fell, pounding him until he shattered into black ash. The winds whipped about, scattering the ash, tearing it into fragments. Even the ash was evil, and those upon whom it fell carried a darkness in their hearts for the remainder of their lives.

"The folk slunk from the withered plain, exhausted, empty. With Solon's death all direction was lost. He was their reason for being, be it as follower or rebel, and with his destruction, they were as loose leaves in an autumn storm. Only one Feyree remained, she whose young son had died at Solon's hand. She knelt and wept, praying for the shattered remains of the folk that lay tossed about and for the son lost to her. And the clouds parted to reveal Lunasa, who took pity on her grief for some unknown reason, when so many also grieved. He shrouded her in silvery light, filling her with his radiance until her tears ceased. And it was she who would become mother of the Twins." Lady Argentyne folded her hands in her lap, eyes misty with memories.

The sprytes blinked away tears, the reek of burning flesh and sodden ash still in their noses, the bitter sobs echoing inside their skulls. They felt as if they had witnessed the battle rather than simply heard a tale. Danai raised her hand. Lady Argentyne gazed at her for a measured moment. "Yes?"

Trembling at her own temerity, Danai arose, stiff with cramp, and attempted a bow. "My Lady Argentyne, are you the Blessed One?" She heard the sharp intakes of breath about her, saw Toron's face go sickly green.

Lady Argentyne rose gracefully, her face expressionless, one finger beckoning. Danai took a quick breath to stiffen her spine and approached the nyad. The Lady reached out and placed both hands on the spryte's shoulders.

Danai jolted as a violent shock wracked her body. She thought she heard Toron's shout. Then lake, trees, even the nyad vanished into a spill of memories flooding her mind. She was swept back to the plain of Sagad, then to a birthing hut where her body writhed to push forth its burden. And then the soft chirps of newborns caressed her ears, and she brushed back the sweat-soaked hair from her face to gaze upon two babes, silvery like herself. Two babes who would become the Twins, the lawgivers, the peace-makers. She felt her shoulders released, staggered, and she gasped for breath. The vision dissipated.

"Yes," Lady Argentyne said simply. "I am."

All knelt before her in homage. She was more than a Hidden One, an Ancient One. She was the Lady of Peace, whom they called the Blessed One, she who had given the fey folk the means to re-build their realm.

"My Lady Argentyne," whispered Pook. "Why have you shared with us this part of your spirit?"

She pondered his question, studying him all the while. Then she glanced up at the silver shell of eventide mist beginning to gather above the lake, and whispered such that her answer went no further than the edge of the group. "Because what has happened once can happen again."

She stepped to the water's edge where the whirlwind reformed, entered its welcoming embrace, then turned to smile at the sprytes. Her gleaming silver eyes were the last thing they beheld as the lumi-nescent figure dissolved back into a silvery mist and sank into the ruffled waters.

No one spoke on the return trail, still in the thrall of an experi-ence they sensed was of legendary proportions. Toron puzzled at the fact Lady Argentyne had touched Danai—he had never seen her touch anyone besides himself in all the Rites. As they re-entered the Dell, he summoned her to him, and motioned the others past, wait-ing until they were out of earshot.

"Mentor Toron?"

He looked at Danai. Her green eyes seemed to retain some of the nyad's opalescence. Visible on her shoulders in the gloaming were oval marks of palest silver. "What did she show you?"

"Her birthing the Twins," she answered softly, for a moment re-living the agony and ecstasy of the vision.

"Look at your shoulders."

She craned her head, eyes widening as she saw the marks. "But what, why...?"

"For some unknown purpose have you been marked by the Lady." He paused, studying her thoughtfully. "Danai, I now speak to you not as a spryte but a Feyree. Once again, you are touched by an unusual happening. There are signs and wonders in this which none of us can yet interpret. But I tell you that the Dolmen does not like the unexplainable. And he will like this newest incident even less. Be cautious around him. If ever you need aid, I will come at your calling." He reached out to clasp her wrist and, to her surprise, briefly inclined his head. "Now let us go. The others await."

* * * * *

Chapter Thirteen

As they entered the Dell, Danai at once sensed something was terribly wrong. The air seethed with grief. Sprytes and Mentors were gathered in tight clumps. She could hear sobs from some. Pook had waited for her, and together they raced over to their huddled friends.

"It was horrible." Elanoria's sobs nearly choked her.

"What?" Pook grabbed her hand, impatient with fear.

Joson answered slowly, still disbelieving the truth. "Aaron's dead."

Danai knew with a terrible clarity that she would remember the next moments for the rest of her life. The smell of sun-baked earth, the chatter of birds flying home to nest, the gaunt looks on her friends' faces. The sharp painful thump of her heart. "How?"

"Aaron just couldn't obey." Damon pounded his fist on the ground. "Our group went to see Hoarus, an oak dryad. Mentor Illion said he was angry at being awoken, but things would have gone all right had Aaron just followed orders. Maybe he thought that something that old and wrinkled-looking with thin twiggy fingers couldn't be dangerous. We'll never know. So he interrupted the dryad during its tale. And Hoarus gave a furious bellow, leaned down, and grabbed him by the throat, roaring about insolence and invaders and other things I didn't hear because we were all screaming and shouting, and Illion was begging the dryad to release Aaron.

"He wouldn't. He shook and shook him, flinging his body about, ignoring those horrible screams as he throttled the life from him...and then there was this snapping sound. Aaron's neck broke. Only when he went limp did Hoarus toss his body aside like a used rag, and then cursing the whole group, retreated into his oak. Aaron's dead. Just like that."

This isn't happening, Danai thought. Not my Aaron. He was laughing at me just this morn, making faces behind the Mentor's back as the groups formed. Her stomach heaved, and as if from a great distance, she saw the others speaking, but could no longer hear them. Aaron's beloved face flashed before her, and she reached out, begging him to say it was all a dreadful prank. That he was there to hold her, to tell her how much he loved her. That they would soon go for their evening amble as they had so many times before. Her Chosen One. Gone. With a bitter sob, she fainted into Damon's arms.

* * * * *

"Danai? Dearling?" It was not the voice she wanted to hear, and Danai wished she could return to the welcoming black of unconsciousness. A cool cloth, smelling faintly of lavender, was placed upon her brow. She forced her eyes open. Triasa knelt beside her.

"Auntie..." She began to sob, curling up in Triasa's arms, weeping her heart to fragments as she grappled with a pain that ripped at her insides. Triasa held her close, stroking her hair, saying nothing, knowing that words were useless. She had suspected that Danai and

Aaron had grown close over the past lumnas, but now realized it was more than it had appeared.

When the sobs changed to parched hacks, Triasa took the filled mug that Mentor Nacci brought and gave it to Danai. "Sweeting, sip this. It will help. Please."

Force of habit made Danai obey, and the cool liquid slid down her throat into the nauseous knot of her stomach. A faint warmth radiated outwards, and she felt a gentle numbness begin to cloud her thoughts. Her eyes felt cracked and tearless. "Auntie, he was my Chosen One," she sighed. "I loved him." Her eyes closed, and she slumped back against Triasa.

Triasa and Nacci swaddled her in coverlets, pillowing her head on a downy catkin. They were a short distance from the Skystone where the Mentors milled about, waiting. Nacci shook her head. "What a terrible waste. He was from my sister's glen, always getting into trouble. But never anything bad—just an over developed sense of fun. And with a good heart. I remember he often took the small younglings off on short journeys to the falls to teach them how to swim. I shall miss him. I overheard the Dolmen saying there will be no more visits to Hoarus. Is that true?"

"Yes. Much good as that does poor Aaron." Triasa smoothed back the wispy bits of hair from Danai's forehead. "I grieve for her. She has never been close to any lad as she obviously was to Aaron. I wonder if she will request to leave the Rites?"

"Would the Dolmen permit it?"

"Were she and I to petition it, I think it likely. Particularly given its suspicions about her."

Nacci shook her head. "Triasa, I don't think Danai will. For all her tendency to be quieter than many of her podmates, throughout the Rites she has struck me as a strong maiden, one who is gaining ever more confidence in her abilities. My guess is she will swamp herself with training and all we have yet to do. And, speaking as a Healer, it is the best way. Sitting and mourning Aaron, alone in her bower, with all her podmates absent? I would fear for her life."

"She is asleep?"

Nacci and Triasa started, turning around to see the Dolmen just behind them. Triasa wondered how long it had been there.

"Good. Then come to the Skystone. We must converse."

When the Mentors were seated, the Dolmen gestured at Toron. "Speak thy tale to all." There were many open mouths and much shaking of heads when he concluded.

"These Rites become stranger with each passing day," Asagion said. "We have lost three sprytes, another is become a babe, and there are yet four Rites to go, albeit two are not dangerous—usually. Dolmen, what is happening? This is more than a mere unusual set of circumstances."

The Dolmen frowned, shook its head. "A death and a birth. And as Asagion points out, omens not before seen among the Rites. And once again Danai is the focal point. We would consult first with the Mother and Lunasa before we speak further. First, we must address the pod about what has happened. Triasa, we trust thee will care for Danai until she wakes? The others are to come with us."

Like a brown eddy, the Mentors flowed through the weathersign bushes to join the huddled sprytes. Above, the clouds changed from dull gray to raw scarlet as the westering sun dipped underneath, while a breeze moved uncomfortably among the branches. The Dolmen clapped its hands for attention. "Ye will recall we spoke this morn of the dangers of this Rite. Had Aaron heeded our warning, he would be yet among ye. His death comes from his own stupidity."

Joson was glad Danai was not present. He doubted she would have held her tongue at such harsh judgment.

The Dolmen felt the sprytes' burst of hostility at its callous statement, and it continued, "Consider thy own experiences with Lady Argentyne and Trom. Can ye deny that had any of these Hidden Ones chosen to do so, they could have destroyed ye?" It paused to watch the glances being cast back and forth among the sprytes. "They are the Ancient Ones! Ancient in time and wisdom, great in strength. To anger them can be fatal. We warned ye, as we have warned so many other sprytes. Aaron is not the first; hopefully, he will be the last to ignore us. His mourning feast will be on the morrow, before the Rites continue."

"Let us now address what ye may have heard befell Mentor Toron's group, and the past wondrous tale told by the Lady Argentyne. She is the Blessed One, the mother of the Twins!" Despite its rigid countenance, it was apparent that strong emotions were stirring just beneath the surface. "And she marked thy podmate Danai, who is at this moment being tended to by the Healers. We know not why. It may be many lumnas before we do. And therefore ye are to regard them as no more than a birthmark, and treat her no differently than before." With that proclamation, it turned and vanished into the gloaming.

* * * * *

Laying prone inside a pale purple foxglove blossom, Danai watched the pod gather and reform into small groups like a flock of feeding birds as they waited to be summoned to Dream Council. If she chose, from her high vantage point she could see over the weathersign bushes to the Skystone, but she had no desire to do so. She spotted Pook slipping away into the woods, something that seemed to have become a habit of his. Even though well over half a lumna had already passed, she instinctively searched for Aaron. The scene blurred with sudden tears, and she forced her thoughts into a different channel.

Triasa had kept her asleep until the next day, waking her in time for Aaron's mourning feast. At the somber gathering, her podmates had a first chance to see the silver marks which had brightened enough to be visible in daylight. Later she had taken Joson aside and shared her sorrow, craving one trusted friend's compassion, but begging him to tell no one else. They had clung to each other and wept.

She had flung herself into the Healer and Weathercast training with an intensity that Mentors Nacci, Illiai and Triasa understood— and they deliberately used it as a focal point to keep her occupied. She felt deeply drawn to the Healer lore, some of it familiar from her fostering with Triasa. Clawcatsbane made into a poultice helped relieve strains, soothe burns, and ease restlessness. Marigold applied externally would help heal small cuts and open, inflamed wounds. Draohadshood could soothe a scratched eye. Bitterwort relieved the pain of a severe blow to the bones. The more Danai learned, the more she wanted to know, and she prayed that this would be one of her Dream Council Callings.

She found weathercasting intriguing, although it was hard to not look at Mentor Salomai and remember Aaron. She tried instead to focus on Mentor Marcelon who being a Tier Four Weathercaster had more knowledge to impart. The pod learned how to read the varied cloud shapes, how to smell the wind to detect rain, and how heat and cold shifts could be sensed ahead of their arrival.

Marcelon startled them all when he introduced them to using plants and trees as well as wood folk to weathercast. "Ye all know how the Guardians' nightwings start life as a wriggly crawler, then hide in a cocoon. We can tell from the cocoon's thickness what winter will be like," he explained during one teaching. "Have ye noticed that the squirrels and rabbits are hairing up early this summer? It foretells a cold winter, and already our Gatherers are preparing. And our friends the birds serve as an early warning to when spring or winter will arrive."

Her attention was brought back by a Mentor selecting and escorting another spryte back towards the Skystone. Dream Council would take three days. Mentor Mehrten had explained that it must occur during solas, when Lunasa's full face would guard over the Rite.

She lay there, listening as the breeze lisped at her blossom, releasing a cascade of fragrant pollen that engulfed her in sweet scent. Danai studied the creep of the plant's shadow along the grass as the sun rose overhead. Maybe if she closed her eyes, she could escape into a dreamless nap.

Prrrrrt! The unmistakable whir of a hovering Feyree's wings startled her awake, her head knocking down a cloud of pollen. When she finally cleared her eyes and stopped coughing, she beheld Melitsa, uncloaked, peering at her.

"Danai, descend. The Dream Council awaits. I will attend you below." Easing gently out of the blossom to avoid a repeat of the pollen burst, she hopped lightly from blossom to blossom in a downward spiral, then shinnied down the long thick stalk. Melitsa, once again robed, gestured towards the Skystone. As they walked through the grass, Danai felt her stomach twist. *I do not want to see the Dolmen,* she thought. *I do not trust it.* She shuddered at her heresy, knowing that to question what it said or did was wrong. But it did not stop her strong feeling that something was not right.

As they approached the Skystone, she saw it standing uncowled, conversing with Mentor Oyon. Her shoulders began to tingle, a queer ripple like still water disturbed by some unseen creature below the surface. It saw her approaching and gestured at Mentor Toron who advanced to stand on his right. Oyon bowed, and placed something in the grass before them that winked in the sunlight.

"Danai. Thee are greeted. Guided by the wisdom of Lunasa and the Mother shall we help thee to perchance find thy Calling best suited to thy skills. Be seated."

Melitsa guided her to sit before a small knob of white stone upon which sparkled a blue-white crystal chalice overlaid with silver wrought in a cunning design. She gazed down into the dark red liquid. It looked like blood. "Drink," Melitsa ordered.

As if from a distance, she watched both her hands clasp the smooth stem, bring the chalice to her lips. The cloying liquid seeped down her throat, and she had to overcome the desire to gag. Slowly it oozed into her stomach—then exploded in pulses of whirling heat. She blinked. And blinked again.

Night already? Why, she was no longer even in the Dell. Beside her burbled the Trykle. They must have completed the Dream Council, then brought her to the creekside so she could slake her severe thirst. She slurped the cool water from her cupped palm, letting it unseal her gummed lips and rinse the sweet-sour taste from her tongue. A paw appeared in her line of sight on the opposite bank. Before her stood a fox, gazing at her with unwinking eyes, its fur silver in Lunasa's patchy light. It barked twice.

"I speak not thy tongue," Danai apologized. She stood up. "And I guess you don't speak mine," she muttered as the fox barked again, then turned and looked back as if asking she follow. For a moment its eyes seemed silvery too, but she was sure that was just a trick of the light. She hesitated. There was no one about, and if something happened, she could be lost. But there was a note of pleading urgency in the fox's next whine that decided her.

She waded across the creek and noticed a strange pouch bumping against her thigh, lumpy with unknowns. But there was no time to investigate. She trotted just behind the silent creature. In a few moments, they reached a sheltered hollow, scooped out by the creek from under the roots of a long dead pine. Danai heard a soft mumble of yips and whines, and caught a whiff of cub musk.

"I take it thee have a problem with thy little ones?" The fox yapped—Danai thought it sounded like 'yes'—then gently nudged her towards the burrow. "I won't be able to see in there. My eyes are not thine," she protested. "Could thee not bring the little one out here, and I'll try to help?" The fox yapped twice and slipped into the dark shadow.

A ball of soft fuzz perhaps three times her size was tenderly deposited before her. It tried to stand, but whimpered when its right front paw touched the ground. Danai reached out her palm for the nervous cub to sniff while the mother mumbled reassuringly. Then she gently ran her hand over the paw, felt its swelling and heat. "Mother, please tell thy little one that I must look underneath his paw." The fox yipped. The cub gave a little protesting whimper, but extended its leg, turning the paw up for Danai's scrutiny.

The row of small punctures, festered and begrimed, were painful to look at. Danai surmised they came from being nipped by his fellows. The cub looked hopefully at her. "We will take care of thee little one," she said, reaching out to stroke its muzzle. "Mother, I need to clean his paw and make a healing salve. Please stay here."

Hastening to a nearby myrtle bush, she tore off several leaves. Then, kneeling by the stream, she untied the pouch from her belt and reached inside to pull out a handful of small cloth bundles. Each was bound by a twist of braided grass, with a stylized plant or flower painted on the side. "By Lunasa," she breathed. "This is a Healer's pouch. But how did I come by it?" The cub whined softly. She shook her head; no time for such questions now. Searching among the bundles she found white oak bark and lavender powders. She tore a piece from one leaf on which she carefully mixed the powders with drops of water until the paste achieved a smooth consistency. Folding it, she tucked it carefully into her belt, then cupped another leaf to scoop water.

It took three trips before the paw was rinsed clean. "Mother, this salve will help draw out the poison and soothe thy cub's paw. After that, I would like to give him a sleeping draught of redcup such that he will rest and stay off his paw. May I have thy permission?"

The fox's eyes flickered silver. "Yes. It is granted."

Danai blinked. How could she now understand? No matter. Crooning softly, she carefully spread the salve over the entire paw, putting an extra layer over the wounds. Next she wrapped the paw in leaves, using a coil of woodbine from the pouch. "This is to protect his paw and keep the salve on. Tell him not to chew it off—it must stay on for two days." She returned to the creek to replenish the leaf cup, and mixed in the redcup. The cub, not yet weaned, sniffed at the leaf-cup of water. At his mother's yip, he lapped it up, and he soon lay down with a wide yawn. Danai laughed, softly stroking his ear.

While the fox carried the cub back into the den, Danai took the remainder of the white bark and lavender powders, wrapped them in a leaf, and secured it under a large pebble. When the fox returned, she explained. "If the wound is not yet well-scabbed in two day's time, then have the little one wet his paw, and pat it in this until covered. He should not move about much for at least four days. Best if thee carries him when he must go out."

The fox touched her nose to earth. "Thank thee Charmer-Healer. In exchange for thy kind service, I give thee counsel. Heed thy silvered self. Dark are the forces gathering about thy folk. From within shall come their greatest sorrow and their only hope."

Mesmerized by the whirling silver eyes, Danai was unable to reply.

"Heed thy silvered self." The eyes receded into a gathering mist as the stream and fox disappeared.

Danai felt a tap on her shoulder. Toron stood there, uncloaked, jade wings folded behind. He beckoned. They walked down an unfamiliar trail, bubbled with rounded stones. Toron led in silence. Night dissolved to day, but no birdsong greeted the light. Halting, Toron stepped aside, motioning Danai forward. Before her, the trail divided in three.

Each trail looked alike. Dusty, yet untrodden, unpebbled, smoothly vanishing over a small rise ahead, offering no clue as to its destination. Danai advanced a few paces, then knelt down at the center of the trails' juncture. Scooping up a fistful of the right trail's powdery beige soil, she held it to her nose, tasting the scent as Tlarg had taught. Under the smell of dust was a hint of sourness. Her nose crinkling, she tossed it back, wiping her palm on her tunic. The middle trail smelt of sweet decay, old flowers past their prime. The left reeked of new cut wood—and fire. Surprised, she dropped the dust.

Turning about, she beheld not only Toron, but Melitsa, both waiting to escort her—but she sensed they would not provide guidance. She knew she must choose her trail. But where did each one go? If only she could see over the rise, she thought, so she could select the best one. She closed her eyes, inhaled deeply. 'Heed thy silvered self' the fox had counseled. She tried to empty her mind and listen to her heart. Slowly she faced each trail. The right and center ones made her rock slightly backward, signaling unwelcome energy. "I choose the left," she announced, and she stepped forward firmly, causing the dust to spurt up. The other two trails rose with a wail, twisted into a knot, then burst apart in a spurt of silver and purple sparks.

Danai strode forward, assuming the Mentors followed, and she crossed the small hill. Before her surged and billowed an opaque barrier of fog, veined with black and silver. Toron and Melitsa linked their arms in hers. She noticed a tingling in her shoulders as they eased into the roiling fog. The reek of rotting flesh engulfed them, causing her to gasp. Black-thorned plants, the likes of which Danai had never seen clutched at the Mentors' wings, forcing them to release her arms and walk in single file, with Melitsa leading and Danai in the center. Toron stared as Danai's shoulders began to shimmer brightly in the darkening fog.

A wet stale wind buffeted their bodies, nearly shoving them off the trail. Danai heard Melitsa's angry shriek, but could no longer see more than a handspan through the fog. Somebody grabbed her arm, yanking her forward into a stumbling walk. Sure it was Toron, she shouted into the formless dark. "Wait. Melitsa!"

He ignored the cry, hauling her forward. Danai glimpsed a shadow of lightness ahead. It brightened until the Mentor's cloak billowed against the dull grayness. Cloak? The thought vanished as he released her hand and turned about. The wind cast back the cowl. It was the Dolmen.

Danai stared. It has a right to be here, she reminded herself. But the look in the Dolmen's eyes pushed her to retreat several steps.

"Thee!" it spat, pointing directly at her head. "Thee who brings ill forebodings amongst our folk, for whom the daemiani search, who turn the Mentors against us. Thee are the spryte who should die! Clearly the daemiani search for thee as one of their own, thus a daemon thee must be. But what kind? Answer! The Dolmen commands!"

A jolt of pain raked through her skull, and Danai staggered as the Dolmen invaded her mind, savaging her memories. "No!" She flung crossed arms before her face to ward off the mind-rape. Her shoulders ignited into a brilliant blaze of silver light that coursed down her limbs and formed a glowing orb where her wrists crossed, shattering the spell's connection.

Foiled, the Dolmen's motionless face cracked with an earthquake of rage. "Then thee shall die as the wraith intended!" It raised both its arms, fingertips flickering brilliant green, the air reeking with a bitter smell of gathering power. Danai knew to run was useless.

"For the safety of the folk!" Shouting, Triasa erupted out of the fog behind the Dolmen, slamming into its back with such force it sent them both sprawling. A blazing arc warped from its hands, disintegrating a thorn bush into black dust.

The late-day sun momentarily blinded Danai. She lurched up from where she lay. Beside her sprawled the prostrate Dolmen. Triasa was getting to her knees, aided by Toron and Melitsa. About them clustered the other Mentors, their voices a confusing babble.

Oyon and Conya knelt to assist to the Dolmen who rose sluggishly. "What means this outrage?" it hissed.

"I was about to ask you the same thing." Triasa enunciated each word to make sure every Mentor heard, dispensing with the formal language of respect. "What were you doing in my niece's dream?"

"It is our right. We are the Dolmen!"

"It is not your right to mind-tamper!"

Shocked silence suffocated the Mentors.

"Do you accuse us?"

Triasa did not hesitate. She crossed her arms, eyes narrow with barely contained fury. "I do."

"And I." Toron advanced to Triasa's side. "At the Trial of the Three Paths, when Danai sought to see where her energies might take her to determine her Calling among the folk, you cast a fog that blotted all sight."

The Dolmen's laugh, long unused, rasped out. "We cast no fog. It was the essence of her evil, drawn forth by the revealing power of the Dream Rite. There was no sight for her, for she can have no future among the folk. Lunasa showed the truth. Saw ye not the colors of black, red and silver? The colors of the daemiani, the forbidden ones."

"Silver is also Lady Argentyne's color and Lunasa's," Danai blurted out.

"Silence daemon-thing, changeling, horror!" The Dolmen back-handed her with such force, she staggered, ears ringing shrilly.

"Then why did you shove me aside and pull Danai away from us?" Melitsa stepped forth to join Toron and Triasa. "I accuse you as well. Since the recounting of the Truthing Well, you have sullied Danai not only in your own mind, but to us all, forcing her to fit some perverse interpretation, determined to ignore what I believe the Mother is trying to tell us! Danai is perchance a messenger, but of certainty, she is no daemon."

Iridescent green glows danced about the Dolmen's robe and on the ground by its feet. "Ye dare! Ye dare to question our actions, we who are responsible for the well-being of the folk, who speak with Lunasa and the Mother?"

"We do." Like shifting brown sand, over half the Mentors strode over to form a wedge behind Triasa, Toron and Melitsa, eyes bright with accusation.

"This cannot be," bellowed Sombron, his face aghast. "It is the Dolmen who speaks! If it says Danai is a danger, it is ours to listen, not challenge." A spattering of 'ayes' issued from some of the Mentors who remained seated.

"The Dolmen is neither Lunasa nor the Mother," Triasa spat. "It is a High Loremaster, chosen by a council of the Lady and her Lord, the Chief Tains, and the Guild Masters. And if it takes actions that for no good reason jeopardize any member of the folk, we have a right to question and challenge—"

"False, false, false," Sombron shouted her down. "As much question the rising of the sun. It has always been so."

"Lady Argentyne would advise you otherwise," countered Toron. "You know that the Dolmen arose under the direction of the Twins in the Days of Dimness after Solon. They tasked the Dolmen to teach the Feyree about the Scrolls of Atonement, to help us recover our shredded selves. All that is now came in the age of seasons after."

"Toron speaks the truth." Mehrten's loud voice silenced the debate.

For a half a heartbeat, the Dolmen seemed to shrink in to itself. The Mentors waited. It reminded Danai of the heavy feeling before a hail storm broke.

The Dolmen drew its magic close, stood tall, seemed almost to grow, billowing its robes although there was no wind. "It is moot. The Rites must proceed."

"How can they if you cannot be trusted to conduct them—and yourself—in the sprytes' best interest?" Triasa followed her angry question with another. "And how can we trust you to accept our counsel that Danai is no changeling, and let her be?"

Studying their doubting faces, the Dolmen felt its power fracturing. Here was no time for battle. There would be one better. It exhaled slowly. At all costs, the Rites must proceed, or the Lady and Lord would want to know the reasons. It would deal with Danai later, in its own way.

It snapped its fingers, and the oak staff appeared in its right hand. It advanced until standing before the entry to the Skystone, then struck the rock face thrice. The staff leapt free to hover between the Dolmen and Triasa, emitting a beam of silver-green light up into the sky. "The Rites shall proceed. Danai shall partake until the end. We swear it." Recapturing the staff, it retreated into the black maw of the Skystone.

Triasa gestured Danai to follow her. "Come. We three will dream speak you." They entered the woods, soon arriving at a small clearing, dappled with shade. Danai recounted her dream in detail, answering their many questions.

"Heed thy silvered self?" Triasa gave a tired rub to her temple. "This is a kryptic. It is clear that your Calling is that of a Healer and perhaps also a Charmer, but the fox giving you such a warning is hardly a normal part of the Dream Rite. I know not what counsel to give."

Toron shrugged, staring at the creek's tumbling waters, flickering silver in the sunlight. "Describe the fox to me."

Danai culled her memory of the silver fox. Silver fox. Her eyes flew open. "She was silver. It wasn't just a trick of Lunasa's light either, although I thought so at first. Even her eyes were silver."

Toron nodded. "So." They waited as he organized his thoughts. "I believe it was a message from the Lady Argentyne."

"But I was nowhere near her lake in my dream."

"Danai, with all that you have already seen, can you even question the power of the Ancient Ones to send their thoughts or minds where they will?"

"So what was she trying to tell me?"

"Silver is the color of the Lady of the Lake," Triasa mused. "She marked you with silver, a lighter hue visible even on your own silver skin. So, she silvered your shoulders. But what about them? Why heed them?"

"They ached when I stood at the trail—"

Toron slapped his thigh. "Triasa, that's it. Her shoulders glowed ever brighter as I followed her along the trail." The three Mentors stared at each other. Lady Argentyne warning Danai against the Dolmen? Was it possible? But why?

"There is much not yet understood," Triasa said. "I think we agree that we can no longer trust the Dolmen to be impartial in this matter. But what do we do next?"

"Could you not ask the Lady herself?" Danai suggested. "Mentor Toron, you seemed to be, um, close to her." She blushed at the Mentor's surprised glance.

Toron frowned. "Not without attracting attention. A Mentor missing during the Rites is ill-advised. We cannot risk more loss of power to the Mentors' Ring—"

"Toron!" Melitsa interrupted. "She is yet a spryte."

"One marked by the Lady! She must know." He continued. "You will not speak of this with the others. That is an Order." Danai gave a tiny nod. "Our role is more than to guide, to train, to test. A Mentors' Rite of Power of which the Dolmen is the focal point precedes the Rites of Krisalys. One that weaves a circle of protection about all the sprytes, and casts a ringwall about the Dell and even a certain distance beyond into the forest to prevent the smell of magic from attracting others."

"Such as daemiani," Melitsa added, her voice flat.

"When one of us departs, as did Armerion, it leaves a gap, and the ringwall is more sheer, more easy to pierce. Were I to go to Lady Argentyne without the additional spell the Dolmen casts when Mentors absent themselves, not only would it sense my missing energy, but most important, it would expose all to greater risk."

Triasa sighed. "As it is, the Mentors not being in accord and no longer having trust in the Dolmen—along with its problems with you—has created fractures throughout the ringwall. We are no longer focused, hence our energies which guide and maintain the magic are not as powerful."

"So what do we do?" Melitsa stood, tapping her foot with impatience. "Send Danai? We must know, must gather what knowledge we can. I do not fear for her safety with the Lady."

"I would not leave Danai exposed alone for any length of time," Triasa cautioned. "I misliked the look in the Dolmen's eyes, although the oath taken is binding."

"Let us think on it." Toron also stood "Perhaps the Mentors' Search can offer a way." The dancing notes of the summoning reed pipe came from the Dell.

"Wait! Please. Before we return, what does this have to do with my Dream Council?" Danai felt an almost desperate need to have something positive upon which to concentrate, something to offset the growing feeling that her life was headed in a direction over which she had very little control. It was like drowning slowly.

Triasa reached out to touch Danai's silvered shoulder. "I would trust the message of the fox. You healed her cub. She spoke with you. Healer. Charmer. Learn more about both. See where your Self guides you."

* * * * *

Chapter Fourteen

Pook kicked a heap of pine cone seeds into the air, sneezing from the dust as the hazel flakes floated above his head, then drifted down in a gradual spiral. When he had been younger, it had been a fine game to kick them up, then see who could duck beneath the darting flakes and balance them on top of their heads until the wind snatched them away. Now all he felt was a prickle of irritation scraping at his emotions.

The Rites had lost their luster, their fascination. In Dream Council, he had nettled the Mentors by playing dumb about his dream. But it had been so awkward to recall. At least in front of a bunch of stuck-in-the-mud Feyree, he thought. Even his escort Mentors Alamai and Nporan had seemed uncomfortable about it. He could still see the females' torch-like bodies cavorting on all three trails, their sheer tunics barely hiding the lush figures beneath. Beckoning him with hard, lurid smiles. He had wanted to bolt down any trail to grab one, anything to release the hot pounding desire they roused. Yet as he had approached the trail's juncture, the three figures joined and danced down the left trail, and so he hastened after them, oblivious to the Mentors' startled shouts.

"Poo-ook." He could almost hear their seductive whispers, feel the hungry heat wash over him again.

"Would you not want to learn more about what you saw?"

It wasn't a memory voice he was hearing. Pook slewed about to find its source. There. Under the deep shade of a burdock leaf, a bluish shape glowed, gathered, formed into a female. She beckoned.

"I would fain show you more. Give me a taste of your skill at fire magic, and I will pull back the gate so that you may peek into my realm."

Pook edged toward her, fascination warring with caution. "Why do you offer me this?" In the back of his mind a voice was shrilling a warning. Yet it was so tempting. Danai seemed to be having all the adventures. Why shouldn't he? A gate to what?

The daemon giggled with a sound of water sprinkled on hot embers. "Pook, Pook. So many possibilities. Why confine your thoughts to just the realm of Feyree? Many are your folk who are among us, having chosen our way instead of," she gave a scornful sniff, "the simple life you lead."

He bristled at her tone, stopping at the edge of the leaf's shadow. "I see nothing wrong with our way." She drifted closer. The heat of her body engulfed him, lifting the hairs on his neck and arms, pulsing his blood. Her skin glowed with the white hot intensity of an ember. He could smell the fresh smoke from her flowing blue hair. What would it be like to mate with a fire daemon? "Are you safe to touch?"

She smiled a slow sultry smile. "Do you try to mate with every maiden you meet?" She let her palm rest above his wrist, not touching him. The heat felt as if his arm had lain too long in the sun. "Wouldn't you want to know my name first at least?" At his nod, she spoke, but the name sounded like the crackle of a distant forest fire.

"My tongue won't get around that. Do you have another name, one I can pronounce?"

"Then call me Balayzia." She drifted into the deeper green shadows by the thick stems. Pook followed a step further, half in-half out of the shadow. He felt bold, daring. "So, can you be touched by a non-daemon?" She came back, reaching out to trail her finger almost along his arm, leaving a trail of heat. His loins throbbed.

"Only if you perform the fire magic." She leaned forward. He could see her full breasts appear and disappear under the ever-shifting tunic.

"Why are you so insistent about that?" Again, a ripple of wariness shivered through his mind. He brushed it aside.

She stepped away, her color deepening back to cool blue, appraising him. "I can destroy you with a hug," she said matter-of-factly. "The fire spell admits you to my realm, and gives me the power to weave a spell that will, ah, protect you from the side-effects of my nature."

Pook considered. To see another realm! Now that would get some attention. What harm could there really be performing the fire magic spell? This daemon clearly wasn't anything like the one that had attacked Danai and Joson. He nodded, and was rewarded by her lush smile.

He stepped completely beneath the leaf, surprised by how cool it seemed, how quiet. The deep silence of a summer late-day, when heat stills everything. Closing his eyes, he gathered his energies within, centering them about his midriff. They coalesced into a knot of heat. He heard Balayzia hiss softly. "Fi-re." Opening his eyes, he wove his hands in flame-like motions, saw the shimmer of energy gather between his palms until a lavender flame fluttered a feylength before them.

Balayzia plunged her arms through the flame, then flung them wide. The tiny flicker spurted free of his control, elongating into a pillar that seared through the leaf, shriveling its center into the crusted brown of dried blood. Pook struggled for mastery, but realized it was out of his hands. *What have I done?* He flung up his arms to ward off the flames.

About him Balayzia danced madly, igniting a swirling cone of sparks that captured him in a seething net of slender flames. Before him the pillar widened, a darker gash forming at its center. Strangling for air, Pook croaked out her name, stretched out a beseeching hand.

"Welcome to Nonetre, Pook," she crackled, before she shoved him with a blast of heated air through the widening gash, then swiftly followed.

It hissed shut. The burnt leaf sagged and collapsed into a crumple of charred fragments.

* * * * *

"Where's Pook?" Joson glanced about the Dell at the gathering sprytes. He was surprised to see Danai emerge from the woods with several Mentors—why weren't they coming from the Skystone, he wondered. He waved and she plodded slowly toward him, as if unbelievably tired.

"Have you seen Pook?" he asked as she came up.

"No." Danai shaded her eyes, peering about. They felt gritty with fatigue, and her cheek ached from the Dolmen's blow. A flicker of light, then a movement near the wood's edge caught at the corner of her vision. She pointed. "Is that him? My eyes are kind of blurry." And why have my shoulders started to ache?

Rhytha began to wave, then paused. "What's the matter with him? He's walking so...so...oddly." Her voice trailed off. They turned to watch Pook approach. He straightened as he drew closer, but seemed to be concentrating on where he placed each step. He made no eye contact with them until just a few strides away. Then he looked up.

For a moment the ache in Danai's shoulders felt like fire, burning to match the embers of Pook's eyes. She gasped, hearing it echoed by the others.

"What in the name of the Twins is the matter with your eyes?" Damon blurted, nearly tripping over his own feet as he lurched backwards.

"There's nothing the matter with my eyes at all." Pook's voice was calm, almost smug, like a creature well fed. He studied them as if from a great distance. "Why do you ask?" Even as he spoke, the embers dimmed, his eyes returning to their familiar aqua.

The four sprytes looked at each other, at Pook, and at each other again. It all felt wrong. But what could they do? Go to a Mentor and say that their friend's eyes had briefly changed color? A Mentor's handclap summoned them to the Circle.

"After evenmeal, ye will gather before the Shehn." Mentor Mehrten permitted himself a wide smile. "The Dolmen has called a skaldmoot, and Yarbrough shall give us a tale."

A flutter of anticipation rippled through the pod, and they hastened to get their food. Yarbrough was the highest ranked taleteller of the folk, the Skald Guild Master. Many were the seasons he had sung at revels and moots, and long had it been since he had been chosen by the Chief Tains as the High Skald. It was an honor for him to come.

Joson hung back as the others went on, lightly touching Danai's arm. "His eyes. Danai, I've seen those eyes before. If Aaron was here..." he swallowed, then plunged on. "Aaron would say the same thing."

"You're right. They're fire daemon eyes." Danai overcame her shudder of revulsion. "And he feels different Joson. His energy is all wrong. If I were to meet him in the dark, I'm not sure I would recognize him—and I would feel afraid. And Jo'?"

"What?"

"My shoulders ached around him."

"Hah? What do you mean?"

"Don't tell the others. Even the Mentors don't know except for Triasa, Toron and Melitsa, who did my Dream Council."

"I was going to ask you why you came from the forest, not the Skystone."

"I'll tell you later. Anyhow, since Lady Argentyne did this," she twitched her shoulders, "they start to tingle when the Dolmen is near. When Pook came at us, they felt for a moment as if they were on fire."

"A warning?" His voice was somber.

"I guess so." They both looked at their friend who was jostling and joking with other sprytes at the trestles. "It happened in my dream too—with the Dolmen."

He stared hard at her. "Explain."

"At the three trails—from what the Mentors mentioned I'm assuming we all face that—he blocked the outcome. He tried to kill me. Called me a daemon, a changeling." She was surprised at the surging anger she felt. "If my aunt hadn't burst into the dream and knocked him flat, I'd be dead."

Joson whistled softly. "So he distorted your dream too." At her stunned look, he nodded. "At the three trails for me too. I had saved Rhytha, and all the signs suggested that I'm to be a Guardian. I'm really glad about that. But as I started down the left trail, this haze got between me and Mentors Poron and Dilyn, and I could hear them shouting. The Dolmen emerged from the haze and accused me of protecting a daemon in our midst. I'm guessing now he meant you. He started doing something with his staff, then the haze ripped away. Poron and Dilyn shredded it by fanning the air with their wings. I can't tell you if they were more shocked or furious with the Dolmen. I woke up sick to my stomach."

"The Most High! What a bunch of toad gas." Danai clenched then unclenched her fists, wishing she could tell her whole pod about the treachery of the Dolmen. "It thinks nothing of destroying anything that gets in the way of its precious idea of how the folk should be. Triasa as much said it is ignoring some sort of warning from Lunasa, and more than half the Mentors sided with her."

"You mean they're against the Dolmen?"

"Pretty much so, yes. Triasa and Toron forced an oath out of it to leave well enough alone until the Rites are finished. But I don't trust it. We're going to have to sham and be careful. We'd better get along to evenmeal." She took one step, then stopped and turned to face him, giving his arm a squeeze. "Jo' let's agree to keep and eye out for each other." He gave her a hug, resting his chin on her hair for just a moment.

"I'd not trust Pook either," he added as they began to walk.

Danai sighed at the heavy sensation Pook's name gave her. "No. But we can't let on. Let's see if we can figure out what's going on first."

They hurried over to join their friends, carefully balancing their trenchers and the small cups of *miel*, a fine honey-mead given out for this special occasion. Pook, already finished, was reclining against a grass tuft and glanced lazily up at them. "We were talking about our Dreams. Rhytha here thinks she may be called to be a Skald. Damon is simply thrilled about being a Weaver. Elanoria doesn't believe she could possibly be called to be a Guardian, do you Ela?"

"Well look at me! If I came riding at you on a nightwing, you'd probably fall over laughing, I'm so skinny. It's simply ridiculous!"

Danai felt a soft shudder run through her shoulders, then heard a voice of quiet intensity issue from her lips, as if she spoke for another. "Strength comes in many forms. It is not always the biggest that does the best."

Pook's eyes narrowed, and Danai was sure she saw a momentary flicker. "Your voice sounded weird. So what are you supposed to be?"

She didn't want to tell him, but knew it would look strange saying nothing. Her tone was clipped. "A Charmer or Healer. Jo's supposed to be a Guardian too, Ela. No, let us eat first, or we won't get done in time. You talk."

She listened as they described their dreams, glad to hear that some were perfectly normal. "What about you, Pook?" she finally asked around a mouthful of sweetseed. "You didn't say." Even as she spoke, she sensed an eddy of heat that set her shoulders a-throb. It ebbed around her and engulfed Pook, stirring his hair and the embers in his eyes.

He avoided her question. "Look at your shoulders Danai! They're glowing silver."

Determined not to be dodged, she nodded. "Yes, they've been doing that from time to time. Don't know why yet. So, about your Dream?"

"My Dream got messed up at the end. I was something like a Chief Tain, but in a place I didn't know." His eyes slid away. "At the three trails, I didn't know which to choose, and then I woke up."

He's lying, Danai thought. But is he the one doing the lying or something else?

"What happened at the trail?" Joson had put down his trencher and was looking intently at Pook.

"Hey listen, there's the reed pipe!" Pook jumped up and started towards the Shehn. "I'll tell you afterwards," he called over his shoulder.

Danai bit her lip, but it was Rhytha who said, "We've got a problem here. I really think we should speak with the Mentors now."

"She's right." Damon jerked a thumb at Pook's back. "You weren't here for a bit, and I don't know who that is, but I can tell you it's not Pook. Talk about a changeling!"

A shiver scrambled down Danai's back at hearing that word again. "How do you mean?"

"He reminds me of somebody who thinks they know so much more than you ever can," Elanoria said. "He wasn't talking with us. He was talking down to us. You'd think he was a Chief Tain already or something. His dream went to his head."

"Noooo," Rhytha said thoughtfully. "I think it's more than that. Pook is there, but there is something else going on. He reminds me of somebody who's traveled and seen things we couldn't imagine, like the Skalds do, or the Northlands Chameleon Feys. One of those actually came back with Skald Aloran and told us a tale about how Lampion is only the beginning of the land. I spent more time watching him change colors as he spoke than listening to his tale."

"But Pook didn't go anywhere," Elanoria protested.

"Maybe not in the way we know. But c'mon Ela. Look at what we've seen and done in a few lumnas. Daemons. Wraiths. Ancient Ones. Truthing Wells that talk. Who is to say what else is out there?"

"But he's our friend, our podmate." Elanoria's voice quivered with dismay.

Damon reached out to gently touch her shoulder. "Look, we've got to get over to the skaldmoot. Let's sleep on it and then morrowmorn, we'll at least talk to a Mentor we trust. Fair?" Elanoria nodded, and the group hastened to take places to the rear of the already seated sprytes. Pook was far up front, and he had not saved them a place as he usually did.

Sunset had left a tracery of rosy clouds trimmed with gold in the sky. Already the larger stars were emerging. Glowflies began to dance about the Dell, freckling the air with sparks, most flying high enough to avoid the hungry tongues of the first croaking frogs. A refreshing breeze set the clover and daisies nodding.

Yarbrough sat upon a comfortable green walnut hull. Glowing knobs of foxfire, poised on top of ornately-carved staffs, were staked on either side. His ice-white hair tossed back any light, and cast his ivory face in shadow as he leaned forward to tune his small lap harp. Moss green tunic, journey boots, and wings allowed him to blend with forest or meadow, for he traveled throughout Lampion carrying tidings and tales. At his belt, sheathed in a heavy silver cloth, hung the braided golden blade of Contort, steeped in legend, said to be a gifting from an Ael-lord.

Behind Yarbrough the uncowled Mentors sat chatting in low voices, enjoying this brief respite from their duties. They ceased speaking as the black shadow of the Dolmen appeared.

"Greetings to ye." Not all the sprytes and Mentors joined the return chorus. "It is not often that Yarbrough is among us with all his travels and duties. We summoned him to share a tale of which you have heard at most only fragments—the Battle of Sagad and the Rise of the Twins. As ye are soon to become Feyree, he will tell ye of things not meant for the ears of younger sprytes. Listen well." It stepped back and cast out its arm towards the waiting Guild Master. "High Skald Yarbrough."

With no preamble, the skald trailed his fingers across the strings, releasing the dissonant wail of a mourning song. In the gathering gloaming, he raised his head to cast a red-eyed gaze across the audience.

"Then rose Solon, mighty in self and power.
Aught of harmony he knew not.
He drove the folk to cower
save for those who swore allegiance born
of fascination or desire.
Of life many there were shorn
in driving hatred and fire."

As Danai listened to Yarbrough's chant, she realized she already knew most of the tale. In fact, as it unfolded, she observed it circumvented some of the facts and masked the battle's brutal violence.

He's not as good as Shamarig, she thought. Doesn't craft the scenes or emotions as well. Or maybe it's because I know more than he's telling that the tale doesn't captivate me. She noticed that those sprytes who had been to the Lake seemed less interested. Especially Pook, who seemed to have trouble keeping his hands still.

Yarbrough ended the first chant with,

"Double tongued were the daemiani
teaching forbidden magics
no care for consequence.
Incinerated. Tragic.
Died by his own hand, Solon.
Blessed be Lunasa."

Everyone repeated the last line. Except Pook. As Yarbrough adjusted his harp for the next chant, Pook flung out a question. "What happened to the Feyree who were loyal to Solon and didn't die in battle? And for that matter, what happened to the daemiani?"

Ignoring the Mentors' sharp gasps at such rudeness, Yarbrough gazed mildly down at Pook, weighing the challenge in his voice. He turned towards the Dolmen. "Most High?"

Advancing to stand beside the Skald, the Dolmen stared down intently at Pook. "Of what relevance is this useless query?" Its voice dripped reprimand.

"Its relevance is that Yarbrough presents only one viewpoint," retorted Pook, staring back with an insolent smile. "A moralistic tale with no accounting for the other participants."

"Thee would care about traitors who forsook our folk, our ways, in pursuit of power?" Its voice darkened. "Thee would care about horrors who taught those traitors how to kill, to maim, to destroy?"

Pook shrugged. "I wasn't there. And unless you're an Ancient One, neither were you for that matter. I'm hearing one perspective. How do I know it is the right one?" He smiled at the reactions his audacity drew from sprytes and Mentors alike.

"It is a fair question," Yarbrough said, before the Dolmen could retort. "Yon spryte has not said he cared about the daemiani. Only that he seeks to better understand. What harm in that?"

"Aye, what harm?" Mentor Qyon agreed. "While none may have before asked this question, it has now been asked. And of what better Feyree than the High Skald? Why may he not respond?" Other voices joined in, debating.

Danai saw the green glow forming about the Dolmen's feet, and guessed what was coming. It clenched its staff, mouth thin with barely controlled anger. "These are the Rites of Krisalys! What we say is an Order! This skaldmoot is ended. Disband!"

Yarbrough's dismayed expression, mirrored in many other faces, was quickly replaced by anger. He said something, but in the ensuing clamor, Danai could not hear. The Dolmen struck his staff on the ground, mouthing some curt response, then stalked away from the gathering. Through it all, Pook remained seated, a contemptuous smirk smeared across his face. She wanted to slap it off.

* * * * *

Sleep eluded her. Even counting stars failed to work, especially with Lunasa's full face dimming all but the most brilliant ones. Finally she dozed, only to be woken by a faint rustle from where Pook lay. He was upright, peering into the dark distance with smoldering eyes. She watched through slitted lids as he glanced once at his podmates, then rose and strode off purposefully towards the forest. The shadows swallowed him.

I should get up and follow him, Danai thought. But now her eyelids sagged with fatigue. Perhaps he's just going off to do the necessary. I'll wait a short while and if he doesn't come back...her thoughts faded into slumber.

She was slow to wake. Remembering, she rolled over and was rewarded by Pook's tremendous yawn. "I could sleep all day," he announced, standing to stretch. "I must admit I'm rather tired of these Rites. We've been at it what...four lumnas now?"

"You want your wings, don't you?" Damon was still irritated with Pook for having curtailed the skaldmoot.

"I guess so. Beats traveling by foot anyhow. C'mon, let's go eat."

"I don't know where you put it all." Elanoria ran her fingers through rumpled hair. "I'd be cheeky as a squirrel."

"But you're not. You're quite a pretty maiden, and I'm sure you'll make a lovely Feyree." His appraising gaze made her blush.

The reed pipe summoned them to the Circle from mornmeal. Mentor Narldon stepped forth. "When the sun rises above the Shehn, ye shall seek your assigned Mentor with no help but your wits and training. Three clues shall each be given. One day's food and water may ye take. No magic may ye use. One clue shall all know— no Mentor shall be more than a day's journey from the Dell. Mentors, call thy sprytes."

One after the other, moving sunwise around the Circle, each Mentor summoned a spryte. Toron beckoned, and Danai dodged through the others to reach him. They moved off towards the Dell's easterly edge, still shaded and dew-laden. Small tussocks of grass partially shielded them from view. Toron took a few more strides, then froze. A short distance ahead, a pair of moss green boots protruded from behind a droplet-clad grass clump. "Danai, remain where you are!" He sprinted forward.

In moments he returned, his jade skin pale green with emotions. Pinching his fingers to his lips, he gave the shrill Guardian's emergency whistle, bringing a flock of uncloaked Mentors winging towards them.

Narldon landed first. "Toron, what's wrong?"

Toron pointed towards the grass hummock. "Yarbrough. Dead. Strangled from the looks of it. I have not touched his body."

Danai stared numbly at the boots, a sinking feeling heavying her heart. The Mentors flowed towards the body. Unbidden, she followed. Even in the shadowy light, the neck bruises stood out starkly against the Skald's ivory skin. His eyes and mouth were open. In shock? Fear? Disbelief? Danai couldn't tell—his self had been gone too long. She noticed his dirq sheath was empty. "Contort is missing," she said, pointing.

Toron looked at her in surprise, began a gesture of dismissal, then decided otherwise. "Aye. Who—or what—would steal that sacred blade?"

"Ask the same as to how could any of our folk kill a Skald?" Melitsa's voice shivered with suppressed shock.

"What is to say it was a Feyree?" Qyon asked quietly.

"Finger size suggests it." Toron knelt to examine the corpse. He extended his hand over the bruise marks without touching the flesh. "But whatever killed Yarbrough would have had a hand within the same size as our folk." His hand moved to gently close the Skald's staring eyes.

"Where is the Dolmen?" Triasa glanced about. "He could not have missed the signal."

"We are here. We are listening." The Dolmen appeared from behind another hummock, still cloaked, in stark contrast to the other Mentors.

Why didn't it fly, Danai puzzled. Doesn't it have wings?

The Mentors stepped aside as it advanced then knelt beside Toron to inspect the body. It pressed fingers on Yarbrough's cheek. The flesh pocked and did not rebound. "Dead for a good while," the Dolmen judged. "Toron, feel underneath him. Is the grass dry or wet?"

"Sodden."

"Yet his body is dry. Therefore long after dewfall." The Dolmen stood. "Toron, Qyon, bring the body to the Skystone. Mentors, join us there. Triasa, advise the sprytes that the Mentor Seek is suspended until the morrow. Tell them they are not to leave the confines of the Dell, nor approach its perimeter on pain of forfeiting their wings. Use the Cordon magic if need be to bar any who should think otherwise. Let us go."

Chaos erupted among the sprytes upon hearing of Yarbrough's murder, some screaming the Rites were cursed, others sobbing hysterically. Triasa whistled for other Mentors and Toron, Illiai, Memnon, and Asagion flew over to help impose order. Some sprytes had to be slapped free of hysteria, and three were downed by sleep-dust when they attempted to flee the Dell. The Mentors finally herded them into the semblance of a circle, and Triasa gave them the Dolmen's Order. Then the Mentors flew towards the Skystone.

Rhytha soothed a sniffling Elanoria, her arm cast around her friend's shoulder, while Danai, Joson and Damon conversed in low voices. Pook sat a little apart, his face still carved by the frown that had emerged since watching Triasa cast the Cordon spell about the Dell's perimeter. The sun crept across the sky.

Looking drawn and pensive, the Dolmen and Mentors appeared mid-day.

They took their customary stance around the waiting sprytes. Toron spoke. "We don't know—yet—who killed Yarbrough. Only that it was likely a Feyree." He searched their faces. "Do any of you recall strange sounds or perhaps something unknown moving?"

Danai recalled Pook's nighttime amble. He was only going to the necessary, she told herself. It was impossible! Or was it? She glanced at Pook, but his face looked as upset as anyone's.

Toron sighed at the silence. "As I expected. Until we gather more clues, you may all be at risk from this murderer. Yet you must complete these Rites, as ill-fated as they have become. We shall resume the Mentor Seek on the morrow. But first we shall train you in the spell of protection, and teach you the Guardians' emergency call. Learn these Teachings well, for your lives may depend upon them."

* * * * *

At the second shrill whistle, the birds had promptly abandoned the Dell, and Danai had shortly wished she could follow. Her ears rang from practicing the bone-piercing sound, her lips were sore from puckering, when Toron finally signaled a halt. Even Danai's tongue ached from the peculiar twist needed to accentuate the squealing noise.

Each Mentor then summoned their Charge to teach the protection spell, and Danai scurried over to Melitsa. "These are ancient words," she explained, "crafted in the ancient Feyree tongue and not easy to pronounce. Listen closely first."

"Ju remo enprit tou be nisons.
Gardimoy desenemi part oo.
Gardimoy Lunasa jenpris. Oed."

Danai's tongue tangled around the words as Melitsa patiently drilled her in the spell. Finally she was satisfied. "Now we invoke the spell."

"Melitsa, how do you know if such a spell is working as there are no visible results?"

"The words of most spells are just that—words—until you add the final gesture or element that invokes it. While many of the Tier One spells are just basic gestures—for example fire magic and Feyree dust—the more complex spells require greater efforts. In the next lumna, you will be introduced to more of the basic elemental spells of which this is one."

"It seems to me that these would be the first spells you would teach us, not the last!" Danai knew she sounded petulant, but she was frustrated by the logic of the training.

Surprised, Melitsa stared at her. "You may not believe me, but there has not been the need to do so in the past."

"Not true, and you know that! Others have died in these Rites—Toron said as much. Even one death should cause the Dolmen and Mentors to review things." She kicked at the ground with frustration. "Although Lunasa knows that the Dolmen never would even consider such a change. We sprytes are just so much nothing to it."

"Danai! That is enough! I will hear no more on this. Let us finish the spell."

Swallowing her retort, Danai countered with a different question. "Does the Dolmen know all the magics?"

Melitsa hesitated, but given Danai's situation with the Dolmen, deemed it wiser to respond. "No. The Scrolls of Atonement forbade this, although it knows more than most. Each Guild Master reserves the right to keep certain spells sequestered in their craft. They may choose to share them, but cannot be forced—not even by the Dolmen."

"What about new spells?"

"Meaning?"

"Maybe as I'm experimenting with Healer spells, I invent a new one. What happens?"

Nonplussed, Melitsa stammered. "I have never heard of such a happening. Granted I am of the Weavers Guild, and no spells are used—that I know of—in making our wares. Your aunt might better know the answer to that." She held up her hand to forestall further comments. "Danai, focus! This must be learned. Repeat the spell once more, and add these movements to invoke it." She quick-stamped her left heel twice, and spread her arms wide. "Fling your arms out fully so as to create a shield through which many harmful things cannot penetrate. Remember it will not protect you against all that intends you harm. And most important, remember the spell lasts only one day, and must be repeated each morn. Do so upon awakening. Now, invoke the spell, and I will prove its power."

As Danai completed the spellcast, Melitsa reached into her sleeve, withdrew her dirq, then plunged it at the spryte's heart. It bounced back. Melitsa then reached out to gently tap Danai's shoulder, encountering no resistance. But when she clenched her hand into a fist, and attempted a punch, she was shoved back so hard she nearly toppled.

"By Lunasa," Danai breathed, eyes wide. "Is this how the Feyree survive in the Wilderlands? Why weren't we taught it before the Truthing Well?"

"Danai as to your first question—only in part. As to the second question, that Rite was a test of your survival training. And much as you think otherwise, magic is not the cure-all—we use it only selectively when truly warranted. All magic drains energy, and, overused, it will leach your very spirit until you join the wandering wraiths. It is not just in the bogs they dwell, I assure you. You must understand that magic is like a two-edged blade—it cuts both ways. If you come to depend too much upon magic, you can forfeit your ability to live without it."

* * * * *

There was little conversation that night as the sprytes settled into a slumber crowded with bad dreams. Pook awoke to Rhytha's moans, thankful they had yanked him from a nightmare where flames devoured him of his own choice. His heart still thumping from the dream's vividness, he eased to his feet, careful not to disturb the others. His throat felt parched. I need a drink and a walk to calm me down, he decided, and set out towards the Trykle.

A bright wink of bluish light flashed once just inside the trees by the creek. Probably just Lunasa's light on the waters, he thought when it didn't return, glancing up to see the oval face sinking into the west.

The deep quiet of late night had settled over the forest, and Pook fancied himself alone in this realm of darkness. He meandered along the bank, listening to the creek's soothing mumble. The woods were wonderfully cool.

"Fi-re..." sighed a strangely familiar voice. Balayzia materialized, a radiant blue so hot she crisped the edges of nearby leaves, sending up wisps of sour-smelling smoke.

Pook lurched backwards into the stream. "Get away from me," he gasped. "I want no more of your pretense nor your daemon realm of Nonetre. A place so parched of beauty it withers the spirit. Faugh!"

The fire daemon's smile did not reach her eyes. "That is because you judge with the uneducated eyes of a spryte mired in the old ways. Not the eyes of a lord."

"It's hard not be what I am."

"It's no harder than trying to be what you're not."

"Come again?" Pook's heart told him to flee, but her statement intrigued him.

"You pretend to yourself that this is the life for which you are destined. And why? Because your elders say that's the way it must be. For somebody as smart as you, it surprises me that you accept such a path when so many others are open to you—if you choose."

"I want my wings, and this is the way we earn them."

Balayzia gave an unlady-like snort. "Please. There are magics and wonders beyond this realm that can give you wings without such sweat and toil. That's just another of your foolish Dolmen's carefully preserved myths. Rites? Bah!"

The water was chilling his legs, but he stayed put. "Be that as it may, it is our way."

She scowled, dimming to indigo. "It is their way. I called you a lord. Are you not at least interested why?"

"Not particularly," he lied.

"Perhaps you're right." Balayzia began to back away, dimming until only her eyes were visible. "Perhaps I misjudged you and your abilities. Maybe you are not the one the Herald foretold to us."

"Who's that?"

"Our prophet. Our highest loremaster if you will. He scries the future in Keothach's fires. Long ago, he prophesied a Feyree would return to his rightful place as our lord and lead us to the forefront of all realms."

"So why do you think it's me?" In spite of his misgivings, he was fascinated.

"Of lavender will he be made
of shadow his roots are wrought
a questing mind unafraid
of desire for what is sought.
Wingless born, winged be
a chasm will he span,
Feyree master, daemiani's lord
He shall all command."

Balayzia ceased her chant. The silence waited.

Pook felt twainsplit. He knew what he must do, yet something inside his mind nudged him to consider the possibility of becoming a powerful lord. Lords and Ladies were made only through the election of the Chief Tains. Lord Andamion and Lady Atelai had long held the high seats at Revelstoke. Unless they ceded their title or died, it was a rare chance any Feyree had to become one. Of course, there were the Warlords, but since the death of the Twins, war was only a word. The role had become a relic from the past due to lack of need. Now the Guardians retained the mantle of defending Lampion.

Observing his ambivalence, Balayzia adopted a conciliatory tone. "I'm not saying our realm doesn't look different from this primitive woodland. You know that yourself from your, ah, visit." Her palms left a trail of sparks as she cast her arms wide in a gesture that reduced the whole of Lampion to a clump of ashy insignificance. "But think of all there is for you to discover in Nonetre. New ideas. Better, easier ways of doing things. Folk to talk with who will challenge your obvious intelligence."

"Daemiani you mean." He shook his head.

"And Feyree and Ael and dwarves."

"Did you ensnare them too, or capture them like you tried to do to me?"

She chose to ignore the last part of his question. "Most were restless with their lives and sought change. A few fell in love with a daemon and followed them."

Pook contemplated. He was wary of the Dolmen and admittedly impatient with the Rites. A lord. It sounded interesting. "What if being a lord is not to my liking?"

Balayzia glowed brighter, releasing a slow smile. "You may return as you did before—I swear it. But there are certain, shall we call them, rules."

"Which are?"

"Your memory shall be wiped clean of Nonetre. Only by our choice can other-realmers enter. We want no Feyree spreading ill about our lands. It is a simple process, with little pain. Our Herald mind-melds with you and extracts those thoughts and anything associated with them."

"And what's to prevent him from inserting 'memories'?"

"See? As I have said, you are wise beyond your seasons. He does put in false memories. Otherwise you would have an unexplained gap and that would cause trouble as you struggled to fill it."

"In other words he mind-tampers."

Balayzia shrugged. "If you want to put it in those ugly words. I prefer to see it as he preserves our chosen way of life."

Somewhere distant, the faint warble of a nightingale riddled the silence. Dawnshine could not be too far off. Pook inhaled deeply, savoring the cool air laden with scents of pine and clover. He stepped from the creek, felt the soft moss sink beneath his feet. "I'll come."

For a moment, it seemed to him the soft light of Lunasa dulled, the shadows grew blacker. Then the air was gashed to such brightness that he cast his hand up to shield his eyes. Behind Balayzia the air split wide, fire lipping along the tear's edges. She stepped backwards through it, her arms outstretched towards Pook.

He followed.

* * * * *

Chapter Fifteen

Pook turned up missing at mornmeal. An immediate search ensued, some Mentors flying into the woods, others trilling the birds down to ask what they had seen. The sprytes warily scoured the Dell, afraid of what they might find. As the hot sun climbed overhead, the weary searchers re-gathered.

"Auntie!" Danai hurried over to Triasa who had flown off before she could catch her. "I must speak with you. I wanted to yesterday, but could not with all that happened."

Triasa massaged the aching juncture of her wing and shoulder. All morn she had flown, pushing against an insistent hot dry wind that came from the west. "What?"

"The day of my Dream Council, Pook came back to our group from the woods at evenmeal summons. He seemed...changed." Her voice foundered at Triasa's frown. "His eyes were odd, almost like embers were flickering far behind them. But after a bit, he seemed better, and his eyes looked normal. But we had agreed we would tell you yestermorn...and then everything happened."

"Explain 'changed.'"

Oh no, Danai thought. She's angry with me again. "Pre-occupied. Distant. Almost condescending, as if we amused him. Not our Pook."

"The others in your little group saw this?"

Danai nodded.

"And you decided to wait to tell me?" Triasa struggled not to give her niece a hard shake. She let her next words do it instead. "Danai, you show remarkably poor judgment at times when we both know you should know better. With all the strangeness tangling up these Rites, you persist in foolishly waiting to speak. How could you not say aught about Pook, if not to me then to another Mentor, especially after his behavior towards the High Skald?"

"But it wasn't bad behavior..." Tears prickled her eyelids. "He just seemed a bit odd."

"Embers behind his eyes? You call that just a bit odd? Spryte, he was more than odd. We have been keeping an eye on Pook since Wag-Tail told us of his possible encounter with a fire daemon. His eyes confirm our worst fears."

"That day you brought him back after all that bird ruckus?"

"Yes. Ever since, we have seen his attitude shifting. Not enough to say beyond doubt he was daemon-touched, but enough that we were discussing his removal from the Rites. Especially after Alamai said fire daemiani danced on all his trails. Now you tell me of his eyes. After he is gone. He has been spellstruck by a fire daemon." Triasa closed her eyes a moment. "Come. Much as I wish to keep you away from the Dolmen at all costs, this is a matter of too great importance. Gather your friends and come to the Skystone."

The review was short and pitiless. Without preamble, the Dolmen castigated their negligence. "Ye fools! Ye may have placed all Lampion at risk! There now be no doubt in our mind we shall not find him this side. He has crossed to another daemension, and only Lunasa knows what will become of it. We can only hope he becomes naught more than another among the lost."

"Dolmen, should we suspend the Rites?" Nporan's face was clenched with concern. "Is it not time instead for council-moot when daemiani seduce sprytes from our sacred Rites?"

The Dolmen contemplated a point above the great Shehn, finally answering. "We must consult with Lunasa." Aligning the staff with its body's center, it closed its eyes and halted breathing, grew rigid, and a faint greenish glow, visible despite the full sunlight, flickered along the cloak's edges, slid up the staff and radiated into the air. From the very tip of the staff a pale green beam vanished into the sky. The moments passed. Then it inhaled, the hiss of breath rasping the silence. "Beware Rites' end. So says Lunasa. We take that as his desire the Rites continue. Let the Mentors Seek commence morrowmorn. There is no need for council-moot."

"And the lost one?"

"Let the Charmers tell all the wood folk to be wary of him if he appears. But Lunasa's orders are clear. The Rites proceed."

"Sounded more like a warning to me," muttered Damon as the sprytes were dismissed.

"I wished we followed our first thoughts and said something." Elanoria's puckered face looked ready to cry.

"You don't tell on friends," Joson snapped. "Pook's always been a bit queer. How were we to know it was more than that?"

"Because sometimes," said Toron, appearing behind them, "you have to look beyond yourselves and realize there is more than just what you hope or want. Working together, as you hopefully discovered on your sojourn, does not just end because the journey is over. It is a constant thing. How think you that the folk have survived? If everyone only looked out for themselves and their friends, how could they see the greater problems or others' needs?"

Joson blushed at the Mentor's reprimand. "Mentor Toron, I didn't know you were behind us."

"Little matters that. You spoke as you believed. I am telling you it is necessary to change that belief. Even more so now that Pook is gone to the fire daemiani."

"You don't know that!" Elanoria shrilled, face taught with anger.

"All signs and omens point to it. Even your accounts confirm it. There are times, Elanoria, that you must learn to deny your heart and listen to your head." He strode away, his cloak swirling about him.

* * * * *

The day dawned amid cool silvery showers that mottled the dry ground. None of the sprytes had any desire to heed the reed pipe and mornmeal was eaten by necessity rather than choice. Even Joson only lipped at his food, and he made no effort to sneak an extra handful of sweetseeds into his rucksack along with his kuis.

The pod shuffled in small subdued clumps towards the waiting Circle, each breaking off to stand before their assigned Mentors who stood unrobed, wings at the ready. Danai spotted Toron, and made her way over to stand before him. His face remained expressionless as he spoke. "Three clues I give you to seek me." His voice was pitched just below a whisper, and Danai had to listen carefully. "Silver. Tale. Lake. Wait until the sun touches the Shehn's second branch. Forget not the protection spell. Turnabout—you may not watch whither I go."

She faced the Dell, watching most of the Mentors trot off purposefully in all directions. A remaining few moved about speaking to the waiting sprytes. A tug on her rucksack brought her face to face with Melitsa. "I come to remind you to cast the protection spell," she said in a loud voice. Then she peered into the rucksack as if inspecting its contents. Danai caught a swift blur of bright green tumbling into the sack from the Mentor's sleeve. "It is a Weaver weapon," Melitsa murmured as she pulled the sack's drawstrings tight. "Keep it hidden. If attacked, fling it at the eyes. Then run." She stepped back. "A good search."

The pod stood silently, not permitted to discuss their clues, watching the sun creep up the branches. Danai counted the dark-leafed clusters of Lunasaberry clinging to the furrowed bark. The plant was sacred to Lunasa, and only the Chief Tains and the Dolmen were permitted to imbibe the sacred Lunasaberry wine that could impart visions. At last the sun's rays ascended the second branch and the pod scattered like sparrows startled by a fox.

I know where Toron is headed, Danai thought, setting out purposefully towards the Trykle. But first I need to get a message off. Once well inside the woods, after making sure neither Mentors nor podmates were about, she gave vent to a raucous shriek.

In moments, a magpie landed behind her. "The Mother's greetings maiden. Why call thee?"

It was not Wag-Tail, as Danai had hoped, but her message could be sent with any magpie. "The Mother's greeting to thee. I am Danai. And thee be...?"

"Crookshank, son of Cloud Chaser." He extended his gray leg, and she could see the odd angle that forced the bird to cant slightly left.

"Crookshank, thank thee for coming. Would thee carry a message for me to Tlarg of the Troich?"

The magpie cocked his head. "I know not this Tlarg, but am friends with young Peymlak. She delves the hills two valleys over. Would that suffice?"

Danai hesitated. She could only hope that Peymlak would pass on the message. "It will suffice. Ask thy friend to tell Tlarg to meet Danai at Windsrest Carrig above the Dell at mid-day on the fourth day from this. Beg him to come in the name of the Anam." With a bob of assent, Crookshank launched with a wing stroke that scattered leaves and nearly knocked her over.

She took her bearings and headed west, stopping occasionally on the crest of a tree root to sip from her kuis, and listen to the forest's mumblings amid the brief cloudbursts. She smiled sadly as she realized how differently she now weighed all the forest's sounds, paused to smell the air, and watched for hunters' movements. Gone was the carefree spryte of seasons past.

By mid-day, she reached the aspen forest. Flashes of gold glinted among the flickering leaves, the first fingerprints of the season of falling leaves, and Danai marveled that in less than two lumnas, they would be facing the final test. Through their trunks, she saw the silvery sparkle of the lake.

On the shore, Toron and Lady Argentyne stood waiting, the Lady skirted with silvery mist. They turned and smiled as Danai jogged towards them.

"My Lady Argentyne." Danai bowed.

"Maiden Danai." Her smile seemed to reflect the sunlight. "I am told that you do more than simply ask nyads impertinent questions. Indeed, you have given the Most High much to think about, and not a little to fear."

"Lady, the Dolmen says Pook has gone to the fire daemiani. How can such a thing be?"

The nyad sighed, a soft sound of water lapping among the reeds. "Toron told me of the questions young Pook demanded of the High Skald. I shall reply to both your and his questions as one." She turned to face the lake, her eyes seeking a shadow tucked in the darker gray of the left cliff. "In the dark days after Solon, the fighting among the folk did not immediately cease. Without a leader, Solon's forces quickly fractured into many factions, each warped by the craving for power they had savored under his rule. They battled among themselves, and against the rebels, casting yet another mantle of blood across an already drenched realm.

"And so, for many winters after the firestar crossed the sky, Lampion stumbled along in darkness. Lunasa's face remained cloud-hidden, only a faint glow revealing his presence. Even the sun struggled to pierce the murky haze. Many Feyree died of hunger and illness, for few Healers had survived. The wood folk and other folk avoided us, we who had so devastated their lands. The woods were silent with grief.

"In a cave by this lake I hid, bearing my son and daughter, accompanied by eight other Feyree. In those, the Days of Dimness, the seasons dulled, and many were the plants that failed to bear their usual bounty. We foraged, shivered, grew gaunt among our memories. Only the laughter of my sprytes kept our hearts alive. Tall Iniyo, the eldest by a heartbeat, was the leader. Alambi early on saw visions, being gifted with future sight—she became a Seer among our folk. She foresaw yet many dark seasons ahead and urged us to gather for more than a few lumnas. I can yet hear her lilting voice. "Mother, into darkness we have gone, and the light will be slow to return. It is coldest and darkest before the dawn. Prepare."

"And we did. We and others who heard of our small gathering and came seeking hope and refuge. For more than twenty strangely cold winters, we eked out our survival, hiding from those who continued to fight. Yet despite all, there were still those among the fey folk who harbored hope for Solon's promises.

"Iniyo drew my attention that Mid-Summer's Eve to another firestar that streaked white across the sky, trailing a mantle of red. It would appear for eight more nights. Alambi stood by my side, and bespoke that a herald of the enemy would arrive on the third day after the firestar, and that our folk—for by then many had settled about this lake—should be ready. "For what?" I cried. "We want no more war. Our land is but a shadow of itself. Lunasa hides his face. Will they still seek that to which they have no claim?"

"Give them more than what they seek," Alambi advised. "You know the ways."

"Iniyo nodded his fair head. "Mother, you have memorized much of the Scroll of Spells, having served long with Loremaster Oshmlin. You know many of the daemensions from which the daemiani hail."

"To sully our fair realm with their presence!" Alambi's scarlet eyes blazed like the firestar in her silver face.

"You speak truly," I replied with great caution, for only the highest of loremasters knew of what I was about to speak. "Nothing can come from nothing. Like segments of a tartberry are many daemensions fitted together, each finely divided by an edge of time. There are ways to open—and seal—gates between daemensions. It is sacred lore said to have descended from the Mother when she crafted all the daemensions in the dawn time. Oshmlin once told me that all realms have daemiani of some sort—even Lampion. You must not speak of this lest you bring down Lunasa's wrath."

"As one my sprytes spoke. "Can you not cast them from Lampion?"

"It is not that simple," I demurred. Yet already I was searching among the spells long stifled in my memory. "This magic must act on a place, not on the folk."

"Then I will gather them for you on the Plain of Sagad." The look in my Iniyo's emerald eyes brooked no argument. How fitting, I thought, that those who had destroyed Lampion should in turn find their ending on the same charred and wasted plain. I nodded. "Gather them by the Pillar of Solon." For his followers had erected a stone to mark the site of death.

"As Alambi had foretold, came upon the third day a herald from Merionis, self-styled ruler of Lampion. Doromon was the herald's name. His grim face I remember as the last to vanish behind the net of fire.

"Lady of the Lake, I bring words from Lord Merionis who would end this fighting and weave together the factions of Feyree into a wholesome new realm." He stood there, clad in a scarlet tunic with frayed edges, left hand ever fondling the hilt of his dirq, feigning disdain of my folk who stood about him. Worn by determination, yet with faces quietly proud of their ability to survive.

"It is good," Iniyo said. "We are willing to meet. Let all gather at the Pillar of Solon." He ignored the listeners' mutter of dismay. "In six days' time, when Lunasa would be in solas, let us gather in peace near night's edge. Will that suffice for thy master?"

"Doromon scrutinized Iniyo, then myself. Too shrewd he was I thought, to not suspect our ready willingness. So I added honeyed words to soften his suspicions. "Will you not bide a short while to refresh yourself? There remains a little of the sweet woodbine nectar we have gathered." I directed one of my maidens to escort him to our guest bower, well-knowing she would be more than willing to spend time with such a handsome Feyree and distract his questing thoughts.

"He left the next morn, and the Twins called a Council among the eldest and the most skilled of our group. To them we told our plan—but not in full lest there be yet traitors even among our own—and all gave approval, some voicing hope that perchance our future could finally begin anew. Then Dashami, our Skald, asked that which we could not contemplate—what if we failed?"

"It shall not be," Alambi answered her, the simple words falling like balm upon our long-frayed hopes.

"Iniyo addressed the Council. "And then shall we make new Laws, in which all shall have a say, and regain the favor of Lunasa." He stood before them, a cloak of oaken green lapped about his silver shoulders, already a lord among the folk. As if he heard my very thoughts, he spoke again. "And let the Feyree choose a new Lord and Lady as they see fit, and to them Alambi and I shall be advisors if they so wish."

"Dawnshine smoldered to light, the ever-present haze shrouding the sun in blood-hued dust. At my insistence, Alambi remained behind. "For though your vision sees far, there are things beyond all vision. If we fail, there must be one left to carry on the hope of Feyree."

"I shall watch from my heart," she replied with her gentle smile.

"The Plain of Sagad had gained little with time. Still upon the withered land stood the blasted, burnt trees, the scorched rocks, the parched earth on which no grass could take root. Only the bodies were gone, perhaps devoured, perhaps taken for burial. The Pillar of Solon rose from a scabbed black patch of earth, a rough-hewn black stone raked with red.

"Scattered groups began to appear around the edges of the battle plain. A few carried ragged banners, once bright, now dulled by time and grime. The remnants of Solon's great plan. Others bore no banner, and advanced with caution, hands gripping dirq-hilts, eyes white with watching. Merionis marched ahead of his scruffy ilk, beneath a scarlet banner emblazoned with a tarnished blade severing a twisted branch. His following was larger than I expected. The westering sun slunk behind murky ochre and brown clouds.

"Merionis sent out heralds, like ants from a nest, each bearing a white swan's feather in their left hand. Towards us came Doromon. "The Lady is summoned."

"Summoned?" My voice was as hoar frost.

"He gazed at me sideways. "I misspoke. The Lady is asked if she will join the other leaders near the Pillar."

"I advanced with Iniyo at my left elbow. How my heart throbbed with fear and hope! I sent Lunasa a whispered request to guard our desperate venture. Upon it hung the fate of Lampion.

"The firestar waxes more brightly," my son murmured. It seemed to be poised high above the Pillar, a glowing scarlet. As we joined the others, there was silence. No words of greeting. The banners flapped in a sluggish wind that shoved about small whirls of dust.

"When all had come, Merionis strode forth. Once a lordling under Solon, quick to follow orders without question—like a fanged snake, hot yellow eyes staring about, wondering whom to devour first. No dream of peace in those eyes! He spoke, his voice harsh and snorting like a boar's.

"It is seven and twenty winters since the fall of Solon. Many have suffered. Not a few have died. Little have we to show for all our grief. Yet there is a better way, even as Solon foretold. Shall we not draw back together, the Feyree folk, and rebuild our realm anew?"

"A murmur rippled among the listeners. "And what promise have we that if we join with you, we will not be destroyed for having dared to challenge Solon?" cried one leader.

"Merionis appraised the speaker before replying. "I give my word that all who have fought shall be forgiven if they will join me to forge a new Lampion. Will those Warlords who fought for Solon first come forth?" Behind him the scorched sun brushed the mountain's edge.

"We without banners, we who had hidden these many seasons, stepped aside to let the Warlords advance. "Let your followers gather behind mine," ordered Merionis. I watched as it was done, sighing at the sprytes I saw. If only the spell could spare the innocents among them. But it could not be, I knew.

"I gathered the energies within. I felt Iniyo's thoughts join mine. Then Alambi's gentle touch. The power of their youth would stand as strength for this great magic. Already the Warlords were arguing with Merionis, hands waving, voices raised in sharp demands. I closed my eyes and spoke the first of the three magics, the spell of Summoning.

"The air began to thicken behind Merionis and his followers, like sheer wet cloth through which the sun, sinking beneath the heavy haze, glared like an angry eye. I spoke the spell of Rift, and the air split down the center with the shriek of metal dragged across gritty stone. The gash widened quickly, fifty, a hundred feylengths, as if pulled apart by the many-hued fingers of flame licking along the edges. Blazing figures peered out with hungry eyes.

"Behind me the Feyree were crying out with fear, pointing. Merionis and the Warlords finally listened to them, but too late. I had cast my arms wide and spoken the spell of Passage, and my gestures had already pulled the edges of the gash forward so that the flames engulfed the supporters of Solon, weaving a net before them through which they could not escape. How I yearned to bring the flames down upon the now-terrified Warlords for all the harm they had bestowed upon us. "Mother, no," my Twins whispered in my mind, their wisdom overcoming my hate.

"Instead I pushed the flaming net back towards the rift. Those ensnared had no choice but to retreat, retreat into that new realm which Solon promised them. A few tried to force their way through, among them Doromon. He reached a beseeching hand through the flaming net towards me, crying my name. But I hardened my heart. And then I closed that terrible gash. The sun guttered and sank. Above, the firestar swelled, streaking down to chase after the sun. About me I heard sobbing, screaming. I was hollow, a reed with no pith. Stinging sweat blurred my eyes. Or perhaps they were tears. I no longer remember.

"Mother, see." It was Iniyo's voice, a guiding note in my darkness. His gentle touch turned me about to behold Lunasa rising in silver majesty, though still yet shrouded by a thinning haze. Yet we could see his face. As one, the fey folk sank to their knees to give thanks. The Days of Dimness were past."

Like a silver statue sheathed in purest crystal, Lady Argentyne stood shimmering between Toron and Danai, her voice echoing across time. "As one," she repeated, her eyes rediscovering the now.

"Lady, to which daemension did you send them?" Toron's voice was hoarse.

"Nonetre. Realm of the fire daemiani. I thought it safer than that of the time daemiani who are the most wise and cunning of them all. There at least, the barriers are less easily passed."

"Why is Nonetre to be feared?" Danai felt she must understand.

"Would you see Nonetre?" The nyad gazed at her with some surprise.

"Yes, if I could do so safely without any risk to Lampion."

"Every encounter you have with any thing will change your life's course no matter how small. Even if you only look, it will nudge your thoughts in a direction they might not have otherwise taken."

"We are convinced that Pook is there, my Lady," Toron interjected. "Would it not be better to see if it were true?"

"Why fear you a lost spryte? He is but one of many who have crossed, even since my time."

Toron paused before replying. "Lady, I knew Pook well. Indeed, although he does not know it, I am his great sire removed by nine. A curious spryte, always thinking, puzzling, but a good heart. To see him now perverted into a liar, ensnarled by daemiani...I would save him from himself if only he can be found in time."

"He is no longer himself." Lady Argentyne shook her head sorrowfully. "He has tasted of Nonetre, and never can you change that. Were you to return him against his will, his heart might yearn after it, strange as that seems."

"Will you not even grant us the chance?"

A trickle of wind stirred the Lady's hair as she watched the lapping waves smooth the sand by her feet. "There is one way. A Joining."

Toron raised his hand in startled protest. "But Lady, your privacy!"

"It is no violation if it be my choice. Remember that your privacy is also cast aside. I can probe where I will if I choose, do as I wish with you, and you cannot stop me. I am master." They stared into each others eyes, forgetful of Danai.

"I do not believe you would rape my mind." Toron eased the words out. "I will submit."

"And you Danai?"

"I have no idea what you're talking about." She was surprised by her own bluntness.

"A Joining. A melding of the minds where one takes charge of all. It is the only way that I can safely show you Nonetre. I must invade your mind and claim all control. Some have used it in ways you should never know. Will you trust me?"

Danai smiled up into the nyad's eyes. "My Lady, I already do."

* * * * *

Chapter Sixteen

"We must not leave our bodies behind for others to molest," Lady Argentyne advised as she led them to a cliff cave cunningly hidden behind a rough-hewn dark gray boulder. Even on land, the nyad seemed to float along, her ever-present skirt of mist guarding her steps. The entry was small—Toron had to stoop to avoid bumping his brow—but inside was spacious, dimly lit by long narrow shafts that entered the roof at acute angles to ward off rain. A musty smell of long disuse permeated the air. They followed the nyad toward the center of the cave, where she assumed a seat on a smooth-crested white rock. "Sit."

To each she gave a small golden kernel extracted from a pouch hanging from her girdle, ordering them to chew slowly. "Your mind will soon lose clarity. Lie down and close your eyes. Release your selves to me."

The kernel tasted dry and bitter, and it formed a thick paste that stuck and tingled in the back of Danai's throat. She felt a creeping languor spread from her mouth down her back, then to her head. Her muscles refused to support themselves, and she slumped backwards with a sigh. For a moment the ground felt cool against her back, then sensation faded. Inside her thoughts she saw a silvery brightness. "Follow me," Lady Argentyne whispered.

I am flying, Danai thought, her eyes opening with delight. She instantly sobered. Below her lay two bodies. I look so frail, so empty.

That is what I shall look like to others when I die. She realized she was seeing through the nyad's eyes.

"Come." The nyad tugged their thoughts out of the cave, and over the lake's center. They descended, sinking into the water.

Danai heard it slurp over their heads. I'll drown, her mind cried. Her thoughts began to struggle for the surface.

"Cease! Break contact with me and you will drown, for I cannot recapture your mind once it is released from your body. Danai, you must trust me."

"Trust her as I do, Danai." Toron's thoughts came through, a reassuring blue.

Danai clung to both thought tendrils, trying to release her terror.

"Spryte, you have not yet drowned!" Lady Argentyne's silvery thoughts shimmered with a hint of exasperation. "By now you would have were you not safe with me."

With a mental shudder, Danai forced herself to relax. I wonder what color my thoughts are she mused, trying to distract herself as they sank deeper into the mere.

"Silver, but a lighter hue than the Lady's," Toron replied. "Your thoughts are usually colored like your Feyree dust."

The clear waters deepened from emerald to blue-black. Danai was surprised she could feel it growing cooler.

"You are a part of me," Lady Argentyne said. "What I feel and see you also do. We are three minds, one body."

"Why this way?"

"Each daemension has many gates. Those known and not sealed are well-guarded. But there be always a crack or crevasse that they have not found. Who would think to guard water in a realm of fire?"

Danai felt a shudder, as if she were stepping through a waterfall. The liquid about her abruptly felt warmer and somehow, thicker. They started to rise through waters that became a muddy orange. She heard the nyad murmur a few words that sounded like rain upon leaves.

"That spell will permit us to walk invisible," the Lady thought to them. "Think softly, for there are those who may sense us. And so we will stay as far away from these beings as we may, and gaze upon what there is to see." Like a bubble, they pushed out of water the color of mud, flecked with gray foam and shards of what looked like burnt wood. "Behold Nonetre."

Edging the lake was a shallow valley thinly shrouded with scrubby grass the hue of tarnished bronze. To the west, twin suns, one scarlet, one ochre, glowed like dirty gems through a smoky yellow haze, casting a tired orange sheen across the landscape. The distant black mountains lay like a dried backbone across the horizon. The dusty air tasted sour and parched, as if water had not scoured it fresh in many seasons. Danai was appalled by the desiccated landscape.

Smoke lazed its way from block-shaped structures that were spaced in an organized fashion, overshadowed by withered trees. Figures hurried out of these dwellings, some climbing into wheeled baskets that were then pulled by others down a path off into the distance; others flew. Beyond the surrounding hills to the east, a black smoke throbbed and billowed in the sky, its underbelly lit by a lurid crimson glow.

No more than a ripple on the water, they glided ashore and advanced towards the path. Up close, the dwellings seemed made of some porous, coarse dark red rock. There appeared to be no openings through which to peek inside. The path itself was coated in a black substance that smelled like pine resin on a hot day. "Do we walk this trail?" Toron asked.

Before Lady Argentyne could answer, a flaming green figure emerged from the dwelling they had just passed and stared straight at them, a quizzical expression on his face. Beside him followed a Feyree, her drooping blue wings neatly folded behind gray shoulders, copper hair close-cropped. She carried a clear glass phial, glittering with a foaming yellow liquid. About her throat hung a collar decked with green stones. Her haggard face bore the look of one without hope.

"Amira!" Toron's gasp of dismay swirled through their minds.

"Silence!" commanded Lady Argentyne. "The daemon senses us." They froze.

After a few moments, the daemon seized the phial from Amira and quaffed the contents. Immediately it began to blaze a paler green, and floated upwards. Amira unfolded her wings and followed behind, flying towards the hills beyond which writhed the coiling black smoke.

"Do we follow?"

"Let us first see if we can learn what we need to know here. I have little desire to be too far from this lake, however foul it is, lest we trap ourselves." They eased forward along the now empty path, straining to hear any voices. The green daemon must have been a straggler.

"I mislike this emptiness," the nyad muttered. "It is normally a noisy land of folk hurrying from place to place, some served by their thralls such as she you named Amira. Something of great import must be calling them to Keothach, the Cauldron of Smokes."

"Keo-what?"

"You will see, Danai. We must fly if we are to discover the meaning of all this. Toron, heft your wings. While we are one, your thoughts have weight."

"I don't have any." The confusion in his mind came through as dark blue, almost black.

"Imagine yourself in flight. I will do the rest."

"And Danai?"

"I will carry her as well."

Lady Argentyne heaved into the air and lumbered towards the smoke column. As they scudded above the dry hills into the next valley, Danai beheld a roiling reddish-orange glow about the seething smoke's root that grew ever brighter. Dwellings clotted the hillsides, clustered around smaller glowing wells of fire or smoking vents that gave off a foul stench as they flew overhead.

At the valley's heart lay a fiery lake, twisted about a jutting outcrop of stone. It boiled scarlet, bursts of scabrous yellow that released great gouts of smoke convulsing the surface, to be swallowed in slurping gulps. Upon the outcrop's apex squatted a hulking black split-spired tower surrounded by smaller dwellings about which writhed a long wall. Torches were scattered throughout the enclosure. "Behold Naloch," murmured Lady Argentyne, "high seat of the Firelord. About it boils Keothach."

Hoards of beings were gathering on the open plain that surround Naloch, fanning out in wide waves. Danai could see the torch-like forms of fire daemiani in flames of every hue. Many collared Feyrees and dwarves were there, and others whom she guessed were Ael or something like. Some non-daemiani had no collars; she wondered why. A roar went up.

"We must land." They began to descend into Naloch's courtyard. "Here we can listen and observe, but will not risk an encounter with that mob." They landed beside the perimeter wall and kept to the shadows, avoiding the troop of fire daemiani that flickered by on a stream of flames. The roar from thousands of throats rattled the air and ground a second time, then fell silent.

From high above, a deep yet rasping voice cried out. They could not see who—or what—it belonged to. "Folk of Nonetre. I give you greetings!"

"All hail, all hail to the Herald," the throng shouted in unison.

"A prophecy this day has come true, as I long ago foretold. One has come to us from a realm rich in those things that Nonetre deserves. He has chosen to embrace our realm, and lead us down new paths of enlightenment, challenge our old way of doing things, make us leaders among realms, even daemensions. Give all hail to Tvashtar Tizon, anointed Firelord of Nonetre!" The air quivered under the onslaught of screams and shrieks of gladness.

Lady Argentyne had slipped along the wall as the Herald was shouting his tidings until they commanded a view of the balcony on which he stood, an ashy wizened figure crooked like a burnt branch. Beside him appeared a tall, glowing figure, clad in a supple black tunic, a red and black mantle draped between his golden wings. A radiant smile slashed his face. He waved his hand, trailing an arc of fire. Later Danai would learn it was called the *Ilan*, the arched salute of the fire daemiani. She stifled her dismay.

It was Pook.

Behind him Danai glimpsed another Feyree, her scarlet skin a gash against the tower's black stone, golden wings and hair a stark contrast. "We have seen more than enough." Lady Argentyne backed into the shadows. "We must flee while the sky yet remains empty. Let us away." The sight that confronted their eyes as they cleared the wall would be forever scalded into Danai's memory.

A tapestry of shadowed and flaming figures capered in mad delight under the smoking column's writhing gloom. Fire daemiani exploded upwards, cavorting in blazing displays that left trails of hissing sparks. The air throbbed with shouts and shrieks and drums. "Tvashtar Tizon, Tvashtar Tizon, all hail our new Tvashtar!" Keothach vomited glowing geysers of red and maroon and yellow-white.

"We must rise above this," panted the nyad.

Danai sensed Toron laboring to help carry them further aloft. She must help somehow! She thought of how it felt to fly on Wag-Tail, tried to imagine herself flying. She heard Lady Argentyne gasp as they soared upwards.

"But you have no wings!" Toron's amazement was sharp and bright.

"Neither...do...you...for a...fact," Danai jerked out, trying to stay focused on the movements of flying, shoving aside the intruding vision of Pook. Stroke down, push up, stroke down, push up. Already the burning valley was receding, the cacophony of sound crashing over the hills like a rogue wave. Ahead through the dusky haze, Danai saw the welcome sight of the brown lake lying dully under the setting suns. They plunged in, the waters sealing off the sound with a gurgle. Again Danai felt the strange shudder, and then they were in the fresh silvery waters of the nyad's lake, rising upwards into the gloaming. An egg-shaped Lunasa cast a soft light across the lake. The damp air was sweet with the scent of flowers.

Lady Argentyne hurried them across the waters to the hidden cave. Inside she advanced with great care—Toron's and Danai's bodyglow could barely be seen. She leaned a moment over each body, reaching down to touch the right temple with her forefinger. "*Lessay.*"

Danai cried out as her released thoughts rejoined her own body's senses. It hurt to breathe. Every sensation felt fresh and raw, her nerves jangled by sound, taste, texture. Is this how a newborn feels, some part of her mind asked. She heard Toron groan.

"Be still, be still," Lady Argentyne soothed, gently holding Danai's shoulders in place. "It will pass in a few moments. Breathe softly, keep they eyes closed, listen only to my voice, daughter of daughters. A wind drifts among the little waves, dancing in their soft silver curves, giving back to Lunasa his blessed light. The birds sleep, save for the night owl who guards my lake. There are yet many dawnshines where all shall be as we have known. Be still, be still."

The nyad's gentle chant soothed like lavender oil as Danai fitted back into her body. Gradually the pain was replaced by an enervating tingle that coursed throughout her limbs. She sat up, pushing against Lady Argentyne's hands. "I think I'm all right. Toron?"

Fist clenched, he lay sucking deep gulps of air, his bodyglow shuddering back and forth over his body, his tunic sweat-darkened. The nyad knelt beside him, stroking his brow, matching her breathing to his. Toron gasped, then relaxed, his shimmer brightening. His eyes opened, and to Danai's utter surprise, glittered with tears.

"He is of the lost, my Lady. He is of the lost." She nodded, her face carved by sorrow.

"What do you mean?" Danai stared from one face to the other. "We can rescue Pook. Bring him back from that awful place!"

"He chose to go there," Toron sighed. "And not as a thrall—there is sometimes at least hope for those that are trapped and forced into being thralls. You heard that mob. He is their new Tvashtar, the Firelord."

"He will be warped by that evil shadow, Eshel," Lady Argentyne added, "deformed until he is everything the daemiani hold dear."

"For Lampion, Pook is dead, and by his own choosing." The finality of Toron's voice sent a shiver through Danai.

"Not truly dead." The nyad spoke more to herself. "For the dead cannot return to lay claim to the realm they abandoned." Her voice grew hollow as she spoke in vision-tongue. "He shall return with sweetened words and promises, and it will be our choice to allow his return. And the Tvashtar will swallow all in a winter of fire, when even the deepest snows cannot overcome him, then from where he least expects it shall encounter tear-filled resistance."

"And the blossom time?" whispered Danai. "Shall it return?"

"It is not granted to me to see that far."

* * * * *

They both stood gazing at the ripple where the nyad had slipped beneath the silvered surface. A gentle breeze eddied through the branches, shuffling a few leaves. An owl hooted.

Danai turned to Toron. "Now what?"

He studied the star-pierced sky a few moments before answering. "I speak to you again not as a spryte but as a Feyree, for it is clear to me that you are to play a great role in whatever the future holds for our folk. You know well that I mistrust the Dolmen. In you he sees great change—and he is likely right—and he deems it for evil. Yet I do not know if you will be the maker of change or perhaps the one who deflects the maker. Even the Lady, with all her powers, could not scry your future that far, or so she told me. For all that, we must involve the Dolmen in this finding—and it is given that he will see it as yet more proof that you are a daemon-sent changeling. Not a messenger. Would that I knew all the answers, for I feel in my wings the ache that comes with only the most fierce of weather, when all wise Feyree stay in their bowers, and only the foolhardy and unlucky are caught without."

"I think we should seek counsel first with my aunt. She doesn't trust the Dolmen any more than you."

"A wise thought. And she is not alone. He has assumed a great mantle of power over the multitude of seasons. Where once he was a loremaster who advised and counseled, teaching from the Scrolls of Atonement, he has contrived to become one of greater import than all others, save perhaps the Lord and Lady, the lawgiver, the final judge. I confess, though it be heresy, I am not always sure that Lunasa's messages are true, or if they are but mouthings that chart the desired course of the Dolmen. Yet I have never seen him do other than what he believed was best for the folk. Until your and Joson's Dream Councils. It is well Triasa suspected him, or you would have joined Aaron in death. Come, we must return to the Dell. We are overlate."

She reached out to stay him. "Toron, could we remain here until dawnshine? Who knows what is waiting among the tree trunks?"

"When you are with a Guardian, you have little to fear." Toron tapped his dirq hilt meaningfully.

"It's not fear. Call it bad energy or a premonition. My shoulders are tingling."

He studied her shoulders thoughtfully, noting their pulsing glow, then glanced about. "Explain, but speak softly. They do more than glow?"

"So far it's ranged from a slight tingle to almost burning. Around the Dolmen and Pook."

"Hmmmm. And who knows what else? The Lady has provided you with an early warning, much like our perimeter sentinels—both wood and fey folk—who help guard the dells. Without them, we could easily be overrun. With them, we have at least time to prepare and send Guardians before the damage cannot be undone. Indeed, as the fox said, 'heed thy silvered self.' How feel your shoulders now?"

"It's gone."

"Then whatever provoked it is out of range—for the moment. We shall keep our converse in safer channels, as your gift suggests."

"A gift or a curse?" Danai squatted to scoop up a handful of sand, then flung it far into the water. It sank with a sprinkling hiss, sending off a litter of ripples in all directions. "Why me?"

"Ah! The question that torments us all in times of unknowing. I will let you know if I find out." He stretched out comfortably beside her, drooping his wings so that he could lay on them, and folded hands behind his head. "Have you ever noticed that Lunasa is most beautiful when he reveals all his wrinkles?"

Distracted, Danai peered up at the creamy orb and its tracery of dark grey lines and pockmarks. "No, I haven't."

"And like any of the folk, his face is ever-changing."

"He looks the same to me as always."

"That is because you are young—what, twenty one or two winters that you have weathered? Lunasa changes in small gradual ways that you can only see if you are long-lived. Your eyes are veiled by youth."

"How old are you Toron?" He was silent for so long, Danai wondered if he had dozed off. The breeze slowed to an occasional sigh.

"I was birthed in the winter that Iniyo's third-born son perished. That he had died in a fashion so like his sire and Alambi sent my mother into shock—as it did many of the folk. The Healers doubted I would survive, for I was no bigger than an apple's seed—and scrawny besides. For many days I wandered between this realm and the Veil of the dead, but the Healers' great skill called me back, and so I survived."

Searching her recall of the Teachings, Danai attempted to determine his age. "That would make you over three hundred winters old!"

"Aye. And yet the nyad and all her kin are far older than that for they came from the time of Solon, and even before."

"You don't seem that old."

He laughed outright, his chuckle dancing through the air among the glowflies. "I thank you, maiden, for that compliment. I am what we older fey jokingly call 'well-seasoned.' We Feyree do age rather well, I agree. What did you expect? Some addle-pated, withered old stick?"

"Well, no, I mean..." She was thankful it was dark, so Toron could not see her blush. "But we usually don't talk about our ages, and you don't look much over one hundred. Is it magic?"

"No, simply a gift of the Mother. She created each with a different life span as she saw fit. My nightwing will fly me at most only one or two lumnas before he passes. The Ael and the Troich live equally long, and are the longest-living among all the two-footed folk. All things in their place. Some of us are just craggier than others, whatever their age."

"Is my aunt as, um, old as you?"

"No, she is over one hundred and sixty winters younger. No Mentor can be less than one hundred winters. I was, in fact, her Mentor at her Rites."

"Really? Have they changed much over time?"

Toron's voice sobered. "Yes. Once they were, how shall I say, more gentle, more kindly. The magics, the trainings were the same. But dwarves and Ael were invited to share of their lore as well, and so keep the bond between our folk. But that has faded under the present Dolmen who assumed his place some two hundred winters past."

"And the Rite of Krisalys?" She hoped he didn't hear the tremor in her voice.

"It was known by that name, but it was a dance where the Mentors would circle about, winding you in the lightest filaments of gossamer—woven for us by the gossamer worms—until you were lightly cloaked and bound. And then the Lord and Lady would cast over that a mantle of nettleweed soaked with *numronbar's* pungent oil that numbed the shoulders, particularly the wing bumps so the wings could be released. The stink of the stuff always brought tears to the eyes of the newly-fledged sprytes, but it was a joyous event."

"Released?"

"That I cannot tell you, nor how the Rite now goes."

"Did sprytes die?"

"Beyond rarely. I mentored at many a Rite where at most carelessness caught injury. The deaths came later."

"When?"

"Ah. That is an awkward question, rooted in changing leaders. The Twins became great counselors, refusing the folk's petition to become Lord and Lady. Alambi advised that it was unwise for two of the same birth tree to share the throne, and that in time became law. In the seasons after Firestar Night, they summoned all the remaining loremasters and Guild Masters and wove together the Scroll of Spells from all these masters knew. They did not ask of their mother, for they all agreed her knowledge was best left dead among the many wise ones who had perished.

"As the realm healed—and that was long in happening—they gathered to them younger Feyree who had shown great promise wielding the magics. For as you must now realize, some are better than others. And they were taught parts of the Scroll, even as rules of conduct were established for how and what and when a spell could be used. Those strict rules formed the heart of the Scrolls of Atonement, and they forbade the use of magic for aught but the betterment of the realm. Each apprentice worked for many, many seasons. Some bowed out, others were given roles as loremasters for the smaller outlying dells, and they in turn taught others. And so the lore carried down through the winters. Among them one shown forth as a leader who could bend magic to his will, and wring from it the last dregs of power."

"The Dolmen?"

"The Dolmen. But not the present loremaster. He arose much later, under the tutelage of the fourth Dolmen. For each in turn selects apprentices and trains them even as did the Twins. The first Dolmen took the name of the standing stones that were once placed as markers about our dells in the days beyond memory or myth, for he said they were the most ancient of guardians and his role was to be the same. Under the mantle of the Twins he rose in skill, but always he used the magic as the Twins directed, and then only sparingly. "Magic attracts magic," he warned the apprentice loremasters. "Never forget. And it need not be from within our realm." That is why the Mentors form protective circles about you and cast spells of preparation before executing certain magics lest they attract—as you did—more than planned.

"For many seasons, the Twins and the Dolmen worked to heal and rebuild the land, always with prior approval from the Lord and Lady. Once peace was safely rooted, the Dolmen received permission to depart this lake, and settle in the Great Dell by the Skystone—believed to be the firestar that fell on that eve of banishment. The Twins never settled, instead journeying about the realm, weaving the folk back together with the new Laws and Teachings scribed in the Scrolls so that all would know—and obey." Toron's voice trailed off into a smothered yawn.

"You said they perished?"

"Yes. But it is late, and that is a tale for another time. The morrow will not be an easy day, and we will need all our wits about us to plot our path. Sleep sweet."

Danai lay gazing at Lunasa where he rested on the crown of cliffs above the lake's western edge. The owl hooted again, and she wondered if it was the nyad's. The thick silence of middle-night lulled her into a dreamless sleep.

* * * * *

Chapter Seventeen

"Yet again we are presented a tale wherein the so-called spryte Danai consorts with daemiani! Can you still doubt she is a danger to our folk?" The Dolmen shoved its face close to Triasa's.

"You see one side, I see the other," Triasa snapped. "The Lady has silvered her for an unknown purpose and bestows upon her a marked preference unheard of for any Feyree, much less a spryte. Her Dream Council summons her to be a Healer, perhaps even a Charmer. Lunasa himself intervened against the fire daemon's assault on their sojourn. Yet you stubbornly insist she is a danger, instead of considering the possibility she may be of vital importance in ways not yet given to us to know. You who are supposed to be impartial instead are more interested in your ill will towards her—rather than the fact that Pook has been declared Tvashtar and will be prodded to pursue the Mother knows what actions against the Feyree."

The Dolmen pursed his lips contemptuously. "Many will be the seasons before one such as Pook can be more than a figurehead."

"You are wrong," Majikian interjected. "Pook demonstrated an unusual aptitude for magic. I was hard put to prevent him from experimenting beyond the First Tier, and despite warnings, I oft' wondered if he was practicing during respites when none could witness. Yet never had I enough proof. In him, this Eshel may have found the perfect blend of vanity and talent to mold something far more dangerous than a so-called figurehead. From what Toron says, Lady

Argentyne told him about this Herald, he is of Solon's ilk and not to be lightly dismissed."

A chorus of 'ayes' came from several other Mentors where they stood gathered before the Skystone. The Dolmen motioned for silence. "We do not ignore the Lady's far-sighted wisdom. But it is not something that can happen quickly. Lunasa told us to proceed with these Rites. At the gathering of the Chief Tains for Krisalys shall we discuss this issue."

"Will you at not least advise Lord Andamion and Lady Atelai?" Toron asked.

"We have kept them informed as required." The Dolmen's eyes shifted. "It is our thought that Danai be eliminated from these Rites."

"Never did I think I would say such a thing, but you are a fool Hnanan!" Toron ignored the gasps that using the Dolmen's birth name kindled. "You dwell on dust specks when a rock is racing towards you. Too long has this realm been at peace if the Most High Loremaster can be so thick-minded."

"Thee dare name us in front of others?" The Dolmen's eyes blazed red.

Toron crossed his arms and assumed the Guardian's defense stance. "I do. For all that you are the Most High, you are also of the folk, and it is our right, no matter one's Tier, to speak if we feel another's actions endanger the Feyree."

The Dolmen jabbed his finger at Toron. "We will hear no more on this matter until Krisalys!" A spurt of green flame arced towards the Guardian, who dodged aside. "Lunasa has spoken to me and we shall obey!" It stalked into the Skystone, ignoring the shocked protests of the Mentors.

"When Krisalys comes, I will send messages to the highest-tiered Guardians of each dell," Toron told Triasa once they were out of earshot of the other Mentors and back in the Dell. "They can at least accompany the Chief Tains as they journey here, and then we will have many wiser minds that can perhaps dislodge this wrong-headed thinking."

"It is my thought that we should summon more than our own folk," Triasa suggested as they dodged around a clover clump.

"Such as?"

"At least the dwarves and Ael. I believe that their sendings come from the Mother, and even if my thought is flawed, it would be well to refresh the old ties in the event—"

"Of attack?"

"Of war," Triasa whispered softly, her eyes bleak. "Of war."

* * * * *

Danai sighed. With the loss of Aaron and Pook, their little group felt sad and silent. Each had tracked down their Mentor and returned by evenmeal. Joson had been all for going out to search for Danai when she and Toron failed to return and had been "as impatient as a rabbit with a blister on his bum," according to Rhytha when his request was denied. Danai mesmerized them with her descriptions of Nonetre, and of Pook turned Tvashtar.

"Should you even be telling us this Danai?" Rhytha glanced uneasily over her shoulder.

"Perhaps not, but I choose to. If something happens to me," she glanced meaningfully as Joson, "I want you to know."

"It's the Dolmen, isn't it?" Damon muttered. "It's disliked you ever since the Truthing Well."

"Hah! Disliked is a mild way of describing it. It tried to kill me during Dream Council." Her voice was bitter with disgust. "The Most High. Now there's a skald-myth. I wonder how many other sprytes have died by its hand because they did not fit in with its vision of the folk."

Elanoria gasped at such heresy while Rhytha reached out to clasp Danai's hand. "I have wondered why you returned so haggard when most of us were relieved to find our Callings. And now I think I know why I always see a Mentor somewhere within sight of you. You are being guarded."

Danai glanced furtively about. "I had not even noticed."

"Is it possible it killed Aaron?" Damon's voice cracked as he shivered in the rising breeze.

It took Danai a few moments to shove her answer past the lump in her throat. "No. You know how he loved life and having fun, often at others' dismay. He made a mistake, and it cost him everything. How much I miss him." She could no longer suppress the tiny sobs that welled up. Rhytha reached to hug her, while Damon patted her hand.

"And now we've lost Pook to the daemiani." Joson made a rude noise. "Somehow I always figured that Pook was too smart to be lured into anything like that."

"Maybe, maybe not," countered Rhytha. "He's always asked questions and wanted to learn things. Remember how impatient he was with these Rites, and how interested he was in how to be a loremaster? I guess he's gotten his wish."

"Hardly!" Danai smeared away her tears. "He has wings and is being worshipped, but that does not mean he is skilled in anything more than he already was—not yet at least. Leaders don't always know more than others—as I have grim reason to know."

"So what do we do?" Damon demanded.

"Triasa and Toron said wait. I don't think there is much else we can do."

"I would add 'watch' to that list, myself," Joson said as they settled for the night.

* * * * *

It was an uneasy pod that answered the dawnshine reed pipe. Rhytha sniffed the wind as they walked towards the waiting Mentors. "Smells like leaf change is starting—that almost smoky smell? Hard to believe we're in our fifth lumna."

"And at the end of the sixth, Krisalys," Joson said.

Elanoria's eyes narrowed as she saw the Dolmen standing among the uncowled Mentors. "I wonder what delightful new adventure it has for us today."

"Shhhh. Somebody will hear you." Rhytha poked her arm.

Within moments of sitting down, Danai's shoulders begin to tingle. The Mentors formed their Circle about the pod. Conflicting energies vibrated through the air. If energy was colored, she thought, the space above me would be crammed with shattered rainbows. There is no harmony, no balance here. Out of the corner of her eye, she thought she saw the air coalesce into a brief blue flicker just behind Mentor Narldon, but she blinked, and it was gone. The Dolmen stepped forward.

"Sprytes, heed us. Nearly trained are ye all in many of the necessary magics and skills fitting for the First Tier. Krisalys awaits ye. There remains yet one other Rite which together binds all that ye have learned. Morrowmorn, after ye have been taught the journey spells, ye shall commence the Rite of the Beast." It paused.

"This sounds bad already," Joson whispered to Danai.

"Ye shall set forth to claim a tear from the Ice Dragon." An explosion of dismayed and angry cries came from several Mentors. The Dolmen held up its staff for silence, then continued. "To Snodon Tor shall ye journey, beyond the Anlyn Hills, and as proof of thy success shall ye bring back a dragon's tear. This is not a journey to be taken lightly. Sprytes have died in the past."

Joson sighed. "Why am I not surprised?"

As if it had overheard, the Dolmen slowly turned its head to stare at them, and Danai's shoulders crawled at the black eyes glittering snake-like from within its cowl. "Behind the Anlyn Hills ascend the Rymple Mountains, the backbone of which are the highest Tors. Ever snow-clad. Ever dangerous. It is at least two sevendays' journey each way—in fair weather. Ye will be set upon the proper path morrowmorn. Fare ye well."

The Mentors gazed after the retreating figure in stunned silence, oblivious to how their expressions were affecting the sprytes. "This is not good," Damon said. "They didn't know what it was going to say until just now—can't you tell? Look. Only Oyon, Mehrten, Qyon, Narldon and Poron don't seem bothered. As if whatever the Dolmen says is right by them."

"Sprytes, ye shall learn the journey spells as ordered by the Dolmen." Oyon stepped forth into the confusion, quickly dividing up the pod and assigning them to Mentors. Danai realized he had put her with Mehrten and Poron—as if keeping me away from those who believe me, she thought.

The day's remainder was engaged with learning the specific incantations that would help them on trail, as well as how to prevent any spellcasting from attracting prying eyes, or worse.

* * * * *

After mornmeal, the sprytes gathered to receive final counsel, then went to get their rucksacks and kuis. Everyone girded on their dirqs. As she collected her journey food, Danai felt a prickling sense of unease. She glanced about, but the Dolmen was nowhere in sight. Mentor Illiai summoned them and gave clear directions. "Fare ye well and may Lunasa and the Mother guard ye." She waved them off.

As soon as they were beyond the Dell's edge and a ways into the woods, Danai suggested a halt so that the protection spell could be cast. To her surprise, none disagreed, and for a few moments the air shimmered with energy as each spryte invoked the spell. Joson then recommended the gathering of additional weapons while they remained safe in the Dell's truce zone. Spears and cudgels were the fastest to make, aind the air was soon cluttered with the crack of sticks being snapped off. Points were rough-carved, and hand-grips smoothed as the sun climbed overhead.

By late-day, the pod had marched to where Joson, Danai, and several others guessed the truce zone would end. About the clearing, the dull green of late summer burnished the leaves, and the hazy air danced with dust and woodflies. Already splatters of gold trimmed the ferns under which they marched, and they had to dodge around the new fall of still-green acorns and hull-shrouded walnuts that dotted the ground as they passed among the trees. They had stopped to enjoy a feast of blackberries, tugging the fruit from the burred branches in teams of two, then dividing the plump fruits into segments and sucking the sweet dark flesh from around the soft seeds.

"Let's spend the night here," Joson advised. "We should still be within the safety of the Dell. But I do think we should set a watch," he added, staring at the deep shadows gathering in the gloaming. Above, the first stars were pricking through the indigo sky.

"Why bother?" yawned Ymeran, a lanky bronze-haired spryte the pale color of freshly-hewn pine. He lay sprawled on the pile of snowberry leaves he had gathered, arms tucked behind his head.

"We're also near the edge, which means there may be creatures who don't feel beholden to honor the rules. Why shouldn't they slip in and gobble up a spryte or two for an early evening snack? I don't know what your Truthing Well sojourn was like, Ymeran, but we collided with a clawcat just along the ridge above here, and it had no interest in Charmers' truces. Trust me on this one."

A sudden gust of wind sent a swirl of new fallen leaves hissing and crackling about, startling several sprytes. Poochigan stood up. "I'll stand watch with you Joson. How long should the watch be, and who will follow us?"

"Let first watch end at Lunasa's high, the second when he touches the hills. Tonight is *Roinn*, so there should be enough light. We should plan to head out at dawnshine. We're all going to have to do this during this journey. Who takes second watch?" After Merlon and Kerion volunteered, Joson grasped his new spear, and strode to the clearing's edge. Poochigan marched to the opposite side.

"Does he really believe there's any danger here?" Siddiqui asked Danai, who was impressed with Joson's foresight.

Danai had to squint to see her. She had the same coloring as Pook and was barely visible in the gloaming. Only her body shimmer and the glow of her eyes catching the rising half moon's light as it filtered through the branches revealed her presence. "Yes. Call it a feeling, but I think we should err on the side of watching everything. There's been too much weirdness."

Siddiqui nodded. "No argument there."

Sunrise found them marching along the ridge. Danai glanced hopefully for Tlarg as they passed Windsrest Carrig, but it was too early, and she had no way to let him know she would not be there.

Six days marching took them well up into the Anlyn Hills. The pod stood on the stony brow of a steep hill, gazing at the distant snow-crested Rymples. "Which one do you think is Snodon?" Damon asked, shielding his eyes from the sun's glare.

Joson pointed. "That tor with the double peak, according to Mentor Illiai."

"Looks forever away. How far would you guess?"

"More than the two sevendays the Dolmen said. He must have been thinking in dwarf strides or something." Joson ran fingers through sweat-clumped hair. "I'm guessing at least another sevenday, probably more. We've got to get across the River Dunakey, follow the Silverstream, and then find the Kairncross Pass trail. I'm pretty sure that's the Dunakey down there."

Below, the forest slumped down to the broad band of a sparkling river. "You're right," Sohain remarked as he came up beside them. "Upriver leads to Tequestar Glen where my folk live. Follow the river west two days march, and it will meet with the Silverstream which pours from the Rymples' heart." A wistful smile crossed his coppery face as his dark purple eyes gazed northwest. "Would that I could keep marching three more days beyond that and return to my dell for good." With a shrug, he proceeded down the steep trail, feet kicking up puffs of dust.

Elanoria briefly paused beside Danai to glare at the mountains. "I can't wait to get these stupid Rites over with. If I didn't want to be able to fly so badly, I'd quit too." She hitched her rucksack over her shoulder and followed Sohain.

As the rest of the pod trooped past, followed by Joson, Danai hesitated and glanced over her shoulder. It had become a habit and was giving her a bit of a stiff neck.

"Still bothered by something there?" Joson stopped to look back up at her.

"Yes and no." She peered around once more, then joined him. "It's both what's there and not there. Even allowing for the south-march some birds start at this season, have you noticed the lack of birds and wood folk? And then there's that blasted blue spark. I saw it again last night after we had settled in, and my shoulders ache on and off. I'm sure we're being followed, but by who or what?"

"Better stay close together then." He picked up the pace, and in few moments they caught up with the pod just as it passed into a tiny glade plump with sunlight. A lack of rain had parched the long grasses to dull straw, and stumps of flowers sat hunched about. Off to the right squatted a bulbous outcrop of reddish stone. The warm air was heavy with scents of dust and sun-baked grass. They approached the stone slowly, dodging carefully among the grass blades that had grown sharp-edged with dryness.

There was a loud crack, and the stone gaped open. Pation gave a shout of warning, then leveled his spear as a silver-bearded figure stepped forth, shielding its eyes against the sun's glare. "The Mother's greeting," said a gravelly voice as the figure raised an empty callused palm towards the pod.

"Tlarg!" Danai cried out with mingled relief and delight. She darted past her podmates to hug the dwarf's legs, Joson three steps behind.

Tlarg blushed and harrumphed, patting their heads. "Maiden, glad am I to see thee. My path had already turned towards the Dell when thy message arrived from Peymlak, and so I marched towards my tunevich at Windsrest. When ye failed to appear, I learned from Flapper that ye had headed north on a quest. A good jay he is, guarding my home when I am absent." A cursory perusal of the pod brought a frown to his lips. "Where be Aaron and Tatia? Or be they with a different group?"

It already seems forever ago, Danai thought. "Tatia was hurt on our return from the Well and is likely be forever a babe in mind. Aaron...Aaron is dead." The word was so final, so brutal. An empty summary of her first love's too brief life.

"So," breathed Tlarg, perceiving the anguish Danai attempted to mask with her brittle smile. So young for the burden Shamarig foresees, he thought. Now is not the time to tell her. "I come to walk with thee and thy friends for a ways," he announced. The sprytes gaped up at him. "Rumors be traversing throughout Lampion that trouble brews, though its source be as yet undetermined. Both Ael and Troich have received sendings thick with kryptics, and in all, the fey folk be the keystone."

Danai gazed up at him, a sinking feeling in her stomach. "What kinds of sendings?"

The dwarf chewed his mustache a moment, then bluntly replied. "Of flames and Feyree, Troich and Ael against their own. Of our realm shattered under boiling darkness through which the Mother cannot even see to weep. Of a silver star charred to red yet once again silver. Beyond that no sending reveals. The Ael pass this chant throughout the land so all folk are given the alert. I was bringing it to thy Dell. It runs rough in thy tongue.

> *"Behold the rising flame.*
> *Mantled glory of new domain.*
> *Shackled will be those who disdain*
> *his rule.*
> *Seasons pass in black.*
> *Behold the silver star, blood dipped*
> *slave of truth, unstripped, unbroken.*
> *Shattered dreams will be reborn."*

Rhytha, who had approached, gave a shudder. "Ugh, it rubs me all wrong. It's so jagged-sounding."

"Warnings often are," Tlarg said with a shrug as he shouldered his knobstick. He turned towards the stone, muttered a few words, and waited until it closed with a brittle snap. Then he turned towards the pod. "Lead. I follow."

"Tlarg, did the Comhairle ever determine what the Anam revealed?" Danai asked, sidling around a shoulder-high rock even as the dwarf stepped over it. He had shortened his boot stride so as to stay with the pod, and it meant watching where he placed his feet.

He glanced at her sideways. "Aye, but here be not the place for such converse."

"Why?"

"Wag-Tail has been shadowing ye along with two sparrows these past days. Yestermorn he sent word that thee are at risk from more than one shadow."

Joson's head jerked around. "Meaning?"

"One be a *cuirna'theine*, fire daemon in the common tongue."

"That blue flame I've seen!"

"Good! At least thy trail-wits are sharper than when we first met, maiden. Where has thee seen it?"

"Only for a moment in the shadows of deep night. It hides."

"Ummm. Or steps behind the veil. To be already so bold." Tlarg muttered half-under his breath. "It is well Wag-Tail sent word."

Joson stiffened. "We've been keeping a watch."

"Well should I hope so." Tlarg swatted at a persistent fly. "The other Wag-Tail cannot see but senses. He is not sure which one bothers him most."

A gabble of tumbling waters began to play about their ears, accompanied by a welcome trill of birdsong. The slope grew steeper, ending in a jumble of water-rounded stones that forced the sprytes to slowly pick their ways around them, pausing in welcome patches of shade under larger bulges of rock and dried flower clumps. Finally they reached the Dunakey's south bank and stood watching the blue-black waters surge over huge rocks and tug at half-submerged branches.

"How in the Mother's name could we possibly cross this without wings?" Elanoria stood staring open-mouthed at the wide river. "Can you imagine how wide it must be in blossom time when the snow-melt pours down the mountains?"

"From where think thee the stones among which we stumbled came?" Tlarg smiled. "Each spring the Dunakey tidies itself, scouring banks free of the chatter of bushes, flowers, and past seasons' leavings. Often it rises as high as that bottommost branch." He pointed to a massive oak hunkered down behind a root-wrapped boulder high upon the far bank. "This be its low time."

"Low? A river can be that much bigger?"

She was rewarded by Tlarg's throaty chuckle. "Are not much traveled, are thee youngling? Nay, nay, look not so affronted—it is but speaking the truth. But to answer thy question, while the Dunakey be the widest of our realm's rivers, there are others far greater beyond our lands, and even the Dunakey widens yet more as it seeks its final resting place through the lowlands into the sea. Yet most times, there be ways to cross."

As they traveled upriver, the sprytes plied Tlarg with questions about his folk which he cheerfully answered, excusing them from using the courtesy speech. "Thee. You. What difference makes it?" he chortled. "I understand thee. You understand me." The going was slow, and the hot sun cresting above added to the heat shimmering from the sun-warmed stones and dead grasses among which they marched. Danai was glad Tlarg had joined them, his size and knobstick reassuring to see. She had dropped back to let the others talk to him, and so caught the first scent of smoke in the gathering breeze that pushed up from behind. "Tlarg! I smell smoke!"

Everyone spun about, noses to the wind. Wisps of smoke that could have been a fine haze—but were not—floated towards them. "Hasten!" bellowed Tlarg. "It be a wood fire. In this dry time it can grow beyond thy imaginings, though how it could start when no storms are about is beyond me. Run, but stay near the river's edge. We may yet need the Dunakey's aid!"

They fled, blundering among the smoothly treacherous stones. About them, the air grayed with smoke, and glancing back, Danai spotted a ridge of fire gobbling the dry bracken and grass tufts, singeing tree trunks, always leaping forward in search of more to devour. Ahead Rhytha tripped and fell. Damon seized her elbow, yanking her up, but she collapsed as her right foot touched the ground. "It hurts," she panted, then shrieked as Tlarg lumbered up, scooped her over his shoulder and kept lurching along, urging the sprytes to greater speeds.

Behind, the flames roared down to the water's edge, then turned to consume the brush along the bank. The cacophony of exploding sap and snapping flames intensified, and they were inundated by billows of choking smoke that bleared the eyes. The fire was gaining. Ahead a small rise appeared, a river-scoured tongue of dark stone that jutted into the Dunakey. "Climb! Climb!" Hoarse with smoke, Tlarg knelt down to help them swarm over the stone. The fire scrambled forward, eager, reaching, searing everything it encountered.

On the other side of the stone, the water eddied about in a shallow elbow, a backwater carved by innumerable floods. "Into the water," Tlarg rasped. "Stay close to the stone lest the river seize ye."

Siddiqui splashed in first. The waters closed over her head. "Too deep to stand," she spluttered as the others leaped into the water like a multi-colored avalanche.

"Tlarg, that branch!" Danai gestured towards the shore. The dwarf vaulted off the stone, a cliff of flames rising just behind. With an oath, he grabbed the branch, yanking it free of the clinging gravel, then plunged into the pool, anchoring the branch with his body as the sprytes clung to it, gasping and coughing.

The fire scrambled around through the brush at the stone's back-side, then seemed to crouch, nibbling about the grass tufts, as if con-templating its next move. The sprytes huddled low, Tlarg holding the branch secure as water lapped about his shoulders, floating his beard like some strange gray waterweed. His eyes narrowed, perplexed by the flames' unnatural movements.

As if hearing his thoughts, the fire heaved itself up into a swirling whirlwind littered with black ash and white hot gledes. At its heart winked a blue flame. It towered above them, teetering back and forth, belching smoke. "Beneath the water!" cried Tlarg, just before it cascaded down in a sheet of consuming flame.

Everything seemed to move slowly as Danai dove. She saw and heard the water overhead bubble and froth as it battled to quench the flames. Her chest grew tight, craving air. Still the water burned. Drown or boil, she thought. No choice. How much longer? Which death would be less painful? Or should she just push herself out into the river's currents and pray not to be dashed to fragments? The bubbling subsided just at the moment she knew she must make some decision. The river claimed victory.

How sweet the air tasted! Still thick with smoke, but it was air. About her she heard harsh panting gasps as the others broke surface. On the smoldering black bank, a desultory wriggle of fire edged away to burn a few strides further upstream before it collapsed upon itself in a cloud of smoke. Tlarg shoved the branch towards the shore, dragging the sprytes along, until they were able to stand. His cap was gone, but he seemed not to notice. Some one whimpered.

Arcieron slowly raised his head from the branch to horrified gasps. His turquoise scalp down to his eyebrows was crisped scarlet, striated with charred black. His silver eyes were dark with agony. "Get him ashore," Joson shouted, plunging back into the water followed by Damon.

Oh, for a Healer pouch, Danai thought, scanning the woods ahead. I must find some numronbar. I know it grows among the damp roots of the water-loving aspens. Some distance up the bank she caught a glint of silver-gray bark and flickering leaves among dark-needled pines. She dashed towards it, and soon came upon an aspen sapling, an outlier of several larger trees edging a small meadow. An older tree would be best, she knew. Glancing back at the pod, she darted into the woods.

The surrounding forest muted the river's eternal mumble as she hurried among the roots, slipping past piles of bronzed leaves until she reached the largest aspen's trunk. Kneeling, she delved along a partially submerged root. The rich smell of newly turned earth cleared her thoughts as she sniffed for the sweetish stink of the healing fungus. Something soft yielded in her hand. She began to dig, revealing a golden bulge laced with veins of gray growing from the root's underbelly. With a glad cry, she used her dirq to hack off a large chunk, then raced back towards the river, clutching the slightly oozing mass to her chest.

The pod was clustered about Arcieron, trying to calm him. Tlarg cradled his body, trickling cool water from cupped hands over the spryte's scalp. He glanced up at Joson's shout to see Danai. She stumbled to a stop among them, holding forth her precious burden. "Numronbar," she panted. "Water. Make a thick paste and slather it on his scalp. It will numb the pain." She knelt to catch her breath.

Sandai scurried up the bank with Elanoria, and they returned with several leaves from a hazel bush. They gave one to Siddiqui who placed the fungus on top and began chopping it into small bits. Poochigan followed them to the river's edge and scooped water into a folded leaf until it was full. As Sandai slowly dripped water from the leaf over the numronbar, Damon and Ujerion used the butt-end of the spears to mash it into a pulpy paste. Siddiqui began to smooth the paste on Arcieron's scalp, crooning softly in an attempt to soothe him.

The other sprytes milled about. Tlarg took charge. "We shelter here for the night. Ye others, forage as a group. Stay within the river's sight. Be gone not overlong. Danai! Where go thee now?"

"To find webs. And I think I saw redcup back in that meadow where I found the numronbar. We've got to get him to sleep before the pain gets worse."

Tlarg grunted approval. "Take Joson and Damon with thee. Thee were foolish to go alone. That fire was of evil nature."

"What did he mean by that?" Damon asked, as Danai lead them back towards the clearing.

Danai glanced about. "Daemiani. Talk later." They entered the woods and soon reached the meadow's edge. Late summer wildflowers topped the waving grasses. "Watch as we pass near flower stalks or shrubs," she advised. "Good places for webs."

"Why webs?" Joson dodged around a tree root.

"Something in them helps to heal," Danai explained, pausing to search among the flowers up ahead for the telltale scarlet. "My aunt uses it to help seal wounds."

"Why redcup? It's always been a great flower to sleep in, I know, even with all that black and yellow pollen it dumps on you."

"Exactly. It's the pollen that makes you sleepy. When you doze in there, the amount you inhale is pretty small, so it's not dangerous. But if you were to eat it, you'd sink into a very deep sleep. Too much, and you won't wake up." She shuddered. "Triasa said Healers sometimes use it on those who are dying to aid them to the Veil of the dead. It's a form of mercy, I guess."

"Over there." Damon pointed at a fuzzy dark green bush towering among the grass. "By Lunasa, we could use our wings just now! There's no tree nearby from which we can jump into that."

Joson drew out his dirq. "We're not here for a comfortable nap. Let's hack it down." He plunged among the spiky leaves and began chopping at the stalk. "It's pretty tough. There—watch out you all. Here it comes!" The flower toppled, the scarlet petals billowing as they caught the air.

Running along the stalk, Danai poked her head between the petals' edges.

A black and gold dumbledore confronted her with an angry buzz. She froze.

"Danai, what...?" Joson halted, hearing the irritated sound. Oh toads, he thought. Just what we need; more trouble. He vaulted over the stalk and ran up the other side, hearing the buzz grow louder. Glancing about he spotted a small twig, seized it, and swung it hard into the petals until the dumbledore's rump brought him up short. With a shrill protest, the dumbledore burst free of the redcup, fluttered above for a moment seeking its new assailant, then departed.

Taking her first breath in several moments, Danai pushed in among the petals. She carefully reached up the golden stalks to pluck the pollen-coated balls and place them in her emptied kuis to prevent the fine grains from blowing away. "Got it," she shouted. "Let's start back."

"We still need those webs," Damon reminded her.

"I wish it were dawnshine." Joson glanced about. "You can't miss those dratted things then. They're everywhere just waiting for you to run into them."

"Over there." Damon hurried forward. "Between the goldrods."

"Careful!" Joson grabbed his friend's arm. "Some of webbers have a thing for Feyree flesh. Don't just go charge into somebody's web without looking around."

They cautiously approached the large empty web, peering about. The slender cords were dull grey with stickiness. Damon raised his dirq. "How much of this stuff do we need?"

"It balls up no matter what you do," Danai replied. "I'll have to wash and separate the threads at the river. About your height and width will do fine."

Damon slashed. The web quivered. He cut again, hacking through the tough thicker strands. One of them curled about his ankle. "Help a fellow, can't you?" he panted at Joson, who bent to cover his hands with dust before attempting to pull the web away.

"I think we'd better hurry," Danai breathed. "We have company, and it's a big one. Don't look. Keep cutting you two." She stared up at the dark brown webber, cloaked with almost wispy fine hairs. Its facetted eyes gleamed red as it ogled the trio. Then it yawned, revealing oozy nippers shiny with venom, and tripped out onto the web. "Will you hurry up?"

Damon and Joson responded with a volley of oaths as Damon lost his balance and fell back against the web. Danai jumped forward to help hack him free. "Stop struggling," Joson shouted. "You're making it worse!"

The webber scuttled to a high point above them, watching Damon writhe about for a moment. Then it began to spin, a filament emerging from its backside. "It's coming down," Damon yelled. "Get out of here!"

"No!" Jason slashed in a wide arc about his friend's head, releasing him. "There! Run!" They bolted.

With an ugly clicking sound, the webber leaped into the air, caught a puff of wind and soared after the fleeing sprytes.

"Around this tree, quick!" Danai shouted, scrambling over a root. The webber, unable to control its flight, thudded with a soft squishing sound into the bark and tumbled to the ground. "Keep going! Back to the river!"

"I hate webbers," Damon gasped as they halted by the Dunakey, aglow with sunset. He turned to shake his fist back at the clearing. "I feel all stiff and sticky."

Danai laughed suddenly. "Damon, I never knew you were so clever." Joson followed her look and joined in.

"So what's so funny?" Damon looked in the same direction, but saw nothing.

"You," Danai giggled. "You have exactly what we need attached to your tunic and your legs. No wonder you feel sticky. You're covered with web! Come on. Only water will get that off you." They hastened back along the bank, Damon grumbling all the way.

* * * * *

Chapter Eighteen

"Praise to the Mother for thy safe return!" Tlarg waved at them. "The others are already back and have had good hunting." Behind him, piled on clean leaves, were an assortment of berries, seeds, and bright green watercress still shiny with damp. A shelter of overlapped leaves protected Arcieron.

Danai looked up at Tlarg. "How is he?"

"Thy paste has eased the burning, and for a little while he recognized some of thy fellows. But now he drifts, murmuring memories. There be no fashion by which he can continue this journey. Such scorchings have I seen before, and always will he be a bald Feyree after this. Be that as it may, he must be returned to thy folk so they can make him whole."

"Tlarg, we're six days away from the Dell," Joson objected. "Even with all your underground trails and longer legs, it must be at least a two days march, and I'll bet that whatever is following us would like nothing better than our waiting here so it can attack."

"Think thee that I have not been considering all this?" The dwarf scratched irritably at his neck. "I would carry him back, yet it is clear that ye must remain guarded until thy shadows play at their next move."

"Can you not summon Wag-Tail?" Danai suggested.

Tlarg's eyes lit up. "My wits are addled that I would not think of my winged friend. Of late the younger Troich have teased me for such slow thinking. Mayhap they have good reason." He threw his head back and nearly deafened them with a cawing screech. Off in the woods, they heard a distant reply. "He shall be here in short time. Hast been following ye all along, which is how I knew where to meet ye."

Danai nodded, then gingerly tapped Damon's elbow. "Time for you to unweb. Joson, get some of the others to help you. Gently peel that stuff off, then hold it in the water where there's a light current to rinse off the worst of the stickiness. Try to keep it untangled. I've got to figure out how to make this sleeping draught." She peeked under the lid of her kuis at the six pollen balls. Much had shaken off and settled like the finest golden sand flecked with black at the bottom.

Elanoria came up behind her. "You mean you don't know?"

"I've no training in this sort of thing yet," Danai said. "My Dream Council may have said Healer and Charmer, but what I know comes from watching my aunt and her Healer friends. Doesn't seem like anyone else here knows much about healing either. Which means, no, I don't know the precise amount to mix."

"You could kill him!"

"Thanks for reminding me."

"Then you shouldn't try it."

"And leave Arcieron in such pain? Are you crazed?"

Tlarg interceded. "Younglings, enough. Maiden, can thee not treat the lad as a babe? Small tastes and wait to see the effect? Better too little than too much."

Danai nodded. "And you said your wits were addled. It is ours that are none too good. Does that satisfy you Ela?" She bit her lip as her friend stamped off. "She's not been the same since Pook went to Nonetre."

"They were mated?"

"No. But I think she was very sweet on him, and he certainly flirted with her a lot. She's been very sour ever since."

"Such thinking clouds judgment. Now what is it thee needs?"

At Danai's request, Tlarg summoned Siddiqui who had shared with Danai that her Dream Council also called for her to be a Healer. She had just finished binding Rhytha's ankle with the tunic strips offered by several sprytes. Procuring a second kuis, she came over to help. Into the kuis Danai placed a tiny pinch of pollen, then slowly added drops of water while Siddiqui stirred until a syrupy sweet-smelling mixture formed. "Tlarg, what if I do make a mistake and kill him?"

"Canst only try maiden, canst only try. Give him but a tiny sip. If my memory serves right, redcup brings sleep in a very short time, so thee can measure the effects."

"And we'll listen to his breathing," Siddiqui said. "If it gets too slow, he's in trouble. We'll need to wake him."

"How do you know?"

"Snail-brain of a brother broke his leg running from an angry squirrel. He was stupid enough to raid its nut pile. The Healers had him in redcup for several days."

There was a whoosh of wings and startled shouts from scattering sprytes. Wag-Tail plopped down a few strides from Tlarg. "The Mother's greetings upon ye all," he glarked, slightly out of breath. Without waiting for the customary response, he turned towards the dwarf. "Thee gave the desperate call?"

"Aye, and a wonder it is that all the magpies in Lughadon are not here with thee," Tlarg growled. "Do thee not find that as strange?"

334 | CLAUDIA NEWCORN

Wag-Tail ruffled his feathers in disagreement. "Nay, not when a haze of sour magic be about. No bird of wise mind will fly casually into that for a stranger's call."

"Look out!" shouted Merion. Two brown balls, nearly invisible in the gathering gloaming, hurtled to the ground behind Wag-Tail, sending up bursts of sooty dust that set the nearest sprytes coughing.

"We are come," twittered the slightly larger of the two. "We heard the desperate call, and are here to aid our folk."

Danai took a half step forward. "Mentor Quenton? Mentor Melarna?" A ripple of surprised dismay came from the pod as they grasped the reality of the two sparrows.

Both bobbed. "We have joined with Wag-Tail to guard this journey. It is the least we can do, since we did not give you proper counsel during fire magic training."

Joson stepped up. "But how have you survived? You were not born birds."

Quenton gave a chirpy chuckle. "The same way all folk learn to survive in the wilderlands, my spryte, be they two or four-footed. Even as you learned—perhaps to an extreme—on your first journey, helping each other is sometimes all that makes the difference. We have stayed in the Dell, seeking food during the day and staying hidden at night in an old hole in the Shehn, and we have watched and seen much."

Tlarg stared a moment and made as if to ask a question, then changed his mind. He thumbed at the shelter. "I called for aid for the youngling under there. He cannot continue this journey." Summarizing the day's queer events, he concluded with a nod towards Danai. "The maiden was to give him a sip of redcup juice in hopes of sending him to healing sleep."

Melarna hopped over and cocked her head at the kuis. "Redcup? It is unusual to find it this late in the season. Show me the pollen Danai." She sniffed over the upheld kuis. "Very ripe redcup, but redcup nevertheless. Perchance it grows later up here. Tell me the proportions of your mix." She bobbed as she listened. "It is too watered down, but that is better than too strong. You did well. Small surprise the Mother gave you the double calling of Healer-Charmer." She twitter-laughed at Danai's surprise. "What, you think the Dell birds don't know such things?" Quenton nudged her with a slightly extended wing. "Well, yes, and Triasa kept us informed as well."

"Are you a Healer?" interrupted Elanoria, shoving through her podmates. "Because if so, Arcieron is in a lot of pain, and I think he could use your help, instead of all this gassing and chatting."

"Yes, of course." Melarna was unruffled by Elanoria's rudeness. "Danai, come. Wings make poor hands." As they moved towards the shelter, Lunasa peered out from some thin clouds, his crescent shape casting little light. Arcieron lay groaning, struggling to pull his hands free from Rhytha and Siddiqui.

"Rhytha, lift him by his shoulders." Melarna's voice was soft. "Good. Danai, let us see if he will sip. Hold the kuis tight. Pain controls the body, and his motions will not be what you expect. Arcieron, Arcieron, it is Mentor Melarna. I have come to help you."

The spryte's eyes flew open, and an arm flailed. "Muime? I tried to duck down. So much confusion. Bodies kicking in the water. The branch clubbed my head. I thought it was just bark scraping, and then the pain, the pain, the pain!" His voice rose to a scream, his body lurching against the restraining hands.

"Arcieron!" the bird screeched. The harsh sound cut through the spryte's agony. "Drink what is being given to you. It will quell the pain until we can get you back to the Dell."

"D-d-dell? B-but my wings?"

"You have completed this journey according to all rules," soothed Quenton, who had joined them. "Your wings are not forfeit. I so swear before witnesses. Now drink. That is an Order."

Arcieron drank. After several moments, they watched with relief as his jaw slackened and head slumped. "Call me if he wakes," Melarna ordered. She watched the sleeping spryte a moment. "My poor fosterling—it has been many seasons since he called me by that name."

As the sprytes ate, the birds and Tlarg sat a little ways off and discussed their choices. "The lad must be returned to the Dell, and right quickly." Tlarg was barely audible among the many night sounds. Manylegs had no regard for any type of magic, good or bad, and went about their affairs. "I mislike any thought of leaving these younglings. Had ye but seen the fire, no doubt in thy minds would there be as to the presence of a cuirna'theine."

"We do not argue with thee Tlarg," Quenton said. "But there is no way we can carry him, even bound to Wag-Tail's back, as thee suggests. The binding would likely loosen."

"Could ye not fetch a Healer and bring them here?"

Quenton clacked his beak. "Can thee imagine the debate in the Mentors' Circle? Some would leap to help, other fools would protest it was a sacrifice of the Rites, and by the time they had argued it out, the lad could be dead. The Mother knows the Dolmen permits no swerving from its path. Look what happened to us!"

"Even I, broad-backed though I be, need my riders to hold on during flight," Wag-Tail added. "Nay, Tlarg, I see nothing to it but that thee transport him back through thy hidden paths."

The dwarf still argued. "It would take two dawns at least to return him to his own. And ye has made clear that even that shortened passage of time may be too long. It is yet my thought that ye fetch the Healers."

Melarna flipped her tail with impatience. "Danai has made enough redcup that Arcieron can be kept asleep the entire journey. The numronbar cap of salve and web, if undisturbed, will protect the scorched flesh."

"And how am I to carry him? Slung over one shoulder? In my watersack? That indeed would do him great good."

Wag-Tail stamped a claw. "Tlarg, stay will I with the younglings and keep good watch. No other way is there. Would thee have the death of that lad on thy head?"

"Better the death of one than of many."

"It can be the death of none." Melarna shivered, then fluffed her feathers. "I will accompany thee through thy tunnels, much as I hate the thought. As for Arcieron, the sprytes can make a *samanth* with woven stems and birch-tree bark. It is what we carry our babes in. A special strap will let it ride comfortably on thy back. Will that suffice?"

"There is no room for thee to fly under ground." Tlarg offered up one last argument.

"Then I will walk."

"More be the like that I would end up carrying thee as well. Rather would I that thee remains here with thy sprytes. I will complete this errand alone for best speed, and at the same time, deliver my much overdue message."

* * * * *

Danai's tingling shoulders awoke her before dawn-shine. The sky was the deep, almost luminescent blue that glows only in those brief moments when the sun's outermost halo hesitates just below the horizon. Stars still studded the western sky. Her shoulders twitched as she gazed into the forest's blackness. For a moment she thought she saw movement, but when she blinked, nothing was there. Only the silence of the windless wood.

Nearby crouched the black shadows of the birds, heads tucked under their wings. A snoring Tlarg lay sprawled, looking more a knobby stone than a living creature, a high black hill among the smaller mounds of sleeping sprytes. The chilly air still smelled of smoke. With a start she realized that the two seated sprytes on watch at the edge of the group were also dozing, propped against their spears. She shivered, then flicked her fingers, whispering the warming spell. An invisible coverlet of comfortable warmth enveloped her. Her next move was to invoke the protection spell.

The tingle was fading, but she still had the lingering sense of being observed. Stepping carefully among the sleepers, she went to the river's edge and cupped handfuls of water to her mouth. It was pleasantly cool, tasting of stone, moss and distant snows. Somewhere a bird stuttered awake, its broken call piercing the hush. The sound set the scene before her in motion. The two sentinels scrambled to their feet, glanced surreptitiously around, and stiffened before

Danai's gaze. The birds jerked to alertness, fluffed huge, then began to plume their feathers smooth. Tlarg awoke with his customary snort and scratch, and a tremendous yawn. About him sprytes stretched and stood.

Elanoria and Siddiqui hurried to Arcieron. Rhytha limped along behind, supported by Danai, as Melarna hopped along beside them. She cocked her head. "He still sleeps," she chirped softly. "The best thing."

The sky brightened to rose, and color gradually returned to the landscape. Mornmeal was a hurried affair. Everybody wanted, as Damon cheerfully remarked, "to get a move on and get this Rite over with." Tlarg and the birds shared their plans with the pod for Arcieron, eliciting a mixed reaction. "You're going to leave us alone with all this danger?" Consternation glowed Merion's black eyes.

"It is not customary to have a dwarf accompany the pod," Quenton said. "There is a good reason for this being the most challenging Rite. As it is, you will have the three of us with you, and that in itself is unprecedented; however, we agreed it was the wise course."

It was also unlikely that most journeys were trailed by at least one fire daemon and probably something else, Danai thought. But this probably wasn't a good time to make that point.

The crafting of the samanth allowed the sun time to climb into the sky and warm the air. Under Melarna's direction, the pod gathered pliable fern stems—no birch twigs being low enough to reach—and peeled a sheet of birch bark as high and three times wide as themselves, careful to avoid harming the tree. The fine white powder that gave the birch its silvery cast puffed about them as they shook the bark, rendering it a translucent beige, scalloped with black twig scars. Working in pairs, the stronger sprytes wove the stems into a long cradle-like bowl and lined the inside with bark and soft moss.

Arcieron still slept, but Melarna instructed Danai to trickle drops of redcup onto his lips, where his tongue instinctively licked away the moisture. "It is best he remain asleep until he reaches the Dell."

"Won't he starve?" Joson asked, as he helped settle the spryte into the samanth. He stepped back to let Elanoria and Siddiqui secure Arcieron with a final wrapping of bark, bound in place with supple leaf stems.

"We can go without food for much longer than you imagine," Melarna chuckle-chirped. "It is liquid we require for survival. Tlarg will use the same trick to get him to consume water and more redcup during the underground march." They watched as Tlarg shouldered the samanth, and settled the strap across his broad shoulders.

"Danai, give Tlarg that kuis of redcup liquid. It will keep fresh in the cool of the tunnels for yet several days. Keep the remaining pollen. We will gather some more pieces of numronbar when we set forth and let it dry as we march, so you also have that if needed."

The sprytes gathered around Tlarg to wish him well. Danai and Joson hugged his leg, unashamed of the tears gathering behind their eyes. He harrumphed and squatted down to stare into Danai's eyes. "Maiden, heed me. No time to talk have we been given. I bear a message. Shamarig and the Comhairle foresee from the Anam's sending dark daemon-shadows upon the horizon. Not yet is the storm to break, but it gathers. Be wary. Ye will all be too many days gone for me to rejoin before ye ascend the higher tors, and there are no tunnels there of my folk of which I know. Hearken well to thy Mentors and Wag-Tail. Heed thy self above all."

Danai started at the echo of the fox's words.

He placed his hand lightly upon her and Joson's heads. "The Mother's blessing upon thee and all ye younglings." He smiled, then he clambered over the stone with his burden and was gone.

The day swelled with heat and dust as the pod hiked along the Dunakey's banks, following its way steadily into the hills. They were wide-eyed and edgy, jumping at the pop of a branch or the slurpy plop of a fish gobbling a careless manylegs. Overhead, the three birds swooped and soared in wide circles, dropping down during the pod's brief halts to report on what lay ahead.

"A season of bright colors it will not be," remarked Wag-Tail on one visit. "Even though we be higher in these hills where the season has already begun, too little rain has fallen, and already the leaves turn brown. It is a good thing ye follow this river. The many small streams that lace the woods are mostly dry." He fanned his tail. "Even the manylegs taste old and dry; the hunting is poor hereabouts."

"Do you eat manylegs?" Joson asked Mentor Quenton during another break.

"I tried a few." Quenton clacked his beak with distaste. "They squirm on the way down. Most unpleasant. I think that while we have these bird forms, in all other ways we are Feyree, so we desire the same foods we know. It is in truth easier to forage, for our eyes are like nothing you could imagine. We see beyond seeing; no motion escapes our gaze, colors are brilliant, and our sight span is wider than yours."

"How do you mean?"

"You see straight ahead and to the sides, but not behind. We see almost all around us with one glance. There are some advantages to being a bird, although I await being myself most eagerly."

At mid-day, they stopped to eat. They had barely delved into their rucksacks when Wag-Tail plummeted like a tossed stone to land beside them, hopping urgently back and forth. "Tarry not long here! I spied a strange thing but a moment's hence. Back near the aspen grove where last ye rested, though it seemed to be naught, a movement caught my eye. A drop of water looked to be crossing the dry ground! The leaves drifted aside with no wind, and through it I could see the soil, but with the strange wavering wriggle that looking through water gives. The drop moved with purpose. It heads towards ye. I watched until it vanished under a thicker cloak of spruce."

The pod needed no urging. There was a quick scramble of rucksacks being heaved back onto shoulders, and they hastened up the river at a jog trot, Poochigan helping Rhytha. Joson moved in beside Danai. "How much farther until we can cross over?"

"Melarna said around gloaming—but that was at a walk. If we can keep this pace up for a while, then maybe before the sun sets. But how is that going to help against whatever is following us?"

"While you were off getting the redcup, Siddiqui mentioned there is a secret cave up ahead, known only to Tequestar Glen. Word of it is passed down only when one goes on a journey. But it needs daylight to be found. That's why she's leading. Whatever is behind us presumably doesn't know we've picked up speed. That might give us just the time needed to find this spot and hide. Maybe it won't see or find us."

"At least we know it's probably a full Feyree," said Damon, just behind them. "No spryte has that magic."

"Nor every Feyree either." Danai grunted as she leapt over a large pebble to avoid bumping into Joson. "Being invisible in motion can only be loremaster magic. We're going to learn how to be invisible when perfectly still, but the concentration that must be needed to move with an invisible cloak...!"

Joson nodded. "You've got an idea who it is, don't you?"

"The Dolmen, right?" Damon put in.

Danai was so startled, she almost tripped over a twig jutting out of the coarse gray gravel. Without breaking stride, Joson caught her elbow and helped steady her. "How ever did you know?"

Damon gave an awkward laugh. "Well, you told us about your Dream Council. And it doesn't care when a spryte dies, as long as we obey the rules. And it's always watching you when it's about—whether with fear or hate, I don't know."

"Probably both. How many others do you think have noticed?"

"You should socialize more outside our little group, though I can't say as I blame you, what with Tatia, Aaron, and now Pook. It's all pretty ugly." He concentrated for a few strides as they traversed a rough patch of ground. "But a lot of the others have seen or sensed its sour energy towards you, even though nobody knows why. And it's probably one of the few loremasters capable of following us as Wag-Tail described."

"You're right. I can't think it would be anyone but the Dolmen. I woke this morn with tingly shoulders—they seem to act up when there's something wrong nearby—and could have sworn I saw movement in the woods. But why follow us?"

"Great way to get rid of you once and for all," puffed Joson, "and if it does the thing right, it can say you're just another casualty of these Rites."

Danai glared at him. "Thanks for sharing."

"By the way, your shoulders glow sometimes too," Joson continued, undeterred. "When you got up—I was awake—they were glowing, then dimmed a bit later."

"I know. Toron pointed it out. We should all jog along together more often," she laughed, despite her misgivings, "so we can learn all sorts of things we never knew."

They halted briefly for a suck of water. Siddiqui and Sohain continued to maintain a brisk pace. They entered a vein of ancient bedrock, cracked and scoured by the river into deep gullies and sharp-edged ridges. Feet had to be placed with care to avoid slipping. Siddiqui told them it was known as the Jharma. "It's a good thing she knows where we're headed," remarked Rhytha, leaning on Poochigan's shoulder as she slithered over a slice of stone. "This place must be a maze of dead ends. We'd probably have to go 'round it otherwise."

"Hopefully our tag-along doesn't know the way." Damon glanced behind.

"It can fly, we can't. Remember?" Joson squeezed through a narrow crack. "Just hop over this mess."

"Not and stay invisible too," Danai objected.

"As you said, it's a loremaster. And if it is the Dolmen, the Mother knows what spells it has up its sleeves. I wouldn't bet on anything but trouble. Toads, how long do we have to wriggle through this muddled shim-sham of rock?"

The cracks widened into a slender basin floored with fine grit. Danai heard echoes of the river rebounding off the dull gray walls, colliding with each other to produce a confused watery murmur. Siddiqui motioned for a halt. "It's a good thing we're passing through the Jharma in dry season. The Dunakey drowns this trail in blossom time. Up ahead, the bend of Cauldron Pool marks the place where the Silverstream meets the Dunakey. We should be there just before gloaming."

As the pod resumed its march, Danai's eye was caught by a brief golden glint near the valley's left side. "You go on," she said to Joson and Damon. "I have to step away a moment." Assuming it was for the necessary, they nodded and trotted ahead. Reaching the sparkle, she squatted down and shoved aside the loose sand. A large flake of gold as big as her head shone forth, its finely etched surface shivering back the light in glittery fragments. It's bigger than any I saw at the Goldsmythes Hall, she thought, tugging it free. Beaten thin by pounding waters, it was supple enough to roll into a tube, and she tucked it into her rucksack, not quite sure why she wanted to carry the extra weight. Wag-Tail landed beside her in a flurry of sand.

"Haste, maiden, haste! The pod is beyond thy sight. And the water drop has shed its cloak upon entering this stone maze. When the hood fell back, I beheld the dead face of thy Dolmen."

Needing no further urging, Danai sprinted the remaining length of the valley's floor to disappear into another gully and catch up with the pod. "Wag-Tail's spotted the Dolmen," she whispered to Damon and Joson as she fell in behind them. "Just entering the Jharma."

Joson scowled. "Not good. That means it may know where we're headed. Let us know if your shoulders start up. We may have to change plans."

The trail climbed steeply to crest on tall cliffs towering some forty feylengths above a swirling cauldron of thundering waters where the two rivers collided. Roiling waves clashed and frothed in the whirlpool's constant spray, striking against the cliff base and sending a low shudder up to their feet.

"We're supposed to cross that?" Elanoria took a step back from edge.

"Not right here, silly flit," Siddiqui scoffed. "Not even Feyree try to fly across Cauldron Pool. Unless you want your bones to join those of the fools that have tried. See that gap in the cliffs just west of here? That's the Dunakey, though much narrower. There is a stone causeway over which we can cross morrowmorn." Below, the waters began to take on a reddish tinge. The sun was sinking. "We don't have much time." She took several steps along the edge, peering for some mark. "Ah, here. Follow me. Have a care. It gets slippery."

She began to ease down a steep trail that clung to the water-polished cliff, flattening her back against the stone, followed by Tyra then the others. The noisy waters masked the clatter of small pebbles kicked loose by their descent. Chill splatters of spray made the footing even more slick. The trail bent, sliding into a deep cleft, overhung by a bulge of dark gray rock that cast confusing shadows. Siddiqui vanished.

Tyra stopped dead. "Siddiqui! Where are you?"

Siddiqui's head popped out from around a rocky outcrop invisible in the growing gloom. "Hurry up," she hissed. "This is no place to try and reach in the dark. Move! While there is still light."

One by one, each eased around the bulge into a slit barely wide enough to admit Joson—who thanked Lunasa that he had lost weight during the Rites. For seven heart-thudding steps they proceeded into an absolute blackness with only faint bodyglows marking their whereabouts inside the steadily thrumming cliff stone. The passage elbowed to the left, then widened abruptly into a cave. Danai gasped.

The top glowed, a medley of crystal facets and foxfire. In some time past, a tree's roots had groped through the cliff's many fissures, and the slow rotting wood had become a host for the luminescent fungus. The gleaming crystals cascaded down the cave's sides, creating an illusion of being underneath a silent, glittering torrent that trembled with the constant vibration of the Cauldron's tumult. The cave, easily large enough to accommodate several pods, was fringed by bubbles of smaller caves. A moving ribbon of silver brought Danai's attention to where a trickle of water gathered in a pool against the back wall's base, the overflow conducted out by an ancient hand-carved channel that vanished into a small crack.

Siddiqui and Sohain bowed formally to the pod. "Welcome to Mahadas-cadeum, safe haven of the Feyree of Tequestar Glen," Siddiqui said.

"Your folk's refuge in the Days of Dimness after Solon," Danai blurted out.

Siddiqui's eyes widened. "How did you know? That is closely guarded lore."

"I guessed because of the tale Lady Argentyne told us. It reminds me of her cave. I wonder what its name is—I never thought to ask."

After studying Danai for a long puzzled moment, Siddiqui continued. "This is a place our dell holds sacred, whispered down through many seasons. In bringing you here, we will have to account to our Chief Tains, for we have violated *interdee* in doing so. I must ask you to swear by Lunasa to never speak of it to others. Swear!" Her eyes glowed aqua with intensity.

Each spryte inclined their head, crossed hands over heart, and intoned the sacred vow in the ancient tongue. *"Namanala jur onsta Lunasa."* The words set the crystals humming softly.

"Siddiqui, is there more than one way out of here?" Joson asked a bit later as the pod rested, eating sparingly of their journey food, and refilling their kuis from the rivulet.

She nodded, quoting the old fey saying. "No creature has a burrow without at least a second entry. See that small cave beside the spring? Through there is another tunnel that twists up to the cliff top. While the Deum is well above the usual flood level, ever so often the waters rise even higher, and the place is inundated."

"What are the chances the Dolmen knows of this place?" Danai asked.

Siddiqui looked at Sohain. "It is High Loremaster, and likely the Chief Tains would consider it above interdee. I would say it knows. Why?"

"Because Wag-Tail said it's following us, and I'm sure it's after me." She gestured for silence amid the startled clatter of voices, and briefly told them her suspicions. Joson and Damon added their observations for support.

"All of us have seen it watching you," Ayulun said. "Much as I struggle with the Dolmen meaning ill, too much has happened for me to trust it, improper as that may be to say." Others nodded.

"Did you hear that?" Elanoria stared back at the entry tunnel.

"Look at Danai's shoulders!" Damon scrambled up.

Joson leaped to his feet, scooping up his rucksack with one motion. "The Dolmen must be near the passage. Everybody out of here. Danai, stay in front. Siddiqui, Sohain get us out of here!"

The crystal ceiling jangled shrilly, reverberating with both their emotions and the sounds of hurrying feet. The thick dust in the tunnel set them coughing as they climbed upwards through the furry blackness. With the exception of Danai's silvery shoulders, fear had virtually extinguished their bodyglows. The others followed behind her as they would a beacon. *Someday I will not run from the Dolmen*, Danai thought. *I swear.*

"Rotting slugs! I can't move the waystone!" Siddiqui shoved her shoulder hard against the tunnel's end. Danai joined her, to no avail. The stone would not budge.

"Joson, Poochigan, you other fellows. Whoever strong can fit in here, get up fast," Danai shouted. Shoving by the others, the largest lads jammed into the small hollow. "One. Two. Now!" Joints popped, throats grunted. A fine shower of dust fell. "Again," Danai urged.

"Smell! Fresh air!" Siddiqui cried. "You're doing it." The stone began to rise. "Heave to the left, onto the ledge."

The rock shifted to the left, and, like ants pouring from their disturbed nest, the sprytes scrambled out. They were back on the ledge overlooking the Cauldron. The waters boiled black and silver in Lunasa's pale light.

"Push the stone back!" Siddiqui and Sohain squatted and began to shove. Others joined. With a gritty protest, the stone slid back and disappeared. In the dim light, it was impossible to see any marks of where it lay.

"Now where?"

Danai realized with surprise that Rhytha had directed the question at her.

She looked at Siddiqui. "Siddiqui, Sohain, how quickly can we get to the river crossing from here?"

"In the dark, I have no idea," Sohain answered. "But we'll find out. In daylight, it would be a short morn's march. Let's go. We will have to follow along the cliff's edge. It will be too dark and risky to go among the tree and brush."

"You don't think we can just stay here until dawnshine?" Sandai suggested. "It took a lot of us to move that rock."

"For all we know, the Dolmen may have some spell that just pops it off," Joson said disgustedly. "I vote we move on."

"What about the hunters?" Elanoria said, peering into the forest shadows.

"We're already being hunted. I'd rather take my chances with the wood folk. At least they're just trying to survive. Lead on, Sohain."

The pod wended along the Cauldron's edge like a dimly glowing beaded necklace. It was hard to practice woodcraft in the dark, but every effort was made to move in silence until they were a good distance from the Deum. Lunasa was just a pale smear behind a scum of clouds oozing over the sky, blotting out the stars. The deeper darkness made for even slower going and occasional curses could be heard as toes were stubbed and shins banged.

"Why do you think the Dolmen just doesn't simply fly after us, instead of following on foot?" Damon asked as they trudged along.

"Actually I'm not sure it can fly," Rhytha said.

"It's got wings," Elanoria retorted. "Unlike us who could sure use them now."

"But have you ever noticed how, uh, dull they are? No, don't look at me like that. I'm not batty Ela. Haven't you ever seen how Feyree wings seem to almost shimmer in waves, as if a pulse is passing through them?"

"Almost like a heartbeat," Damon added.

"Exactly. Maybe that's why. Well, the Dolmen's don't. They just sort of flop there, almost as if they're stuck on, instead of a part of it.

I was thinking I've never seen it fly, even at the great revels. It just sort of presides over them. In fact, it's usually attired in its black robe which hides the wings."

"I always thought it was just being standoffish," Damon said.

"That too, but maybe there's more to it than that."

"Wouldn't it be wonderful if you were right, Rhytha." Danai squeezed her friend's hand.

"We can only hope," Elanoria muttered.

* * * * *

Chapter Nineteen

The first strands of dawnshine pierced the clouds, glowing the sky an angry crimson. "Red sky at morn, all journeyers be warned," Tania announced, citing the old saying.

"Let me guess," said Poochigan, his dark green skin reflecting strangely in the red rays. "Weathercaster?" He laughed at Tania's pleased smile.

The nearby brush gradually shifted from black to greens and yellows, dulled by the lurid light. As they rounded a sharp bend in the trail, Siddiqui cried out with dismay.

"What's wrong...?" Sohain's query trailed off as he came around the bend, followed by the others. A short distance beyond, the narrowed Dunakey had gashed the bedrock into a deep gully, hundreds of feylengths deep, and perhaps a hundred wide. The remnants of a slender natural stone arch spanned the gully like a broken bow. Upstream, the river widened again. Squeezed through the gully's rocky confines, the galloping waters clattered and splashed across jagged crumbling boulders. It was the perfect place to die instantly.

"Oh, this is just great." Elanoria threw her hands up. "For our wings."

"Will you just shut up about wings," Joson snapped, ignoring her sour glare. "That's why we're here in the first place. We're trying to earn them. And in case you haven't noticed, even without the Dolmen chasing us down, this is a Rite, and we would be facing this problem anyway."

Damon gazed upstream. "How close is the next crossing Siddiqui?"

She shook her head slowly, still stunned. "I don't know. I've never crossed anywhere else."

"Four days upstream," Sohain answered. "A tree spans the Dunakey above Tequestar Glen, but it's not much used."

"Too far a march," Danai decided. "Then we'd have to come back. With the Dolmen following, we'd best cross here. Ideas anyone?"

Gray daylight had replaced dawnshine's red glare. A chill breeze blew up, knocking loose a shower of leaves, some of which twirled across the gully, while others spilled down to be gobbled by tumbling waters. Something long and white wavered by. Then two more.

"Look! Webber-puffs!" Danai jumped with excitement. "Little webbers are riding on the wind. If they're nearby, and we can catch enough, we can float across this gully."

Elanoria tapped her forehead. "Lack of sleep has made you loopy!"

"No, she's right." Joson caught Danai's enthusiasm. "If the wind picks up, the force might be strong enough to carry us." Even as he spoke, another webber-puff floated by. "Quick! Dust your hands so you won't stick too much to the webs. Does anybody see where they're coming from?"

"Back behind that oak," shouted Alemeron. "There's lots. Must be a newhatched nest." The pod hurried towards the tree.

"Keep an eye out for the mother webber," Tyra cautioned. "She may or may not be dead yet."

Gathering around the nest, the sprytes watched as the tiny palm-sized webbers struggled free of the fibrous gray sack, pointed their backsides to the strengthening breeze and began to spin the fine puffs that would carry them off until the wind dropped them at their unknown destinations. The filaments tangled themselves into a bulb which would swell out and catch the wind once large enough.

"Sorry, but I need this more than you right now." Joson snapped free the billowing web-puff. The startled webber scurried a few steps away, then instinct took over and it began once more to spin. "Hey, it's not quite as sticky as I thought it would be. Ugh, but sticky enough."

"Maybe you had better grab four or five," Danai teased, hoping to relieve the tension.

"Good idea." He moved to grab another. "Everybody better grab several. We're all a bit heavier than these little things."

As they returned to the broken bridge, the sprytes struggled in the rising breeze to keep from being yanked into the air. They stood looking at each other. There was a distant grumble of thunder.

"Oh well. My idea, so here goes." Danai leaned forward with the wind, letting the web-puffs billow out, feeling them tug against her grip. There was a gust of wind, and, with a sudden jerk, she was airborne. The open maw of the ravine yawned beneath her feet, then was gone. She flew above a smooth stony bank towards some underbrush. "Oh toads! How do I stop this thing?" she muttered. She was too high to safely drop off, and her attempts to slow down did little. The web-puffs writhed and twisted, hauling her towards the woods. Then with a sigh, the wind slowed, dumping her into an aril bush laden with poisonous pink fruits. Now I know how little webbers must feel, she thought, carefully untangling herself from both the branches and webs.

She hastened back towards the river, where one after the other the sprytes were launching. Sandai and Dlargon's web-puffs collided and they plummeted to the ground just beyond the ravine, a tangle of bronze and purple limbs. She sprinted towards them, but slowed as they stood up, shook themselves and laughed wildly.

"Get me out of here!" Behind her, Elanoria's web-puff had wrapped itself around her slim frame then spread across a birch sapling's trunk. She kicked and struggled to no avail, looking, Danai thought as she suppressed a smile, like an angry mottle-faced babe in a samanth. Joson was already there and shinnied up the trunk, then sawed through the filaments until she could swing free and drop to the ground. She kept up a steady stream of curses as she sought to peel the sticky threads from her hair and arms.

Those sprytes that had landed with little mishap scampered to help the others in various predicaments, and shortly the group regathered around Siddiqui and Sohain, several still scraping off patches of web. "Now where?" Tyra asked, twitching her brown nose. "I think I smell rain and soon."

Siddiqui thumbed north towards the dark green mountain slopes. "We'll work our way back towards the Silverstream and follow that into the tors. I've heard our bards speak of a trail that follows that river. Better to cut through the woods I think, than double back to the Cauldron and look for the trail. I don't think we want to risk the Dolmen seeing us." Another rumble of thunder punctuated her last words. "At least we'll be under the trees, and maybe avoid the worst of this rain. Look—you can see the rain veil already at the Cauldron." The smell of wet dust blew by them as they gazed at the rippling gray rainfall's edge. "Come on. Let's go." The pod trotted into the moaning woods.

* * * * *

The rain began while they were marching through a grove of aspen and birch. The storm raked the branches free of leaves, allowing the fat drops to pour through. For a short while the gold, bronze, and copper leaves swirled and rattled about them, then the deluge soaked them into stillness.

"I just thought of something, Joson," Danai said. "What about the birds? We snuck out of there so quickly, I forgot about them completely. In this heavy rain, they won't be able to fly. How will they find us?"

He patted her rain-slick arm. "They'll find a way. And after all, we are supposed to be on our own. And there is one bright spot to this weather." He shook a large droplet off his nose. "Kind of hard to start a major fire, wouldn't you say?"

Without the sun, it was hard to sense the precise time of day. Finally a halt was called to eat and rest. Tired clumps of sprytes huddled under still golden ferns or large russet oak leaves that remained stiff despite the rain. Some nibbled half-heartedly at bits of miyacan, but most leaned into each other's shoulders or lay back for a short nap. "No need to take water from our kuis," Damon smiled, cupping his hand to catch a bead of water suspended on the frilly leaf of their fern.

The steady downpour softened to a gentle sprinkle, but the sky remained a rumpled grey when they finally set out again. The trail grew steeper, the leafy trees gradually replaced by pine, and they appreciated the dryer ground as they passed underneath among the needles and cones that littered the floor. "Another positive about the rain," Joson said, glancing around. "Hunters also tend to stay in their burrows."

"And we think we're the smart ones," Elanoria groused. "Wouldn't it be nice to be snuggled in a bower under feather coverlets right now? Instead, here we are, tramping along in the soaking wet rain. Bah!"

Rhytha tried to console her. "But think, Ela. In a little over one more lumna, it will be *Verlunasa*, when day and night are equal. And as soon as Lunasa reaches solas, Krisalys!"

"Thanks awfully. But right now, if you don't mind, I'm thinking about surviving a little thing called an ice dragon."

Joson and Danai rolled their eyes. "Nothing escapes you Ela," Damon said cheerfully.

Danai was glad Damon had spoken. She had almost told Elanoria to stifle it, but his was the better way. She shivered in her damp tunic, small bumples rising along her arms. Joson noticed.

"Considered using the warming spell any time recently?" He prodded her side. "One would think you're some dumb spryte instead of a Feyree-in-the-making."

"Ha-ha." She stuck out her tongue at him, then muttered the spell. The welcome cloak of warmth enveloped her. A shout came from up ahead. Siddiqui stood triumphant. "The Silverstream!" Swollen by rain, the waters slid almost silently along, a river of molten silver that gleamed despite the sky's dullness. No waves or surges broke the surface, no trees or rocks jutted forth to disturb its sheen. Siddiqui pointed upriver towards the not-so-distant tors now swathed in heavy clouds. "Yonder lies the ice dragon's lair."

"And yonder we march," said Rhytha. "There's still a good part of the day remaining, and I'd rather be marching than twiddling my thumbs." A chorus of ayes started the pod northwards.

"You think the Dolmen made it across?" Joson asked Danai later.

"Probably not. I doubt it guessed how we got across, and the rain would have washed away any scents or marks. It's likely the Dolmen would assume we're continuing up the Dunakey. By the time it finds out, especially in this weather, we'll be too far gone—I hope."

* * * * *

Four days later, they stood on a ridge among the tors. Behind them, lost somewhere in a sunny autumn haze, was the distant Dell. The Silverstream was now a thin shimmering thread, slipping deep inside a ravine on their right. A chill wind tousled their hair as they stared up into the snow-crowned peaks.

Danai and Joson had resumed the lead shortly after setting out along the Silverstream. "You should stay leader," Danai had protested to Siddiqui. "Look how you got us out of that mess."

"No thank you." Siddiqui shook her head emphatically. "My Dream Council said Healer, not Guardian, and I don't want the responsibility. What if I did something wrong, and got everybody hurt?"

Now they stood searching among the tors for Snodon. "Taller than the rest, silver brow along its crest, twin-topped towards the west," Danai recited. She shielded her eyes from sun glare. "There! See it? Slightly off and behind that one to the right."

Joson peered, then nodded. The tors seemed near enough to touch, but he knew there was yet several more days march before they reached Snodon. "Probably five to seven more days," he said to the pod. "And I thought the Truthing Well was a long journey! Well, let's get going." They resumed their march.

"Have you ever wondered why the journey back usually seems easier?" Danai asked Joson a while later as they plodded uphill. "The unknown path always seems longer."

"That assumes you take the same way back. These Rites have me thinking that time may actually be flexible, not rigid and fixed." He flushed under Danai's confused stare. "Consider this. It's been fourteen days since we left the Dell. But it seems much longer, correct? Forever ago, as Ela frequently reminds us. Yet haven't you had days that fly by while others drag on and on? How could that be unless time is not a rock, but more like a river that slows or speeds up depending on the inflow of energy? Maybe we each have our own time thread and what we do with it dictates the speed at which it really goes."

Intrigued, Danai warmed to the notion. "What if there is no such thing as time at all? Maybe we have created the concept so that we can measure progress and what happens to us."

"But everything progresses," objected Damon, who as always was close behind.

"By definition, progress means advance," Danai argued. "What if it's actually a simple circle repeating itself season after season, overlapping the preceding circle? Change doesn't necessarily mean progress. Just because you're taller or a tree is wider doesn't mean things are necessarily growing older—they're just changing."

"So why even create time?" Damon frowned as he wrestled with the idea.

"Can you imagine how Feyree would feel if the truth of their reality was not forward, but circular?" Joson said. "That in fact, no matter what you do, you are not advancing but simply following the same path over and over. Learning and changing, but always 'round and 'round. It would make us no different than any other wood folk—which the Elders insist we're superior to. They would define it as existing rather than living, when in fact by existing, we *are* living."

"Flexible time or no time. What a head-banger! All right, how about this thought?" Damon moved his hands in a circle to emphasize his point. "If we are moving in a perpetual circle, and there is no true fixed time, shouldn't we be able to move back and forth between layers of time?"

"Wouldn't it be hard to go forward, not knowing if we'd been there?" Danai said.

"But if we are just things in a great ever-repeating circle, then whether we are there or not isn't relevant. The essential things—the earth, trees, waters—they are the foundation upon which the circle is built. So by attaching yourself to something that has been there a long time and is likely to be there going forward—at least for a while—you could adjust your place in time."

Danai and Joson's eyes sparkled. "I wonder if any of the loremasters have thought up this one?" Danai asked with a smile. "What would be the spell that could let one slip through the walls of time?"

"Something extraordinary, that's for sure," Damon said. "You'd become a Timemaster. Ugh! It just occurred to me—the time daemiani may have the spell and already know how to do this. But I hope I'm wrong about that!" They looked at each other and shuddered at the prospect. Danai wondered for a moment if Lady Argentyne might know.

"Speaking of time." Joson slowed as they entered a stony clearing sparsely flecked with grass tufts. "It's probably about time to call a halt and look for a bower site." He raised his hand to signal the pod. "That old maple looks good. We can climb it easily."

The setting sun stained small puffy clouds rose and gold as they chatted through evenmeal. A jay squawked nearby. "Have you noticed how there have at least been a few birds since we got up into the Rymples?" Rhytha remarked.

Danai nodded. "Hopefully it means the Dolmen and whatever else was following us got stymied by the broken bridge."

"I wonder where Wag-Tail and the Mentors are though?" Rhytha looked skywards towards the south. "I would have thought they would have found us by now."

"How would they know where to look?" Damon asked. "A broken bridge we couldn't supposedly cross. Several days of rain. Not a lot of birds about. And now we're somewhere in the Torwilds of the Rymples, a bunch of pretty small objects trooping along under pine trees. Small wonder they haven't a clue."

Later, as she lay stargazing from a comfortable bend in one of the maple's branches, Danai thought back over Damon's comments. *Maybe we should ask the local birds to pass the word. I could try. I'm supposed to be a Charmer as well as a Healer. All I can do is try.*

Just before dawnshine, she worked her way down among the craggy bark folds, remembering sadly about another time when she had taken Aaron's dare and grabbed the maple spinner. She recalled Aaron's laughter and admiration. *Was it possible it was already over two lumnas ago? Focus on the matters at hand,* she ordered herself, walking cautiously into the clearing's center. She stood and listened. The sun's first rays produced only the rasp of a nearby jay perched on a pine bough, evidence of how the advancing season had already sent most of the bird folk further south. Oh well, here goes. She rasped back a greeting.

There was a startled silence, then a loud flap of wings. A plump jay, azure wings steeped for a quick halt, plopped down before her, crest raised for battle. Danai bowed and again gave greeting. The jay cocked its head, seemed to think for a moment, then clacked its beak twice. "Who be thee?"

How rude, Danai thought. "Sprytes from the Great Dell on a journey to Snodon Tor."

The crest smoothed back. "Why called thee?"

"We have friends among the bird folk who may be seeking us. Is there a way thee could pass a message along to let them know our whereabouts?"

The crest flared. "Of what like be these birds?"

"Wag-Tail, the magpie, and with him fly two sparrows."

"Magpie! Magpie!" the jay shrieked, dancing about in agitation. "Nest robbers! Food snatchers! They think they own the skies, but are less than the flies I eat. Send a message to bring one into our nests when they have left—and good riddance—to escape the cold like frightened fledglings. Never, never, never!" With a curse, the bird vaulted up and vanished into the woods, its harsh scolding fading into the distance.

"Touchy, wasn't he?" Joson approached. "Guess you do have Charmer in you, to summon a strange bird in the Torwilds."

She tried to shrug away her irritation. "Oh yes, I really charmed him. So much for letting Wag-Tail know where we are. Like you said, we're going to have to do this one alone. Let's get mornmeal done with, and get going. I think I smell weather. Where's Tania?"

"Here. Let me sniff." Tania turned windward and took deep snorts, her rose skin darkening with concentration. "Clear morn, but by late-day, cold rain, maybe snow." She opened her eyes and smiled. "Dream Council was right. I can do this. Most times," she amended.

"We'll need more than a tree for shelter then. Hustle up folks," Joson called to the pod. "Tania is scenting wet times ahead. Let's get on trail."

* * * * *

Blustery weather followed them for the next three days, sweeping down from the north and changing from chill rain to a mushy mix of sleet and snow as they continued their ascent. The trees became squat, dark firs that huddled more and more closely to the cracked stone landscape scoured by the harsh winds. The sprytes discovered they had to repeat the warming spell more than once a day as the weather grew colder.

"You think they could have timed this Rite in the middle of summer," Tyra said to Elanoria as the pod gratefully dropped into the shelter of a small vale. A blade of late-day sunlight bit through the lumbering clouds, and they turned their faces to its welcome brightness.

"Some journey," Elanoria grumbled. "We still haven't reached the ice dragon's cave, and there's not much journey food left."

"Good thing Danai and Joson reminded us to forage as we went along. Although there's not much left, it's more than we'll find once we get up into the snows."

Elanoria glanced about and lowered her voice. "Tyra, I'm afraid of snow."

"It's just frozen water. Your warming spell will melt it away."

"Well, yes. I hadn't thought of that. But it's likely to be well over our heads."

"So, we'll manage. We have so far."

Elanoria continued as if she hadn't heard Tyra, her opal eyes dimmed by memory. "I nearly drowned in snow as a youngling. Our bower was in an oak knothole, about twenty feylengths above the roots. Snow was heavy that year, and there had been a major fall that night. I was leaning forward to look at it, lost my balance, and fell head first. I couldn't see or breathe. It poured into my mouth, nose, and eyes. I remember screaming, but the sound went nowhere, just back into my head. Had my sire not flown down and pulled me out, I would have smothered. I hate snow." Her voice was fierce.

Tyra clasped Elanoria's clenched fist. "Just take it a day at a time, Ela. You want your wings, and it means we have to get that tear from the ice dragon. I promise I'll stay with you if it will be of any help. But it's not just the snow that's bothering you. What else is it?"

Elanoria's face pinched shut. "I miss Pook. He really was special. Treated me like a Feyree, not just a spryte. I wish he'd come back. I still can't believe he would join the daemiani. There has to be something they're not telling us." They both turned at Alemeron's warning shout.

Over the edge of the vale strode a lean long-legged hooded figure. A leaf-green cape whipped and snapped in the wind, revealing an earth-brown tunic belted over tawny breeches, a sheathed blade hanging from a wide belt. A sudden gust shoved back the hood.

Tightly braided green hair streaked with gold framed the fellow's face. He noticed them and halted.

"What is it?" Rhytha gasped. "It's as tall as Tlarg."

"Weapons at the ready," Joson commanded, even as he couched his spear forward.

Seeing their movements, the figure raised both hands over its heart in the age-old salute, palms out, empty of weapons. Then it started towards them. "The Mother's greeting to ye all. I am Rynok, son of Tauzin, third bard of the Southern Ael. Whither are ye bound, and if I may ask, why?"

Danai hesitated as she stepped forth, uncertain what to reveal to this stranger whose eyes were the color of newly-sprouted spring grass. His name tugged at her memory. "The Mother's greeting to you, Rynok of the Ael. We are sprytes on a journey from the Great Dell. And where are you bound?" She decided it wouldn't do to say too much—not yet at least.

Rynok studied her briefly, surprised at her shrewd side-stepping of his question. A wise precaution for one so young, he thought. "I carry a message from my folk of another sending from the Mother that warns us of approaching danger. She counsels us to prepare for battle, but that is all. The enemy is yet unknown."

"The chant Tlarg taught us," Joson remembered, then clapped a hand over his mouth with embarrassment.

"Ye know Tlarg?" Rynok said, raising his eyebrows. "And he told you our verse? Then why are ye here and not yet returned to thy bowers?"

Danai found herself irritated by his overbearing tone, as if he were talking down to foolish younglings caught doing something they shouldn't. "As I said, we are on a journey. We have no choice but to finish it."

"Kyllgohr is not an ice drake to be trifled with. He cares little for anything but his own well-being, and will right gladly welcome thee to dinner. I marvel that thy Dolmen should take such a chance with younglings."

"You know where we're going?"

Rynok gave a small snort. "A pod of sprytes, traversing the Tor-wilds late in the season on a journey which they must complete. My good maiden, while commerce between our folk is less than it was in times past, we are well-acquainted with thy customs and the Rites of Krisalys. In another time, thy bards and those of the *Nainabiju*—the gem dwarves—trained with our folk. And merry were the songs we sang. But I wander. Now is not the time for wings, but flight to safe-ty. Heed my counsel."

"We thank you for your well-meant words, but we have jour-neyed more than half a lumna. To return when we are so close would make little sense. And it is my understanding that the warnings fore-tell of trouble, but not this soon."

"And what say the others?" Rynok plucked at the strings of mixed emotions he sensed among the pod.

"She speaks for all of us." Elanoria stepped forward, chin jutting out, both hands on her hips. "Know you, Rynok, that we may not yet have wings, but we've gone through a lot of things these past five lumnas. Maybe you lead a sheltered life in some pretty meadow, but we have lost friends and gotten a lot older in a short time. We stay together."

Rynok threw his head back with a shout of laughter, then squat-ted down so his head hung just above the pod. "Many pardons, little maiden. I ask thy forgiveness for giving orders. I only want to shield thee from the gathering storm clouds." He gave a wry smile. "And as for sheltering in a pretty meadow for what thee imply are the short years of my life, know thee that I saw the rise and fall of thy tyrant Solon, though I was then reckoned but a stripling."

Elanoria blushed a dark bronze. "I'm sorry if I was rude. But we all just so want to get this journey over and get our wings."

Rynok nodded. "So be it. In the end, we all must take accounting for our decisions of choice and action. And now I must hasten onwards to pass word to the Tor-Ael of the North Reaches. Is there aught I can aid ye with before I leave?"

"With the weather, we've not had much luck foraging," Joson said. "Would you have any journey food to spare?"

"I can only offer *mazidouces*, our wayfarer cakes, if they will meet with thy approval. At my last halt, they were over-generous, and I would be grateful to give some away, how little ye may be able to carry." He removed a bulky brown journey sack slung across his back, and rummaged through it before pulling forth a squarish bundle tied by woven broadgrass. A delightful sweetness emerged as he opened it, reminding them of high summer morns filled with dew-kissed flowers, and ripe berries bursting with sweet juice. "Summer honeycomb, indigo berries, the pollen of night-blooming *Elsheiratoual*, and a blend of finely-ground nuts," he answered their unspoken question. "We eat meat only at high feasts, lest we empty our forest with hunting."

"What is Elsheiratoual?" Danai asked, as she tucked chunks of the mazidouces into her rucksack.

"The name means flowers of Sheira."

"Sheira?"

"He whom ye call Lunasa."

Astonished, Danai stared at him. "You would name a flower after Lunasa?"

"What greater way to show our respect for the most treasured beauty of Sheira but to give her name to a flower that we hold dear as well?"

"But Lunasa is the most high!"

"Among thy folk, that is true. Among the Ael, it is a slightly different tale. But come. We have not time to banter about our folk's differences. I must away if I am to cross the Dentcasser, the ridge of broken teeth before sundown. If we have one this day." He glanced up. Already the gloom of impending rain was lowering the clouds towards them.

"The ridge of broken teeth?" Even to her own ears, Danai's voice held a quaver.

Rynok stood and pointed north. "Beyond the next rise, ye will see a ridge spiked with spines of weathered gray rock. The Dentcasser. There the last of the trees relinquish their rootholds, and ye will at most find withered grasses and thornybrush in which to shelter." He scrutinized the heavy clouds. "And like as not the snow-line. While you have chosen not to follow my counsel and return to thy folk, at least heed me here. Behind that stone spur yonder is a cave we Ael sometimes use in our travels. Stay there this night. And on the morrow, when ye start over the Dentcasser, set thy bearings for the middle teeth—two spikes so close together, they resemble front teeth, though not a pair I would wish in my mouth." His grin flashed briefly. "Follow the trail ye see there, and it will lead ye to Snodon Tor. Kyllgohr's cave lies on the western face, where he can gaze each night at the land of sunset from whence his ancestors came. One other thing. Can any of ye whistle? Good. Then trill me this."

He gave a high whistle that descanted down, then back up, and terminated with three short notes. He waited the few moments it took the sprytes to master the tune. "That is the *Heald*, the query call of the Ael. If any of our folk or friends of our folk are within hearing, they will attend to ye. Now I must away, and be through Kairncross Pass ere nightfall, lest the ice drake forever interrupt my errand. May the Mother's blessing guard and guide ye."

"May Lunasa guide and guard your footsteps," chorused the sprytes. Within a few moments, the Ael had vanished over the rise.

* * * * *

Chapter Twenty

The cave was chilly but dry, well out of the wind. They skirted the blackened stone hearth ring, and found a comfortable nook where Danai guessed the Ael bedded down. Even as they set down their rucksacks, the first splats of rain could be heard outside. "Smells like snow is right behind it," Tania said.

Darkness arrived just before the snow, and the cave grew icy. Their warming spells lasted for only a short time, and the cold nibbled at fingers and toes. "We have a problem." Joson came over to Danai. "Tania smells it's going to freeze tonight, and I think we're going to need more than just warming spells."

"You're suggesting?"

Joson hesitated, looking down at his feet. "Fire magic. I saw some old bits of charred wood in that stone ring, and noticed a small pile back over behind that rock. There must be some pieces we could lift if we work together."

She stared at him a long moment before speaking. "Joson, how can you forget what happened last time? And with Pook and everything else, we're even more likely to attract a fire daemon. In this cave we'd be burnt to a crisp."

"But we were taught the spell-mask magic—finally," Joson argued. "If several of us exercise that spell in a circle with you in the center invoking the fire magic..."

"Joson, I agree about the need for fire, but I will not be the one to do the spellcast. I think it will attract the attention of whatever is following us—me really. It's a bad idea. Better you do it."

"I'm lousy at it. You know that. Mentor Quenton nearly failed me in that training."

"So I'm the only spryte here? There's twenty-two others you can ask. But not me. I think it's just too risky." Her tone brooked no further discussion, and Joson took himself off to find another spell-caster. Torqlan agreed after several of the sprytes told Joson how he had excelled in the magic under Mentor Shanaron.

Even as she chanted the spell-mask magic with the others, Danai shivered. In her mind's eye, she could see that terrible fiery pillar that would have incinerated the whole pod were it not for Tlarg. Please let nothing happen to us, she said, sending a silent prayer to Lunasa.

Torqlan kindled the fire just outside the hearth ring, tucked into a triangular nook at the base of two large stones. It crackled cheerfully, emitting a welcome warmth that allowed shivering muscles to relax. Soon the stones were reflecting the heat several feylengths out, creating a comfortable cocoon between the fire and the back wall.

Tania trotted back into the reddish glow after a short visit to the cave mouth, her golden hair flickering in the firelight. "It's snowing like all anything," she announced. "Sticky and piling fast. I hope Rynok made it over the pass in time."

As the pod settled in for the night, Danai's busy brain kept sleep at bay. She listened to the wind skirl outside, its cry reminding her of clawcats fighting for their mates, up and down, whining and wailing. She turned her thoughts back to the Ael. Rynok, Rynok...the image of Pook telling of his Ael encounter swam back into her memory.

Could he have been that Rynok? But there hadn't been a lyre. Unless it was in the sack. Still wondering, she drifted into an uneasy dream.

She was alone, back in Nonetre, in the valley of Keothach, walking along the molten lake's shores. Waves of heat shivered across its surface, yet she felt no discomfort. From behind came a hiss of heavy fabric brushing against rough stone. She spun about. It was Pook.

But she was looking at a golden-winged stranger. About his brow, contrasting sharply against his black hair, nestled a twisted circlet of red gold. A ring of fire hovered just above the circlet, the tiny flames spitting and flickering, emitting occasional sparks of brilliant blue. He was garbed in a tunic with matching cape that ended just above the knee, its purple so dark as to seem almost black. About the hem was an intricate filigree of flames, stitched in gold. From his braided golden belt hung a scarlet-sheathed dirq, a large ruby sunk deep into its hilt. The ruby pulsed with its own inner fires—almost, she thought, like the Anam. She was surprised to see he wore black hide boots, ending just below the knee, polished until they reflected the fires of Keothach.

But it was the intensity of his eyes which struck her most. Gone was the contemplative look she knew so well, replaced by a calculating stare that darted and slid about. She felt she was being appraised instead of meeting a dear friend. The smile that crawled across his lips only reinforced the sensation. Yet it was Pook. Surely he could not have changed so much, so quickly? She took a hesitant step forward.

"Danai! You've come at last. What a pleasure to have you here in my beautiful realm of Nonetre." His hug felt genuine, though he smelt oddly of burnt wood and another unpleasant scent that reminded her of bad eggs. "I have so looked forward to your coming here."

"What has happened to you Pook? Why did you leave us, leave the Rites? We're so close to our wings."

"I already have them—or haven't you noticed?" His smile was smug. "But the best of it was I didn't need to go through all that stupid foolishness, risking my life for the Dolmen to prove a point. Eshel, my trusted councilor, simply worked his great magic, my wing-bumps burst open, and out they came."

"Did it hurt?"

"A little," he admitted with a flash of his old grin. "I was going to say not at all, but you'll find out soon for yourself. Unless you'd rather stay with me, and I'll have Eshel take care of you."

"Who is this Eshel?"

"My most valued advisor and court loremaster—our folk call him the Herald." Pook's voice deepened and swelled. "It is he who recognized me as the Prophesied One and anointed me Tvashtar Tizon, Firelord of Nonetre. Under his tutelage I am learning the magics of our loremasters and the laws of my realm." His voice softened, became almost sleek. "Danai, you have no idea of what we don't know. The daemiani have taken magic to a whole new level. They are willing to try new ways to improve on things. None of those rules about 'dangerous barriers' or 'why it shouldn't or can't be done.' If it will benefit the realm or make lives easier, it's worth exploring."

Danai frowned, uncomfortable with how easily he referred to Nonetre as 'my realm,' as if he had discarded Lampion. "How do you know when you've gone too far?"

Pook shrugged. "A few may die, or something be damaged, but everybody recognizes this is the price of discovery, and it is worth the risk. It's a risk they're willing to take."

"They themselves or have others take for them?"

"Always up for a debate aren't you?" His hand rested a moment on his dirq hilt. The ruby glittered, then subsided. "Not all daemiani are spellcasters. Like the Feyree, they have magic Tiers, or engage in other crafts to support our lifestyles. The barrier-pushing magics are by the *Talushim*, the highest Tier loremasters. Eshel ranks highest, like the Dolmen."

"Are you one too?"

"Not yet. But I'm training to be." The ruby pulsed hotly as he clenched his fists at her continued frown. "Can't you see, Danai? This is what I've always wanted to do. Become a loremaster like no other. And now I have the chance. Who would have thought that little Pook, the one who had so much trouble directing Feyree dust, would one day become the greatest loremaster of all?" He tossed his head back and laughed, a hollow sound unlike anything Danai had ever heard from him.

"And the collared Feyree?"

Pook's eyes narrowed. "How did you know of that?"

In her growing anger Danai realized she'd almost revealed her visit. "What does it matter?" she stammered, alarmed by the sudden blaze in his eyes. Like the fire daemon's.

He seized her arm in a bruising grip. "I asked, how did you know?" He began to shake her. She screamed, struggling to break free.

"Danai! Danai!" Joson was shaking her. "You're moaning and struggling in your dreams. Are you all right?"

He was a like a dark shadow leaning over her. She recoiled, seeing another, and tried to claw aside the thick clouds of sleep. "Pook," she gasped. "I saw Pook."

"You've been here the whole time I've been on watch. It must have been a bad dream. Hey, you're really shaking!" Without thinking, Joson cuddled her close, whispering soothing words.

She felt rather than heard his heart's steady thump-a-thump. For a moment she rested, glad to remain in the safe circle of his arms. If only it were Aaron there to hold her.

"Feeling better?" Joson was glad she couldn't see his face. Feeling her nod, he reluctantly released her. "Try to go back to sleep. I'll stay right here."

She knew she would not sleep again that night.

* * * * *

The noises of waking podmates dragged her eyes open. She had finally slipped into a doze as the first whispers of dawnshine changed the cave's blackness to gray. The storm had blown itself out, and brilliant silvery light glittered on the walls.

"Oh fish feathers!" Danai heard Elanoria's exasperated shout. "If it's not one thing, it's another." She rose and followed the other curious sprytes beyond the hearth ring. A wall of snow at least four feylengths high blocked the entry, glowing blue-white in the sunshine. "Anyone got any ideas on how to get out of this?"

Alemeron approached a part of the drift that had eddied into the cave, stepped on to it, and immediately sank. "Mush. If we try to crawl on top, we'll sink in less than a wing beat. So that's out."

"What about using our warming spell to melt a path through it?" Rhytha suggested. She pointed her palms towards the drift's base, murmuring softly. A small trickle of water began to puddle.

"We'd have to keep it up constantly or be trapped," Joson said. "What if this snow goes all the way upslope? And how are we going to keep our bearings, moving along in a snow tunnel?"

"Shadows?" Tyra suggested.

"Only if we're close enough to the surface."

"We could wait until it settles," Alemeron said. "Feel that breeze? It's warm. Hey Tania, what's the weather going to be?"

After a few sniffs, she announced, "Definitely warmer. Too warm for snow. Alemeron's right. It will settle, but I don't know how much."

"We could wait until tomorrow," Sandai suggested. "If there's no more snow, a good hard crust will form and we can easily walk on that."

"I hate the idea of waiting a whole day here," Damon said. "Look, let me see if I can scramble along the outside wall and climb to the top of that rock outcropping that shields this cave. The snow shouldn't be too thick there. I can get a lay of what the trail looks like. Hey Rhytha, are you all right?"

She staggered slightly before nodding. "This definitely isn't the way to go," she panted. "It takes everything out of you. I was fine until a couple of moments ago, and then everything started to spin and flash."

She stepped out of the puddle of water she had melted. "Look! Tania and Alemeron are right—it's starting to melt. Damon, why don't you wait until after mornmeal? I think it will be easier for you."

After a brief meal of the Ael's mazidouces—which everyone pronounced excellent and a delicious change from miyacan—they walked back to the entry. "By the Twins, Tania, you sure have a nose for weather! It's sunk almost halfway down." Damon prowled several paces into the snow until he found a good spot from which to view the outcropping. "Just as I thought—no snow on top of it at all. And look, there's a narrow passage forming between the outside stone and the slumping snow. I'll follow that. Watch for my signal— thumbs up to get on trail, down to stay put." He vanished into the shadowy crevasse, and in a little while appeared clambering up the rocky face.

Watching him survey the area, outlined by a sky so intensely blue it glowed, Danai half-hoped he would signal thumbs down. This is ridiculous, she chided herself. We have to finish this journey. Although nobody could blame me for not wanting to cope—at least not yet—with an ice dragon. She sighed.

Joson tapped her arm. "Damon's signaling to join him. Everybody's ready. Here's your ruck. I'll carry his." He saw how tired she looked. "Why don't you let me lead?"

One by one the sprytes eased into the crevasse. The blue-silver of sunlight filtering through the snow enshrouded them, causing their skin to glow with a weird light, and the air was almost too cold to breathe. Tiny puffs burst from their nostrils and mouths, hung suspended for the briefest moment, and vanished. As she turned sideways to slip through a narrow stretch, Danai could see individual snowflakes in the loose-packed snow. She marveled at their myriad designs, more elaborate than the frost crystals she loved to look at. Her tunic brushed against one, and the filigree disintegrated into a drop of water that hung poised, and began to crystallize—until Tyra knocked it off. The creak of settling snow, and its melting gurgle, filled her ears.

As they emerged from the passage, shards of sunlight scattered from the snow, nearly blinding them. One by one, they scaled the rock face to join Damon and lay resting in the warm sun. Already patches of brown were appearing in the vale below.

"I think it just drifted a bit by the cave's mouth," Damon said as Danai came up. "See? We can follow along this outcrop, climb the rock ledge over there, then up over the crest, and spy out what the Dentcasser holds for us."

With Damon leading, they soon reached the hill crest and gazed up at the rock-toothed obstacle. Snow drifts streaked the muddy ground. A little to the right protruded the middle teeth Rynok had described. "Onwards and upwards," Joson shouted, stepping forth.

They reached the teeth at mid-day, and found the trail as Rynok had described, passing through the gap between. They had agreed to nibble as they marched and take only occasional short halts. Once through the gap, they beheld the crooked snow-clad twin pinnacles of Snodon Tor, which had been hidden behind the Dentcasser.

"Look!" Danai pointed. "Cairns. I wondered how the Ael could follow this trail over stone. I thought it might be some special magic. They've marked it with those. That means we should be coming near to Kyllgohr's cave."

Elanoria glanced about uneasily. "And if he sees us first? A bunch of moving black specks against a white background. Not exactly invisible."

"Don't you remember your dragon lore? Dragons have trouble seeing in bright sunlight. They're more a twilight creature, preferring to snooze during the day. As long as we're well-hidden by gloaming, and don't make too much racket approaching his cave, things should go fine."

"If I had a feather for all the shoulda-couldas on this journey, I'd already have a full set of wings, and probably a pair to spare. Still, you're right. We should avoid talking too much. I remember they are supposed to have superb hearing. Can anybody see the cave up there?"

They peered up the relatively smooth mountain side—no cave was in sight. "Must be on the other side," Damon suggested. "Mentor Toron told me it's called Glaceturm. Means something like 'ice cavern.'"

Joson interrupted. "Shall we cut the jaw and get moving? I don't see any shelters from here, and I, for one, don't want to spend the night in the open."

Clambering over occasional drifts, they marched along, keeping conversation to brief whispers. Danai pointed out to Joson how the Ael had mixed dark and lighter rocks in their cairns to allow contrast whether against snow or rock.

It was Siddiqui who first noticed the large bruise on the lower western shoulder of Snodon Tor. She squinted, shading her eyes. "Doesn't look like a rock fall to me or a solid outcropping. Ummmm, didn't Rynok say something about Kyllgohr's cave being on the western slope? Well, that's definitely a cave. Big one by the looks of it. Seems to be smoking slightly too."

"I would say the dragon is at roost," Danai murmured, trying to ignore the clutch of fear in her gut. "I hoped it might just be snow smoke. You know—when the snow changes to mist because it's so warm—but I guess not. Let's continue along the trail, unless it starts to turn away. Keep silent."

Glaceturm loomed gradually larger, a dark eye overlooking their progress, sheltering some brooding presence that hackled their neck hairs. High above the cave, Snodon's pinnacles seemed to scrape at the cloudless sky.

Scouring her memory for dragon lore, Danai regretted not having had a chance to ask Triasa or Toron more about them. Could I charm a dragon, she wondered. No. It was too great a risk to take.

The cave's surroundings grew better defined, and she noticed the entry was partially protected by a wide overhanging ledge, crowned by recent snowfall that seemed ready to tumble off at any moment. Large drifts poured down on either side of the cave, giving the uncanny impression of a hungry creature's wide open mouth. Danai saw—and doubted. How in the name of all Lampion are we going to do this? A soft 'sssst' caught her attention.

Joson stood by a double cairn that lined up directly with Glaceturm. The sprytes clustered about. "Eventide isn't too far off," he whispered. "Personally, I'd rather tackle a dragon at the start of a day, preferably when he's asleep." Heads nodded. "I haven't seen a hint of anywhere to hide or shelter. Anybody?"

"Whatever may be here is buried by snow—if there is anything," Siddiqui said. "Rynok sounded like he would cross the pass in short stride, so perhaps the Ael don't worry about night shelter, knowing better than to risk being near a dragon. This trail is not designed for fey folk."

"What about a snow cave?" Everyone turned to look in surprise at Torqlan, who rarely spoke unless asked. "Kristal Glen lies on the flanks of the westernmost Rymples; it's where crystals are dug free from the frost-shattered rock and borne to our Kristal Guild to be smythed, some shaped into the scrying globes the loremasters imbue with magic. The finest crystals are found only among the higher peaks. There the snow lasts for most of the year, melting and freezing, chipping away at the surrounding rock until the crystals are revealed. Crystal hunters must often overnight on the slopes, and the fastest shelter is a snow cave. It is part of our training."

"Doesn't the snow just melt about your ears?" Damon wanted to know.

Torqlan half-smiled. "Not if it is built with enough room that your breath freezes against the top."

"Well, it's better than standing here waiting to become dragon food." Elanoria jerked her fist up at the cave. "Torqlan, show us what to do."

Sandai, also from Kristal Glen, joined him in scouting the area, testing various drifts by measuring them against the taller Torqlan, and studying the width and snow slope. The pod watched, intrigued by the process. Sandai and Torqlan worked their way farther down the trail until they reached the next cairn. Just beyond they found a drift that suited them.

"Only two can start to dig at a time, for the tunnel to the cave should be kept a narrow passage," Torqlan explained. "As I dig into the tunnel, each of you line up and we will pass the snow out to clear a hollow. Make sure you dump the snow on other snow so that it blends in and does not attract unwanted attention this night." He rooted around inside his rucksack. "We'll need at least ten empty kuis—we'll use them to dig and carry out the snow. See? Like this."

Like an eager squirrel searching for a long-buried nut, he began to dig, flinging the loose snow behind him in kuis-fulls. Sandai brushed it away into a snow drift on the opposite side of the trail, then fell in beside Torqlan and began to dig.

The exercise kept them warm as the pod worked its way into the drift, passing empty kuis in and full kuis out, in what became a fairly smooth sequence after a few dropped kuis and bumped body parts at the start. The light inside deepened from silver to icy blue as the snow depth increased overhead. When Torqlan and Sandai judged they were far enough in, they summoned four sprytes to join them, instructing two to dig left, two right, while they continued forward. "We're starting the cave," Torqlan explained.

As the hollow grew, others moved in to join the digging, and in short order a cave roughly ten feylengths wide and deep and an arm's length higher than the tallest spryte was excavated. "Pat the snow hard using firm yet gentle pressure," Torqlan directed. "This compacts it so it will resist our warm breath. Tonight the snow will freeze, and we will be in a cave of ice—our own Glaceturm."

Joson poked his head in through the narrow entry way. "Just to tell you the sun is about two handspans from the horizon."

Hurrying out, Torqlan gave quick orders. "Smooth away our tracks and do all you can to make the trail look unused. The dragon Mohrdryd has claimed a cave in our mountains. They have keen night eyes and any disturbance will bring them down in hopes of an easy meal. No snow cave exists that can outlast a digging dragon. I have reason to know," he added, more to himself.

Only Joson heard his last remark. "How so?" he asked as he bent to whisk away the snow with a tuft of dead grass, while others smoothed the snow tossed by their digging.

"My birth mother was crystal hunting with six others in the High Reaches. They had found a good crystal vein, and failed to keep an eye on the sun. Gloaming came before the snow cave was completed. Only Asuon escaped. He said Mohrdryd made great sport with them after he broke open the cave as a snake does an egg. They tried to fly away, but he caged them between his cupped claws, laughing as they begged for mercy in the Mother's name. Then he ate them."

Joson stared at him, shocked. "But we are so small!"

"Mere tidbits to a dragon," Torqlan agreed. "But prey is prey. Asuon had stepped out of the cave to attend to the necessary, and hid in a rock cleft. When he returned to the glen, his hair and skin had turned from indigo to white with horror. None have dared to crystal hunt in those High Reaches since."

"And Asuon?"

"He could not free himself from the terrible memory. The Healers tried everything, even dream-melds, but could not break its hold. He flung himself from the Dyamant, a crystal-tipped cliff that overlooks our glen."

"I admire you," Joson said after a pause. Torqlan started and stared. "Why? Because if there is any spryte in this pod that has reason to want out of this Rite, it would be you. Yet here you are, calmly directing us to make a snow cave."

Giving an odd smile, Torqlan shrugged. "I have a score to settle with Mohrdryd. I will need my wings to accomplish it." He raised his voice a breath louder so others could hear. "Come. The sun is near the edge. We must hide within, and block the entry."

Once the pod had settled in the chilly confines of the cave, Torqlan gave final orders. "Speak not until dawnshine. Talk only with your hands. Try not to use a warming spell unless your hands and feet grow numb. Some dragons can smell such magic. As you can already feel, our breath and bodies are warming the space. And if you hear anything, anything at all, play dead." About them the blue light dimmed to black.

Danai clutched Joson's arm as a sonorous bellow sounded far above. It crescendoed in a wail, sank to a deep, guttural grumble, and then ended with a fullthroated roar. Moments later, a sharp clap of wings sounded overhead, followed by the rumble and hiss of a small avalanche that hurtled past their cave, shaking the walls such that a fine shower of ice crystals cascaded down. The Mother keep us, Danai thought. It was going to be a very long night.

* * * * *

Chapter Twenty-One

Not until the snow cave was once again filled with blue light would Torqlan permit them to speak. "It is beyond dawnshine now, for the sun will have climbed the eastern slopes of the mountain, and Kyllgohr will again be at slumber. Let us discover what there is to see at Glaceturm."

The snow plug at the tunnel's end was frozen, but a few hard smacks with the butt ends of their spears finally smashed through. Outside, another chill day of brilliant sunshine and clear skies greeted them. A snow crust reflected back the light in rainbow bursts. They turned to stare up at the cave. "I would say let's climb up the southern flank," Sandai suggested, her voice a soft whisper. "That way we are downwind, and Kyllgohr should not see nor smell us."

"How are we going to avoid sinking into the snow?" Elanoria asked.

Sandai tisked and shook her head. "You southern sprytes really don't know much about snow, do you? Didn't you notice the snow crust? It will bear our weight. Look." She walked over to a shallow drift, and hopped up, raising out her arms to get her balance. "See? It will be slippery, but if you lean forward and go carefully, it should be fine. The sun will melt it only a bit on a day so chill, but enough to help us better keep our feet."

"Since you know so much about snow," Elanoria sniffed, put off by Sandai's superior tone, "why don't you lead?"

Nonplussed, Sandai looked askance at Danai and Joson. Both nodded without hesitation. She began to creep her way upslope, hunched slightly forward like a crooked twig.

It was slow going. Each foot had to be carefully placed. More than once, a spryte lost balance, and was saved from a wild ride down slope only by the grip of their fellows. Danai found the view breathtaking. The air, polished to gemlike clarity by the recent weather, seemed to magnify everything. She saw the distant spire of Pyre Tor. South, the Wynndowns lay like a rumpled coverlet, daubed with orange, gold and crimson. Even further beyond was the Great Bog, a brown-yellow smudge, edged by what she guessed was the silvery flicker of the Great Waters at the farthest reaches of her vision. She wondered what lay beyond.

Their eyes ached from snow glare, their feet were chafed by the coarse ice. At mid-day, they reached a snowdrift that ran parallel with the cave. Several peeked over it. They could hear the steady chuffing of the dragon, stippled with the steady patter of drops pouring from the cave's snow-crested overhang as the creature's warm breath melted the snow.

"Now what?" Damon's voice hung below a whisper.

With surprise, Danai realized they were all looking expectantly at her. She shrugged. "I honestly don't know. Any ideas?" There was a shuffling of feet and chewing of lips. Joson ran his hands through his sweat-soaked hair, looked at her, made as if to speak, then stared off into the southlands. "Speak out Joson," she prompted as the silence grew overlong. "You've got an idea. Anyone can see that."

"It's too dangerous."

"Let's hear it first, then decide," Elanoria muttered, disregarding Rhytha's poke in the shoulder.

"We should scout out his lair. Maybe there are dragon's tears lying inside, and we could sneak in at night, steal one, and get out safely."

"Scouting out the lair is a great thought," Danai nodded, ignoring the faint ripple of startled gasps at the temerity of Joson's suggestion. "At the very least it would give us some sense of the cave. But I don't know about the night visit—what if he returns? I'll go. No Joson, you tend to trip and fall at the worst times. Wait for me here." She held up her hand at her friends' protests, slipped over the drift and started up.

Following a narrow ridge of snow, she eased her way along. I must be out of my mind, she thought. What if the dragon isn't asleep at all, has known all along we're out here, and is just waiting for his midmeal to arrive? Stopping to catch her breath, she studied the way the overhang projected only part way out over the cave's entry—the cave's lower ledge extended well beyond, creating a perfect place for a dragon to lay out and watch for dinner. As she drew near the cragged lip of the cave, a rising wind blew the sour stench of dragon breath into her nostrils. She stifled a cough. The plop-splat of snow slithering off the overhang served as a backdrop for an odd jumble of sound. It reminded her of icicles clattering on stone, followed by a steamy hiss. She crept closer until she had reached the cave mouth, then peered around the edge.

The cave was not as deep as she had imagined—perhaps two dragon lengths. Kyllgohr sprawled on his back midway, presumably asleep, clawed feet splayed towards the cave roof that had been worn smooth by his countless comings and goings. He was the icy blue of their snow cave with transparent silvery-frosted wings and claws of matching silver. He seemed to glow, the shimmer of sunlight through heavy frost, so that the cave gleamed with a quiet, shifting radiance. The strange jumble of sound she had heard was his breathing.

She started to take a tiny step forward for a better view, then froze as his tri-tipped tail twitched. She realized the wind had shifted slightly and was now blowing into the cave. Better to stay back and see what she could.

Behind Kyllgohr, piled to the roof, lay a shining heap of crystal spars that flickered with rainbows from the dragon's radiance and the bouncing beams of sunlight. Large. Small. Jagged. Faceted. Sticking every which way. And I always heard that dragons slept on their gatherings, she thought. His weight would turn that into crystal crumbs. She peered harder with a mounting sense of dismay. How could she tell if any were dragon's tears, having no idea what a tear would look like?

The sun crossed overhead, the warm rays melting a sheer waterfall from the overhang. A thunderous roar on a nearby peak startled Danai, and she watched as an avalanche stormed down the mountain side, to disappear into Kairncross Pass, leaving behind a frosty plume of snow. She thought of Torqlan and Sandai describing how avalanche snow turned into stone when it halted, and was the last to melt in the spring. Above, a large clump of snow broke free and landed just beside her. It gave her an idea. She headed back towards the pod.

They clustered eagerly about. She described the lay of Glaceturm, the hopeless pile of crystals, the melting snow, and outlined her plan. "We have to do it now, while the snow remains mushy," she urged.

"We'll have to work in pairs," Joson agreed. "Everybody keep far enough back so that you don't get sucked under."

Siddiqui shook her head. "It's too risky Danai. For sure, you'll get smothered, and then the dragon will be raging around and kill us all. There has to be a better way." Several sprytes nodded agreement.

"I'm listening." Danai controlled her impatience. Time was wasting. There were several moments of awkward silence. "Well?"

Joson stepped beside her, turning to face the pod. "You've trusted us to lead you this far. Without the tear, no wings. Unless you can offer some other choice, we must move forward. Speak or hold your peace."

The silence drew bowstring-taut, the air among the sprytes brittle with upset emotions. Another avalanche roared in the distance. Damon stepped forward. "We follow." He dropped in behind Joson and Danai as they started back towards the cave. After a pause, the rest of the sprytes followed, Siddiqui, Elanoria and Tyra last.

* * * * *

Danai stood watching her podmates pick their way among the jumble of ice, snow, and rock as they worked their way up-slope and above Glaceturm's overhang. Lunasa guide us, she thought, then started back towards the cave.

Peeking inside, she caught her breath in wonder. The westering sun flooded the cave with golden light. Inside, Glaceturm was on fire. Sunbeams ricocheted off the crystals in shimmering bursts of color, blues colliding with reds into purple, or yellows into green—a glittering, shifting rainbow. Everything sparkled, and the sun's warmth drew crackles and tzings from the crystal. Kyllgohr gave a tremendous yawn, belched, and rolled over on his belly.

She took several paces back and looked up, searching for Joson. After a bit, she saw him lean out from the overhang. He waved his hand; she waved back, and he vanished. Closing her eyes for several heartbeats, Danai gathered her courage. Here goes, she thought. I guess I *will* be trying to charm a dragon. She took a half-step beyond the edge, full into the wind that was now blowing directly into the cave.

Kyllgohr's eyes flashed open. Their sapphire depths looked bewildered as he took mighty snorts of the strange wisps of scent that trickled on the wind. Something in Glaceturm! Unheard of, in all his days, that any creature of right mind would actually dare enter his domain. True, there had been a foolish Ael once who had challenged him to a duel. He had been armed with spells and weapons for a fire fight, never realizing ice dragons did more than flame; they froze. It had been a simple thing to vomit ice over the shocked Ael, then knock off his frozen head and shatter his body into bite-sized morsels. Kyllgohr smacked his lips at the memory, long silver tongue flashing in the sunlight. "Who goes?" The rumble of his voice shivered small icicles dangling off the overhang, some snapping off to plunge like silver dirqs into the snow. He blinked, and finally spied the tiny figure near the corner of his cave entry, a shifting silhouette edged by the blazing sun, nimbly dodging the deadly icicles.

"Danai of the Feyree, come to ask a boon of the great dragon Kyllgohr." Her shout echoed faintly about the cave.

"Come into my home, little one," the dragon purred, "that I may see you more closely."

"Many thanks for your offer of hospitality great lord," Danai replied, instead retreating until she was well clear of the overhang, and off to the side. "But one such as I cannot presume to enter such a sacred place. Will you not come forth a few steps that we may converse?"

Kyllgohr laughed until the crystal hoard behind him tinkled shrilly, his throaty chortle setting the cave a-tremble. Entertainment before dining. How refreshing. That only happened at the great conclave of dragons once every *Talanamach*, when the sun's orb was swallowed by shadow, and daylight travel could happen safely. He would grace his victim with a little time, rather than toasting her this moment. Tromping forward, he came part way out of the cave until his hindquarters were just under the overhang. The ground trembled as he lay back down, forepaws comfortably crossed. His bulk loomed like a waiting wave above Danai. She did not move.

"Why have you come to my cave?" Kyllgohr demanded, lowering his massive head so that his eyes were on a level with Danai's head.

They were at least three times her height, fringed by long dark blue lashes. She felt dizzy, wanting to walk in the endless azure depths that glittered and whirled beside her, reflecting countless Danais. Kyllgohr exhaled, and the sharp hot smell of fire cleared her mind. "I came to ask a boon. I crave a tear from my lord."

Kyllgohr blinked and snorted. "A tear? Have you any idea what you ask, bit of nothing that calls herself Danai?"

"Only that such will bring me nearer to my wings, my lord."

"Know you that my tears hold great power? They are not just some play thing for a spit of a Feyree such as yourself." He slitted his eye so that now only her face reflected back.

Only sheer force of will kept her from bolting. "It is not for me, but for the Dolmen, most high loremaster of our folk, that I make this request."

"Ah, yes. The Dolmen." Kyllgohr gave an unpleasant smile that revealed teeth the sickly hue of old ice. "I know of him. You are not the first Feyree that he has sent to me that he wanted gone. The fools come across Kairncross on some trumped up errand and are exposed to me. Easy meat. I admit you are the first spryte he has sent. And none have ever dared enter my cave."

Danai gasped. "Are you saying that...?"

"He wants you dead? Exactly. And of course, I will oblige him, although I must say I appreciate your courtesy and honesty. What have you done to run afoul of the Dolmen, I wonder?"

"This." She pointed to her silvered shoulders, fury replacing fear. "They are a gift of the Lady Argentyne, and the Dolmen sees me as a bearer of evil, a changeling to be destroyed." A large splot of snow fell from the overhang onto the dragon's shoulders and neck; several others followed. The dragon paid them no mind, entirely focused on Danai. Thank the Mother he thinks I'm alone on this quest, she thought.

"Such a shame," Kyllgohr commiserated. "Ah well—such is life. I will give you a choice. Flame or ice?"

Another splot of snow fell, and Danai could see a steady trickle starting off to the left of the dragon's shoulder. A little longer, she thought. I must keep him talking. "Choice for...?"

"Your way of dying. If you will kindly step into my mouth, I promise it will be quick and painless. Flame or ice?" He opened his mouth wide, revealing a shockingly red throat. Danai seemed to ponder, her head cocked. More snow tumbled down. The dragon's tail flicked with impatience. "Choose. I have other duties to be about."

"I choose...neither!" Danai shouted, then jumped back and raced away from the avalanche that frothed down off the overhang, piling smothering snow upon Kyllgohr. Bursting white powder obscured her vision. She kept running, slipping on the hard ice crust, desperate to avoid being entombed.

Finally the snow settled, an occasional swirl whisking away into the breeze. She looked up and saw the pod almost tumbling over themselves in their haste to climb down to her. From near the overhang, she thought she heard a muffled whine from under the mound of snow. But there was no sign of the dragon.

"Fire magic worked just like you thought!" Damon crowed. "Although it took less time than we expected to melt through that crust and down into the snow until it started to crumble, then slide. Where's the dragon?"

Danai jerked a trembling thumb at the cave. "In there. He was about to eat me." The snow-muffled moan came again. "I don't know if he's stunned, or shamming. But we've got to try and force the tear from him. For the moment, I'm hoping the weight of the snow will keep his jaws closed—otherwise he would have already burned his way out. Come on. Let's try to find an eye."

Joson, Damon, Rhytha, Sandai and Alemeron agreed to help her as the whole pod hurried towards the cave. Based on her recall of where Kyllgohr's head had been, they produced a concentrated warming spell that began to melt the snow where they guessed the eye might be. They found an ear instead, and the dragon's moan became a muffled yelp as the heat singed its tip. Concerned that the spell might damage the eye, they began to dig using their kuis and soon the dragon's eye blinked azure in the sun light.

"Kyllgohr, if you can hear me, blink twice," Danai ordered, putting on a stern expression. It would not do to show fear at this point. The dragon obliged. "Being that our roles have, um, changed just a tad, I shall again ask, will you not grant me a boon and give me a tear?" The eye remained unblinking, and a growl shuddered the hard snow beneath them. She shrugged. "So be it. I cannot make a great one such as you do anything you do not wish. So we shall leave, and return to the Great Dell, with only our story to prove we were here." To the waiting sprytes she said, "Let us go while the sunlight yet remains. He is of the ice and will not mind the night freeze." The pod began to move off, Danai lagging behind.

The muffled bellow of protest caused Kyllgohr's eye to bulge, and Danai was glad the snow muted the sound, else she would be forever deaf. She turned and walked back. The eye was blinking frantically. "You do not want us to leave?" Two blinks. "But then what would you have us do? You will grant no tear, yet keep us here until we freeze solid beside you in the night? I think not. We will not tarry." Again she turned away.

"Mmmm-hmm-hmmm-hmmmmmm," the dragon moaned, the last hmm plaintive. Danai counted to five, then looked back. Kyllgohr was crying! For a few moments, a trickle of moisture ran down. As it met the snow, it changed into rough-shaped crystals the size of a Feyree's hand. With a shout of delight, she scooped up the seven that had formed, scattering a confused jumble of color across the snow. She quickly tucked them into her rucksack, and prepared to leave.

"Mmmm?"

Something about the sound caused her to stare back into the dragon's eye. It was brimming with sorrow. "You can't get out, can you?" It blinked twice. Be careful, she reminded herself. Dragons are clever, crafty, wise in the ways of the realm. Yet wouldn't he have burst free and consumed them if possible? Could the weight of the wet snow be that great? "Wait," she said, and hurried back to the waiting pod.

"You got one? By the Twins, that's wonderful!" Elanoria exulted, doing a little shimmy in the snow. "Now let's get out of here before the sun sets and we're dragon fodder."

"He can't get out," Danai said.

"The better for us," Elanoria grinned. "What mercy would he have shown us if we'd been out yesternight?"

Danai could sense Kyllgohr's eye boring into her back, awaiting the outcome. I must be sun-touched, she thought. Wanting to free a dragon. What right have I to risk the pod? "He will die if we don't release him."

"One less dragon is no great loss to Lampion," Torqlan said, an ugly smile on his face. "I'm sure that others will gladly take his place, but perhaps for a while, Kairncross Pass will be safe for journeyers. I, for one, will rejoice."

"Rejoice? In another's death? Perhaps the fire daemon who attacked us found Arcieron's terrible burn something to rejoice in too. After all, it wanted us dead, and were it not for Tlarg, we would now all be charred bits floating in the Dunakey. That wouldn't be something to rejoice in, though, would it? One of our folk's deaths?"

"It's just a dragon," Torqlan spluttered, flushing dark green with anger.

"And you're just a spryte! Don't prate two standards to me!"

"Danai—" Joson started to intervene, but she ignored him.

"In battle, were he or we killed, it is the fortune of war, or so the bards will sing. But we have won. The battle is done. Should we at least not give him a chance to redeem himself? Would we not want such a chance?"

"A dragon's promise is not worth a puff of smoke. Once a dragon, always a liar." Sandai nodded agreement with Torqlan.

"I could say the same thing about the Dolmen, who is supposed to protect our folk. Yet as I have told you, he has tried to kill me more than once!" She was shaking with rage. "He decided to kill me in the name of what he believes is right. Kyllgohr himself told me that the Dolmen has deliberately sent other Feyree to their deaths." Behind her, the eye blinked twice. "And think a little further—in the purest sense, he sent us all to our deaths. Remember how upset the Mentors were when he announced what beast we were to go after? So you would all just be a casualty of the Rites, thanks to our Dolmen. And you would so easily murder another? I say again. Give Kyllgohr a chance. And if you will not, then leave that I may do what I believe is right. Then only my life may be forfeit."

"And mine," said Joson quietly, standing beside her. Damon and Rhytha stepped forward, followed by most of the pod. Torqlan stood mutinous.

"Are you all completely mad?" His eyes swept them with scorn. "You will let this spryte, this one marked by a nyad for who knows what end, tell us to take a risk that could well cost our lives?"

Sandai, who had held back, turned on him, furious. "How dare you criticize Danai for being marked? That is no fault of her own. She has led us to success when the Dolmen would have had us dead!" Disgusted, she strode over to stand beside Joson. Only Elanoria, Dlargon, Thran and Ujerion hung back.

Ignoring them, Danai directed her next words to the eye that had followed her every movement. "Kyllgohr, even dragons must have sacred beings by whom they swear. Lunasa and the Mother are sacred to us, and to take their names in a vain vow is perilous. Do you honor the Mother?"

If two blinks could shout yes, these did.

"Then in the name of the Mother, will you swear that if we free you, you will neither attack nor seek to harm us, and grant us safe passage from Snodon Tor, now and always?"

Blink. Blink.

"Joson, Damon, everyone, half of you work on melting the snow in this side and across the top, and the other half of us will dig with our kuis' as you soften it. If we can get his head free, I think he can break out. Kyllgohr, do you think that will work?"

Blink. Blink.

The sun was settling low in the sky by the time they had freed the dragon's head. He yawned, clicked his jaws a few times, then turned to gaze at Danai for a long heart-stopping moment. Steam fizzed from his nostrils as he puffed them clear of snow. Had Torqlan spoken the truth about dragons? She prepared to be charred or frozen.

"Little maiden, beyond great is your courage. Most would have left me to smother as most surely I would have when the snow froze solid tonight and sealed off all air. At best, I could have hoped for a blade rammed through my eye and a swift death. You have more than bested me in fair battle. Stand back all, for I come forth!" They scurried to obey. He began to puff hard, heating himself, blowing downwards, melting the snow by his forepaws until they broke free. Then, like a fox shaking itself off, he scattered snow in all directions, heaving himself loose and extending his wings with a tremendous flap.

Frightened cries pierced the air as the sprytes recoiled from his enormity. He stamped. They were knocked flat. He roared, the bellow bouncing endlessly off the mountain peaks, until it faded into its own echoes. The sun sat on the edge of the world, the color of new-spilled blood.

Danai rose and stepped forward to face Kyllgohr. She was surprised at how calm she felt in the face of likely death. They confronted each other for several moments. Then, he bent his left foreleg and bowed, his snout touching the snow. "In the name of the Mother, I swear sacred friendship to you and those that accompany you."

Stepping forward, she placed her palm on the translucent webbing between his claws. "And in the name of the Mother, I swear sacred friendship to you. Small though I be, if ever you are in need, send word, and perchance I can be of some help."

Kyllgohr smiled, but not in mockery. "Night falls, and I must go forth to hunt. It would bring honor to me and my cave if you will accept the use of Glaceturm while I am gone. I shall even light a small fire for your comfort. Come!" He turned and lumbered back into the cave, the sprytes keeping well clear of his swinging tail. Torqlan lagged farthest behind, scowling to himself.

Kyllgohr plucked a smallish crystal spar from his hoard, and inserted it firmly into a hole he bored out with a single claw close the cave wall. He gave a short puff. A gout of blue fire seared the crystal. With a high-pitched crackle it ignited, burning with an aqua flame. Kyllgohr stepped back and waited courteously until the pod had gathered around the strange yet surprisingly warm blaze. "I will return just before sunrise. I doubt you would wish to see me at feast."

Turning, he trundled out to the far end of the ledge. In one swift leap he was out, then with a tremendous down sweep of his wings, he vanished skyward. The last hint of sunset was swallowed in darkness.

* * * * *

The dragon returned at the promised time. Poking only his head into the cave, he smiled at the sprytes sprawled about the still-glowing crystal. His rumbling chuckle brought them awake and to their feet in a startled scramble, grabbing for weapons. Most laughed off their fright, but Torqlan and Ujerion glared, then sulked about until it was time for departure.

"Would you like to fly to the Lower Reaches?" the dragon inquired as they stood at the cave's mouth gazing at the distant southlands faintly lit by the first suggestion of dawnshine. "I will not descend beyond the Torwilds, but at least I can save you a part of your journey home. The cold nights are marching further down the mountains, and deep snow is as likely as not nowadays."

"We could never hold on to your back ridge," Danai protested, at the same time wondering what it would be like to soar into the sky with a dragon.

Kyllgohr snorted a burst of blue steam. "I doubt there lives a creature that could. When I am flying full sweep, the wind flattens down my ridge such that any attempting to grasp it would indeed be lost. No, I thought to carry you in my pouch. There are few enough that you could all even look out if you choose."

"Pouch?"

"How did you think we carry the treasures and trove that we gather? It would be a weary many flights back and forth if our only choice was to convey them by clawfulls. We fill our pouch—which, as you will see, can hold a great deal—and that keeps the journeys few. See?" Rearing on his haunches, he bent forward and pulled at a cunningly hidden flap mid-belly. The pouch yawned wide, like an oversized mouth.

"By the Twins!" Joson stared into the belly cavern in amazement. "It looks as if you could fit all the Feyree folk in there."

"It is not as big as some," Kyllgohr said modestly, "but it serves me. What say you? If we go, it must be now, while the sun is yet still young, and not too great a blind for my eyes. Else we must wait until the morrow, and unless I miss my guess, there are those among you that would prefer to avoid that." Danai could have sworn she saw a twinkle in his eyes.

Without hesitation, she and Joson stepped forth into Kyllgohr's outstretched claws, followed by the rest of the pod. The dragon deposited them carefully into his pouch, then spoke down to them. "Crawl forward to the pouch lip. This skin is hard-ridged and you can stand upon it as we fly, and peer out. 'Ware the wind—it will be strong. Ready?" He waited a few moments until Danai waved her hand, then leaped lightly into the air.

Danai gaped as he circled twice around Snodon Tor, and she caught sight of the jagged white-cloaked mountains that clambered beyond Kairncross Pass, though none seemed as tall as the dragon's lair. They sank back to darker green in the hazy distance, and she wondered what lived north of Lampion. Kyllgohr banked then zigzagged among the peaks, keeping wind speed to a minimum so that the sprytes could look without being blown back into the pouch. The ground raced by, and Danai glimpsed the small vale in which they had weathered the storm. They passed the fringe of scraggly trees which marked the headwaters of the Silverstream, and she had the oddest illusion that the trees were growing upwards as Kyllgohr descended.

Making for a muddy patch of ground just west of the Silverstream, Kyllgohr landed with a soft thump and skidded about a dragon's length in the mud, leaving a deep furrow. There was a burst of startled birds in all directions and the bleat of a fleeing deer. He leaned over and opened his pouch. The sprytes, slightly breathless, jumped out.

Kyllgohr leaned his head down and Danai ran up to stand beside his great eye. She placed a hand upon his jowl, wondering if he could even feel her touch. "Thank you," she said simply. "My offer to you will always be."

"As will mine, brave maiden. Fare you well. Be guarded and guided by the Mother." He raised his head and his voice. "I must leave. I wish you all safe journey. Squat down, lest the wind from my wings knock you about like leaves." They barely had time to obey before he launched skywards, circled once, then raced back into the mountains. There was a momentary blue flash of light upon his wings as the sun cleared the horizon, then Kyllgohr was gone.

"Well, he saved us several days, no doubt," Damon said cheerfully, pulling off a fragment of muddy grass that Kyllgohr's departure had plastered to his brow. "We know where we are, and Siddiqui and Sohain can lead us back through the Jharma. I, for one, am glad we're coming to the end of this journey."

"Do you think the Dolmen may still be about?" Tyra piped up. They all looked at each other uneasily.

Joson shrugged. "I guess we'll find out. Keep your eyes open. And if he is, Danai's shoulders should let us know."

After the cold of the Rymples, the air seemed balmy, and it was a relief to no longer need their warming spell. Siddiqui remarked that they should expect to make good time marching downhill, and at least now they knew where they were going. While the Silverstream was yet more a runnel than a river, they crossed a fallen tree to the main trail shortly after setting out, then continued down stream, their feet made light by a sense of relief.

Late the third day, they reached the broken bridge over the Dunakey and agreed to wait until morrowmorn to decide how to get across. The sun was sinking into a ridge of black clouds mounding high on the horizon, but Tania felt that they would not bring rain that night, and so the pod prepared their bower site on the stony bank.

Danai's shoulders felt strange, not with the tingle that the Dolmen brought on, but a deep ache, like the feeling of an old, poorly-healed wound. "There's something unfriendly nearby," she whispered to Joson.

"Stay in the bower site's center," he urged, scanning the woods that were being quickly swallowed by the hurrying darkness. He raised his voice. "Danai's sensing something. Keep a sharp watch."

Gloaming flowed over them, the damp air thick with the scent of leaf mold. A net of mist eked from the ground, wandering aimlessly about the underbrush and trees, crawling slowly over the stones. Danai shuddered. It reminded her of the Great Bog. The mist floated over and above them, blotting out Lunasa's oval face and the budding stars.

There was something odd about the mist, Danai thought. Something unnatural. It seemed to swell and thicken off to their right, condensing until it became almost solid. There was a spark. Her shout of alarm was joined by others as a rift of white light fissured the mist, blazed scarlet, then ripped open with the sound of tearing cloth.

Pook strode through the gash, flanked by a guard of four blue fire daemons. One carried his standard, a gold crown diademed with red flame on a field of black. Naked curved blades that reflected no light swung from their belts. He stood there, letting them digest the impact of his arrival. The flowing raiment, the aura of command.

They gaped. Except for Danai, who sensed rather than saw that her shoulders were glowing.

He flung open his wings, eliciting a startled flurry of gasps. Then Elanoria darted forward. "Pook, you're alive! Oh, I am so glad!" She flung her arms about his neck, not seeing his quick gesture that stayed the guard who had already half-drawn their blades.

Danai did see, and hung back, noticing how he scanned the pod's faces, even as he hugged Elanoria, seeming to assess them. She felt his embered eyes rested longest on her, and she looked away after a few moments. His lips seemed fuller than she remembered, and his eyes smoldered with an unpleasant hunger.

"Toads!" Thran strode up and grasped Pook's arm. "Where did you come from, and where in the name of the Twins did you get those?"

Pook grinned back. For a brief moment, it was the familiar face of their podmate. "I got tired of the Rites and was invited, you might say, into another realm. It's called Nonetre."

"Invited by what?"

"A lovely daemon." Pook's grin slid to a more practiced smile. "Why go through all this risk, she pointed out, for a pair of wings that could be so easily granted? So I went. The folk—there are Ael, Feyree, and dwarves—all liked me and gave me my wings. Didn't even hurt."

"You do look like you've done well by yourself." Elanoria stood back to admire him, clad in the purple-black raiment Danai remembered from her dream. "Of what Guild are you?"

Pook's smile thickened. "Well, I'm more of a loremaster in training, you might say. The daemiani heralded me as their Firelord. My new name is Tizon. I am the Tvashtar."

The guttural hiss in his voice clutched at Danai's heart. He was already pronouncing his words more like the daemiani, a sound of fire scalding water.

"Strange word," Joson remarked, folding his arms across his chest. "Something like the Dolmen I presume?"

Pook's eyes slitted, his smile replaced by a sneer. "That one! Over-bound by tradition, afraid of change, mired in a realm that should have evolved long ago."

"Define 'evolved.'"

"So much more can be reaped from Lampion if only the folk are better organized. The gem-dwarves mine only as needed, yet the wealth of their tunnels could launch Lampion to leadership of other realms. The Ael pluck their lyres, the Feyree flitter about, dancing in Lunasa's light. But for what? Unproductive frittering of time that could be turned to so much more, bringing wealth and great things to all."

"But why? What need have we of wealth and things when what we need is there with simple effort and by working together?"

"I expected as much from you Joson," Pook scoffed. "You dream of being Guardian for a stale folk. With your strength, you could rise above such a lowly Calling."

"What could be better than protecting my folk?"

Danai wanted to hug Joson for his quiet firmness.

Pook shrugged. "What about you others? Why wait for your wings? I can promise them not long after you come to Nonetre. Join me in the wonderful new realm in which I live. You will all be given useful tasks that will in the end help improve our realm. You need fear no wayward creature hunting you through dark forests, or foolish old Feyree who live in lakes and trees and mourn the past when the future is so promising, or worship Lunasa, remote in the sky, who truly does not care whether you live or die. In Nonetre, many are the dances, the feast days, the celebrations. We work hard, we play hard. And," he paused to assess their reactions to his words, "if you find it not to your liking, why you can return any time to Lampion and the old ways."

He's lying, Danai realized. But to what end? Unbidden, the memory of the collared Feyree thralls appeared. She had to warn them that Pook was lying, of what Nonetre really was. She saw Pook's eyes upon her, and suddenly her tongue felt hot, dry, choking off the words. "Jo'," she managed to whisper. "Stop them." But it was too late.

There was a shuffling of feet. Torqlan pushed through the pod, his posture radiating challenge. "I will come to your realm on one condition." Pook's smile shifted to that of a hungry snake. "I be allowed to return to Lampion to finish my business with a dragon who murdered my birth mother."

"In due time, once you have become used to the ways of Nonetre, I swear that shall be granted. Clasp hands on it." He reached out. His hand glowed violet-red.

Torqlan hesitated, then clasped it. For a moment, the acrid stink of burning hair filled the air. The glow expanded to engulf Torqlan's entire body. He stiffened, then a glazed smile drifted across his face. Pook released his hand as the rift widened behind him, then stepped aside. Torqlan moved past him, walked through the rift, and was swallowed by the shifting shadows.

Through the gash, Danai glimpsed darkness-clad trees draped in pale mist. But it doesn't look like that, she thought. What magic is this?

"I'll join you Pook." Elanoria approached him, her smile coy.

"Ela, no!" Damon cried out to his half-sister. "This feels all wrong."

She turned on him, her face twisted with anger. "I'm sick of the dying and violence of these Rites! For what purpose? I trust Pook— if he says I can get my wings without all this, then I'm going!" She swung back to face Pook. "Shall we see more of each other?"

Pook smiled, reached out his glowing hand. "We shall assuredly see each other."

Danai, still struggling to speak, watched with utter dismay as Ujerion, Thran and Dlargon followed, ignoring the protestations of their podmates. Her dismay changed to anger as Pook turned towards her. She was stroked by waves of heat. A heady fragrance, like burning cedar, tickled her nostrils.

"Danai, will you not join me as well? We have need of strong folk such as yourself."

Joson gripped her arm, and the coldness of his hands pierced through Pook's seductive warmth. She felt her throat relax and knew she could speak. Her anger grew as she realized Pook had spellcast her silent. "No. I will not. It is not the time."

"But the time will be soon when you come to me." Pook's voice was sultry with promise. "The Tvashtar is granted the gift of seerage when crowned. I have seen much."

"Perhaps. But no future sight reveals all." She stood tall, her shoulders blazing silver, and was pleased to see a momentary shiver of uncertainty in his eyes.

"Be it as you will." Pook stepped back among his guards. "Send my greetings to the Dolmen. Tell him I will most assuredly see him soon." The guards stepped aside, two on each side, forming a ceremonial pathway. Pook stepped through the rift, followed by the guard, then turned once more to stare at Danai.

She felt a swelling pressure somewhere in the back of her mind, and a vision of Lady Argentyne gathered. Unbidden, a voice, hollow with distance, pushed forth from her mouth like dark waters. "From tears shall thee fall, Majerion." Danai's arms lifted of their own accord, her hands clapped thrice, then gestured sharply at the rift. She felt an unknown power flowing through her.

Pook started at hearing his birth name, took a half-step forward, then leaped back as the rift snapped shut with a hiss and coil of foul-smelling smoke.

* * * * *

Chapter Twenty-Two

Shocked silence held the sprytes motionless as the last smoke wisps were swallowed by the thickening mist. Somewhere across the river, an owl hooted, startling them into action.

"What did you mean by that?" Damon stood, fists clenched, still staring at the vanished rift.

Danai shook her head, a strange feeling of emptiness drawing tears to her eyes. "I don't know. It wasn't me speaking." Damon whirled about, and for a moment she thought he would strike her.

"They just walked out of our lives! No looking back. No farewells. As if we didn't matter any more, not in any way, shape or form! They were so close to their wings! What in the name of the Mother possessed them?"

"Possessed is the word." The sprytes looked at Joson. "Pook was spellcasting. Couldn't you feel it? Did you see their faces once he glowed them? They looked like, like..."

"Mindless ones," Siddiqui finished Joson's sentence. Others nodded. "I think we had better stay close to each other and post double-guard this night," Joson said.

"I don't want to stay here," Atelya burst out, teeth chattering, eyes whirling scarlet. "Pook felt all wrong. Twisting fire, pain-torn shadows. Couldn't you see how the air warped around him? He is only a strangled shell of Pook, threads of our friend holding together this new thing he names Tizon." She spat. "I name him Poison. He

411

brings darkness to Lampion. We must warn the Dolmen and the Chief Tains." She sagged, leaning against Rhytha, who encircled her with comforting arms. "Oh, why I am cursed with being a Seer?"

Siddiqui cocked her head towards the Dunakey. "We can't cross at night with the bridge gone, and I doubt we'll find webber-puffs this time. But I have no doubt we'll figure out something." There was something soothing about having to deal with a real problem which could be solved.

Joson and Damon took first watch, but sleep held no sway over any of the pod, and they peered into the sighing shadows with glowing eyes, praying for a quick end to the night.

* * * * *

Dawnshine brought only the gloomy gray fog that still ebbed and pulsed around them. It made sense to wait for the fog to lift, but the pod agreed it was better to get going. Taking turns, they hewed down a sapling which toppled over the roiling Dunakey to create a slender bridge. Agile Siddiqui and light-footed Damon crossed first, and held down the branches while Joson and Danai secured the trunk, following only after all the others were on the other bank.

"Is there a faster trail to the Dell?" Danai asked Siddiqui. "The sooner we can get back, the safer we will be."

"Ummm. I think if we go through Silver Wood then by Red Nose Rock, it could cut off at least two days. But in this dratted fog, I don't know if I can find the trail without losing sight of the rest of you." At her words, the fog billowed and seemed to thicken.

"We'll have to try," Joson said. "What are you looking for?"

"An ancient dead birch tree. It's straight ahead from the bridge. It's so white, it's easy to see—but I can't see much beyond my nose in this mess."

"Fine. Let's work our way along the bank until we find the bridge."

Linking arms, the pod moved slowly along the bank keeping at least a feylength's distance between them and the river gully. The leaders could not be seen by those at the rear. "Found it!" Siddiqui shouted. "From here, the tree would be that way." She pointed south, trying to peer through the fog.

"Anything between here and the tree we could try to find?" Damon suggested.

"There's a boulder about midway between here and the tree," Sohain offered. "Big gray thing banded with white. An arch of brambles lies a little beyond that. Then a rumpled trail of packed stones. My older brother said it carries a stream early in blossom time."

"Any guess at how far the boulder is?"

Sohain made a face. "Not sure. Somewhere around twenty-five feylengths, maybe?"

"Then how about this? Let's hold hands, and stretch out as far as we can. I'll stay right here, Sohain, Siddiqui, you'll be at the far end. Let's see if we can find that boulder."

"No luck," Sohain bellowed a bit later, his voice muffled in the fog. "We need to go farther out."

"Everyone back," Joson shouted. When they had returned, he offered another idea. "Let's haul the sapling over, and we can use that to extend our reach. I'll hold down the end here, and the rest of you can walk along to its far branches to continue searching."

"Good idea, Joson!" Poochigan thumped him on the back. "Let's make it happen."

As he watched the others fade into the mist, Joson ignored the sensation of being watched. He thought back to last night. Pook's going to turn them into thralls from what Danai described, but to what aim? Why did he even come back? He doesn't need us. But he wants something. From Lampion. I don't get it. He's got everything he wanted, especially his wings, but still he wants more. Joson sighed. There was a kryptic in all this, but he didn't have enough to figure it out—yet.

"Found it!" Siddiqui's voice was so faint, he had to hold his breath. Again came the glad cry. Following the sapling, he soon joined the other sprytes clustered around the boulder.

"Wouldn't it be nice to be snug in our bowers with nothing more to worry about than mornmeal?" Tyra stared wistfully into the curling fog. "Ah, well. So where's these dratted brambles?"

"Hey, I think the fog is thinning." Sohain peered ahead. "See the brambles? Over there. Drat, they're gone again. There! That's it." He scraped a line in the moist dirt with his toe, marking the brambles' direction as the fog tightened about them. "Let's form another line folks."

Crouching to avoid the wicked brown thorns the length of their forearms, Danai gave a sigh of relief when she heard Sohain call out he'd found the streambed. She stumbled as her feet encountered the froth of pebbles.

"Look!" Siddiqui sang out. "I see the birch trees of Silver Wood. There's the ancient birch. And the fog's lifting. Finally." Sunshine poured down through golden leaves trembling in a soft warm breeze.

Glancing behind them, Danai frowned. The fog was retreating back towards the Dunakey. She elbowed Joson. "Look at it. It was only a patch of fog. There's none else about."

"Pook?"

"Maybe."

* * * * *

"**D**o you think we'll run into him again?" he asked later as they slogged up a steep slope, leaving Silver Wood behind.

"Not for a bit. I'm guessing he got whatever he wanted—for the moment," she panted back. "But I wish there was a way to get back more quickly so we can tell the Mentors." The trail circumvented a massive oak, its scarlet-mottled leaves rattling in the stiffening breeze.

"Why not call for Wag-Tail?"

Danai gaped. "Where are my thoughts? We should have thought of that sooner. Everybody, halt!"

Moments later the pod erupted first with the magpie's raucous squawk, then the jay's harsh rasp. They repeated the sequence three times. Tyra pointed at a streak of blue heading towards them. "Jay!" It circled once, then landing on a twig above their heads.

"Stellar am I named. Who gives the call and why?"

"We did, good Stellar. I am Danai of Feyree. We are from the Great Dell and in need of aid. Could thee carry a message to the Dell for us telling them where we are, and that a Mentor is needed in all haste?"

Stellar cocked his head. "Why not have one of thee fly with me?" He chuckled at their surprised expressions. "The word went out to the bird-folk to keep an eye out since ye were last seen at the meeting of the two rivers. But early rains, while much welcome, have kept most huddled in their nests. Who will come?"

"You go," Joson urged, pushing Danai forward. "You know more than any of us. We'll rest here until Stellar comes back with orders." The jay bobbed in agreement, looking expectantly at Danai.

She hesitated. "Stellar, who gave the word?"

"Tlarg."

"I will come."

* * * * *

The Mentors converged upon her like dumbledores on a just-opened redcup as Stellar landed.

"Thank Lunasa you are returned." Triasa nearly hugged the breath from her niece. "Where are the others?"

"Waiting by the great oak above Silver Wood near the Dunakey. They must be brought back as quickly as possible. Can you send sixteen birds out to fetch them? Stellar can lead."

"The rules of the Rite require that they return here unaided, unlike yourself," Oyon huffed.

"Are you deaf?" Toron jostled past Oyon. "Danai, if that is one bird for each spryte, then you have lost five sprytes. Where are the others?" The import of Toron's question stilled the Mentors.

"I do not know if they are dead or alive. Pook appeared from Nonetre yestereve at gloaming and persuaded several sprytes to join him, promising them their wings. Ujerion, Thran, Torqlan, Dlargon and Elanoria went." She ignored the flutter of dismayed gasps. "And I believe he will return. That is why I chose to fly back with Stellar and give warning."

"Bah, bah," Oyon protested. "This is a decision for the Dolmen whether to send aid, not some troublesome spryte or even the Mentors."

"Oyon, you're as dense as the Dolmen," Triasa snapped. "Blindly mired in rules even as a storm gathers. Have you so quickly forgotten Tlarg's message?" Oyon sputtered as she joined the other Mentors who were already crying down the birds. Stellar launched to intercept the arriving flock, and escorted them northwest, even as the Dolmen emerged from behind the weathersign bushes. It studied the milling group of Mentors, stiffening when it beheld Danai, then strode towards them.

"What means this uproar?"

"We have sent the birds to retrieve the remaining members of the pod," Triasa replied, turning her gaze from the disappearing flock.

"Remaining?"

"Five have joined Pook in Nonetre."

Danai would not have believed the Dolmen's face could be any whiter—until now. Like fresh snow on old snow, she thought, watching its jaw muscles twitch.

Toron stepped forward. "Dolmen, the Chief Tains must be summoned."

"For the defection of a few foolish sprytes?"

Toron took a deep breath to control his temper. "I do not call the summoning of sprytes by one of their own turned Firelord a 'defection.' I call it an invitation to worse."

Nporan sniffed. "Guardians always see fighting as the outcome of everything."

"It is our duty to prevent fighting," Toron shot back. "When a fire daemon fries your skin from your bones, will you still whine and wheeze denial? That Pook could so casually enter Lampion, and so easily seduce five sprytes shows a failure on our part as Mentors to properly teach them daemiani lore, and why such realms are to be at all costs avoided. Too complacent have we become." He turned to the Dolmen. "And answer me this. Why have the spells that sealed Lampion from the daemiani for so long now weakened such that they can cleave through the barrier?" Without removing his gaze from the Dolmen, he directed his next question to Danai. "How long was Pook among you?"

"Some time. Enough for him to boast of being Firelord, describe the niceties of Nonetre, hand clasp five sprytes, and urge yet more to join."

"What stopped thee from returning to thy own?" the Dolmen hissed.

Danai raised her eyes to stare at him. I'm no longer afraid of you, she realized. "I denied him. Then another spoke through me, words that sealed the rift."

"Who?"

"I believe it was Lady Argentyne."

"Preposterous," Oyon exclaimed. "Another inside your head?"

"There is much precedence for such a mind-meld, although over such a distance is difficult," the Dolmen said slowly, brushing aside Oyon's remark. "One can travel with another even when the body is not there. As did Toron and Danai with the Lady when they went to Nonetre. Or have ye so quickly forgotten Oyon?"

Toron drew them back to the matter at hand. "The Chief Tains, Dolmen. I urge you to summon them."

"So be it. But tell them that it is for the Rite of Krisalys, to be held in two days on Lunasa's next solas."

"You will not advise them?" Melitsa's tone was brittle with outrage.

"We had not yet finished speaking. Advise them of what has transpired, and that it is in part the reason for Krisalys being advanced one lumna. Request that they be escorted by their highest Tier Guardian—the one that would assume the mantle of Warlord if such a need arises. Is that sufficient Mentor Melitsa?" She flushed and nodded.

It was not over-long before a racket of mixed bird calls could be heard approaching. The Mentors and Danai watched as the wedge of burdened birds cascaded over the tree tops into the Dell to deposit their sprytes. Spying Wag-Tail, Stellar and Mentors Quenton and Melarna together among them, Danai raced over, dodging among flapping wings and prodding bills. She quickly explained events, her conversation masked by the general hubbub. They bobbed and vaulted back into the sky, Wag-Tail and Melarna heading northwest, Stellar and Quenton north, their determined flight lost in the cloud of other departing birds.

A series of three sharp claps brought an end to the noise. "We will hear the tale of Pook from each of you now," the Dolmen ordered. "Proceed to the Skystone." It turned, striding up-meadow, with the Mentors and the sprytes following.

The dragon's tears! Danai decided to lag behind. The pod had been too far away to realize she had collected more than one, and she had never mentioned it. She did not want to give them all to the

Dolmen—not by any means. Delving into her rucksack, where she had carefully secured the leaf-wrapped tears, she plucked out a single packet and hugged it to her heart. Hurrying after the pod, she caught up with them as they passed through the weathersign bushes.

The Dolmen gestured Joson forth. "Tell what ye beheld." It issued the same order another sixteen times as the sun crested overhead. After Tyra had concluded, the Dolmen spoke. "And so each went of their own free will."

"He offered them reasons best suited to their desires," Triasa said. "Even though it is unlikely he will grant them other than thrall-collars."

"Perhaps not," Majikian said slowly. "If Pook plans more than the simple capture of a few sprytes, then it would not do well to relegate them to drudgery. He is no fool. He knows the tale will spread faster than a summer blaze, and if he appears again, others may challenge his promises and demand proof. What better than sprytes-turned-Feyree to serve as his tale tellers?"

"Spells can be cast to make one do or say anything," Toron pointed out. "While they are lost to our folk, I much doubt that the daemiani have the same scruples."

The Dolmen struck his staff down hard, casting a shower of green sparks. "This is a matter for council-moot, not idle sprytes' ears. Where is the tear, the proof of this Rite's success?"

Danai rose, wishing she could have handed the tear off to Joson rather than having to approach the Dolmen. She calmly walked forward, stepping through the seated sprytes. Ignoring her shoulders' tingling, she concentrated on the single tear she was to hand over.

The Dolmen extended its hand.

She unwrapped the tear, releasing its silver-blue radiance. For a moment the hazy sunlight seemed to dim, the birds hushed, the eddying breeze slowed. There were murmurs of amazement from Mentors and sprytes alike. Danai sensed that even the Dolmen was slightly startled to actually see the tear—or, she wondered, was it something else? She dropped the tear into its outstretched palm and stepped back.

The Dolmen dragged its eyes from the glittering tear. "The Rite of Krisalys is in two days, at next solas. The Mentors are to prepare ye. The Chief Tains have been summoned to attend thy passage into Feyree. Or thy failure." It spun about and disappeared into the Skystone.

* * * * *

Chapter Twenty-Three

"Learn how to fly? We don't even have our wings yet! They're suntouched!" Damon tapped his forehead as Mentors Alamai and Tamilyn called the pod to order.

"It is better to learn the basics while yet ground-bound," remarked Alamai, who had overheard Damon's remark. "Especially as Krisalys has been moved forward one lumna. Were all as it should be, it would not be held until Verlunasa, when day and night are equal. You would have had time for this and other final training—now that will fall after the Rite. New-fledged Feyree are very giddy—understandably so—and we do not want you to damage your wings or yourselves." She paused to let that statement sink in. "Remember the most important rule of flying. If your wings fail, you fall. Like any other part of your body, they must be attended to. But unlike the rest of your limbs, you have not had them all your lives, and will have to learn not only how to fly, but how to care for them until it becomes second nature."

Tyra raised her hand. "Birds know right out of the nest."

"They do no not," Tamilyn replied. "Consider how many dead nestlings you have seen among the tree roots. They jump, they flap, they fall. If they have a soft landing or a parent to intervene, and no hungry creatures about, they may survive. And then they start with short hops, developing their muscles. No more than you were able to walk the first time you stood—although I doubt you remember it. Flying is the same thing. You begin at the beginning. Now attend!"

Alamai and Tamilyn doffed their robes and turned sideways, presenting profiles of translucent wings, one pair topaz, the other amethyst. Tamilyn assumed the role of teacher, gesturing at Alamai's wings to illustrate his points.

"After your wings are released—"

"How does that happen?" Kerion interrupted.

Tamilyn smothered a smile, fully understanding the spryte's eagerness. It was like this for all sprytes perched on the abyss of flying. They saw only the wings, not what followed. "You will find out at Krisalys. It may not be spoken of. Now, as I was saying, after your wings are released, they will be soft and beyond delicate. Much like those of newborn flutterbies. They will ache as your body pumps blood into them and they unfurl. And you will be dizzy and light-headed until your body adjusts to the new demands being made upon it. Avoid the urge to jump and dance—more often than not, such caperings result in new-fledged Feyree fainting."

The sprytes were enthralled. Slowly he explained each part of the wing and how it functioned, how they could be stiffened for flight, or drooped as needed. Danai wondered if she had ever truly looked at Feyree wings. Then Alamai took over the training as Tamilyn demonstrated simple aerial maneuvers.

"Like any muscle, you will have to build your flying strength. Short shallow hops, a basic down thrust to lift off. It will take practice to learn how to maneuver, so stay in the Dell. Do not go among trees or shrubs which can tear your new wings."

"How long does a wing take to heal?" Tania asked, eyes wide.

"It depends upon the Feyree's health, but a torn wing is prone to stiffness at the scar, and few Feyree recover the full control. In two words, do not. Now watch how Tamilyn alights. Do not plummet, but curve your wings, catch the wind—ah yes, you must always watch the direction of the wind, for it can help or hinder your movements. Take time to study the birds—they are the true loremasters of flight." Tamilyn made landing look so simple, but as Alamai pointed out each step, they realized how complex the maneuver was.

"Once you have fledged your wings, you will stay in training for at least one more lumna to ensure you have acquired all the basics. Trust me—it looks far easier than it truly is. Perhaps it is wise to once again remind you that Feyree are not birds, and our wings are not designed for long distances. Like the manylegs, we flit, we make short journeys, we rest. The great sky belongs to the bird folk, not to us."

The day flew by under the Mentors' tutelage. Danai noticed that the other Mentors were largely absent. As the sun began to sink, the pod found it harder to concentrate. Krisalys was morrow's eve! The Mentors continued their teaching until evenmeal, then excused them. Gathering around the trestles, Joson nudged Danai. "Look. By the weathersign bushes. I wonder what's in those bulky bundles the Mentors are carrying up to the Skystone?"

Every spryte was up at dawnshine, none needing the reed pipe. "Eat," ordered Mentor Nacci, as she saw that few sprytes were interested in mornmeal. Even Joson only pecked at a few sweetseeds. "You will need your strength in more ways then you know this eventide."

The Dolmen appeared and summoned them to the Mentors' Circle. "This gloaming begins the final Rite. The Krisalys. Ye have passed all other Rites to the satisfaction of thy Mentors. This eventide the Chief Tains will arrive, gathering to witness thy fledging." It paused, glancing at each spryte, then continued. "Or thy death, as it may be. Once more, ye have the choice to leave this Rite if ye so will. Go ye and think on it. At gloaming, ye shall be asked one final time. This be thy final day for contemplation. Stay within the Dell. That is an Order." It started towards the Skystone, signaling the waiting Mentors to follow.

An unoccupied day was the last thing any spryte wanted. "It gives us too much time to dwell on tonight," Rhytha grumbled as she sat with her friends beneath a golden fern whose curling edges were a light brown. "My stomach is one large knot, and no matter how hard I try to think of something else, I keep imagining the Krisalys. What if I can't escape?"

"You mustn't panic," Danai urged, hoping her aunt wasn't anywhere within hearing. "If nothing else, the one thing these Rites have taught us is to think before reacting. Remember the Hunted Rite? Do you think you'd do the same thing now?"

"No-o-o-o," Rhytha said, after a moment's thought. "I'd ambush Arlymyria, get the whip, and tie her up with it, instead of trying to use it on her."

"Danai's right," Joson said. "I feel so old when I compare myself to how I was back in blossom time." He stuck his tongue out at Rhytha as she tried to unsuccessfully stifle a snort. "Seriously. I've watched a friend become a babe, others die, yet others vanish into another daemension, and I've seen things I thought were only Skald and Orpheii tales. Laugh if you like, Rhytha, but I feel ancient." She lightly touched his forearm in apology.

"What happens right after Krisalys do you think?" Damon asked, hugging his knees, enjoying the sun's warmth on his back.

They gazed at each other. "You know, I never thought to ask," Danai confessed. "I've been so focused on all the Rites and then this thing with Pook..." Her voice trailed off. They all sighed.

"You said the Dolmen summoned the Guardians as well as the Chief Tains," Damon said. "But what is it expecting to happen? Danai, what really puzzles me is that with all you told us about Nonetre—and Pook was there—they still chose to go. Including that dimwit half-sister of mine, Elanoria." He shook his head with disgust. "When that rift opened, I saw trees. But you described it as an ugly, barren land. I don't get it."

"Who knows what magics he has already learned?" Danai twisted a bit of grass. "He needs such illusions to convince folk to go there. And perhaps his folk have persuaded themselves that what they have is wonderful, unwilling to face the reality. I don't know."

"It's hard to believe Pook could allow himself to be so..." Rhytha searched for the right word, "warped. What joy could he find in a place so structured and defined, so empty of the Mother's beauty?"

"Maybe that Eshel cast a spell on him? Was he a daemon too?"

Danai shook her head. "Not sure, now that I think on it. Lady Argentyne seemed to recognize him. As to the spell, yes it's likely, but you know Pook was impatient, especially when it came to learning the spells. If somebody presented you everything you thought you wanted on a trencher of gold, and they said it's yours in exchange for coming to such a place, what would you do?" She gave a crooked smile at their confused looks. "Triasa once told me the unknown can be very seductive. But she cautioned me that all new things are like a double-edge dirq, and too often one forgets—or ignores—the back slash. Perhaps Nonetre was once as fair as Lampion, but the folk followed a different path—one that seemed right at the time—and those who live there now don't know any better?"

"The daemiani could have made it that way," Rhytha argued. "Look at how the one chasing us scorched everything it touched."

"Yes. But presumably somebody had to let the daemiani in first. Consider Solon and the time daemiani. He let them in, and once they were here, well, you know."

"Look at Ela and the others," Damon said. "They actually chose to go with Pook. He didn't cast any spell on them until they clasped his hand. Then it was too late."

"And did you see those bizarre smiles on their faces? Ugh!" Rhytha shuddered. "Danai, I wish you had told everyone about Nonetre. Maybe that would have prevented what happened."

"It was forbidden to me. As it was, I took a risk telling you. And a lot of good it did with Pook. But yes, I wish now I had ignored that Order."

Damon tossed aside the bits of catkin he had been tearing apart. He lowered his voice. "So don't make the same mistake now. You feel something, I can tell. Maybe it's those silver shoulders of yours, but you sometimes seem to sense things ahead of others. What? You've got to tell us. We're your friends."

Their eyes are so expectant, Danai thought, wishing she could unburden all her worries. "I believe Pook will return. I saw him in what I thought was a dream that night in the Ael's cave. He will not be satisfied to be Tvashtar of one realm, for he is convinced—perhaps by magic—that Lampion should come under his dominion.

He will return. That the Dolmen has summoned the Warlords is proof of that, I think." She hesitated.

"And?" Damon prompted.

In the distance of her mind, Danai heard a mother weeping. She whispered one word. 'Sagad.'

There was a shout behind them. A running quail burst into the Dell, two winged figures nestled among its neck feathers. "Eldrich Symnon! Manichia!" Siddiqui and Sohain hastened towards the bird with loud cries of welcome.

Mentors appeared, even as other birds began to arrive, some bearing the Chief Tains, others a Guardian.

A gleaming raven coasted down, the sinking sun at its back, but only Sandai ran over to greet them. "They must be from Kristal Glen," Rhytha sighed. "I wonder if they know where Torqlan is gone to. And poor Arcieron is still under the Healers' care. Oh, look! Eldrich Treana." She bolted towards the jay that had just landed, Poochigan, Tania, and Tyra joining her.

More birds arrived until the Eldrich and Guardians from all nine dells were present. A general hubbub of greetings and laughter replaced the tension of the day. Danai hurried towards Eldrich Shealor and Nishai, and was surprised to see Toron approach. I had forgotten he is the highest Tier Guardian, she thought. Out of the corner of her eye, she noticed the Dolmen observing the gathering, yet also scanning the sky. I wonder who else it's waiting for? She followed its gaze, and gasped.

A huge silver bird appeared over the Shehn, and descended in gradual circles, wings outspread. Even from a distance, Danai could see the glitter of its golden eyes, and caught a flash of scarlet as it beak opened to scream out a greeting. A ripple of excitement filled the air.

"Behold the Hyrald, bearer of our Lord and Lady!" The Dolmen's voice was deep with respect. "Give ye greetings to Lord Andamion and Lady Atelai whom are come to attend Krisalys." As the Hyrald landed with a strong backstroke that caused the tawny grasses to ripple, the Dolmen knelt on one knee, and everyone did likewise. They rose, and the Dolmen strode forward to proffer its hand to the Lady. With a smile, she grasped it and dismounted.

Danai stared. It had never occurred to her that the Lord and Lady of Revelstoke, High Seat of the Feyree, would attend Krisalys. The silver of her skin was so bright, Lady Atelai seemed almost made of crystal. Her golden hair bordered on almost white, while her wings seemed a rippling cascade of sunsplashed water. She reminds me of the dragon's tear, Danai thought, or a star wandering about in daylight. Lady Atelai stood in stark contrast to Lord Andamion's dark green skin, citrine eyes and bronze hair. His copper wings seemed like thinly-beaten metal. Both wore full-length robes of ceremony the same color as their bodies, girdled with gem-studded sashes. About their brows were bound intricately braided circlets of silver. Crystals and sapphires were woven in the Lady's, while the Lord's sparkled with a single round emerald, green as new grass. It reminded Danai of the Anam.

There was a flash of black, and a large raven landed behind the Hyrald. Three ladies and four fellows, richly clad, with sheathed dirqs prominent on their braided belts, dismounted and assumed positions that formed a half-circle about the Lord and Lady. Danai guessed them to be the Guardians of the High Court. For a moment Pook's guards flashed into her mind, and she cringed with some undefined premonition.

The pod was ushered forward, with the Mentors following. Lady Atelai smiled at the nervous sprytes' faces. "Greetings all ye who will soon bear the wings of Feyree." Her voice was unexpectedly deep, like the quiet rumble of distant summer thunder. "We are honored to be here at thy Krisalys, and will be there to welcome ye to fledge-hood and freedom." She gestured to her Lord.

"Once every three Verlunasas, when Lunasa is in solas, are sprytes offered the choice to become Feyree," Lord Andamion spoke, his voice even deeper than his Lady's. "Know ye that it is not a mantle to be assumed lightly. Thy Dream Councils foreshadow thy roles among the folk, and ye will embark along many paths. When ye return to thy dells, there are those who are yet sprytes that be thy friends. They will hasten to ask about Krisalys. These queries ye are forbidden to answer, for the Rites must not be tainted by fore-knowledge lest their purpose be defeated.

"When Lunasa rises this gloaming, the Rite of Krisalys will com-mence. Are their aught of ye who feel as yet unready?" Lord An-damion studied each face, and Danai had the sensation of something gently probing her thoughts, a slight pressure behind her eyes, and then a lightness filling her heart. One by one, the crinkles of worry were smoothed from each spryte's face to be replaced by a radiant smile. The Lord bowed his head a moment then looked up. "Go then with thy Mentors now, to prepare thyselves for this, the final Rite. No food or drink is to pass thy lips save that which thy Mentor gives ye. When next we meet, the final Rite will commence." He inclined his head once more, then the Dolmen escorted him and his Lady towards the Skystone.

Melitsa tapped Danai's shoulder. "Come. It is time."

* * * * *

As the sun set behind the great Shehn, Danai had the strange sensation of having gone through this once before. Except that now the wind hurried bronze and scarlet leaves across the grass, carrying with it the scents of autumn. The pink and cream-colored blossoms of spring had been replaced by golden tormentil, yellow wood sage, and purple lavender.

She wasn't sure if her trembling was caused by the cleansing in the cool creek waters or her nervousness. Melitsa brushed the rough crop of her hair smooth, crooning a soft soothing tune just under her breath. Danai tried to ignore her dream image of the smothering white threads, but they kept intruding on her thoughts.

The first star pricked forth. "It is time," Melitsa said. "See?" She pointed at the silvery shimmer rising above the trees. "Lunasa is already arriving for the ceremony." Melitsa placed a steadying hand on Danai's shoulder. "Let us go." They began to walk towards the Skystone, joining other silent pairs.

Danai longed for Joson or Damon or Rhytha. Somebody to ask, 'are you as scared as me?' Fear feels so lonely, she thought, swallowing hard against the ache just under her heart. She wished Aaron were among them and blinked away the rush of tears. They passed through the weathersign bushes.

Glowing foxfire had been laid about in a large ring before the Skystone in front of which was seated the Dolmen, flanked by the Lord and Lady, with the seven Guardians standing just behind. The Chief Tains and their Guardians were seated around the outside of the foxfire ring, leaving a small gap at one end through which the Mentors escorted their Charges. They then stepped out and stood behind the seated Feyree to form the Mentors' Circle.

Gazing about, Danai gave a start of joy. Among the Mentors stood Melarna and Quenton. They returned her smile and nodded.

The Dolmen made a slight gesture, and to Danai's amazement, the Lord and Lady rose, each bearing a large, capped kuis. Entering the ring, each stopped before a spryte. "This eve is the last ye be sprytes," cried the Dolmen. "Drink the brew that will bring ye to Feyree."

The kuis were uncapped and a flickering silver radiance bathed the Lord's and Lady's faces. Each spryte drank deep from the proffered kuis then stood, swaying slightly, as the Lord and Lady advanced onwards.

It was almost syrupy, Danai thought, feeling it slither down her throat to land with a warm slosh. A gentle tremor seemed to spread from her belly to her nerves, reminding her of the time she had gulped Shamarig's mead too quickly. She stood swaying, determined not to make a fool of herself. Lunasa rose in majesty, bathing the scene in silver. From a distance, Danai noticed the etched black shadows that each figure and object cast to the west, then realized their edges were blurring. Her knees buckled, and she sagged to the ground. About her, forms seemed to swirl and move in a silvery dance, frosted threads trailing from their hands. Then everything faded into warm darkness.

I am being born, she mused. Wrapped warm under my mother's heart, soon shall I see the world beyond her spirit. She tried to open her eyes, but they were stuck fast. Her nose was pressed against her face, making it difficult to breathe. What little air there was had a musty odor that left a sour taste at the back of her throat. Her skin felt slathered in a mushy stickiness. She tried to move her arms, realizing they were crossed over her chest, fingers facing outwards, as if she were protecting her heart. Her mind cleared, her heart began to thump.

I am in a krisalys.

I cannot see or move.

I can barely breathe.

I must not panic. Must not, must not, must not.

She concentrated on her breathing, slowing down the quick pants. How am I going to get out of this? She wanted to scream, but the thought of the Krisalys threads entering her mouth stopped her. About her she heard muffled cries, and swallowed hard. Don't panic, don't panic, she chanted in her head. They'll make it. We all will.

She focused her thoughts. My hands are my only tool. Try clenching fingers. Ah good. They move a bit. Try moving wrists. Some give. That's a start. I want out, I want out. I hate this. I don't want my wings. Stop thinking like a fool. Yes, you do. Don't panic. Don't panic. Focus on your hands. You can do this. Remember. You faced down an ice dragon. Grip. Pull. Poke. Did it give a little? I think so. Grip, pull harder. Yes. I feel cold air on my finger. Tear harder, harder! Pull! One hand's out. Grab this stuff and tear it away. It won't trap me! My other hand's free. Oh, yes. Get it off my face. Oh yes. Air.

She tugged the clinging threads free of her eyelashes and mouth, gulping deep draughts of moist night air. Then she rested a few moments, grasping the fact she had escaped and now only had to peel the rest of the Krisalys from her body. Through blurry eyes, she saw sprytes tearing free, while others yet struggled with their shrouds that glowed weirdly in the light. Lunasa was now directly overhead. Sitting up, she began to strip herself clean and realized her tunic was gone. Her wing bumps throbbed as she squirmed her arms to yank the threads off her back. Finished, she sat watching the others.

Three sprytes' krisalys remained unopened, their forms yanking and twisting about like some grotesque maggots. Danai and the others watched with grim fascination, whispers of hope pouring from their lips. A collective sigh broke forth as fingers, then hands pushed forth from two of them. Yet the last still struggled, although with less and less energy. Danai glanced about, identifying faces, seeking her friends, missing one. Her gaze returned to the three jerking shapes. The two peeled the threads from their faces. Neither was Rhytha.

The silvered silence pounded at her temples. She watched her friend's Krisalys twitch and struggle, but no hand broke free. Mentors' and Chief Tains' faces swam into her sight, all staring at the swathed form, sadness beginning to dim their features.

No! Danai cried from her heart. I will not allow her to die. This is senseless. The memory of Lady Argentyne and their mind-meld journey flashed through her thoughts. Mind-meld. Maybe in Rhytha's sluggish state she could connect with her. Danai's shoulders began to glimmer as she closed her eyes and concentrated all her energies on her friend. 'Rhytha, Rhytha, Rhytha. Hear me listen to me hear me hear me hear me.'

The form stilled. A soft sad sigh from many throats gossamered the air.

'Danai?'

Danai wanted to weep at the faint questing touch, but dared not to release her concentration. 'Your hands. Tear, grip, pull at the threads.'

'I'm so tired...'

'Try try try try.'

'So...tired...'

'Rhytha you're going to die! You must try!'

The form quivered at the waist.

'Try try try try. That's it! You've poked a finger through! Feel the air? Don't stop. Pull at that stuff. Keep going. You can do it! You can you can you can you can...'

She gasped with hope as Rhytha's hand followed her finger. She kept projecting encouragement, terrified of letting go. Not until Rhytha had pulled the threads free of her face did she allow herself to stop, her shoulders slumping with relief, listening to the welcome sound of her friend gasping for air. A dull ache radiated from her shoulders up the back of her neck.

Looking up, she encountered two pairs of eyes. Lady Atelai's were as approving as the Dolmen's were enraged. How could they have heard me, she wondered. She focused her gaze on the Lady, the quiet smile a balm to her frayed energy. Lady Atelai nodded once, a secretive smile trickling across her lips.

"Stand ye for *Oisillon*!"

The pod rose unsteadily, filaments and rags of their torn Krisalys undulating from their bodies like sticky mist. There was something haggard that creased their faces, a reflection of having hugged death and emerged alive.

We can never be the same, Danai thought.

Lunasa's silvery light seemed to brighten about them until the Dell swam in luminescence. Oisillon, the Ceremony of the Wings, commenced.

The Mentors moved among them in pairs, one bearing a crystal basin filled with warm fragrant liquid, the other a soft cloth which was dipped in the liquid and used to wipe each spryte clean. The liquid left a tingling trail as the cloth dragged across her body, and Danai felt the fogginess clear from her mind. She straightened, head held high.

Mentor Melitsa approached, bearing a shimmering silver tunic, Toron following a step behind. Her smile spoke beyond words as she dropped the tunic lightly over Danai's head, the wing flaps flowing loose about the shoulders. Danai's wing bumps began to itch and burn, as if something were pushing against the tender skin.

Toron bowed to Danai, holding forth a dirq that seemed cut from a single emerald, flashing green in the light. Gripping the hilt with both hands, he raised the dirq and held it above the center of Danai's forehead, gathering Lunasa's rays in a triangle of emerald fire. Thrice he circled her, then stopped behind. Her heart pounded. She sensed rather than felt the first downward cut. The second was complete before she had time to gasp at the pain.

The burn of tearing flesh, the warm trickle of copper-scented blood, a sudden sense of new weight pulling her shoulders back. Twisting her head, she peered over her shoulder to see a jumble of silver and black thrust free, droop downwards, then begin to expand slowly. Waves of dizziness blurred her sight. Her stomach heaved. "Sit," Melitsa ordered, after wiping away the blood. Danai obeyed.

We're not sprytes any more, she suddenly realized. We're Feyree. A rush of exultation flooded her from tip to toe, even as she fought down another surge of nausea. Finally. We are Feyree.

She focused on Rhytha's back, seated off to the right. Her wings drooped like crumpled wet river moss. Before Danai's enthralled eyes, they seemed to swell outwards, then slump, then surge again, spreading up and out, ribbed with pearl, filling and flowing until they sat poised upon her shoulders, drooping slightly, like a motionless flutterby.

Again the Mentors moved among the pod, making each take a long draught of yet another liquid that smelled of berries and sunshine, and seemed more like inhaling air than quaffing liquid. It flooded Danai with energy, and she rose to her feet, wanting to dance and shout and laugh.

Lord Andamion flung out his arms. "Rise, all ye rise," he shouted. "Thrice welcome are ye, new-fledged Feyree of Lampion. Uphold the Scrolls and the Laws, honor Lunasa and the Mother. Treat each other, the younglings, and thy elders with courtesy and respect. Let each Mentor now bring forth their Charge!"

Danai wished Triasa could be the one to escort her. Each new-fledged Feyree was brought before the Lord and Lady. Ribbons of sparkles draped across Lord Andamion's forearms. The Dolmen stood slightly behind the Lady, holding a carved wooden basin in which something glinted. As each new Feyree was presented, Lady Atelai stepped forward to bestow a kiss upon their brow. Then, plucking a belt from her Lord, and receiving a sheathed metal dirq from the Dolmen, she girdled the newly fledged, snugging the tunic's wing flaps under the belt, and adjusting the dirq over the right thigh.

When all were girdled, they stood looking at each other, wondering what could possibly come next. A merry laugh of relief burst from Siddiqui, and a moment later, everyone was laughing. Only the Dolmen stood impassive.

"Now come to feast," Lady Atelai cried, gesturing towards the Shehn. The Mentors hurried ahead while the Chief Tains and Guardians advanced to congratulate and welcome their new Feyree. The throng moved through the weathersign bushes and back into the Dell.

The Mentors had tossed their cloaks in a heap near the Shehn's roots, and were removing the coverings from the trestles. Foxfire torches were set all about, and several more were clustered near a troupe of Orpheii softly tuning their instruments. Then a reed pipe twittered, twirling cheery notes into the air; a tambour thumped. The Orpheii played a wild tune, adding windhorns and harps. Feet began to stamp, hands to clap. Soon nearly everyone was whirling about in a sparkling dance that was perhaps three parts celebration and one part relief.

Danai found herself pirouetting with Joson, and she impetuously gave him a hug, carefully threading her hands beneath his still-soft wings so as not to crush them. "We did it!" They laughed at each other, giddy. Rhytha danced up to them, then paused a beat to incline her head to Danai. No words were needed.

Danai danced with the Lord, the Lady, Damon, and Toron. She flung her arms about Quenton and Melarna, expressing her delight at their safe return. Eldrich Nishai hugged her breath away. Triasa's embrace made both weep with joy. It was over, over, over, the thought skipped through her mind. For a moment, she thought she sensed a smile of approval from Lady Argentyne.

Not until she paused to catch a breath did she remember to wish once again that Aaron could have been among them. His wings would have been golden, she thought, even in the silvery light. And his smile would have lit the Dell. Her heart twinged, and she sent a whispered prayer in his memory to Lunasa.

There was a lull in the music and laughter as Feyree paused to eat and chatter.

A sudden crackle split the air, and a hairline of flame appeared just beyond the trestles. Shouting a warning, the Guardians leaped forward to form a protective line between the widening gash and the other Feyree, dirqs drawn.

Pook strode through, followed by two of his guard, their blades sheathed. He halted to survey the frozen scene, to savor the impact that he had on the celebrants. He gave a laugh, cast wide his arms. "I beg you, fear me not. I come to congratulate my fellows, now Feyree, on earning their wings. I wish only permission to join the celebration."

The Lady advanced until she stood before Pook. He was fully a head taller than she, but to Danai, the Lady seemed of greater stature, radiating a calm beauty and assurance that dimmed the hot purple-blue radiance shimmering from Pook's skin. He inclined his head.

"Greetings, Lord...how shall I call thee? In my memory, I see clever Majerion, oft' called by his friends Pook, dancing at the Mid-Summer's Eve Feast last summer, even daring enough to ask the Lady of Feyree to dance. Yet only the most blind would say you are that spryte now. How shall I call thee?"

Pook seemed uncomfortable, his embered eyes dimming. "Grant me thy courtesy to call me by my old name as all celebrate. My new title has no place here."

The Lady nodded. "So it shall be. Join us in Oisillon, Pook, and reminisce of old. But where are our musicians?" At her bidding the sprightly tune refilled the air, although to Danai, the music had lost some of its luster.

Pook's guard retired to the edge of the Dell, sinking into the shadows, discernible only by their blue radiance. As they retreated, it seemed as if Pook's formal demeanor peeled away, and the mischievous spryte of old sprang forth. Danai saw him whirling and twirling, his full-set firm wings distinguishing him from the new-fledged Feyree. She preferred to avoid him as long as possible, feeling awkward and questioning why he had really come. He finally caught up with her, and, seizing her about the waist, they swirled in a giddy spiral. Then both began to laugh.

"I've missed you, Danai." She glanced into his smoldering eyes, then off to one side. He assumed a lighter tone. "So how does it feel to be winged?"

"Off-balance." She grinned. "Like somebody stuck two very heavy rucksacks on my back. I cannot imagine using them to fly. But, you know, I can hardly wait."

You'll love flying." Pook recaptured her hand after another twirl. "It's better than riding bird back, because you are in control, you determine where to go. It does take a bit to build up the muscles—I ached for days—but you'll soon be flapping about."

"Flapping or flopping?" Danai laughed, glad when Joson whirled in and smoothly spun her away.

"Danai, how can you be so sociable with him?" he demanded in a low voice. "Is what has happened of such little meaning?"

"Don't be a silly, Jo'," Danai retorted, her exuberance a bit dimmed by his heavy words. "But the Lady has approved his presence and I, for the moment, want to enjoy the amazing fact that we are Feyree. Smile! You look as if you had eaten honey gone bad." Joson harrumphed, and they danced a few more steps in silence, until she chose to whirl off to Damon.

As if some delighted magic powered their feet, Oisillon lasted until dawnshine. The food was replenished, refreshing draughts of goldenvine dew served, yet none felt drunk, only light-headed.

The rising sun brought new delights. Under Lunasa's light, the color of their wings could only be guessed at. But now they revealed themselves a riot of colors, almost like the walls of the dwarves' Delving, Danai thought. Her own wings were a vibrant amethyst, threaded with veins of lavender and indigo. Joson's were the slate blue of a stormy sky, while Rhytha's shone a glorious moss green. Damon's unusual wings startled everyone—they were a magnificent swirl of rainbows, trimmed in silver. "It is a blessing from the Mother," Lady Atelai counseled. "You will see and do much in your lifetime, and learn that all colors blend to the pure silver-white of Lunasa."

As the sun rose, the Mentors took charge, ordering the excited pod to lay down and rest. "No attempts to fly," admonished Mentor Melitsa. "Talking is fine, sleep is best."

Pook rejoined his old group, obviously enjoying the familiar chatter of his peers, keeping his part in the conversation to questions about the final Rites which he had missed. As the air warmed, Danai found her eyes growing heavy with exhaustion and relief, and apologizing, she walked a short distance away from her friends, and curled up beneath a fragrant clump of bright yellow meadow vetch.

When she awoke, it was already late-day, the trees casting long hazy shadows the width of the Dell. Her friends were all asleep. Pook was gone. She listened as a sparrow trilled, stopped, trilled again. Somewhere a magpie squawked. Above her, the brilliant cobalt sky provided a glorious background to trees cloaked in gold, scarlet, orange, and bronzy-green. A breeze wandered about, stroking the brown tasseled grasses until they softly hissed and nodded.

Danai savored a wonderful sense of calm, the satisfying knowledge that the Rites were complete. Yet it was almost bittersweet. All her life she had dreamed of Krisalys, fearing it. Now it was over. The fullness of her wings tugged against her back, a reminder that she would soon be learning to fly. What new horizons would she see? She smiled. It was time to look beyond Krisalys and discover her future.

# # # # #

Glossary

Glossary, Main Characters & Places of the Chronicles of Feyree

Lampion

In addition to the wood folk, there are the Feyree, the Troich (gem-dwarves) and the Ael (elves). All folk speak the common tongue as well as their own languages. Certain terms are specific to each folk: (f) – Feyree; (d) – dwarf; (a) – Ael.

Anam (d) – sacred emerald

Ard-Clarsair (d) – High Harpist

Anyisa (f) – special Healer drink

Beahn (d) – blessing

Beahn bron (d) – the mourning blessing

Bionas (f) – food storage bins

Ceol (d) – music

Clahaich (d) – the Delving; council chamber

Clarsair (d) – harpist

Col/ cols (a) – dwelling within a hill

Colet (a) – dwelling cave

Comhairle (d) – High Council

Cuirna'theine (d) – fire daemon

Cura – Self Heal, small creeping purple flower

Dirq – dagger

Dom-hainn (a) – cave where the Lord and Lady are chosen

Dormarai (a) – sleep herb

Drashgalas (a) – dragon

Draoidh (d) – druid, loremaster

Drucei – Thyme, aromatic flower

Dumais (a) – High Council

Dumais-shwa (a) – the choosing of a new Lord and Lady

Eisteddfod (d) – great music competition

Eldrich – elders

Elsheiratoual (a) – flowers of the moon

Fa-mancebo (a) – fostering mentors in Ardmoor Vale

Fathanna (a) – Talan's maidens of light

Glowstone – luminescent rock

Heald – Ael query call

Hyell (a) – dwelling within a hill

Interdee (f) – forbidden edict

Komparda (f) – metal tuning prong

Krisalys (f) – the 9 Rites to earn Feyree wings; also a ritual cocoon

Kryptic – riddle

Kuis (f) – hollowed out acorn shell

Jumo (f) – twins sharing a body, with separate minds

Lirupai (f) – foster mother

Lugh (d) – the moon, their most sacred deity

Lirupai (f) – fostering of spryte for an apprenticeship

Lumna (f) – time for Lunasa to wax and wane

Lunasa (f) – the moon, their most sacred deity

Maidan (f) – open gathering space

Mancebo – Ardmoor Vale fostering method

Manylegs – insect folk

Maighstir (d) – dwarf-lord

Mazidouces (a) – a sweet wayfarer cake

Miel (f) – a celebratory honey-mead

miyacan (f) – mix of honeycomb, nuts, and dried fruit

Morlios (a) – Col Shamrolyn's great garden

Morval (a) – the cave of the dead

Nainabiju (a) – Gem-Dwarf

Noiray (f) – Lunasa's dark face

Null (a) – a numbing salve

Numronbar (f) – a numbing salve

Oisillon (f) – concluding ceremony of the Rites

Orason/Orasaona (a) – Lord, Lady of the Ael

Pod (f) – group of 27 sprytes going through the Rites

Ponchantanyisa (a) – powerful Healer drink

Pusans (f) – a Feyree able to amplify magic

Ramas-Sheira (a) – when day and night are equal in autumn

Rehanna (f) – welcoming chant

Roinn (f) – Lunasa's half face

Samanth (f) – carry-cradle

Semblant (f) – protection spells

Sheira (a) – the moon

Shehn (f) – Sacred great oak in the Great Dell

Sidhiche (d) – Feyree folk

Solas (f) – Lunasa's full face

Solelas (a) – Ael name of the realm

Sprytes (f) – young wingless Feyree

Slanaighear (d) – Troich-healers

Srath Orach (d) – the Vale of the Sun; great garden

Suathglas (f) – a touchstone or stone of power

Talan (a) – the sun, the Ael's most sacred deity

Talanamach (dragon) – solar eclipse

Talan-lumis (a) – 'may the sun shine upon you'

Talan-tas (a) – 'the sun sings praise'

Trideug (d) – 13th face of Lugh (the moon)

Troich (d) – Gem-Dwarves

Tuil Mor (d) – Great Flood

Tunevich (d) – dwarf dwelling, a small cave

Verlunasa (f) – when day and night are equal in autumn

Nonetre

Amsaras – a request for clemency

Andastariq – leader of an incendis

Batoras – battle arena near Naloch

Carcairic – prison cells under Naloch

Carriol – cart, carriage

Chamask – sling thrower

Cheall – board game similar to chess

Chevosarras – sacred day when suns overlap in the sky

Creashas – crystals' pedestal.

Cromosh/Cromoshor – High Council/Council Member

Hsask – heated drink from fermented fruits

Ilan – fire daemiani salute

Incendis – ten stryker troops

Incendyallume – transforming potion

Liosarras – harvest festival

Maishan – courtyard

Meagashk – honey-drizzled nuts and fruits

Moldrask – ebony drink from fermented blackberries

Nantrath – the longest night

Nuchall – a Lampion-born thrall

Pach, Pacha – high-ranked lord or lady

Pirash – Naloch's twin-spired tower

Riag – secret dwarf language

Selgaich – barrier stalkers

Stryker – a troop of 100 warriors

Talushim – high loremasters

Tariq – leader of a stryker

Talushim – high loremaster

Tercera/Terceras – 30 days (a month)

Folk of the Krisalys Chronicles
Fire Daemiani

Tizon (Tee-zohn) – Tvashtar, firelord of Nonetre (formerly Pook, a
                Lampion spryte)

Eshel (Eh-shel) – the Herald, highest Talushim; councilor to Tizon

Saia (Sa-ee-ya) – sister of Syar, consort to Tizon; half fire daemon,
                half Feyree

Syar (See-yar) – brother of Saia; Chief Taskmaster of Lalach

Rial (Ree-all) – Second Taskmaster of Lalach

Dwarves

Tlarg (Teuh-larg) – Danai's friend, Shamarig's brother

Shamarig (Sham-a-rig) – Danai's friend, Tlarg's brother

Finavirig, Mingor, Mushag, Trew – Forgeroch thralls

Feyree

(Guild and dwelling noted)

Dolmen – Highest Loremaster of Lampion. Great Dell

Lord Andamion (An-dah-mee-on) – Lord of Feyree and Guardian
Guild Master. Revelstoke

Lady Atelai (Ah-teuh-lay-ee) – Lady of Feyree. Revelstoke

Lady Argentyne (Ar-jzen-teen) – Lady of the Lake

Damon (Day-mon) – New-fledged Feyree. Mireer Vale

Danai (Dah-nah-yee) – New-fledged Feyree. Goldyn Vale

Farrell (Feh-rell) – Healer Guild Master. Tequestar Glen

Joson (Joh-sun) – New-fledged Feyree. Gliffshado Glen

Kerion (Keh-ry-an) – New-fledged Feyree. Mireer Vale

Majikian (Mah-jee-ki-ahn) – Charmer. Darlding Glen

Melitsa (Meh-lee-tsa) – Weaver. Mireer Vale

Nacci (Na-chee) – Chief Healer. Goldyn Vale

Rhytha (Rih-thuh) – New-fledged Feyree. Darlding Glen

Siddiqui (Sih-dee-kee) – New-fledged Feyree. Tequestar Glen

Tarlokyn (Tar-loh-kin) – Gatherer. Ardmoor Vale

Toron (Toh-ron) – Chief Guardian. Goldyn Vale

Triasa (Tree-ah-sah) – Charmer. Goldyn Vale

Quenton (Kwen-tun) – Seer. Revelstoke

Chief Tains, Guardians, Guilds

Ardmoor Vale: Chief Tains Beriel, Lahiri; Chief Guardian Ilynei
Guilds: Warework, Hearth

Darlding Glen: Chief Tains Taleo, Treana; Chief Guardian Pazin
Guilds: Tracker, Sentinel

Firebaugh Vale: Chief Tains Tauzin, Ibilsi; Chief Guardian Aliya
Guilds: Scryer, Seer

Glyffshado Glen: Chief Tains Daralyn, Amira; Chief Guardian Tallac
Guilds: Skald, Orpheii

Goldyn Vale: Chief Tains Shealor, Nishai; Chief Guardian Toron

Guilds: Charmer, Goldsmythe

Kristal Glen: Chief Tains Anoran, Indamia; Chief Guardian Teril

Guilds: Kristal, Stonesmythe, Weathercaster

Mireer Vale: Chief Tains Edigen, Miatia; Chief Guardian Shadia

Guilds: Weaver, Gatherer

Rymple Dell: Chief Tains Morval, Biagi; Chief Guardian Mailyn

Guilds: Messenger, Metalwork

Tequestar Glen: Chief Tains Symnon, Manichia; Chief Guardian Diestel

Guilds: Healer, Woodwork

# # # # #

The following is an

Excerpt from Scroll 2 of the Chronicles of Feyree

Dark Fire

_____

Claudia Newcorn

Available from Theogony Books

July, 2017

eBook, Paperback, and Audio Book

Came the dark thunder of the drums.

Bronze gates groaned open on either side of the arena. From their rows of stone seats sweeping up the steep hillside, the fire dae-miani leaned forward in hungry anticipation, their torch-like multi-hued flames flickering in the dwindling light. Excited murmurs flared to a roar as the contestants paced forth to meet in the center, two black shadows backlit by Keothach's heaving orange waves of fire. Spurts of scalding yellow and scorched scarlet burst free of the fire lake's seething ooze, clutching at the sky's smoky brown pall, only to fall back in slurping gulps.

The drums throbbed a second time, the deep boom reverberating off the High Seat's blood red stone. Upon it reposed the Firelord, Tvashtar Tizon. From beside him, the Herald Eshel stepped to the edge of the dais and raised his arms, flickering gray flames outlining his familiar crook-shouldered figure. "Folk of Nonetre!" The rasping voice commanded immediate silence. "Behold the condemned! This eve they do battle for their offenses here in *Batoras*. To death, the loser. To the winner, life. Approach ye the Tvashtar!"

Clad in snug ebony tunics, the two feyree advanced to stand be-fore the High Seat. The heavily muscled golden one, with deep blue wings, grasped his curved blade with practiced ease. The other, the green of a just-unfurled leaf, clutched the hilt with both hands, a tremor visible through her entire slender body. Her pale yellow wings seemed to shiver, Keothach's light flickering through them as sun-light through a tear. Both bowed before raising their blades to salute. Stone-faced, the Tvashtar gave a slight nod. The Herald clapped once. "To life!"

The feyree faced each other, blades up in brief salute. Then the golden feyree lunged. Blades clashed, edges screeching with a flash of silver sparks. Back and forth they slashed, amidst the crowd's groans

455

and cheers. Vaulting into the air, soaring, plunging, tumbling over and around each other like ferocious dueling birds, then plummeting back to the ground to hack and strike. Threads of dark blood writhed down the green feyree's left thigh; her arms struggled more and more with each lift of the blade. With an ugly laugh, the gold feyree dropped to one knee and took a vicious swipe at her legs.

So swiftly she was a blur, the other sprang high. For a heartbeat, she hung suspended over him, hefting the blade above her head. Then down she hurtled, her weight adding to the slashing cut that sheared off his right wing. He screeched, dropped his blade, and crumpled forward, face crushing into the crimson dirt. Landing beside him, the green feyree stood panting, wings slumped, blade yet tightly clutched. Keothach vomited hissing flames.

Slowly she gazed up at the fire daemiani who had risen to shriek and cheer. Wearily she lifted the blade above her brow in victory. The crowd stamped, trembling the ground so that pebbles danced. Something brushed her foot. She glanced down. "Kill me," begged the gold feyree. "For if you do not, they will cast me into Keothach, a death far more terrible than your blade's swift mercy. In the name of Lunasa and the Mother, I beseech you, kill me."

Shuddering, she looked up at the exultant fire daemiani soaring skywards in spurts of flame, spinning and tumbling about like some grotesque mockery of a revel in her now-lost realm of Lampion. "May you meet the Twins beyond the Veil," she murmured, bringing the blade down with her last scrap of strength.

The Tvashtar gasped, amethyst-hued hands clutching his knees so tightly, the knuckles gleamed lavender. He recoiled as she stared up at him, silver eyes brilliant with hate, even as exhaustion dulled her bodyglow. Her blade drooped, bloody tip propped on the ground.

"*Amsaras!*" The fire daemiani's shrieks shuddered the air. "Tvashtar, amsaras!"

Eshel looked to Tizon, frowning slightly at the rigid face. "My lord? They cry that Andalorosa be awarded life." He released a slit-thin smile. "At least until the next Batoras. Your decision?"

The Tvashtar swallowed hard. About his brow, the ring of tiny flames hovering just above a twisted circlet of red gold sputtered indigo sparks. He stood, black cloak writhing beneath golden wings, and advanced to the dais' edge. He raised both hands, gazing at the feyree. The immediate hush was disturbed only by Keothach's belch and burble, its sharp reek threading the hazy air. "Amsaras, Andalorosa. Well fought!" Again he lifted his hands to quiet the bellows of approval. "And now two choices I give ye." He ignored Eshel's sudden scowl. "Will ye remain here as a warrior for Batoras, or will ye serve in one of the great gardens as thrall to the Firelord of Nonetre? Choose!"

Andalorosa hesitated. In the under-caves of Batoras where she had been trained for battle, she had been given to understand her only choice would be to fight over and over until, like Oros, she finally fell to another condemned thrall. That the Tvashtar was presenting her an alternative left her breathless.

"The Tvashtar has demanded an answer!" Eshel's voice was harsh with coiled anger. He already guessed her choice. She should not be permitted to leave – her unexpected performance guaranteed at least one more good battle; he was loathe to let her escape. Why had the Tvashtar even offered?

"Tvashtar Tizon, I choose the gardens!"

A groan dribbled from many throats. The Tvashtar ignored it. "To Rualach ye are condemned. Such is my order; such is my command. Now, return ye to the under-caves." With a final salute, Andalorosa retreated.

"My lord, surely you will reconsider...."

Tizon whirled about, aqua eyes orange-embered with fury. But he kept his voice low such that it reached no further than Eshel's ears; not even Falaise, Thrak or Ashnarg, who were waiting a short distance behind the High Seat, could catch his words. "She fought bravely. She fulfilled the conditions of Batoras. Be not so ready to fail in rewarding those who serve, for most surely you will regret such actions in the end."

Inclining his head to conceal blazing eyes, Eshel gave a curt bow. "My lord is wise. It shall be so." He faced the crowd. "It is finished!"

The drums thundered three times, then fell silent.

* * * * *

ABOUT THE AUTHOR

Claudia Newcorn currently runs her own business and marketing consulting firm, Acorn Enterprises, and is a freelance writer as well as an author. Her first fantasy novel, *Crossover*, was published in 2007 and won the 2008 Reviewers Choice Award for Sci Fi/Fantasy and was optioned for screen rights. Her second, *Dark Fire*, was released in December 2009 and won a silver medal in Sci Fi/Fantasy from the 2010 Written Arts Awards literary contest. Scroll 3 was published in 2011 and won the 2013 Written Arts Award, the 2012 Reviewers Choice Award, and the 2012 Royal Dragonfly Award for Sci Fi/Fantasy.

Her published short stories include "A Cat's Gift of Faith," in *Chicken Soup for the Cat Lover's Soul,* and "The Christmas Tree Nobody Wanted" in *Stanislaus Magazine.* She writes regularly for a variety of publications, is a magazine editor, and is a popular community columnist for *The Modesto Bee.* A former private helicopter pilot, Claudia has lived around the world, collects antique fairy tale books, attempts to garden, and is passionate about health & wellness, hiking, animals, and the environment.

Titles by Claudia Newcorn:

"Crossover" – Available Now

"Dark Fire" – Available Summer 2017

"Firestar" – Available Fall 2017

* * * * *

Catch up with Claudia online:

Website: http://www.CNewcornFantasy.com/

Made in the USA
Columbia, SC
10 August 2019